TINFOILS

BOOK ONE OF THE BRANCH

JACOB CLOSE

PRESS

Published by Vulpine Press in the United Kingdom in 2020

Cover by Claire Wood

ISBN: 978-1-83919-038-4

www.vulpine-press.com

PRESS

For Dad, Cara and Rachel, without whom this book would never have been possible.

I am blessed to be the dark space between the beautiful stars of you.

ACKNOWLEDGEMENTS

There are a lot of people to thank for this book. First and foremost, my beloved in-laws Rich and Lisa, who welcomed me into their family and culture, and financed travel to the USA which proved absolutely invaluable for research.

Thank you to Emily Dowd, the world's best and shortest meteorologist, without whom this book probably would have never seen the light of day.

Special thanks also go to Joe Mcaulay, Marina Johnson, Katherine Bull, Liam Rees and Chris Armitstead for taking me on amazing adventures, and stopping me from going mad with loneliness when the work was hardest. I'll see you all in the Hotel California.

This section wouldn't be complete without David Pengelly, Sarah Hembrow and everyone at Vulpine Press, who have worked tirelessly to make *Tinfoils* the best it can be, and graciously decided to publish it in the first place. They are just excellent.

And finally, thank you to the dozen other kids who paid 20p for my story about Vikings on the playground when I was 7. You suckers don't know the monster you made that day, but I sure as hell do.

PREFACE

I couldn't tell you what it is about the road that does it.

Maybe there's something in it. A sickness, suggested by its unsettling, serpentine curve through the landscape.

You might think it's the same thing that turns people back from other places across Pennsylvania's old coal belt. The same overgrown logging roads and quarry scars. No future, no present. Just the past, gone brittle and faded in the long grass, crisscrossing over itself as it wilts.

Elsewhere, that's the sum of it. But not there. Not on that road.

Because as you make the final, blind turn just south of town, something happens. It always does: the radio screams in static and the lights go off. An animal hits the car. A hundred dead insects drop from the air, and the next thing you know you're turned around, a mile back the way you came.

But make no mistake, no matter how unsettling, those events are blessings in disguise. When they happen, it means you still have time to turn away and never come back.

I couldn't tell you what it is about the road that does it, but people seldom cross it twice.

CRICKETS IN THE BUSHES

VIETNAM, 1968

They hid them in coke cans. On the side of the road, or in the grass. Waiting.

Somehow the Vietnamese had worked it out from scratch: that very particular part of the American psyche that still lived far away from the water and the weeds, amidst manicured yards and suburban streets, the part that was stupid and exhausted enough to remember. It only took a second to forget you weren't a kid walking back from school, kicking a loose can into the leaves. You'd be put right a half second after, when the grenade inside busted your legs open.

Yule watched the can from his perch, nestled in the grass, the aluminum glinting like an anglerfish lure. He shuddered and looked away. Half-seen, Corporal Slackley came and sat down beside him.

"You got a spare stick?" he asked. He had a warm, careful Texan accent like a cowboy from a black-and-white movie. Yule always liked that about him. He didn't curse and spit for nothing, at least not as much as the other GI's.

"Nah. Ran out," Yule replied. Slackley gave him something between a smile and a grimace.

"Guess that's why you look so nervous," he replied. Yule didn't respond, and Slackley nudged him.

"I don't know if you looked around recently," he insisted, gesturing to the men around the road, "so's everybody else in this shit-show. You go getting distracted by it, that's a one-way ticket to a rubber bag."

"Guess so," Yule replied absently, his attention still fixed on the deadly glint in the grass. Slackley sighed through his nose, and the sound carried through the swollen canopy.

"Christ, I'd kiss a Gook for an Old Gold," he said.

The addict in Yule perked up a little at the name, like a dog responding to a bell. He could almost taste them. Despite himself, he smirked.

"I hear that. Not been able to get 'em since Hanoi," he replied.

Slackley chuckled and folded his arms. His gray teeth glistened in the wet jungle light.

"You a Golds guy too? Didn't know they stocked 'em outside Mai—"

A sharp, watery 'ting' sound echoed around the suddenly silent road.

Slackley froze, expression vacant. His eyes rolled back in his head, as if to examine the little bullet hole punched an inch above his ear. He crumpled forward, and Yule felt the corpse's face relax against his shirt. Something hot gushed through the sweat-soaked khaki fabric.

The sounds that followed all seemed a hundred miles away. Somebody shouting, and the crackle of machine guns ripping through the under-growth. Bodies dropping to the dirt, survivors fogging the air with noise and smoke as they returned fire at an enemy they couldn't even see.

Yule didn't scream. Not at first. He just sat there, stunned, looking at his own reddened hands. He didn't know if it was his or Slackley's. There was just so much of it, he thought. So much blood, all over him, like boiling sweat, and clinging sheets.

Yule's hands scratched at his side, trying furiously to beat away the dull fever on his belly. Then, he fell, limbs tangled in his bedclothes. The im-pact knocked the wind out of him, blanket flying away as his arms and legs arced away from the mattress and onto the floor.

Breath came in desperate, strained groans. His hand closed around the glass on his bedside table and, without hesitating, tipped it onto his up-turned face. For a moment, the probing shock of cold water filled his senses. The monochrome buzz of terror receded like a drawn curtain and Yule laid back down onto the floor, hands pressing and probing at his face as if he'd just woken up.

It was cold, he thought. Not hot. Not organically sticky like blood, just… water.

Cold water.

Leaden terror lifted away from his chest, and suddenly he was back. Aware. His hands fell down and away, and Yule realized he was staring not at the venomous jungle canopy, but at the flaking apartment ceiling. He lay there for a few minutes, letting the cold blue nightscape flood in through the window and over his naked skin. He named things he could hear, just like they'd taught him to. Cars passing. The warm thrum of night air lit with streetlights. The feeling of the floorboards against his back. Crickets in the bushes.

He lay there for some time, trying to re-solidify himself in the present. The year was 1977. A Tuesday morning, he didn't know the time. He was twenty-eight years old.

That thought made something twinge. He'd been nineteen in 1968, he thought. Nineteen goddamn years old. Nine years later, Yule still couldn't believe they trusted him to tie his own shoes, let alone hold a gun. But there he'd been: a kid who'd never been on a plane before the one that dropped him into the jungle, feeling the M16 pulse like a boiling heart in his hands as he…

…Cars passing, he thought. Crickets in the bushes.

After what seemed like hours he climbed to his feet and found the pack of Old Golds, already open on the table, next to his lighter. His hands shook as he teased a cigarette out from the foil, lighter flame shivering as he raised it up to his lips.

Scalding and dry, the smoke felt almost cleansing, he thought, if you ignored the cough.

After a few test puffs he grabbed his bathrobe off the hook and tied the cord tight around his waist. With nothing but the glowing end of the cigarette to guide him, Yule picked his way through the apartment hallway, hand hissing against the wall as he went. The pitfalls were familiar to him, even after an episode: a pile of old magazines to the right; extension cords; Ornell's car repair stuff. Yule knew they'd never get burgled; the poor bastard would probably break their neck within the first thirty feet.

He crossed the living room and through the screen door onto the balcony, if anyone could call it that at all: it was more of a tight, empty rectangle of space with old iron bars around it. It was like the building had a tumor, and they turned it into a selling point. It was good enough, he supposed. It wasn't as if they were planning to host cocktail parties on it anytime soon.

He looked out over the town, though there wasn't much to see. Even from three stories up, he could just about see over the top of every building, all the way out to the tree line. They'd all been closed since six pm. Present day 1977 was a long way gone from 1968, he thought, but you'd never know it in Amesville, Pennsylvania. Apart from the Kennedy assassination, the decades after 1955 were something that had largely happened somewhere else. Even when the military draft came to drown their children, nobody really talked about it. The ones that survived just reappeared one day, and that was that.

The cigarette, burnt down to a stub, nipped at his fingers. He pushed it out on the rail and threw the butt down onto the street below, where it tumbled out of sight into a storm drain. He'd sleep, he thought, but later. For now, he'd wait until the sky started to mellow in thick puce and purple just before sunrise; see the day coming before it came for him.

MORNING COMES TO JOYTOWN

AMESVILLE, 1977

"I'm telling you, man," said Ornell, sputtering through a mouthful of cereal, "half dog, half boy. It's in the bathroom, take a look for yourself."

"And I'm telling you that shit's in *Believe It or Not.* It's a hoax," Yule replied, messing with his tie. It always sat crooked. Ornell turned around, gesturing sharply with his spoon.

"So, if it was in the *New York Times* or something, you'd believe it?" he said.

"Yeah. I would."

"Why?"

"Because one's the *New York Times*, and the other one's got a lady with three tits in it, Ornell. Jesus," he said, cinching the tie up to his throat. He took his hands away, like a magician expecting doves to fly out of his sleeves.

Still crooked. He guessed he was a pretty bad magician.

He glanced at the clock and sighed. It'd have to do, even if Mister Robinson was going to bust his balls for it. He went over to the hook and pulled on his coat, keys jingling reassuringly in the pocket.

"Shouldn't you be at work already, instead of looking up some dog-boy garbage?" he said, adjusting the sleeve. Ornell shook his head and took a slurp from the cereal bowl. He looked like a bulldog sniffing around in a puddle.

"Nah, I got a late shift today," he said, grinning, "twelve hundred til nineteen-thirty baby. Daddy's making paper."

"You're a lumberjack, not the Godfather," Yule said, pulling out a cigarette. Ornell turned around again, thick eyebrows raised.

"Alright, first of all, I ain't a 'lumber jack.' I'm god's own motherfuckin' lumber *artist*. When I chop lumber, it's like making love to a fine woman, only with a saw," he said. Yule grimaced.

"I'm really not likin' this simile so far, Ornell," he replied.

"And second of all," Ornell insisted, pointing, "you can't go laughin' at me, you crooked-tie-wearin', arcade-job-havin' son of a bitch. What's your career lookin' like?"

"Alright, alright. You're a lumber *artist*. I'm cutting it close as it is without a speech," Yule replied, opening up the front door. "Don't go falling in a woodchipper."

"Don't crash your broke-ass truck into a tree," replied Ornell. Yule smirked as he closed the door behind him. The stairwell creaked and whined on his way down and out of the building. He had no idea how that thing took Ornell's weight every day—maybe they made bolts stronger back then.

At this time of morning Clarence Street was starting to stir to life. Familiar motions started to whir in the neighborhood. The old guy with no hair, walking a dog with too much. The off-white Chevy that would do rounds of the neighborhood with a snoozing baby and exhausted-looking father up front. And, of course, the woman who watched Yule through the blinds as he passed by her house.

Something in her look said she didn't like him very much, but Yule didn't really feel any way toward her. He didn't even know her name, all he knew was that she called him "spook." After about three or four seconds of waiting, she would say it to someone behind her, didn't need to hear it because the phrase made a specific twist of the lip, a sort of unmistakable snarl. "That spook," she said. Every damn day, for nearly four years.

Joytown Arcade sat on the corner of 8th and Clarence, next to a hardware store and a budget dry cleaner. If you had to describe the place with a noise, it would be a wheeze, followed by a sigh, and then whatever the sound of gentle disappointment is.

The neon sign swung out like a dislocated thumb, clicking quietly even when it was off. Mister Robinson got it from the guy who used to own the barbershop and had only ever changed the writing; the bright orange pair of scissors in the corner remained. Whenever Yule asked about them, he always got the same answer: Mister Robinson would loop his thumbs through his braces and cast a withering eye at any one of the dozens of kids gathered round the arcade boxes, muttering a little mantra under his breath.

"Kids these days don't know their ass from their elbow," he'd say, smirking, "little bastards probably think the scissors are some kinda… movie spaceship, or somethin'."

Yule didn't know what a 'movie spaceship' was. Mister Robinson probably didn't either, but God knew it never stopped him.

As Yule fumbled the keys out of his pocket he noticed a small, dark shape out of the corner of his eye. Thin and crushed into a corner like a detached shadow. He snorted under his breath, only half pretending not to have seen him.

"Shouldn't you be in school, Ollie?" he asked. The pale little teenager wiped some black hair out of his face and looked up.

"G-guh… gif…" he said. He then paused for a second and drew in a breath, like he was about to jump out of a plane. "Gifted puh-program. I start an hour l-late."

Yule smirked, key clacking loudly in the lock.

"Seems like everybody's got the morning off but me," he answered with a chuckle and a shake of his head. With that he opened the door, and the thick smell of old carpets and knock-off Windex bundled past him in a rush to escape.

His finger cut a familiar path through the air and tapped against the light switch. There was a heavy *ka-chunk* as the building's busted up wiring buzzed to life, and the arcade jerked awake like an old man woken from his chair. At eye level, the room was lost amongst a tangle of greasy neon, in every off-color of the rainbow. A field of backlit plastic panels and flickering tubes hummed to jarringly different notes, barely revealed by the light of pocked yellow bulbs in the ceiling.

Yule exhaled out of his nose and crossed the threshold. Home sweet home.

"So, you gonna take another crack at Sky Diver, or what?" he asked, flipping the sign.

Ollie shook his head, drifting in beside Yule as if to hide in his shadow. His hands were still fixed awkwardly on his bag straps.

"N-no. I already hit ni... nin... n-n..." he began, face falling as the word stalled on his tongue.

"Ninety-nine?" Yule said, turning to him. Ollie took a sharp inhale, and then just nodded in reply. Maybe being cut off like that embarrassed him. It would embarrass Yule, that was for sure. He made a mental note not to do it again.

"It's a hell of a score. You're running outta machines to beat," he insisted, going behind the desk.

"M-maybe they make them too easy."

"Well they make 'em hard enough for most folk. They oughta get you to test the things down at Atari," he said, trying to sound as casual as he could. Ollie perked up and gave him a smile.

"Y-you think s-so?" he asked. Yule felt like grinning but kept it down. He just gave him a relaxed shrug and a raised eyebrow, just like his brother's friends used to.

"Why not? Probably wouldn't involve much talkin', you'd be good at it," he said, wiping down the counter. Ollie didn't say anything. He just stood there, gripping tightly at his backpack and radiating like a shy little sun. Ollie might not have been able to say it so well verbally, but you could always tell when somebody like him was happy.

Yule glanced at the clock. Mister Robinson wouldn't be done with his morning ritual of cheap coffee and even cheaper cigarettes for another twenty minutes at least. He reached into his pocket, fingers clasping over a coin.

"Hey, Ollie—you wanna help me out a spell?" he asked. Ollie nodded, smile fading into something more tentatively curious. Yule put the quarter down on the counter and nodded towards the back of the arcade. "We just got a new Blasto machine in. How about you give it a spin, see how it handles?" he said, sliding the coin towards Ollie with a finger. His eyes widened, and he snatched it up immediately.

"Thanks!" he said. His voice didn't get any higher, but the breathy echo said it wanted to. Yule snorted and went back to wiping down the counter.

"Hey, don't thank me, you're doing me a favor so get your ass on it," he said, grinning. Ollie laughed and nodded in agreement. Then he tore to the back of the arcade, disappearing behind the high cabinet backs. Yule chuckled and shook his head.

He was a good kid. A damn good kid. Yule wondered what his home life was like—nothing in depth, he just… he hoped it was nurturing. That his old man didn't give him a hard time about the stutter thing he had going on, and that his mom made him soup when he was sick. Storybook shit. Yule would've asked, but the last thing he needed was to get a reputation for asking kids where they lived.

It was good enough for him to know that, at least whilst Ollie was there in the arcade, somebody had his back. That was something he could do just fine.

He smiled to himself and went back to wiping down the counter.

Ollie didn't stay long after that. He racked up a good run of points and then disappeared, lingering by the door for a second to give Yule a wave. Yule stood alone in the shop and watched him go. He'd done a good job, he thought. At least, it was gonna be better than anything else he did behind the counter that day. In between nine and noon, Joytown should have been called Ghost Town. And, like every ghost town, it had its fair share of the angry dead. Or at least, the nearly dead.

Mister Robinson came shuffling in around ten wearing his usual stained shirt and old dress slacks. He stank of tobacco and knock-off Chinese cologne, although Yule reckoned the old, peanut-looking bastard had probably lost his sense of smell years ago. He sniffed as he closed the door behind him and gave Yule a stare with one bug eye.

"What time you get in this morning?" he asked, taking off his hat. Yule gave him a warm, saccharine smile.

"Well, I'll be darned if it wasn't close to eight am," he said. The demeanor change felt like crashing a car into the wall, but Yule was practiced at it. People called it 'military discipline' but the concept was familiar to him long before boot camp: taught by teachers who called his white buddies 'loud' but him 'aggressive'; doctors who stopped smiling when they realized 'Ulysses Lincoln' wasn't some rich white kid from Aspen; cops who seemed to arrive looking for a reason rather than responding to one. A man in his situation had to make it work somehow.

At least being nice probably annoyed the old man more than disobedience; he couldn't fire Yule for reasons of pleasantness.

Robinson, heedless, gave a hoarse grunt in reply and blew smoke from his vulture nose.

"So what, you just been whacking off this whole time or somethin'?" he asked, flicking cigarette ash. "Place is filthy."

"If you want me to stop prepping the register, I can do another sweep," Yule said, almost sing-song. He could hear Robinson's blood pressure increasing from across the room.

"Just do all of it, dammit. I've got a business call," Robinson replied. He started towards the office door, and Yule slid around the counter to follow him.

"You ain't got one of those in a long time. There a faulty cabinet?" he asked. The reply was short, and somehow more annoyed than usual.

"No."

"We gettin' sued?" Yule insisted. Robinson's greasy brow furrowed, and he stopped in his tracks.

"No. Why? You *do* something?" he asked, finger flying up. "Because I swear to God, if you did somethin'—"

"I didn't do nothing, Mister Robinson, no need to panic. I'm just makin' small talk."

Robinson looked flustered for a second, before turning back to resume his stunted walk to the door.

"Well, make it smaller," he muttered, awkwardly lurching through the doorway, "and go throw a bucket of ice water on that bum out back! I don't want him scaring off customers!"

The office door slammed shut. After a few loud scrapes and a couple of banging knocks, the ambient hum seeped back into place again, and the arcade returned to its usual sleepwalk. Yule brushed off the counter a few more times and picked up a pair of trash bags. He couldn't help but empathize with them.

He turned on his way out of the glass doors and was confronted immediately by the alley. The bricks were black with mold which crept up from exhaust fans inset into the wall. A couple of boxes, half-melted by rain, were stacked up by the side; strewn to reveal the off-color neon sleeping bag hidden behind them.

As he approached, for a yawning second Yule thought the guy might be dead. Frozen to death out in the cold, or something. That dread lasted until the bag turned around, to reveal a whiskey-tinted nose poking out from a mad fray of hair. Yule felt a groan rumble up from his ribs. Three dollars an hour wasn't worth this.

"Come on, man," he said, prodding the sleeping bag with his foot. The homeless guy turned and coughed. Didn't wake up, but as he shifted, a shoulder rose. A familiar olive drab flashed dull against the bright sleeping bag; a half-torn fabric patch drooping against the sleeve. A bar of yellow, orange, and green lines, gone threadbare and dirty.

Yule had one of those. Some woman had given him one when he... when he got home.

Something in his stomach turned. Was this guy...?

Maybe not, he thought. Maybe he was just dressed like that. You could buy those things, right? The shirts, and the patches. He'd met plenty of nutjobs who'd never set foot in Vietnam with a patch like that on their vest. They usually congratulated him and bought him a drink for "melting all those gooks." He could imagine those guys ending up drunk in an alley too.

But, then again, a lot of the others drank like that. The other guys, the ones who'd come back with him from 'Nam. Word was that corporal Nesbitt had gotten liver disease. Shakey Stephenson drank himself out of house and home, same with private Anderson, and that was just the ones he knew about.

They'd all been like Yule. That's what was scary about it. Being the same was pretty much entirely the point. Doing the same thing as everybody else at all times, like a coordinated machine. They'd all done it, and done it so damn well that they'd come back in a plane and not a body bag.

Then they started dying. One by one, drink by drink. The guys who shook their heads whenever they saw an old buddy lying in the gutter were the same ones there a year later. Over time it dawned on them all that the spiral wasn't an *if*, but a *when*. It just depended when the ghosts of gunfire became too intrusive and started bleeding in through the walls. How tightly chained the nights spent awake became, nourishing the hot, dense fear that they really *were* all the same.

When Yule finally spoke again, it was hesitant and quiet. He found himself reaching out, though he didn't intend on touching the guy. It was just something unconscious. A helping urge.

"Hey," he began, but the rest of the sentence didn't make it out. A loud bang cracked off the wet brick walls as a car door slammed shut at the end of the alleyway. Yule immediately straightened up and wheeled around, startled. A police officer peered over the top of the driver's side door and adjusted his hat.

"What the hell are you doin', boy?" he asked, staring at him. As he spoke, a second cop emerged from the passenger seat, cigarette held between his lips. Yule glanced between them for a moment and cleared his throat.

"I was just checkin' on this guy, I thought he was dead—"

"You just take a step away, now. Go on and keep your hands where I can see 'em," said the second officer, walking slowly towards him, nightstick ready in a belt loop. When Yule noticed the first cop's hand very conspicuously near his gun, he held up his palms and took a step back.

"Look, I just work here. At the arcade," he said, pointing with a thumb. The police officer stopped, and his voice dropped.

"And I'm telling you to get your hands up, and step back," he said slowly. The first cop stayed by the car, watching. Yule screwed up his face, and raised his hands higher, trying to ignore the seething fear that the guy was a lookout rather than backup.

"Alright. Whatever you say," he said. With that, the first cop finally moved in, stepping awkwardly past the boxes on his way to the sleeping bag. The other jerked forward and turned Yule around, pressing his chest against the moist brick. The cop's cigarette, burnt mostly to a stub, hovered a stinging inch away from his cheek.

A small, half-dead part of Yule flickered and told him to resist. He didn't.

"Hands against the wall," said the cop. He patted Yule down and went into his pockets, pulling out his wallet with a sharp tug. Tense seconds ticked by before the cop spoke again.

"Uly... Yoo-ly... fuck, Terry can you read this shit?" he said, audibly turning to face his partner. "It's some crazy African name."

"Ulysses. Like the dude from the Greek myth," Yule said, trying to keep his voice neutral. "People call me Yule."

The cop laughed quietly to himself, grunted, and flipped the wallet closed.

"Checks out, I guess. You can go on and put your hands down now," he said. Yule hesitantly took his wallet back and stuffed it in his pocket. The cop smiled at him but there wasn't much warmth in it.

"You can get back to work," the cop who handed back his wallet continued. "We'll take it from here."

To the side, Officer Terry was examining the homeless guy, one sleeve held up to his nose. Yule screwed up his face a little.

"So, are you gonna get him to a hospital?" he asked. The cop snorted and shook his head.

"Nah. He's fine," he replied.

"He don't look too fine to me. You hear his breathing?" Yule said, pointing. The cop leaned back a little on his heels and called over to Terry.

"He look fine to you?" he asked.

"He looks fine to me," Terry replied. The as-yet nameless officer turned back to Yule, smile thickening.

"A couple days in the hole for vagrancy to sober him up, he'll be right as rain. No better place for him."

"Who even called you people?" Yule asked.

The cop laughed, but this time it was different. Like the kind of laugh you'd give a cashier who got your change wrong.

"Look," he said, leaning in a little closer, "I've given you the okay to walk away and told you we're handling it. So you should get going before you get yourself in trouble. You hear me, *boy*?"

Yule stared at him for a few seconds. He could feel his fists clenching and unclenching, alternating between useless and a one-way ticket to getting shot. But, eventually, logic won out.

"I hear you," he replied quietly. The cop nodded and stepped aside.

"Have a nice day," Terry said from the side, half sneering. Yule started walking out of the alleyway, willing his stomach to un-knot. The cop's hand had been on his gun more times than he wanted to count. He looked over his shoulder a last time before he turned the corner, and sure enough the cops were watching him go, like they were waiting for something.

Yule made his way back inside. Whatever it was, he didn't care. He didn't need to see it or hear about it.

If Yule had cared to see it, he would have seen the man being dragged into the car, still unconscious. He would have seen the two police officers get inside. And, if he'd cared to wait ten minutes, that would have been all that he saw.

Two cops, just… sitting there. Not saying a single word, for ten whole minutes. Staring forward down the road in stony, knowing silence. And finally, after the long quiet, he would have seen them turn the ignition, and drive wordlessly away.

MISSING THINGS

AMESVILLE, 1993

Cal had never been on a plane, but the moment his bike peeled away from the road and hit the slope between Hope Meadow park and Clarence Street he felt as if he was flying.

He was pretty sure that hill was what got him through the day. He'd stopped believing it was magic by the time he was fourteen, after a brief but powerfully awful phase of believing a topaz necklace would give him good luck. Like most things from the back of a magazine, the gaudy little pendant had almost definitely not been magic, in the same way that a "100% REAL" samurai sword, or a bong shaped like Bill Clinton's head probably weren't magic either.

Even if all the homemade runes and tarot decks had ended up in the garbage can, the Hope Meadow hill still seemed to exercise some kind of hold over him. It was the only part of his route to school where you couldn't see the backs of houses through the trees. And even during the morning rush, nobody ever seemed to be down there except for a group of younger kids, building stone dams in the creek.

If he dared to close his eyes for just a second, he could imagine he was someone different, somewhere different. Someone who was bigger, or stronger, or less afraid heights.

The Hope Meadow hill wasn't magic, but it was easy to think it was.

His bike tires moaned and bounced as the uneven hillside flattened out, and all too suddenly Cal heard the whoosh of leafy canopy passing overhead. He opened his eyes and pulled a tight turn, barely curving out of the path of a brown Ford Taurus, which blared its horn at him on its way past. Cal held up a hand and waved at the back window as it sped away.

"Sorry!" he called, voice cracking. He slowed down a little and looked around. At least nobody had been around to hear it.

Definitely himself again.

Cal cursed under his breath and tried to pick up speed down the road. The town rolled sleepily beside him as he went, shifting in perfect time with the bike chain.

On one side, the State Game Lands stretched out in the distance, dotted with squat concrete towers around the new power plant, like sentries posted just beyond the long flats on the eastern edge of town. That span was all knotted up with old tree stumps and tire trenches, the desperate final kick of an ailing lumber industry before business had finally moved elsewhere altogether. On the other side of him, Clarence Street waited in weathered pastel tones.

A lot of people who visited Amesville thought all of it looked like Clarence Street, but it wasn't because Clarence Street was particularly good looking; far from it. The real explanation was that there was no reason to visit anywhere but Clarence Street on your way through. The police station, the drug store, the Great-Valu Market—pretty much the best of what the town had to offer had circled the wagons and banded together on that road, hoping to ward off whatever evil force had killed the coal mine and the sawmills.

And even as Cal pedaled down the street, he could see flashes of whatever doom had swept over much of the rest of town like a sickness, long before his time. The remains of store signs watched over empty side streets, splitting off the living road like so many dead limbs. It was Mordor out there.

As he made his way down, he turned his head to look at the one element of the street that seemed out of place. Solid and dark, like the tower of Isengard or Barad-dur: a reminder of the boundless, waiting evil in the middle of supposedly safe territory.

In reality it was just an obelisk, dedicated some time ago to some war or disaster, standing maybe seven feet tall. The original intent of it had long been forgotten, replaced in the public mind by the dripping white letters painted on its surface.

"WHO TOOK LESLIE O'NEIL?" it demanded in full, eggshell capitals. Cal didn't know who wrote it. Nobody did. It had been cleaned maybe a dozen times over the last decade, but the writing always returned, like a weed whose roots survived every pulling. This iteration had lasted nearly two years, give or take. Maybe they'd just accepted it was part of the town.

Either way, Cal's knowledge of Leslie O'Neil was shaky at best. She was some girl who'd gone missing when he was a baby, whose disappearance and resulting graffiti was mysterious and entertaining enough that people would get out of their cars to take pictures of it. Aunt Pam said it was "homicide voyeurism." Uncle Terry didn't say anything about it at all. Cal barely ever thought about it, except for the eerie feeling he got sometimes when he was alone with the obelisk. As he pushed his bike forward, he found himself looking over his shoulder as he passed it. Just in case.

Amesville High was a five-minute ride from the main street, and when he came in sight of it, half the road was already choked up with cars. Mostly it was people who couldn't smoke in the school parking lot, but still enjoyed the ambiance of cheap vinyl interiors: goth kids, whose nose piercings flashed against the glow of clove cigarettes; the cheerleaders pairing every stick with a coffee, hoping to stay thin; three local stoners, who simply eyed him nervously as he passed. All of them human, maybe. But if you asked Cal, they often looked and acted like entirely different species.

Cal didn't know where he fit into the ecosystem. He sometimes liked to think he was like a lone wolf, but he knew he was more like a tortoise. Unimpressive, unattractive, but unnoticed. Even if he didn't like to admit it, being able to hide in plain sight was more of a blessing than a curse most of the time.

It was bad luck that day, then, when the bright red Dodge Neon spotted him from behind. Though he did not know it, something of the prey animal inside of Cal flinched. An unheeded reflex that noticed the whine of a window sliding quietly into a door, and the deadened gravel-crack of tires slowing to a stalking pace.

But although those instincts might have stopped his ancestors being eaten by tigers, by now they weren't even enough to protect him from pouncing fast food. It came flying out of the window and hit the side of his head with a wet, explosive slap. Cal yelped, and flung his face to the side.

Beneath him, the bike juddered and bucked against his hands; one trying to wipe whatever had hit him away whilst the other desperately tried to maintain control. Neither was a one-handed job. The front wheel jerked sideways, and Cal threw himself over the side, praying to hit grass rather than pavement before he landed in an awkward tangle, skidded a few inches, and finally came to a stop in the dirt.

Inside the Dodge, somebody was laughing. The window rolled back up again, and the car sped off towards the parking lot.

Cal lay there, wiggling his fingers and toes and making sure nothing was broken. After a half minute, he was satisfied that the only things out of place on him were a sore foot, a few book-shaped bruises on his back, and an oily slick of pink special sauce pooling in his ear.

The same couldn't be said for the bike. It lay on its side like roadkill; front wheel bent and back wheel still impotently spinning. As he considered the damage, a cold realization shot down Cal's spine and he immediately dropped down to one knee, fumbling with the clasp on his bag. Pens and notebooks spilt out onto the grass as he dug for something more precious.

It was wrapped in an old, gingham dishcloth. The box had been too big to fit, and Cal didn't have anything softer. Breath held fast, he pulled open the top of the bundle and narrowed his eyes to examine the precious cargo. His fingers ran over the smooth, gray plastic, expecting cracks but finding none. The knot of anxiety in his throat unfurled, and he sighed in relief.

At least his luck wasn't that bad, he thought, pushing it safely back into the depths of his bag. The thought only lasted as long as it took for him to remember the wheel, still bent pathetically out of place. He gave the bike a mournful stare and stood up. With a final, heavy sigh of resignation, he slung the backpack over his shoulder, and pulled on the handlebars.

Looked like he was gonna be walking the rest of the way to school.

The inside of Cal's locker looked like a dystopian science fiction novel in miniature, filled with old discs and cartridges, scraps of wire and dust. He didn't do it on purpose. Like any guy his age, he had an almost supernatural ability to accumulate dirt, and it all seemed to find its way into that little metal box. There were still nearly five minutes until first bell, so the hall was as full as it was going to get. Sneakers and high heels scuffed their way over the grimy diamond-tiled floor, on their way from who-knew-where, talking about god-knew-what. None of it really interested Cal, which was good, because nobody cared much to talk to him. He'd gotten very good at working out snippets of conversations as people passed by, like working out what notes the ambulance was hitting in its doppler wail.

In a weird way, it made him feel less lonely. If he listened hard enough, and often enough, little plotlines started to appear like currents ebbing and flowing below the surface, cresting for breath every so often in clandestine hallway conversations. People seldom noticed he was there, and even if they did, Cal guessed his low social standing made him the equivalent of a mute. Even if he knew, who would he tell?

That day, Annie Gleeson was worried Bill Hayman had gotten her pregnant. She huddled with a couple of friends, drawing in her yellow cardigan around her as she spoke in hushed tones. They were no more than two feet away from Cal's locker, but at least she was making the effort to keep her business private.

"After that thing in his Corolla," she recounted, "and in the hot tub."

Cal held onto a breath and pressed his head up against the locker door. He waited there for a good few seconds, just relishing the cool press of the metal on his skin. The noise washed over him like an obscuring tide over a stone, and for a few seconds he was comfortably invisible in it. Not for long, though. It never was.

"You lose a fight with a breakfast sandwich again?" came a familiar voice from beside him. Cal smiled, and raised his head.

"Ten for eight," he said, wiping some sauce from his ear. "Looks like I'm winning this semester."

He turned around to see Trevor's moon face beaming at him. If Cal's goal was to be low-key, Trevor was the happiest mistake he ever made: five-seven on his tiptoes, two hundred pounds and fond of flannel shirts; that was a neon sign and a half.

"You're lucky you got that internal bike helmet," he said, reaching forward and tapping Cal's head. Cal laughed, and swatted the hand away.

"For the hundredth time, it's a titanium plate. It's not gonna stop bullets."

"Or breakfast," Trevor replied, wiping a little sauce from his fingertips. Then he leaned forward and gave an exaggerated shifty look.

"So… did it come?" he asked. Cal put on a mock-offended face.

"Auto accidents kill thousands every year, Trev. I could've died."

"I'll be sympathetic after I know you've got the goods," Trevor replied.

On cue, Cal pulled out the cloth bundle and revealed the square-ish thing inside. It was a gray, plastic-clad camcorder, with a ratty fabric strap and a scuffed lens cap, but to Trevor's eyes it must've seemed like a gold bar.

"It's beautiful," he said, wiping an invisible tear from his eye. "When do you wanna test it out? Tonight?"

"So we're just gonna forget about watching *The Giant Claw*? And *Basket Case*?" Cal replied, pushing the camera back into the depths of his locker. Trevor looked halfway physically wounded and mortally offended, fingers curling as he counted off his points.

"*Giant Claw*'s monster is lame. *Basket Case* is some Frank Henlotter bullsh—"

"Why do I get the picture you have your heart set on *It Came from the Pit*?" Cal laughed, closing up his locker with a kick.

From its high perch on the wall, the school bell wailed. The stagnant sea of people rippled and flowed, before it rushed every which way into puddles and lakes behind laminate doors. Trev didn't seem to notice.

"It's a masterpiece, Cal," he said, voice rising to get over the swell, "you know it, I know it. God's perfect mistake: the script, the effects…"

"Alright, Trev. You win, I've gotta get to English," Cal replied, cutting him off. As usual, it didn't do much to stop him.

"I'll come with you," Trevor said, starting forward. "I've got German."

They skirted the side of the hallway, separating to avoid the more dangerous herds: football players, the hockey team, and the guys who hung out at the gates heating up paperclips with lighters and branding each other. When the crowd began to thin and the predators dispersed, Trevor hiked his way back to Cal's side, his enthusiasm undamaged.

"So, some guy on the boards posted up a pic this morning," he said, pausing dramatically, "photo of frickin' dog boy."

"A what?" Cal asked, screwing up his face.

"Dog boy. A boy who's half boy, half dog. Gum?" Trevor said matter-of-factly, stuffing a few sticks into his mouth.

"Like… a real one?" Cal asked, taking a few.

"I dunno. It looked real enough," Trevor replied with a shrug. They came to a stop outside of room 209, and Trevor loitered by the door.

"So, meet at my place at eight? My mom left pizza money," he said.

"Well, I'd probably have to cancel that date with a supermodel I had penciled in, but I can probably work something out," Cal replied. As they parted ways, Trevor flashed him a hand to the forehead, eyebrows raising as if in some kind of arcane greeting.

"Make sure you come back, traveler," he intoned. Cal smiled.

The Martian Visitors, scene six. Word for word, the worst goodbye in cinema history.

"I *never* never come back," he finished. They snorted, and then split. Disappeared into the deluge, hoping to surface again at three pm.

~

The problem wasn't that Cal didn't like Shakespeare; it was that he *hated* Shakespeare. It didn't matter how many times Mrs. Michaels theatrically plopped the model human skull on her desk, or insisted a boy read 'hilariously' for Ophelia, he just didn't get it.

That day, a short kid called Owen Carruthers had been chosen to play the part and, to his credit, he was getting into it. The few laughs he'd gotten when he raised his voice to a scratching pitch had made him confident that, while he was definitely going to be humiliated, it at least wasn't going to end with an after-class trip to his own locker. As he squawked "my lord" for the hundredth time, the bell pealed. Immediately, every still body in the room jerked to life, shuffling their feet and rustling bags. Mrs. Michaels twitched a rouged lip and clasped her ringed fingers to the page.

"The bell is for my benefit, not yours, ladies and gentlemen," she announced, sweeping over to her desk. Most of the other students stopped moving in their tracks and the ones that didn't really give a shit kept going. Mrs. Michaels put her book away and started writing on the chalkboard.

"Reports, reports, reports—and I'll thank you not to groan so loudly, Vanessa, if you'd be so kind," she said, shooting a withering look over her shoulder. "You now have nine days until I want a first copy in. Remember, it can be about something that really happened, or it can be made up, just as long as it's evocative, well-written and...?"

She stopped dead in her tracks. After a few seconds, the word "creative" muttered across the room in a halfhearted chorus. Mrs. Michaels snapped her fingers and sprung up her fist, as if catching the sound in mid-air like a fly.

"Creative! Exactly," she said, underlining the writing. She turned around to the class, and gave them a long, hard stare, like she was waiting for something more. Then, a wry smirk pinched at the side of her lip.

"Alright," she said, taking her usual perch beside the door, "now you can go."

Immediately, some were up and out so fast they almost left people-shaped clouds behind them. The rest got up in patches, slowed slightly by the fact that Mrs. Michaels insisted on saying goodbye to each of them. Even if he found it a little annoying, Cal kind of liked it. That was, except, for when she wanted to do more than wish him a good afternoon.

As he passed, her huge green eyes lingered on him.

"Cal," she said, adopting that unsettling humanness that teachers sometimes get when all isn't well, "would you mind staying back for a minute?"

Cal felt his stomach drop. That was the death phrase. No matter what, it wasn't good.

He lingered awkwardly in a corner whilst the rest of the class filed out, looking at the floor tiles. When the door finally closed, Mrs. Michaels turned around and clasped her hands together. When she spoke, her voice was unlike itself. Less authoritative, and softer.

Shit.

"How are you doing today, Cal?" she asked, sitting on the side of her desk. Cal put his hands in his pockets like he was searching for the right answer.

"I'm, uh… yeah. I'm alright, thanks," he said quietly, nodding. Mrs. Michaels smiled.

"Good. I'm glad," she said. Another pause. Whatever was going to land on him had reached the top of its arc, he thought, the silence was just the sound of it coming down.

"So, the ladies at the principal's office wanted me to talk to you about May 13," she said. After a few seconds, she cocked her head a little, and Cal realized she expected him to react.

"What about it?" he asked. Mrs. Michaels bit her lip, as if pained on his behalf.

"Well, obviously that's a… a *significant* date for you, and that kind of thing affects people in different ways, so they just wanted to know if you wanted to… to take a day off?"

Cal rubbed his neck and looked at the floor again.

"Thanks for the offer, Mrs. Michaels, but—" he began.

"It wouldn't be any trouble. The principal is happy to sign off on it."

"No, no, seriously," Cal insisted, giving her a halfhearted smile. "I'm fine. I won't need the day off, I'm alright."

"Are you completely sure?" she asked insistently. Cal drew himself up a little and tried to look more relaxed.

"Yeah," he said. "I'm good."

Mrs. Michaels looked him over for a moment and took in a long breath through her nose. Then, she nodded.

"If you're sure," she asked for a third time. Cal nodded before motioning to the door, eyebrows raised.

"So, can I…?" he asked. Mrs. Michael's smile returned, looking almost relieved. Maybe she thought there'd be more crying and keening.

"Yes, of course. I hope you have a great day, Cal," she said.

"You too, Mrs. Michaels," Cal said quickly, pulling his bag onto his shoulder.

When he came out into the hallway, he couldn't help but notice a wriggling, uncomfortable sting in his chest. Not physical, like a heart attack, but something deeper and more persistent. He pushed it down and away, focusing on dodging through the crowd instead.

And eventually it faded. Just like the lingering feeling of awkwardness at having a teacher touch his hand, not quite forgotten, but unobtrusive. Ambient.

Days in Amesville usually went like that. Like a time lapse with familiar routines coming in bold but hazy edges, bleeding little by little into the shifting blur. That day on May 11, 1993 would likely be the same as the one the year before, and the year before that.

Or, at least, that was how it seemed.

ROADKILL

AMESVILLE, 1977

When Mister Robinson emerged from his office, it was like a cut-price Wizard of Oz: a wizened little man, erupting out of the back room in a cloud of cigarette smoke to the tinny sound of 'Fever Girl' on the radio. Not quite the wonder of the Emerald City, but there was something about the image of Mister Robinson strutting out to pounding disco music that made Yule smile.

"You're the best at what you do… I got a fever and the cure is you…"

Robinson came over and slapped two piles of paper onto the desk. On one side, a set of hastily printed forms sat bleeding ink. On the other, a black-and-white photograph of an impossibly ugly dog sat gawping up at him, bug-eyed and snaggle-toothed. In large, striking letters above, it read, 'LOST,' and below, in much smaller text, 'no reward.'

Yule looked down at them and tried to stop himself smirking.

"Had as much as I can take… Prayin' for that shake, shake, shake…"

"You get that bum out back?" Robinson asked, coarse voice raking against the music. Yule smiled and nodded humbly.

"Yes sir. Just like you asked," he replied.

"KRRRRRRRRRRRRRRZT," squawked the radio. Robinson's eye flicked momentarily to it, before falling back on Yule.

"And you do a trash run?" he asked. Again, Yule gave a precious little nod.

"Yes sir."

"You got me fading, sweet and low…"

Robinson adjusted his spectacles and sniffed. Then he picked up one of the forms in his gnarled old hand and waved it in the air as he spoke.

"I need you to load up a machine, and—"

"KRRRRRRRRRZT."

Robinson raised his voice a little.

"I need you to take the—"

"KRRRRRNest at whaTKHRKRRRZTt feverZZT."

"What's that?" Yule asked, raising his shoulders and squinting in mock confusion. Robinson's face went purple, and when he shouted his head looked like it might fly off like the top of some chain-smoking pimple.

"I. Need. You. To—"

"KRRRRRRZT"

"For god sakes, would you turn that fucking radio off?" he screamed, screwing his eyes shut. Yule waited for another precious few seconds, determined to milk the joke for all the frustration it was worth. Then, as if a cartoon lightbulb had just lit up over him, his face brightened, and he nodded.

"Ohhhh, you said the radio!" he said, clicking the dial off. Robinson huffed and coughed. The shout seemed to have pulled apart whatever evil force was giving the old bastard life, and now he needed a moment to recuperate. When he spoke again, his voice had downgraded from 'furious' to a more usual 'highly annoyed.'

"I just need you to pack up one of the machines and deliver it uptown. *Uptown* uptown, maybe a mile out on Innsmouth Road," he said. Yule cocked his head back.

"Didn't know we did deliveries," he said.

"We do now," Robinson answered, pushing the forms over to him. Yule picked one up and scanned it over, before pointing to the top with a long finger.

"Is it legally binding if you misspelled delivery?" he asked. Robinson snatched the paper back and cocked an eye at it. Then, with a dismissive grumble, he put it back on the counter.

"Just get him to sign the damn things when you drop it off. He'll give you two grand, cash."

"That's not suspicious at all," Yule remarked. Robinson raised his palms and shrugged.

"Look, if some freak wants an arcade machine for hard cash, I don't give a damn," he said. "It's not like you can build a bomb outta these things. Hell, you can barely build a business out of 'em."

He laughed throatily at his own joke, though it soon became a gurgling hack. After he was done coughing, Robinson swept a vulture eye over the arcade, picking out which kid to put on the train.

"That one. The Polybius machine," he said, pointing. Yule let out a groan of disappointment.

"Really? We can't give them another? Nobody's even played it yet," he asked. Robinson didn't seem swayed. Then again, he was an evil lizard that looked like a person, so of course he didn't get it.

"Exactly, nobody's playin' it. It's a money sink to the tune of two grand," Robinson said, popping a cigarette into his mouth.

Yule's eyes wandered back down to the ugly dog on the posters gazing out longingly at him. Or hungrily. It was hard to tell when its eyes were pointing different directions.

"You, uh… you want me to give him these, too?" he asked, picking one up. Robinson rolled his eyes.

"Christ no, he'd have a heart attack," he said, glancing at the picture. "No, I need you to post 'em over town."

"You lose your dog?"

"My wife's dog," Robinson insisted, grimacing. "I can't stand the damn thing, but apparently the woman's not gonna get off my back until the ugly furball's back chewing my shoes, like it's my fault it's missing."

Yule laughed politely, then leaned in a little.

"And… it wasn't, right?" he asked. Robinson let out an oily chuckle.

"I wish. Ran out the front gate a couple nights ago, and I mean ran, like a bat outta hell. Little bastard. I mean, what kinda dog does that?" he said.

"I couldn't tell you, Mister Robinson. Maybe your neighbors got a cat."

"Maybe," Robinson grunted, blowing out a cloud of smoke. There was a brief pause before he slapped the pile of posters into Yule's hands, which swayed and tottered like cherries on a melting sundae.

"Put all those up and get the arcade machine delivered before five o'clock. I want you here for the rush," he said, reaching under the desk. He brought out a pair of black straps and draped them over Yule's shoulder. "And you'll need these. Apparently, the Waylon brothers both got food poisoning, so you'll be doin' the move by yourself."

"What?" Yule said, dropping the papers on the side counter. "Mister Robinson, I don't know if you've noticed so much, but the Waylon brothers weigh three hundred pounds apiece, and it ain't lard weight."

"What's your point?" Robinson asked, disinterestedly puffing on his cigarette.

"It takes two of those monsters to haul these things out of the truck. How am I supposed to get one in by myself?"

Robinson chuckled, spraying vapor through his cracked, old lips. Smoke wreathed, he patted Yule on the arm and treated him to a mocking smile.

"Like I said, that's what the straps are for," he told Yule, turning to re-enter his office. As he reached the door, he swung himself around on the doorframe, leaning like a stunted ape so as to make his voice heard.

"And don't you think I'm not gonna count out all two thousand dollars of that money when you get back. I find a single cent missing, I'm gonna come down on your ass so hard your nuts'll trade places," he warned.

"Wouldn't want that," Yule replied sweetly. Robinson gave him a withering look, and then slammed the door closed. Immediately the facade dropped, and Yule's entire body relaxed.

Jesus.

He put the papers on the side and wandered over to the machine. It looked heavy as a motherfucker, that was for sure. Yule sighed and put his hands on his hips as if he had a choice in the matter, and it wasn't a decision of suffer now, or suffer later. No time like the present, he thought, bracing his shoulder against the side of the cabinet.

One. Two. Heave.

The next hour was a lost space. A vicious, sweaty battle punctuated by blinding flashes of cramp and mildly crushed fingers. Once the machine was miraculously in the bed of the truck, Yule paused to wipe his brow, wincing at the feeling of the wet shirt against his back. The noonday sun was hot and harsh, but at least there was a breeze out there. When he picked up the order form, wet ink wriggled beneath his thumb. His eyes flicked down to the address column, where it read 'Howard Triptree, 1 Collier's Mill.'

Yule leaned on the truck and frowned thoughtfully.

He'd never heard of Collier's Mill. Or, maybe he had, and just forgotten. It rang a bell, like he'd seen the planning permission someplace, or heard about it on the local news. Leastways, he'd never been there before, and he'd never heard of a Howard Triptree either. Neither of those things was notable, he thought, but enough time spent in Amesville made the new and unknown, however, small, seem world-endingly strange.

He sighed and threw the forms in the glove compartment. Either way, he thought, Robinson didn't pay him enough to be concerned with what was normal or not. Hell, the old buzzard barely paid him enough to warrant driving the truck at all. He climbed in behind the wheel, and the engine clattered to life, cabin juddering like an old man's hand. In the passenger seat, Mrs. Robinson's ugly dog slipped around on its paper pile, drooling at the ceiling.

At that point, Yule meant to start driving. His hands were on the wheel, foot resting on the pedal, but for some reason he just sat there. Sat and stared out into the sunlit pastel tones of 8th street with an unmistakable yet wholly bewildering feeling of dread. It all looked so still, but he was now suddenly and acutely aware of something that wasn't. Something electric in the air, a charge, and not the good kind either; the kind that builds and builds until something bursts. The signs of a storm in a cloudless sky.

But heavy as it was, the feeling fled as quickly as it arrived. It only lasted a few seconds, just until Yule shook himself from his stupor enough to hit the gas. He pulled jerkily away from the curb, swerving to avoid the empty black van parked some ways across the street. He barely gave it a second glance as he made his way around the corner, stopping only to notice the fact it had tinted windows.

Yule grimaced. Now he was definitely back in the normal world, where some people were apparently born without taste.

He slowed to make the corner, battling against the truck's stripped out brakes. The aged Ford picked up speed only as the tires straightened out onto the old road, momentum finally fully forward, and in a moment, he was gone.

For a few seconds, the street lay in dusty silence as the sound of the truck faded away. Then, quietly and unnoticed, the black van swept sharply away from the curb in a purposeful, noiseless crawl.

When he was eight, Yule's Auntie Ray had stayed with them a while. Dad said she'd gone to prison once for robbing banks, but Yule hadn't believed it. Auntie Ray was a forty-year-old woman with a cheap weave and a soft spot for menthols; not how he imagined a bank robber to be.

Over time though, he became aware of an unsettlingly energetic gleam in her eyes whenever she wasn't looking at anything. That gleam was why Yule never forgot what she'd told him the last time they ever met.

"Keep this in your head, kid," she'd said, jiggling the cuffs against her pink nightgown, "you can run fast in a bad car, but you sure as hell can't run far."

Years on, the advice seemed oddly appropriate as he sat listening to the truck's engine die. By the time he'd hit the coarse dirt verge, the entire thing was just coasting on leftover momentum. Yule leaned his head against the wheel, fighting the frustration trying to worm its way out of his temple vein. Deep, centering breaths, he thought. Don't put a dashboard ornament through the windscreen. Deep... centering...

After a while he sat up again and stared through the smeared glass. There was nothing but bare road ringed by trees as far as he could see, with more of the same behind him. On either side the undergrowth rose in a thick green wall, barely kept at bay by the ever-eroding strip of black asphalt. Silence loomed: no wind, no movement, just him and the road and nothing else.

He waited in the car another minute or so, almost melting into the thick swell of quiet. He checked the rearview. No cars. He hadn't seen another person out there the whole drive.

Yule chewed the inside of his cheek and laid his head up against the seat rest. Idly, his one open eye wandered down and met with one of the missing posters. The dog answered to "Fancy," apparently, in a detail that almost seemed cruel. He exhaled through his nostrils and put a hand into his jeans pocket.

"What do you think, Fancy?" he asked, fingers curling around the papery skin of a twisted stick. "Should I be a model citizen, or make bad decisions?"

The dog, predictably, didn't answer. Yule smirked and chuckled to himself. He pulled the joint out of his pocket and popped it in his mouth, fingers already curling over the familiar contortions of his Zippo lighter.

"Bad dog," he said with a laugh, lifting the dancing flame to the joint's tip. With his free hand, he rolled up the window.

Yule liked marijuana. He knew it was a stereotype, and god knew that being black and committing petty crimes was the lazy man's bank robbery when it came to being given a sentence. But he liked it, and he could never get away from that fact.

These days it was less to chill him out, and more to make him normal. It made the feeling of impending dread dull and the ghosts of gunfire abate. At least, most days. Sometimes it just made it worse, but at least he'd stop shaking. It didn't help his paranoia that the threat of prison time hung over the act like the whistling few seconds before an airstrike hit, but it was worth it.

The tip of the joint flared in front of his eyes, brooding red light made misty by the vapor haze. Yule exhaled and let his eyes flutter closed. The entire truck cabin was milky with off-white smoke, hung in perfect stillness, as endlessly quiet as the faded concrete outside. He felt it in his bones and the damp humming in his brain. In that quiet, he didn't hear the bushes parting at the side of the road.

BANG.

Yule's eyes snapped open, and he jerked forward. The entire truck cabin shook as something hammered into the driver's side door, nearly shattering the window. At first, Yule thought somebody had clipped him on the way past, but that notion fled when he saw the blood running down the misty glass.

He cried out in disgust and kicked his way spasmodically away from the door. Instinctively, his hand found the handle behind and yanked, sending him toppling out of the dope-soaked truck cabin and into the coarse roadside dirt. A wispy tail of smoke traced the arc of his fall like in an old cartoon.

He lay there for a few seconds, wide-eyed and panting. Then, he scrambled to his feet and rounded the truck. Prepared for the worst as he was, when he finally saw what hit him, he couldn't quite piece it all together. He just stood there, slowly raising a palm against his forehead.

There was a huge dent in the car door, like somebody had hurled a bowling ball at it. A thick, high pressure spurt of blood splattered up the window and over the roof, dripping in fingertip-sized droplets from the wing mirror. Lying in the quickly moistening dirt below was the body of a whitetail doe. It couldn't have been older than two years, judging by the size of it, and it was a pitiful thing to look at; all bent up next to the car. Its neck was all… wrong. Broken and angular. A little nub of bone had punched its way out from beneath white-flecked fur and left a thick trickle-line of death across the snow white.

Yule stared at it, dumbfounded. He'd hit dozens of whitetail deer over the years, and some had been in even worse shape than this one. But all those other times, he'd been moving.

Behind him, the undergrowth rustled. He wheeled around but didn't see the girl at first. All he saw was the rifle in her hands. The sight of it made his heart pound. He fell back against the truck as if by reflex, putting his palms up. Whatever noise he intended to make wouldn't come, so they stood there for a moment, gawking at one another. The girl broke the silence when her eyes found the deer.

"Oh my god," she said, putting her rifle down by the side of the road. "Oh my god."

Yule lowered his hands and felt the coiled breath in his throat unwind. The girl ran past him and knelt by the cooling body, ghosting a hand over its fur.

"Oh my god," she repeated a third time, eyes straying to the blood-stained door. "I am so, so sorry! Did you hit it?"

"Hit it? I was parked!" Yule replied, gesturing sharply to the truck. Then he leaned forward, one eye squinting as if appraising a diamond. Now that the gun had gone, the girl was somehow familiar.

"I know you from someplace?" he asked. The girl took a step back and shook her head.

"No."

"Nah, nah…" Yule insisted, pointing. "I think I've seen you round the arcade. Bradley's sister, right? Bradley O'Neil?"

Her eyes widened.

"No," she said again, shaking her head. Yule laughed and wagged his finger.

"Yes! I knew I recognized you, you're what… Leanne… Loretta… Le…" he said, snapping his fingers. "Leslie? Leslie!"

Leslie deflated a little. Her once oh-so-bright face of concern soured into something more sedate.

"You've got one hell of a memory for a store clerk," she said, putting her hands in her pockets.

"I never forget a kid," Yule replied, laughing. Leslie snorted.

"I don't think you wanna go around saying that," she said. Yule's smile faded, and he leaned against the truck again.

"Alright, GI-Barbie, maybe I'll say somethin' different. Like maybe I'll say how you was skippin' school, which is wrong, and hunting deer way out of season, which is full-blown illegal," he said. Leslie sniffed, and nodded to the hazed windows.

"More illegal than reefer?" she asked. Yule went to answer but stopped upon realizing he didn't have one.

"Well, you're still skippin' school. That's morally wrong," he said, gesturing to the misshapen pile of fur beside them. "Just like scarin' deer so bad they brain themselves all over my damn truck door."

"My dad told me it was fine to miss school for it, and I swear, I didn't do anything to that deer," Leslie insisted. "Even if they get spooked, they don't…"

She trailed off, as if catching an aftertaste of the word "spook" on her tongue. She glanced at him as if to gauge the size of misstep, but Yule didn't flinch. At least somebody gave a damn at all. Leslie brushed some hair from her face and glanced again at the body.

"This thing ran a half a mile at full sprint. I don't even think it saw me, it just up and ran."

"So what was it running from? Wolf man?" Yule asked.

"Maybe it had a disease or something. It just went crazy, all of a sudden. They don't do that normally unless there's some sorta parasite in 'em," she said, unconsciously rubbing her arm as she appraised the carcass again. Yule stared at the deer too, and for a second he could feel the hairs on his neck rise. Then, Leslie took a few steps back, and motioned with her thumb.

"I should probably go," she said, backing across the road. She picked the rifle back up, and Yule gave a start.

"Whoa, whoa! Hey!" he yelled, holding up his palms "You can't just pick that damn thing up and not warn me. I'm downrange, you could blow my goddamn head off."

Leslie looked sheepish, and then gestured to the door.

"Sorry. And I'm really sorry about your truck," she said.

Yule looked at his hand. Animal blood glistened darkly against his palm. For a moment he'd felt angry or something close to it, but she was just a kid, he thought. What did he expect her to do about it?

"This?" he said, wiping it on his jeans. "Buff right out. Don't worry about it."

With a slight smile, she turned away. Then, as abruptly as she had arrived, Leslie headed back into the undergrowth and out of sight again, the pantomimic wave of waxy green branches the only evidence she'd ever been there at all.

Yule took a few steps into the road and put his hands on his hips, sole concern resting on the blood-spattered truck again. He didn't want to think about what would happen if he rode into town with it like that. Might as well just paint a big target on his back while he was at it.

A gentle wind rolled across the back of his neck, and Yule realized he was shifting his weight nervously from one heel to another. He just wanted to get out of there. Off that stretch of road. Couldn't exactly say why, other than the obvious. He got back in the driver's seat and the engine spluttered to life, somehow recovered from whatever problem killed it before. As the truck crawled forward, he could hear the deer's head slide against the metal and fall to the ground.

When Robinson said Collier's Mill was uptown, he was only half right. It was definitely up, but there wasn't any town proper for more than mile. By some miracle, the truck managed to coast on luck the whole way, although he almost missed the turning, the small white sign half-hidden by undergrowth. There the path split off the main route, vein-like, and wound into a thick green belt of trees.

Yule slowed, rounding the corner at a crawl. The road was only large enough for one car at a time, and with the brakes the way they were he didn't like his chances going faster than ten miles per hour. As he peered through the leaves, Yule could just make out whitewashed walls and gleaming windows somewhere on the other side.

The road ended abruptly at a large gate made of red bricks and wrought iron. An off-white CCTV camera kept silent survey over the entrance, sweeping back and forth like a horizontal pendulum. The gate was open, but something told Yule that didn't happen too often. They never did in places like this.

Well I'll be damned, he thought, pressing on the gas. A gated community in Amesville, of all places. Day just kept getting stranger and stranger.

Number 1 Collier's Mill lay at the end of that strange track, meaning Yule had to drive the whole way through to reach it. The further he went, the less at ease he felt.

There were no cars in any of the driveways, and none of the asphalt was peppered with the telltale dust of use. Every window lay dark, and curtained. And, perhaps most strikingly of all, there were no people. No evidence of people save for the fact there were buildings there in the first place. It was a little ghost town of nearly two dozen houses; whitewashed, gated and perfectly preserved like a bug in resin.

The house he intended to reach was just as whitewashed and unremarkable as the others: two stories of perfect, dollhouse symmetry from red door to roof tile, unsettlingly unmarked. Yule pulled to a stop outside and looked over his shoulder a final time.

The entire place was, and remained, empty.

He got out the car and walked to the red door, order form pressed against his chest. He hesitated before knocking, almost unwilling to break the sleepy silence. But it was nothing, he thought. Something childish in him.

Tap, tap, tap.

For a while there was no answer, or sound from within. Yule waited on the porch, idly looking around. There was another camera, he noticed. Hanging like a squat claw out from the wooden porch roof, the glassy eye fixed in all its deep and unending square blackness upon him.

As he considered it, the door opened.

The man before him was short and lined. Old but not aged, his harsh blue eyes the color of the summer sky mixed in with fresh, cold snow. Sharp, and alive.

"Mister Triptree?" Yule asked. For a half second the man didn't reply, as if he didn't understand what he'd been asked. But then, a satisfied smile spreading over his features, he nodded.

"Yes, that is me," he said. Yule pointed a thumb over his shoulder toward the truck.

"I'm here to deliver your arcade machine," he said. Triptree nodded and shook his hand.

"Right, of course. Please come in," he replied airily, stepping out of the way. Yule went inside, giving a final glance to the glossy camera eye as he passed beneath its gaze.

The inside of the house was clear and airy. Modern-built, or so it looked like. The walls were still rosy with the sheen of fresh paint, and he could see all the way through to the window-paneled kitchen at the other end, which glistened variously with well-polished surfaces. A handful of pictures hung in the hallway, mostly European-looking landscapes. The carpet in front of the door was stiff underfoot, bristles resisting a little before yielding. This guy didn't get many visitors, Yule thought.

"Where should I put it?" he asked. Triptree gestured down the hallway, fingers ticking to the left.

"Just through there, in the garage," he said.

Yule wandered down the hall and stuck his head around the garage doorway. It was the only room so far that looked lived in; oil stained tools lay out on the bench, among what looked like handwritten notes and diagrams. Triptree was a busy man.

"So, uh… what are you planning to do with this thing?" he asked, turning around. Triptree was looking out the window, and almost seemed surprised Yule had spoken again. When he answered, Yule detected a twang in his accent. Something continental.

"I'm what you might call a hobbyist, I suppose. Disassembly, reassembly. That sort of thing," Triptree replied, looking through the open door. Yule grunted and adjusted his belt.

"Well, I can get it hooked up in there, no problem. So long as you got an extension cord?"

"No, no. That won't be necessary, I don't need it turned on," Triptree replied. Yule smirked to cover his surprise and shrugged.

"Alright. You're the boss," he said, making to leave again before stopping at the door, suddenly aware of how much his palms ached. "You wouldn't mind giving me a hand, would you?"

"Certainly," replied Triptree, following him out. They walked down the path and down to the roadside, where Yule set about unstrapping the Polybius machine from the truck bed. Triptree lingered awkwardly to the side, eyes fixed on the door.

"Your, ah, truck appears to have blood on it," he said. Yule paused and looked over at the swirled red stain.

"Yeah. Had a run in with aspiring roadkill on the way here," he grunted, undoing the last strap.

The next half hour was just as lost as the first. After much pushing and sweating, they managed to haul the arcade machine inside and dragged it through into the garage. As the cabinet juddered to its final standing place, Yule let out a long, exhausted sigh.

"Y'know, I thought I was gonna miss this thing," he panted, wiping sweat from his brow, "but now? Not so much."

"I'm sorry I couldn't be of more help. I was never particularly athletic," said Mister Triptree, downcast. Yule gave him a tired smile and shook his head.

"It's more than I'd usually expect to get. Plus I'm not paying two thousand dollars for the privilege," he said. Triptree twitched as if something had shocked him and held up a finger.

"The money!" he said, turning for the door. "My apologies, I nearly forgot!"

He disappeared for a few moments, light footsteps creaking up the unseen stairs. Yule lingered at the edge of the room a while, listening to the muffled sounds of footfall and drawers opening on the floor above. He didn't pay it much notice. His head was still spinning a little from the exhaustion.

A few moments later, Triptree returned with a large brown envelope tucked under his arm. He gave it to Yule, face creased into a well-meaning smile.

"You'll find it's all there, if you want to count it," he said.

"Nah, that's alright. I trust you," Yule replied, taking it from him. He then reached on top of the machine and waved the papers in the air. "I wouldn't mind it if you signed these, though. Saves me getting fired?"

Triptree considered him for a moment, looking him up and down like he was assessing the quality of an antique dresser. Then he perked up a little, and his smile deepened.

"I can go read these over and sign in my office, if you do not mind waiting downstairs a moment," he said, gesturing to the door. "If you'd like, I've got a jug of iced tea in the kitchen. You look like you could use something cold."

That struck Yule a little. He wasn't used to people letting him be in their houses unsupervised. As if the accent wasn't enough, that was all Yule needed to know that Triptree wasn't from around here by any stretch.

"Much obliged," he replied, twisting the moment of shock into a friendly smile. Triptree raised up the papers as if in an imaginary toast, then headed out of the garage. Yule followed, giving one final look at the Polybius machine, stood alone in the center of the room. Outside of the arcade's stuffy carpet décor, it looked desperately out of place. He'd have felt sad, except for the fact it had tried to break his spine in a dozen different ways.

He passed through the main hallway, and into the window-paneled kitchen. The entire east-facing wall looked out over the shallow lip of the hill, filling the whole side of the room up with verdant green. He waited there a while, alone and idly wondering what the rest of the house looked like. His eyes flicked up to the ceiling, listening out for the sound of footsteps. But he heard none, and curiosity prevailed.

Yule turned on the spot and found himself staring through the open living-room door. With a final glance upstairs, he went inside.

The mantle atop the fireplace was a rustic-looking wooden beam, like from a barn roof. A number of photograph frames stood in jumbled lines across it, most of which featured Triptree in varying stages of age. In one, he had his arm round a smiling old woman and was flanked by a graying man stood proudly beside him. His parents, or something close to it, Yule thought. There was a series of photos of Triptree with a young girl, first as a baby, and eventually all the way into a smiling, blonde teenager stood at the base of a blue-rocked mountain.

Yule smiled. Something in him stirred. The same thing that woke up a little whenever he imagined the lives of other people going on behind backlit windows at night. No more than a dozen pictures to suggest an entire, vibrant life. And, he thought as he saw the tarnished old wedding ring sat dusty beneath a photo frame, perhaps other, less vibrant things.

His eyes traced over the rest of the mantle, finally coming to a stop on a framed certificate. It was a dull cream color, with a shiny gold seal in the lower middle. The word HARVARD was written in bold red letters at the top, followed by spidery black text.

"The fellows of Harvard University confer to Henning Van Hallan the degree of Master of Science."

Yule paused and squinted at it.

Wrong name. Either Triptree had stolen a man's degree, or Mister Triptree wasn't Mister Triptree at all. But... that didn't make any sense. Why would anyone use a fake name to buy an arcade cabinet?

Soft footfalls called from the upstairs landing. Yule clenched his jaw and crept out of the living room, trying desperately to silence his steps on the hardwood floor. He made it far enough to look like he'd just wandered out of the kitchen when the-man-formerly-known-as-Triptree appeared once more.

"Done!" he said, holding up the papers. "Although, you should let your manager know that he has made a few misspellings."

"Yeah, I don't think that'd do much good," Yule replied, taking them from him. His eyes lingered on the man for a moment. He seemed different now. Like the bright exterior was hiding something. Triptree had been a pleasant enough guy, but whoever Henning Van Hallan was, he didn't want anyone knowing.

Yule gave a big, fake smile, and held up the glass.

"I should probably get going," he said, thumbing towards the exit.

Triptree considered him for a moment, seeming to detect the sudden awkwardness, but they both committed to the fake smiles enough for neither to suspect too much.

"Of course," he said, showing him to the door, "thank you so much for your help. Here."

Before Yule could respond, Triptree shoved a crumpled twenty into his palm, and clasped it shut. His hands were strangely cold and clammy, but the unexpected money at least made Yule's surprise genuine.

"Oh, uh…" he muttered, looking at it.

"Please have a nice day," Triptree insisted brightly. With that, the red door closed again. Yule lingered on the porch for a second, trying to put together what had just happened. Then, he climbed into the driver's seat and took off back down the road without looking back.

He'd had enough strangeness for one day.

THE THING IN THE MILL

AMESVILLE, 1993

"You're gonna electrocute somebody," she said.

"I told you, nobody's gonna get electrocuted!" he replied, jamming a screwdriver in the back of the TV.

Cal sat on the sofa and watched the air outside turn from burnt twilight warmth to cold, prickling night, the sunset shading the living room in honeyed half-shadows from amidst the pines. The smoke from his aunt's cigarette danced in place, slipping in and out of the haze as it thinned and bloated towards the ceiling. She took a draw and turned to him, brow mostly hidden below a bright pink bandanna.

"When your uncle electrocutes himself," she said, giving him a crooked smile, "call an ambulance."

"What'll you be doing?" Cal asked.

"Tellin' him how I was right about ordering crap from those phone-in catalogs," she said laughing. At that, Uncle Terry's head shot up from behind the TV.

"I told you, sweetheart, it's the future, we gotta get on board! Otherwise we're leaving money on the table."

"So how's the future gonna write a fifty-dollar check for repairs?" she asked. Terry gave her an exaggerated wink.

"I work for free, baby," he said. Pam giggled, and faux shooed him away.

"Get back in your TV, I don't wanna miss *Cheers*," she said. Terry let out a quick, snorting laugh, and went back to tinkering. It was good to hear him laughing with her again. Maybe it was retiring, or something in the water, but they were arguing a lot less than they used to. That was fine by Cal, even if it meant he didn't get sent to the movies alone anymore when they wanted to scream at each other.

From the corner of the room, there was an electrical crackle, a beep, and a hum. Terry jerked back from the TV and clapped his hands as the blank screen lit into a pool of static snow. Pam covered her ears, wine slopping in the glass.

"What'd I tell you? No repairman needed," he said proudly, raising his voice over the fuzzing. Pam flapped her hand at the television, and grimaced.

"You're very talented, now turn that thing down!" she shouted.

Terry did so, and Pam's shoulders dropped back down. The picture crackled and spat for a moment, and then snapped into something else: a video of some turbines, and a pleasant voice.

"...hundreds of jobs when the plant becomes fully operational next month," it said. The screen switched to a middle-aged, gray-haired man in a mustard-colored sweater. He smiled awkwardly at the camera, forehead shiny with sweat. Had to be local news.

"Uh, and, now for something a little more cultural," he said. Beside him, a picture faded into frame. A familiar obelisk, with stark white writing spray-painted on the side.

"WHO TOOK LESLIE O'NEIL?" it asked, unanswered. Pam rolled her eyes, sinking into the couch as if by sheer force of disdain.

"...demonstrations against preserving the historic street art..."

"Do you hear that?" Pam asked, turning to Cal. "Historic street art. Honestly. I've been saying this from day one, it's just not right, it's so... *morbid*. And if that were a young man that had died instead of some little girl—"

"I'm sure he gets it, sweetie," Terry interrupted, taking a sip of his beer. Pam smirked.

"Your uncle gets sick of this stuff, but that's what he gets for marrying a reformed hippy," she said, lying back into Terry's arms. He didn't even look at her. For a second, all Cal could see in his eyes was the yellow reflection of the newscaster's cardigan.

The picture in the corner changed from the obelisk to a portrait. A teenage girl in front of a vomit-inducing flecked backdrop.

"...in broad daylight. Despite a county-wide search lasting nearly six months, the sixteen-year-old was neve—"

Click.

Terry's finger twitched atop the TV remote, and the screen went black. For a second there was nothing but their own reflections staring back through the tint. Then, from a bright center line, the picture returned.

"It's a little-known fact that the tan became popular in what is known as the bronze age..."

Onscreen, Cliff Clavin took a drink of his beer while the canned laughter from the audience rippled in approval. Pam, as if in chorus, yipped in excitement and buried herself further into Terry's arms.

For a half second more Terry still looked far away, trapped somewhere. But it was brief, so brief Cal even questioned if he saw it at all. Terry kissed Pam on the head and put the beer can up to his lips, grimaced, then set it down.

"Papa's empty. Shift your ass, hippy," he said.

"You don't have pepper spray this time," Pam said, grinning. He moved her aside and gave her another kiss. Then his eyes fell on Cal.

"Hey, buddy—before I forget, could you gimme a hand taking that compressor out? I ripped it out the old fridge, but... I guess my knees ain't up to the task anymore."

"Sure thing," Cal replied, getting up. Pam watched them go, giving them a coquettish wave.

"My big strong men. Keep up like this I'll be able to start a moving company," she said. *Mom had never liked Pam,* Cal thought. *Maybe it was because Pam was always happy.*

Terry limped into the tiled kitchen, steadying himself on a chair when he stopped. He acted like he hated that limp, but Cal knew he was proud of it. Only officer in town to get shot on duty and, technically, that meant he was the first to survive being shot, too. He'd halted beside a large metal box sat in a tangled wire nest on the kitchen counter.

"Here it is, in all its glory. Watch the left edge, there's grease or somethin' up the side," he warned, opening the back door. Cal tested the weight and felt his back crick a little. It probably wasn't any heavier than thirty pounds or so, but Cal wasn't used to lifting anything day-to-day, except for the crushing weight of his own awkwardness. Terry came over and heaved it up slightly, using his free hand to prop open the back door.

With a few grunts and some shuffling, they passed out into the cool evening air. A final, swinging heave, and the compressor went skittering towards the garbage can at the end of the drive, where it landed with a slopping, hissing skid. Terry wiped his hands on his jeans and let out a long, relieved exhale.

"Well, that's that done with," he said, looking out over the peach colored clouds. It was nice. The breeze was cool and Cal could hear crickets starting to chirp awake in the overgrown front yard, creaking to the rhythm of dandelion sways.

Terry lingered for a second, and then coughed.

"So, how's work?" he asked. Cal hesitated. Terry never asked stuff like that.

"Delivering pizzas?" Cal asked. Terry nodded.

"Yeah. How is that?" he insisted.

"It's delivering cheese pies to hicks, Terry, what do you think?" Cal replied. When the joke didn't get a reaction, Cal coughed and nodded his head. "Yeah. It's good."

"Good. Good," Terry agreed, nodding into the middle distance. It was a few more seconds before he spoke again, and when he did it was with all the gusto of an acrophobic skydiver.

"I just wanted you to know I'm there for you. My old man was never gonna win any parenting awards, and I know your dad always felt the same way. I dunno. This was… stupid, just forget about it," he said finally. The two of them stared at each other for a few seconds, hoping the masculine discomfort would fade.

"So…" Cal began, slowly gesturing to the door with his thumb, "you wanna go inside, and pretend this conversation never happened?"

"Yeah, I'd love to do that," said Terry, putting his hands in his pockets. They crossed the yard and lingered for a second by the steps up the back door. Cal smiled at him and inclined his head a little.

"Thanks, Uncle Terry," he said. Terry ruffled his hair, and for a second all the awkwardness seemed to melt away. There was just a welcoming warmth.

"Don't mention it. Now get back in, your aunt's probably gonna wanna order in dinner soon," he said, taking a step inside. Cal stopped, and nodded at the road.

"I won't need it; I'm sleeping over at Trev's tonight. His mom's out of town."

When he didn't get a reply, Cal turned around. Terry's brow was all creased into folds.

"You boys ain't gonna be drinkin', are you?" he asked. Now he sounded like a cop again. Cal felt a lump rise in his throat.

"No?" he replied. Terry's stern glare remained.

"Well, good. Because otherwise you coulda gone to the Wondermart on fifth, and not get ID'd by the stoner they got working there. But because you're not…" he said. The hint of a smile broke the glare, but his deadpan was almost flawless. Cal tried to mirror him, giving him a stoic nod.

"Right. Because I'm not," he confirmed.

"Good," replied Terry, turning to face the horizon again.

Cal lingered by the door, half inside the house.

"Are you coming in?" he asked.

Terry chuckled and put his hands in his pockets.

"Gonna stay out here a while, I think. Get some fresh air," he said. Cal nodded, and went back inside.

Terry stood at the edge of the yard, alone on their little hill. Nothing more than a dot astride a shadow, before the yawning, burning sky; all but lost in the lilac streaks of fire on the horizon. Below, the wood waited in yearning, hungry blackness, dragging the road down its cavernous throat.

God, how he hated those woods.

—

The door rattled and quaked, doorknob shuddering as something huge pounded on the other side. He screamed, but it was too late: a gigantic yellowed eyeball was already at the window.

"See?" said Trevor, nodding at it. "They always wait until it's too late."

Cal took a sip from his cup, and immediately gagged. A tingly, burning kind of warmth slipped and bloomed like fire in his chest.

"How much gin is in this?" He coughed, putting the cup down on the side. Trevor raised it to his lips, and his face screwed up.

"About five seconds worth," he replied, cheek twitching, "too much?"

They both visibly suppressed the urge to gag, faces twisted up in a mixture of silent laughter and cringing regret. If there was anything that could've described them without a single word, it would've been that. You could say it was the blooming feeling of warmth and relaxation, but that was less kinship and more the liquor.

On screen, *The Thing From The Pit* had started to cocoon. Organic blisters of flesh wrapped across the fake cabin walls, tinged with plastic slime. Trevor burped, and settled into the couch.

"And they never use fire on stuff. Always use fire," he said, shaking his head. With a theatrical flick, he started another line on a long list cradled in his lap.

"Are you gonna list every single one of those things?" Cal coughed. Trevor clicked the pen again and turned to him.

"How are we supposed to make a good movie if we don't meticulously research what went wrong in other ones?"

"I dunno. Be good at it?" Cal answered.

Trevor gave a blustering laugh, like he'd just seen a wiener dog fall into a kiddie pool. He put down the pen and took up his cup.

"I'm gonna need more of this," he said, taking a sip. The tough face didn't last out, however, and ended in the hook-pull of revulsion at the side of his lip. For a few more minutes they turned their attention back to the grainy TV screen. Two cops were arguing in the station, throwing themselves around in overplayed anguish.

"What even is this thing!" asked the less macho of the two, flinging his hand over to the door. His rugged, handsome partner grabbed him by the lapels, and the camera leaned into a dramatic zoom. Fat, fake beads of sweat rushed down his chiseled brow.

"The pit, you fool!" he said, through gritted teeth. "The thing from the pit!"

"And, roll credits," Trevor said, clicking the screen off. Cal let out an angry gasp and elbowed him.

"What'd you do that for?" he asked, gesturing to the screen. Trevor rubbed his arm gingerly.

"The movie jumps the shark after that scene, nothing happens!" he said.

"What do you mean, nothing happens? A guy's head explodes! Plus, I'm pretty sure you see a full boob when the lair caves in."

Trevor looked like he was about to reply, when the house shivered. The buzz of power in the walls gave way to the halting judder of empty space piling up in the wires. The TV sound distorted and then clicked off, pulling all the lights away with it.

Then nothing. Quiet. For a few seconds they waited there, bathed in the dull, thick stillness. Then, as quickly as it had fled, the power returned: lights flickered back to musty brightness, TV screen flooding up a bright, electronic blue.

"Well that wasn't creepy at all," Trevor said, eyes flicking over the ceiling. Cal got up and grabbed his backpack.

"Power plant. Safety grid. Watch the news, Trev," he said, picking up the gin. "Either way, I'm taking it as a sign. C'mon."

Trevor shifted in his chair and turned to the window. He eyed it with a strange, wavering suspicion, before facing Cal again.

"I think we should wait," he said.

Cal screwed up his face. "Why?"

"It's getting dark," Trevor answered, somewhat timidly. Cal laughed, and stopped what he was doing to smile mockingly at him.

"You afraid of the dark?" he asked.

"What? No!" Trevor insisted, gesturing to the window. "It's just that it can be dangerous out there. Especially in the wilderness, y'know? There could be pumas or bears or… something…"

"Sure. The wilderness. The one kids have Easter egg hunts in," Cal replied, opening the front door. Trevor scoffed, and picked up his shoes.

"I'm just saying," he insisted, tying his laces, "there's a reason that people wandering to their doom in the woods after dark is a trope."

The evening air was warm, and still. Out in the great beyond, the sky settled black where it met the horizon, darkening the tree line stretching from it towards them like a furry shadow. For a while they said nothing, and when Cal next spoke, his voice was softer. Kinder.

"Hey, Trev?" he asked.

"What?"

"Don't shit your pants, but it's pretty dark out here," he laughed.

Trevor shoved him, and soon the night air was filled up with the sound of their voices peeling away into the slowly thickening gloom of the old road. The route took them maybe a half mile down the side of the steep hill. At the end of Trevor's street, it descended, hugging the earthen heap as it ran down into the tree line. The dirt path at the side of the track only lasted maybe a third of the way before it was swallowed up by a long, wriggling lip of clay-brown roots and dull green weeds, and they were forced to walk on the dirt.

They didn't see a single car on their way down, and took no issue stopping at the blind corner. Trevor fumbled a flashlight out of his backpack and checked his watch.

"Think we can get to the old lumber office before nightfall?" he asked.

"Sure. Should be straight down there, maybe ten minutes," Cal replied, grabbing the camera out of his bag. "I got a good feeling about that place. The pond out back, too. It looked nasty."

He flicked the switch, and the camcorder screen lit up. He swung it to and fro, mapping out the path through the camera's glassy eye. In the LCD tint, the road ahead looked grainy and swollen with murk.

"I don't mean to call it early," he said, eyes still glued to the viewfinder, "but I'm getting a serious *Eraserhead* vibe from this thing, Trev."

Silence.

"Trev?"

Cal took his eyes off the camera and turned around. Trevor was stood some paces behind, in the middle of the road, bag slung limply in his hand. He was staring up somewhere at the treetops, maybe at the trees themselves, or the sky behind. Cal couldn't tell.

"You alright?" he asked. At once, Trevor snapped out of his trance and gave Cal a worried look.

"I don't know," he said, eyes straying back to the trees. "Something's off. The air seems weird down here, don't you feel it?"

"Maybe the titanium dome plate stops me picking up on bad vibes," Cal replied, smirking.

"I'm being serious," Trev insisted. If only to humor him, Cal turned around again, hands on his hips. He stared up at the monolith-face of the wood and squinted between the branches as if to spot some previously unseen danger, but there was none. No face in the bushes, no group of cultists watching from the undergrowth, just the same woods he'd known in every shade of morning to night for as long as he could remember. Nothing stirred in him.

At least, not at first.

But as he stood on the edge of the road, the sensation set in. Quick and distinct, like feeling a finger of cold water in a heated pool. The feeling had no definition or word: a moment of noticing everything at once, all the things that shouldn't have been. Fat specks of dust floating in a sky made crowded by emptiness. Dense, wet anticipation that clutched the air in a close, tight grasp. And the smell of burnt ozone: acrid and stingingly sweet.

The signs of a storm, amidst an empty sky.

"I'm only going in there if you promise not to make us investigate anything weird," Trevor insisted, hands planted in his pockets, "or make us go looking after you hear local teens getting eviscerated."

Cal sighed. He could feel the fight going out of him. Trevor had a peculiar way of wearing a person down like the ocean eating away at a cliff face. Cal gestured to the wide dirt path with a hand, camera hanging limply at his side.

"I promise the police aren't gonna find our last words on a bloodied videotape, now can we please just get to reinforcing our positions as weird outcasts already?" he said. Satisfied, Trevor hiked his bag straps up, and began to walk. As he passed, he gave Cal a smirk.

"Don't worry, buddy. The virgin always lives to the end," he said. Cal grabbed at him, and he laughed, breaking into a loping run down the path.

~

O'Brady Mill was a sad, broken place. It lay in what was once a large clearing just off the track, pressed into the overhanging rock face like a dead spider. By the time they first broke ground for the public path, the mill had already been deceased for nearly a decade: its sagging roof and tire trench scars consigned to little more than distant scenery on walking trails.

As they passed under the gate sign, garnished with graffiti, Trevor unhooked his flashlight and shone the beam to and fro over the old millhouse front. Gashes of purple-and-red spray paint stared back, half-obscured under swollen piles of moss and weeping streaks of roof tile rust.

"This was a good idea, it looks creepy as hell," Cal said, grinning. Trevor punched him in the arm.

"Don't say that!" he whispered.

Cal went forward a few steps, sweeping the camera slowly over the broken panorama. Old saw blades leaned against stumps. The shell of a car chassis, half-sunk into the hungry earth. Out to the right of the main building, a ragged fence patrolled in staggered intervals; wooden stakes bent at crooked angles by wind and age, half sunk into the mud. Beyond that lay nothing. Or at least, so it seemed.

It looked like a circle of murky green, extending out for maybe a hundred feet until it hit a far bank of trees. But it only seemed solid until you first stepped past the threshold, and then plunged through a quilt of pond scum into the stagnant depths below. Cal didn't know how far down the water went: after once seeing it swallow up an old bike, he'd never cared to find out.

He walked over to the edge of the stagnant pond, sucking mud underfoot. He stopped when the ground started to seethe around his shoes, groaning with a wet *thwock* every time he lifted his sneakers. He brought up the camera, twiddling with dials. On the screen, rotting green turned white, then sepia, then into a strange, dark blur. Behind him, Trevor walked around the main building, waving the flashlight from side to side.

"Do you smell something?" he asked, sniffing the air.

"Smell what?" Cal replied, half-listening, attention still locked on the camera screen. Trevor sniffed again and coughed.

"I dunno," he said, wiping his nose. "It's like old lunch meat."

"Gee, maybe it's the rotten pond, Trev," Cal replied. His finger stroked across the humped plastic shoulder of the camera and brushed against something pitted. There was a click, and the camera screen lit up. All trace of color snapped into a strange, alien grayscale.

"I've found the night vision setting! Or 'IR,' whatever that means," Cal said proudly, pointing it at Trevor. Trevor frowned; face pitted eerily white on the screen.

"Dude, get away from there, you'll fall in," he protested, taking a cautious step forward.

"Come on, Trevvy. What's the point of hanging around the abandoned mill if you can't tempt fate?" Cal asked, eyeing him through the camera.

In the sickly glow, Trevor's eyes were bright pinpricks on the screen, darting back and forth before he turned back to picking through the grass. Cal chuckled to himself and continued surveying the mill through the stark LCD screen.

The building loomed in high contrast grayness, lit up against the pure black backdrop of the night sky. It was perfect. He could already envision a claw rounding the side of the door, or a horrible, lurching shape lost in the gray fuzz, and experienced a sensation of cold around his feet.

Cal looked down and lifted up a shoe. A splutter of brown water came squelching out of a small hole in the sole. He let out a quiet groan of disgust and stepped back. As he did, his eye happened to crawl back down to the camera viewfinder, frozen up at chest level.

He stopped. Squinted.

There was something strange on the screen.

At the other end of the pond, barely cresting the surface of the water, there was... something. Cal wasn't quite sure what exactly. It looked like a glitch: a flickering mass of pure white light, about the size of a car just sort of sat there, half in the water, half out. Not moving, just... *flickering*.

He glanced above the screen, eyes taking a moment to adjust to the darkness. He couldn't see anything on the other side of the reeking water. Just trees, and dirt. Not even a shadow. He turned the camera off, and then on again.

Still there. And yet, not there at all. He let out a short, sharp sigh, and turned around.

"Trev, I think the camera's busted!" he said, cupping a hand to his mouth. Trevor turned, inadvertently dazzling him with a flashlight.

"What?" he called, inclining his head a little. Cal looked over the camcorder, turning it in his hands.

"Yeah, I dunno!" he said loudly. "Maybe something hit the screen, or—"

He was interrupted by a noise behind him. A slopping heave, and the chattering hiss of falling water. He twisted around, camera dropping to his side.

The scabbed algae moved. Rising and falling together a drooping ripple, clotting in green clumps where it had cracked apart. On the far side a dark hole swirled in the pondweed, as if something had just climbed out of the water.

Cal stayed frozen for a few seconds and stared out at the dark. He thought he saw the trees moving on the far bank, but it was impossible to tell if it was real or a trick of the light. Cal lifted the camera up again and glanced at the other side of the pond.

The glitch was gone. Now, all he could see was the curdling turn of evening to night, in fast darkening tones of gray-black static. The surface of the rotting water settled and returned to perfect, deceptive stillness, as if nothing had happened.

Nothing *had* happened, right?

"I think we oughta hurry up," he said, squelching back towards dry land. "It's getting dark out."

"Who's afraid now?" said Trevor, smiling smugly.

"And you're not?" Cal replied. He raised his eyes up to the mill and pointed to the door. "I wanna see how the inside films."

"Seriously?" Trevor asked. Before he could do his usual eye-roll and explanation, Cal held up a hand.

"I get it, I know, they always go into the creepy mill. But the sooner we're done, the sooner we can go home, and actually plan this thing out," he said.

Trevor looked over at the mill and let out a quiet whine.

"Why couldn't we have been into sports? Or chess, like all the other reject kids?" he said. Cal clapped him on the shoulder and pulled him forward as he began to walk.

"It'll be fine. In and out," he promised. As they pressed further in, Cal gave a final glance over his shoulder at the pond. Still and silent, just like always. No sign of the light.

The door to the old sawmill lay ajar, waving halfheartedly in the breeze. On the wall, a black spatter of shotgun pellets painted the wood, lead slugs nestled in half-burnt holes. A few feet away from it, Trevor stopped dead, light held at his chest in a fearful claw.

"I don't think we should go in," he said. Heedless, Cal went towards the doors, pulling them apart with a rattling creak. Trevor grabbed him by the arm, pulling like a scared dog.

"What if there's a dead body in there?" he asked.

"Then we'll run away, really fast," Cal said, peeking the camera through the gap. Inside, rusted box-shapes threw black shadows on the floor. He stood in the doorway, looking around a while before he turned back to Trevor, still some feet behind.

"Would you come on already? It's empty," he said. Hesitantly, Trevor came forward, swinging the light from side to side as if to catch something lunging out of the shadows. Together they entered, each step disturbing the ancient sawdust underfoot.

Inside, the smell of something coppery pervaded the air. The acrid sting of nature gone raw and rotten. A large conveyor belt dominated one side of the room, bandsaw now absent. Glittery little insect shapes skittered on the walls beside their heads, fleeing from the sudden light, and as their footsteps slowed and the sounds calmed, Cal realized he could hear something else.

Drip. Drip. Drip. A quiet, wet sound jumping from ceiling to floor, one unseen drop at a time.

They paced around the empty floor, occasionally jumping at the clatter of kicked spray-paint cans or jingling chains. Cal hit the record button and switched the infrared vision off. Immediately, the inside of the sawmill was lost, replaced by a strange, angular collection of half-shapes in the LCD screen. With a slow, steady hand, he surveyed the mill like a documentary cameraman taking in the sweeping vistas of decay.

Rainwater had left long, filthy streaks of moss over the off-white walls, and even caved in some of the ceiling beams. Nearby, a broken generator sat in a square of sunken space in the floor, where the water had collected into a stagnant pool. As he peered into the yellow-green surface, he noticed something ragged in amongst the murk.

It was a dead fox. Just floating there, face down in the grime.

Drip. Drip. Drip.

What lay below the cloudy surface was still orange and covered in matted fur, but where its hunched back crested out of the water, it was nothing but ribcage. The same yellowish-gray color as an old smoker's back teeth. No wounds, though. No trauma. Like it had just walked into the pool to drown all by itself. Cal caught a tang of something sharply rotten and held a hand to his nose.

Drip. Drip.

"I think I found your meat smell, Trev," he said, voice nasal and muffled. Trevor came over, took one look, and retched. He wandered to the far side, clutching his face in a tightly knotted fist.

"Gross! Ugh, god!" he said, followed by a light dry heave. Cal smirked at him.

"What's the matter, Trev? It remind you too much of—"

Drip.

Cal flinched. Something ran down his cheek. But not something cold; something warm.

Drip, drip. Two more pattered just below Cal's eye. Noticing, Trevor turned his light upwards, and his expression immediately widened out into something horrified.

"Cal…" he whispered, voice choked. Cal frowned, and wiped a couple of fingers over his cheek.

"What?" he asked, looking down at them. "It's probably just…"

He stopped. Gasped, but terror took most of the noise. Cal took a few unsteady steps back, agape and mute. Slowly, Trevor shone the flashlight up, and something moved amongst the sagging rafters. Before either of them could react, a wet mass of blood and hair tumbled to the floor.

It looked like it had been ripped almost clear in two. Dark clumps of thick, dried gut rimmed the sudden end of its torso, knots of broken rib sticking out wide like a hitchhiker's thumb. A flopping, swollen tongue lolled from its jaw, underlining black eyes gone glassy with sudden death.

A deer. Or, more accurately, *half* a deer.

Cal screamed. It was panicked and jagged. No matter how many times he paused for a gasp of frightened breath, it just kept coming. In an instant, they were out. Both boys tore from inside of the mill, furiously running their hands over their arms as if to scratch away the coppery stink of blood.

Then came the noise. Far off and echoing, unlike any Cal had ever heard before. Like an animal, but... *wrong*. A dog howl and a bull moose roar, mixed with a deep, throaty screech.

For a moment the two boys just stood there looking at each other, panting, terrified and slick with sweat. And then, as if the idea had been telepathically communicated, they broke into a sprint. Across the undergrowth, through the weeds, tearing through the chill night air as if the devil himself were hot on their heels. For all they knew, he was.

Somewhere behind, Cal was sure he heard a faint scream. High and shrill with sudden, surprised terror. He didn't think about it. He didn't think about anything. What the deer meant, what the other noise had been—the fear had clouded over his mind in a thick, grease-smeared haze, and all he could bear to think was to run. Run, and run, and keep running, until the old road and O'Brady Mill were far behind them.

His house in sight, Trevor suddenly veered right out of Cal's peripherals and behind the front door, slamming it shut behind him. Cal barely even registered it. He definitely didn't blame him.

Run half-ragged, he pressed down the empty road, occasionally glancing over his shoulder. Didn't dare stop until the front lawn of Terry's was in sight. The moment his feet touched the grass, he fell forward. Collapsed from his knees onto his stomach, going down face-first into the scratching, dry dirt.

He turned over and sat bolt upright, wheezing. The road behind him was empty.

No headlights. No people. Nothing.

He stayed there for what felt like hours, breath coming in hard, sharp gasps. The haze of horror began to lift. The moment the adrenaline stopped he felt his stomach sink. The sensations of the world around him became imminent and nauseating: the outer surface of the house pressed against his sweat-soaked back, the clutching pain in his head, and the acrid taste of vomit teasing at the back of his throat.

He let out a quiet groan, leaned his head against the wall and passed out.

DELUGE

AMESVILLE, 1977

Getting older was basically like being a teenager, Yule thought, except you were more tired. That, and instead of going home to a prom queen, he had 'the lumber artist.' Didn't seem like a fair trade to him, cosmically speaking.

Ornell was sat watching TV when he came in. Yule made the mistake of looking at the screen, to see what could only be described as a terrible accident at the offal factory. A feral dog raised its head up from a pile of steaming guts, spilled messily out over the Savannah dirt. Yule shivered internally and looked away. He hated dogs.

He collapsed onto the sofa, kicked off his shoes, and let out a long groan.

"The people in this town are nuts, Ornell," he said, head falling back against the cushion. "A kid tried to eat my shoelaces today, what the hell kinda person does that?"

Ornell laughed and ate another fistful of chips.

"Tell me 'bout it," he replied, "I nearly got shot today."

Yule's lowered eyelids snapped open, suddenly awake.

"What?" he asked. Ornell laughed and waved a hand at him.

"Calm your ass down, I'm alright," he said, chewing loudly. Yule sat up; his shoulders hunched over with sudden tension.

"What the hell happened? You get robbed, or mugged or what?"

"Nah," Ornell grunted, shaking his head, "down at the sawmill. You remember Reggie Tugman?"

"*Reggie Tugman* tried to shoot you? The dude with the lazy eye?" Yule asked. Ornell shook his head a little, like he was rolling his reply around in his mouth.

"Wasn't so much me as it was, uh, more the side of the building. Apparently, he was one of them twenty guys that just got laid off last week. I was just working the saw, heard this dude screamin' about how the foreman was a no good son-of-a-bitch, and then *boom*. I swear, man, I heard the damn buckshot go clean through the door and straight past my head."

"Holy shit," said Yule, looking Ornell over for bandages. "Are you alright? You hurt?"

"Nah," Ornell replied, waving dismissively. "Ain't nobody got hurt. Second, he got the shot off, about a dozen guys tackled that sucker right there. Hit the ground so hard I think they knocked his lazy eye back into place."

He laughed at his own joke and took another gulp of beer.

Yule didn't know how Ornell was so nonchalant all the time. He had the same tone whether he was discussing a narrowly averted shooting rampage or the time he saw a fat horse fall over. Maybe it was all the glue he huffed when they were teenagers.

Yule deflated and leaned back into the couch, fingers laced over his lap.

"Well that kinda blows my shit outta the water," he said. Ornell nudged him with an elbow and gave him a gap-toothed smile.

"Ain't no thing. Just because the magnitude of a problem may differ, the emotional impact on the individual remains important," Ornell replied. Yule stared at him, dumbfounded.

"The emotional what?" he asked.

"Motherfucker, we livin' in the new age of self-help. Ornell *reads*," he said. Yule rolled his eyes, and sighed.

"I dunno, man. Had to move an arcade machine yesterday and I feel like my goddamn back's on fire," he said, looking up. "And did you know I had to pay a man to buff blood outta my truck? Nearly fifty bucks."

"The deer thing?" Ornell asked, looking back at the TV.

"Yeah. The deer thing," Yule replied, letting his head fall back. They sat in silence for a while, as the white noise of the television crowd went slithering around their heels. When Yule next spoke, he wasn't quite sure why.

"You ever get the feeling something ain't right in this town, Ornell?" he asked, getting up to cross the room. Ornell thought about it for a moment, and then shook his head.

"Nah," he said decisively.

"Nah. Right," Yule agreed, shaking his head as he rounded into the kitchen. As the fridge door opened, he paused, struck by disappointment.

"Bad news, man, looks like we're out…" Yule began, his gaze cresting over the counter. He trailed off as his eyes unexpectedly met Ornell's, half framed by a single finger, pressed tight against his nose. Yule felt all the goodwill in him go out like a spat-on candle.

"Seriously?" he said. Ornell shrugged.

"Wish there was something I could do for you man, but rules are rules. Slowest man does the job," he said, finger still up against one nostril, "ain't pretty, but it's necessary."

"You were literally just telling me to take a load off."

"And I got shot at today, man," Ornell replied, smiling at Yule's almost horrified expression of defeat. "Yeah, I ain't afraid to pull weight. You been outplayed, son."

Yule stood there for a moment, trying to formulate some way out. But it didn't come, just a half-toned groan of dismay as he went to grab a coat off the wall. Ornell turned on the couch to address him as he moved to the door.

"And none of that lite beer bullshit. You know what I mean?"

"I hate you," Yule replied flatly, buttoning his coat. Ornell grinned.

"Hey man, it's okay to be jealous of my catlike reflexes. You gotta embrace those feelings to grow," he said. Yule didn't answer, for fear he might say something that'd leave a bad taste in his mouth. Scowling, he swept out into the cold clutch of the outer hallway, a fly crushed under the wheel of apartment law.

⁓

The liquor store was surrounded on all sides by black, rain-slick woodland. Some old bylaw from prohibition said there couldn't be any in town, and so it was relegated nearly a mile down the Innsmouth Road; a squat, angular pock of sin on the otherwise uniformly tangled landscape. But more pressingly, tonight it seemed to be empty.

Yule stood under the porch; his shoulders were already soaked despite the short walk from his truck. Through his cupped hands, he could see no movement behind the darkened glass, not even the erratic flicker of faulty cooler lights. He swore, went another few steps around, and repeated the act. Same outcome.

Nobody around, with hours left of opening. What the hell was going on here?

He stopped dead as something squished loudly under his foot. He looked down and picked it off his sole, taped edges greasy with drowned glue. "*Power Out,*" it said in hard pressed, frustrated letters, "*closed until further notice.*"

Yule groaned and let the note flop back onto the floor. *Great,* he thought. *Just great.* Now his back was killing him, and there wasn't any beer in a five-mile radius.

Just. Great.

A brief cold shock ran down his neck as he hurried back to the truck. As the door closed, sheets of white noise became a low, muffled drone, and the world seemed to become comfortably close again.

He sat in the driver's seat and watched the reflection of the dash lights melt endlessly down the glass, running tracks on the blur beyond. With the engine off, it felt like he was the only person on earth, kept company only by the gentle fingertips of water on the windshield. With a key twist, he filled the night with the aggressive, hot burble of the engine as he disappeared down the Innsmouth Road and left the unlit concrete in standing silence once more.

Yule couldn't help but breathe a sigh of relief as he passed beneath the hunched town gate, and the sting of electric light waited to greet him: grinning brightly, bleeding watercolor tones down into the storm drains and gutters.

The streets were completely empty. They were huddled inside, behind backlit curtains and shuttered windows. As he passed, Yule noticed that the bars seemed empty too. That night, nobody in Amesville wanted to be out, not in that god-awful rain.

He pulled into his usual parking space and waited in the truck a moment, bracing himself for the cold torrent. Then, he pulled up his collar, and got out of the truck.

The night shone brightest on Clarence Street; neon lights frozen in midair by diving sheets of rain. Shopfronts selling brand-new toasters and homewares blared a stark, homely yellow onto the sidewalk, glow melting at the edges in the rising water. The wind was rising, too, tugging at loose fliers and posters tacked to telephone poles, occasionally tearing them away like a curious house cat. Looked like that storm had finally arrived, he thought. Yule just hoped he'd get inside before the worst of it hit.

A few minutes into his walk, Yule stopped dead. His feet were cold, and not in the usual way. He groaned, and jerkily turned his sole upward to examine the damage. The bottom of his shoe had split, and now it pulsed water like an open wound. He leaned in closer to see how deep it went. Then, he didn't see anything at all.

At first, he thought he'd gone blind, but it was only as Yule looked up and saw the faint splatter of stars in the sky, that he realized the problem wasn't his eyes. It was the street.

The lights had gone out. Just gone, all of them at once. No backlit windows, no neon shopfronts, just darkness and the sound of rushing water all around him.

And then, a white sting. Yule grunted and shielded his eyes, a stabbing pain scratching back behind his corneas. The ambient hum of electricity throbbed in the air again, and when Yule finally opened his eyes, he found Clarence Street just as it had been: lit, and alive.

He rubbed his eyes and shook some rain out of his hair, trying to get his bearings again. Hands firmly in his pockets, he walked quickly down the street, occasionally looking over his shoulder. He didn't know what for. He just had a feeling he should get home. Something in the air didn't feel right that night, as if something more than a storm had rolled in.

By the time he reached the end of the road, he was soaked through from top to tailbone. On his way, he barely noticed the two cop cars parked opposite the apartment block. One empty, one not.

He skidded to a halt in the building's entrance hall, glass-panel doors buffeted by the wind as they closed behind him. Yule stood in the middle of the gray toned room, listening to the sharp crack of water dropping from his sleeves to the tile. A fat puddle had already started to drain from the cuffs of his jeans and the fabric on his shoes, running down the grouting like sewer gutters. He shook off his clothes, cringing at the way it all clung to him.

As he climbed the stairs, the feeling of bad luck was replaced by more specific and angry ideas. The dull, almost funnily pathetic *slap* of something on the bottom of his shoe only made it worse.

He was gonna kill Ornell. That was it. He was the reason he was out at all. *Slap.*

He'd just go right back up there, *slap,* and get his gun, and just, *slap,* shoot the dumb son of a bitch in his big, *slap,* stupid head.

He could face prison. Sure, he'd realistically end up getting stomped by some fridge-lookin' asshole. *Slap.*

But he'd never have to worry about rent. Or rain. Or whatever was slapping against the goddamn floor. When he reached the top of the stairs, he brought his shoe up again and found a waterlogged piece of paper stuck to the sole. As he peeled it off, soggy pieces came away in clumps, sticking to his fingers. Looked like the storm must've blown it off a telephone pole and onto the stoop outside. Casually curious, Yule turned it around in his hands.

His eyes widened.

It couldn't have been right. A trick of the gloom-swelled hallway, or his tired, blinking eyes. But long as he watched, nothing changed. The truth stood concrete.

At the top, the words, "HAVE YOU SEEN ME?" bled out over the page in thin black rivers, collecting in the smudged physical description below. At the bottom, a young woman stared up at him, features disfigured by the acid touch of water yet horribly unmistakable.

Leslie O'Neil. The girl from the Innsmouth Road.

He stared at it as long as he could bear, not even breathing. Reading and re-reading, taking in what information he could. She'd disappeared late yesterday morning, it said, maybe… maybe just after they'd met. He tried to hold on and decipher more, but soon her face warped and tore as the wet paper parted in his fingers.

Yule let it drop, and it hit the floor with a wet, pulpy splatter. Eyes still fixed on it, Yule fumbled out his key. He felt sick.

"Ornell!" he said from behind the door, swinging it open, "we gotta call, the police, I thi—"

He stopped dead. The police officer sat next to Ornell stood. His partner, already across the room, had his hand on his gun. And Ornell was just looking at Yule. Like he didn't know what to say. That was what shook him most. Yule hadn't ever seen him like that.

"Stop right there," said the officer, hand steady on the pistol's grip. "I'm gonna need you to put your hands up on your head and get on your knees."

Yule froze in the doorway, looking between the cop and Ornell.

"What?" he asked, quiet with disbelief. The officer advanced a step.

"Put your hands up on your head and get on your knees. Now," he repeated, louder this time. Yule did so, slowly. He never took his eyes off Ornell.

He looked so sad. Ashamed, almost.

There were footsteps coming up on the stairs behind him. Reinforcements. The first officer grabbed Yule roughly by the wrists, clamping a pair of cold steel handcuffs together. Then, his hands started to probe down, slapping hard against Yule's ribs as he searched down his shirt and over his waist.

"No weapon, we're clear," the cop called to the others, who immediately moved in to drag him up.

Yule wanted to scream. To shout and run and hide. Even just to ask what he was supposed to have done. But it never came. He just retreated. Hid away somewhere inside his own skin, far away enough that it felt like it wasn't going to hurt him. But it did. God, but it did.

As they moved him out of the front door, Ornell turned away. That was the last Yule saw before the front door closed, and they marched him down the stairs. Getting into the police cruiser was little more than a blur. He felt numb. The voices and colors all merged together, like he wasn't really there, like it wasn't real, but it *was*. Despite hope and despite desperation, reality left no room.

He was here, he thought, listening to the rain wash over the car window. Realer than real, with no escape.

THE NUMBER ONE MISTAKE

AMESVILLE, 1993

"What were you thinking?" Pam asked, cigarette ash floating lazily into her coffee. "You could've frozen to death out there!"

Cal sat hunched over his cereal, chewing as quietly as he could. His head throbbed with every jaw rotation. Pam huffed angrily, painted fingernails clinking on the mug.

"I swear, you come in at god-knows-when in the morning, freezing—and did you throw up on yourself or something?"

"No, Aunt Pam," Cal muttered, shaking his head.

"Well what happened?"

"I told you, I fell over on the way home, and just... passed out," Cal said, wincing internally. Even *he* didn't believe that story, and it was clear Pam didn't either.

"I swear, Cal, I'm not your mother, but I've still gotta put my foot down," she said, pausing to draw on the cigarette. "You can't act like that without there being consequences, you could've been robbed."

"In Amesville?" Cal asked, bemused. Pam gave no quarter.

"I'm serious, Cal. Now I don't gotta know what you were doing out there, just promise me you're gonna be safer from now on," she demanded, staring him down. Cal went to speak, winced, and clutched his head.

"Yeah, Aunt Pam. I promise. Sorry," he said. Pam took a sip of her coffee, then sighed.

"Look, I messed up a lot as a kid, too. I'm not gonna be a hard ass about it," she said, nodding to the door, "and your uncle doesn't have to know anything. Alright?"

Cal smiled weakly at her and nodded.

"Thanks," he said, returning to his cereal. No sooner had he done so, Terry came through, pulling up his tie.

"C'mon, kiddo. I'm driving you to school," he said.

"You are?" Cal asked.

"You… are?" Pam echoed. Terry gave them a lopsided smile and held up his palms.

"I'm going to a meet 'n' greet down at the station, thought I'd give him a ride on account of his busted bike situation. Unless I'm suddenly too old to drive?"

Pam smirked at him and got up. She gave him a kiss on the cheek as she passed, stopping momentarily to put a hand on his chest.

"You're definitely not too old," she said, smiling at him. Cal cringed, and busied himself putting his bowl on the side counter, before Terry came over and clapped a hand on his back.

"Don't wanna be late, grab your stuff," he said, before swiftly exiting. Cal swayed in front of the kitchen sink, lips pursed. He could still feel the clap, radiating through his back, down his spine, into his stomach.

Ugh.

He straightened up and took a deep breath, air tucking nausea under his ribs like an old suitcase under a bed. He tried not to bend down too fast as he took his backpack from down by the stairs and followed Terry out to the car.

As they drove, Cal laid his head against the window, praying for a lack of potholes. After maybe five minutes of silence, Terry tapped his shoulder with the back of his hand.

"Wake up, kiddo. Can't sleep in class," he said, eyes flicking over the road.

"Isn't that an argument *for* me sleeping in the car?" Cal replied, sitting up. He could feel his stomach shifting in time with the gears.

"So what'd you and Trevor get up to last night?" Terry asked, turning a mercifully slow corner. Cal didn't reply at first.

The deer was missing the bottom half. Bloody, torn and encrusted with a dusty layer of fat, black flies.

"Tested out the camera," he said eventually. "Y'know. Watched a couple movies."

Terry chuckled and shook his head.

"Sounds wild," he said. Cal grunted in agreement and propped his head up on his hand. Outside, Amesville crawled by, battered houses stretching to life in the morning heat. The same faces, the same routines. The familiar blur, tinged with nausea though it may have been, was exactly as it always had been.

Until, it wasn't.

Cal sat up. Red-and-blue flashes winked by the side of the road. Three cars, all blocking one of the exits. As they approached, one of the officers hailed them down. Terry frowned, and wound down the window.

"Morning, Harry," he said, craning his head out. The police officer tipped his hat politely and put his hands on his belt.

"Mornin' Terry," he said, looking the car over. "You takin' your boy to school?"

"I was meaning to, yeah," Terry replied, gesturing to the blocked road ahead. The cop shook his head and adjusted the tobacco chew nestled in his lip.

"Can't take Whitmore right now. We got it all shut down from there to Innsmouth Road," he said. Terry scoffed.

"You kiddin' me? What, did a cattle truck fall over or something?"

"I can't really say," the cop replied flatly.

"C'mon, Harry. I was on the force for twenty years, it's not like I'm gonna go blabbing," Terry insisted. The cop's eyes strayed to Cal and stayed there.

"I mean I *really* can't say, Terry," he said. Terry's smile faded.

"Oh," he muttered, glancing at Cal quickly. "You... oh."

The police officer leaned on the car window, and his sunglasses slipped down a little. His eyes were red rimmed and tired.

"You should try going down fifth," he suggested. Terry nodded, turning his eyes back to the road.

"Right. Thanks, Harry," he said, rolling the window back up.

They drove mostly in silence after that. As they pulled up to the school, Terry stopped the car, and waited. Just sat there, brow hard in contemplation.

"Have a good day at school, kiddo," he said, voice soft and monotone. "I'll, uh… I'll pick you up here again when school's over, alright? Don't walk home."

"Yeah. Sure," Cal said. Terry looked at him for a moment, like he was memorizing Cal's features.

"Alright," he said, not breaking eye contact.

"Thanks," Cal said. He got out of the car, bag slung loosely over his shoulder. Terry watched him disappear into the seething adolescent crowed gathered out by the front gates. His gnarled hands tightened on the steering wheel; eyes still fixed on where he'd seen Cal last.

It was all noise. His cloudy head made everything that was usually distinct blur together: places, people, voices, all of it. For the fifth time that morning, Cal made a promise to himself never to drink gin and sprint ever again. And all the while, he tried not to think about… what had happened. The deer, and the noise. And the strange light in the camera.

He and Trevor had just been seeing things, he thought. The booze and the atmosphere got to them, and it had just been a deer. A dead deer in a place it shouldn't have been. That was all.

He trudged down the hallway to his locker, barely concentrating. The combination was all wrist reflex. The door swung open, rising out of the wall like a stained metal shield to block out the rest of the crowd.

Cal pushed down the acid twist of nausea and leaned up against the shelf. In his corner at the end of the hall, he was safe. Now he could just stand and listen a while. Hear all his stories. That'd make him feel better.

And so he stood. Listened.

There was noise, but not like chatter. Nothing above a mutter, cloistered away behind hands and in the shadow of doorways. Something felt wrong. Like an unspoken, shared tension in the air.

The odd feeling pervaded over the entire morning. Everyone just seemed on edge. That was, of course, except for Trevor. He slammed his tray down at their lunch spot, eyes wide and wild with anticipation. Cal winced at the loud noise and clutched his head, half-eaten sandwich drooping.

"Just once, could you not?" he asked, massaging the heel of his palm against his temple.

"We gotta talk about last night," Trevor said, leaning in. "I think it was an alien."

Cal sat in bemused silence for a few seconds, waiting for a punchline. That never came; only a pregnant pause while they sat there, eye to bloodshot eye, the myriad sounds of the cafeteria congealing around them.

"You realize that's the craziest goddamn thing you've ever said, right?" Cal said after some time, resuming chewing. Trevor raised his brows and folded his arms.

"Well alright smart guy, what's your explanation for finding half a deer in a goddamn roof?" he retorted. Cal considered it for a moment, then shrugged.

"Bear did it," he said. Trevor looked at him like he'd just shot a puppy from a firework cannon.

"A bear?" he said, cocking his head back.

"Yeah. A really big one. Just flipped that sucker right up there," Cal explained, popping the top of his pudding cup.

"Oh yeah? Well what about the noise, huh? That didn't sound like a bear," Trevor pointed out smugly.

"You ever heard a bear before?" Cal asked, pointing his spoon at him. Trevor rolled his eyes.

"Yeah, of course."

"Cartoons don't count," Cal added, slurping on a furtive spoonful. Trevor's smug grin faded, and he shuffled in his seat, as if he could physically wriggle his way out of the argumentative corner he was in.

"Well, not in real life, but—"

Cal didn't wait for him to finish.

"Animals make crazy noises, Trev," he cut in, waving his spoon. "Foxes sound like someone stepping on a baby. I wouldn't be surprised if a bear could make a noise like the one we heard. Especially if it's big enough to slam-dunk a deer carcass."

"Didn't sound like a bear," Trevor muttered, moodily opening his lunchbox. Cal smirked.

"Don't worry, buddy. Bright side, I think you came up with a really good movie idea," he said. "Dark side, I think you might've killed some brain cells for lack of sleep."

The bell wailed on the wall. Cal put his stuff away and got up, but Trevor wasn't done talking.

"But *what if*, Cal?" he asserted, rounding the table. "We should at least tell somebody! The police, or the parks service, or someone."

"Or, on the other hand, we could not," Cal replied. They began to walk down the hallway into the science block, Trevor switching sides constantly as if to confuse him into agreeing. When he was excited, that butterball sure could move.

"This is the number one mistake they always make in movies!" he argued, deftly sidestepping. "They never tell anybody until it's too late, and the evil's already spread!"

"Then it's good we're not in a movie. Can you hear yourself right now, dude?" Cal replied, shaking his head. Trev stepped in front of the door, blocking it like a chubby bouncer.

"We could just tell the cops we heard something," he insisted. Cal sighed, and pinched his brows.

"Sure, Trev. Whatever, we'll go tell the cops we heard an inexplicable alien visitor, whatever you want. But can it wait until after class? Please?" he said, pushing past him.

As they entered the room, they found it dim. The blinds were drawn tight, leaving only enough light to make out the silhouette of Dr. Ogden sat hunched at his desk, and the wheeled TV stand looming next to him. As the two boys found their seats, excitement grew in the room, only strengthened by the telling groan and slow gait of the good doctor. Paying the debt for happiness borrowed the night before.

Ogden checked the clock, grimaced, and gestured to the hastily printed quiz sheets on their desks.

"So, today we'll be taking a break from the textbooks for something a little lighter," he said, waving vaguely at the TV. "Instead, we'll be watching this news story I taped last night. In front of you, you'll find some questions about it: how acid rain is formed, what the future of power development is, and, uh, extra credit if you put the formula for sulfuric acid at the bottom."

With that, he sat back down and clicked the remote. The TV tuned onto a news announcer mid-sentence, his bald patch shiny with sweat.

"—Tom Shapiro on scene to get the scoop. Over to you, Tom," he said, smiling. The camera lingered on him a few seconds too long, before cutting to an overweight man in a tan suit. He smiled and nodded to nobody, seemingly alone in an empty parking lot.

"Thanks, Kenny. It's the new development that's got the county talking, but what's really going on at the newly built Sledmore Energy Plant?" he said.

The camera swung left and the silhouette of a building lurched into frame beside the reporter. And in front of it, something more inexplicably strange: a man, tall and angular, his white suit standing out amongst the gray tangle like a snowflake in soot. He smiled gently at Tom Shapiro as he glided into frame, his eyes tracking against the camera lens. The reporter shook his hand, before returning his gaze back to the invisible audience.

"I'm here with Sledmore Industries' CEO Mister Carnassus, how are you doing today?" he asked. Carnassus' perfect face turned warm and smiling, like the picture definition of friendliness.

"I'm very well, Mister Shapiro. May I call you Tom?" he asked. Charming. Almost playful. Every emotional beat was distinct and perfectly timed. Purposeful.

Tom smiled.

"Sure you can. Now, Mister Carnassus, there's been a lot of questions about the exact impact of your new venture on the town and the surrounding environment. Ecologically speaking," he said. Carnassus nodded, and his warm expression slid into one of deep, well-meaning concern, as complexly and effortlessly as an insect shifting its wings.

"I'd hate to think anyone's worried. We've had numerous talks with the Amesville Preservation Society and the EPA, and we're working to minimize the impact on local deer and bird populations," he said, mouth forming a more cautious smile. "Sledmore One is… well, you might call it a fusion plant. A little bit of coal, a little sulfur dioxide, sure, but most of our power comes from geothermal sources underground. It might as well be energy for nothing."

"I suppose people are just wondering why this kind of project isn't being pursued in places like Philadelphia or Pittsburgh; somewhere that isn't so close to state game lands and reserves."

Carnassus' smile sharpened. Well practiced, and perfectly landed.

"Well, Tom, I guess it's for a number of reasons. Amesville and its people are close to my heart, that's certainly part of it. But, honestly? If the Sledmore Project can work in Amesville, and I mean really work?"

Carnassus' eyes flicked almost imperceptibly towards the dead eye of the camera lens, and for a moment it was like he saw the unseen audience beyond.

"We could take it anywhere," he finished.

KKRRRRRZZZTK.

All attention in the room snapped to the crackle of the PA system, wailing from its corner of the ceiling. Dr. Ogden groaned loudly and put a hand to his head.

"All faculty and students, please be advised," it announced, *"buses will be taking students home following third period today, owing to an incident on the Innsmouth Road. Students are advised to take note of the longer route and contact their parents as necessary."*

Kkkkrrrkzzshht.

The speaker whined in echo tones, then died. Dr. Ogden, expression still flatter than new paper, turned a heavily lidded eye over the class.

"You all get that?" he asked. Most nodded, knowing he didn't care what the response was. "Good."

The news footage started up again, but Cal wasn't paying attention anymore. Neither was Trevor, they both just looked at each other, faces lit by the dancing glow of the TV.

"Innsmouth Road. That's—" Trevor began, voice hushed. Cal held up a hand.

"Bear attack, Trev. That's it," he said. In the flickering light, Trevor's wide-eyed stare remained insistent. Cal rolled his eyes and turned back around to the TV.

The camera was back in the studio, away from the strangely perfect man, toward normality. And yet, as Cal watched shapes move behind the glass, he felt unsettled. Something pinched in his gut.

It was weird, he thought. Even if he didn't want it to be true, he couldn't get away from the feeling that something was happening. Nothing ever happened in Amesville, he thought, but now it felt less like learned wisdom, and more like a secret, fearful wish.

BLACKLIGHT

COUNTY HOSPITAL, 1993

Mister Daisy hated the smell of hospitals. It was the only thing he could smell anymore. Years of cigarette smoking had stolen the scent of blood, rot, even gasoline, but somehow the antiseptic chill of hospital air still registered in his skull. He adjusted his hat and walked towards the lobby desk. It'd be over soon, at least.

The woman at the desk looked old and disinterested, pink hair shining ever so slightly in the scathing halogen lights. She glanced up from her magazine as he approached the desk, his yellow-tinged smile filling the room.

"Hello," he said, holding up a badge, "I'm Officer Doe, from the Parks Department. I need to see somebody."

The woman chewed the inside of her lip and shrugged.

"Sorry, honey," she said, glancing through the window and into the flat blackness beyond. "It's way past visiting hours."

Daisy's smile never wavered. People responded to smiles, but they responded even better to badges. He held it up, this time for a few seconds.

"Like I said," he insisted, "I'm on official business. I just have to ask them a couple of questions."

The statement settled between them. As the brass glint reflected itself in her eyes, her lips loosened, her hands flexed slightly on her pen. Signs and signals. Like a railway, he thought, smiling to himself.

"You're here about the Innsmouth Road guy, right?" she asked. Daisy smiled.

"The remaining one. Yeah," he said. She considered him for a moment, shrugged, then glanced at a piece of well-thumbed paper on the desk.

"He's in room nineteen. Keep it short, he needs rest," she said sternly. Daisy gave her another smile and tipped his hat to her as he left. He didn't need to say anything more, nor did he care to.

The plastic-clad hallway was lined with empty rooms, tinted orange by the floods outside. *Regional hospitals*, he thought. Probably saw more Oxycontin addicts than broken bones. Whether or not that was what made them so easy to get into, he didn't know, and in truth, he wasn't much concerned with thinking about it. He didn't need to know how a car worked to drive it.

The man in room nineteen looked less than a man. A collection of casts and tubes rigged up on the bed like a Halloween prop. He was still awake, eyes glazed over and shiny with the reflection of the television screen by his bed.

Daisy crossed the threshold towards him and stopped a foot shy of the cot. After a moment of nonrecognition, Daisy coughed loudly into his hand. The man in the bed gave a start and groaned in pain.

"I'm sorry," Daisy said politely, "I thought you heard me come in."

"No, no I... I didn't," the man in the bed replied, eyes looking over the figure before him. "Who are you?"

Daisy smiled, gloved hand squeaking as he drew the badge from his pocket.

"My name is Mister Doe. I'm from the Parks Department," he said, drawing a little closer. "I'm sorry to hear about your accident. I was hoping to ask you a few questions."

The man in the bed shook his head, and his rigging trembled.

"I already talked to the police," he said.

"Like I said," Daisy repeated, "I'm with the Parks Department. I just have a few questions. They won't take long."

The man in the bed chewed his lip. One of the bags slurped, spitting relaxation through the plastic tube. Whether or not that coaxed him into agreeing didn't matter, Daisy thought, only that he agreed.

A badge and a smile. Repeat as needed.

Daisy pulled up a plastic chair and set it beside the bed. The clipboard at the bottom probably had the man's name on it, he thought. Daisy didn't check it. Instead, he went into his pocket again, and set a tape recorder on the bedside table.

"Where exactly did it happen?" he asked clearly. The man took a moment to think. To sink through the chemical curtain and back into the cold, wet fear of it all.

"Near the O'Brady Mill," he said quietly, "between two hills. Don't know more exact than that."

"At what time?"

"I don't know," said the man. Daisy took a deep breath in through his nose and smiled. He already knew the answer to that one, anyway.

"What do you remember about the accident?" he asked. Immediately, the man in the bed shrunk away, head bobbing side to side in unconscious, feverish refusal.

"I can't. No. I already talked to the police about it, I can't," he rasped.

"I understand it's difficult, but this is official business. What you tell me could stop somebody else getting hurt," Daisy replied. The man clenched his jaw, chewing the quiet for a few moments. Then, hesitantly, he nodded.

"It weren't no accident. Something attacked us out there," he said, eyes lost somewhere in the middle distance. "We were out huntin', we had all the permits, we had permission, and... and all of a sudden there was this... this *sound*. Like a giant animal or something. So we stopped, but we didn't see anything, and... I didn't see anything. Something came out of the trees, ripped through 'em like they were paper, ripped *Bobby* up like he was paper, and I didn't... God, I swear I didn't see it at all."

"But you saw what happened to Bobby," Daisy insisted. The man nodded, unwilling tears glistening at the corners of his jaundiced eyes.

"It… it got him on the floor somehow. I didn't see how it happened, I just heard him screaming all of a sudden. Screaming and… and shaking, like he was having a seizure, but there was smoke, and his skin was…"

He trailed off. Daisy leaned forward.

"Was?" he prompted. The man turned to him, eyes frozen wide with barely contained horror.

"Melting," he said, voice trembling. "Just… just melting off him. Like bacon fat."

Daisy sniffed and teased disinterestedly around his pockets for a cigarette packet.

"And you think it's an animal? Not an electrical accident or something?" he asked. The man shook his head, this time almost feverishly.

"No pylons. No underground wires, neither, and the weather was clear. Bobby was attacked by something; it wasn't no electricity. It was an animal," he said. Daisy, unheeding of the man's nervous energy, took a few long draws.

"You see where it went after?" he asked eventually.

"No," the man replied quietly, "I… the Lord knows cowardice is a sin, but something hit me, and I just… I ran. Called the police when I reached the road, they were the ones what found out Bobby was…"

He leaned forwards and held his face in his hands, lip trembling.

"Oh god," he repeated. "Oh god, what did I do?"

Daisy stubbed out his cigarette on the metal leg of the cot and popped another into his mouth, free hand quietly stopping and stowing the tape recorder back into his bag. Then, he felt around for something else.

It was only after a half minute of sob-punctuated silence that the man in the bed turned around, and his tear-slick face tautened into something more confused.

"What's that?" he asked. The box was heavy in Daisy's hands, more so than it looked. Probably lead lined, but he'd never asked. A little button and a power pack jutted from the back like an angular tumor, pointed towards his waiting thumb. At the front, the door stood shut with a latch.

Daisy smiled.

"It's a blacklight," he said. "Shows if certain chemicals rubbed off on you during the attack. Nothing painful."

Slowly, gently, his fingers teased the latch open.

"Just relax," he said. The man in the bed opened his mouth to say something, but it never made it out. Neither did the scream that interrupted it.

Nobody but Daisy saw what happened next. There was nobody in the hallway, and nobody outside. No one to glance up, and see the windows swell an unsettling, sickly green, glowing not with light but a strange, incomprehensible shine.

An *unlight*.

SPECIAL DELIVERY

AMESVILLE, 1993

The grave stood underneath the boughs of an old, twisted willow, stone cross erupting from the puckered earth like a petrified flower.

Cal barely remembered May 13, 1983. He had only been eight years old.

He got flashes of it in fits and starts sometimes, pulled up by the certain tone of a car engine, or the smell of smoke-stained upholstery. But he didn't remember it the way he thought he should, like a movie played over and over in a continuous, devastating narrative. Instead it had all fallen away, in bits and pieces. Now all he remembered were little details, stuck out like weeds.

The playful clack of the seatbelt buckle as he struggled to connect the pieces together. The purple-and-red folds of the creased coloring book rubbed together by a dozen journeys spent shoved against his leg. And the bright green sign on the way out of town, seeming to flash and lunge past the headlights before it disappeared back into the wriggling black evening shadow.

He didn't remember the crash. He didn't remember the blood, or the pain, or the cold kiss of asphalt against his cheek as they dragged him from the car. He didn't even remember the fear.

The only thing about it that frightened him anymore was the Innsmouth Road. It felt cursed. Whenever they had to drive down it, he'd feel himself shrink away from the windows, as if looking at the path would alert it to his presence. That it would become psychically, unknowably aware of returning prey, left previously unkilled.

But that was the only thing.

Apart from that, it was almost worrying how little he thought about it now. It felt like Dad had always been dead. He had been for as long as Cal could really remember. There was no jarring memory of the moment he found out, or a longing for what the world had been before that, because he'd never really lived in that world. Life just… went on.

He pulled awkwardly at the bottom of his shirt and looked at the grave.

"Hi, Dad," he said, smiling weakly, "that time of year again."

The grave, predictably, didn't reply.

"I'm sorry I don't visit so often. I never really know what to say, or, whether I should say anything at all."

He paused.

"Mom's still in the hospital. Uncle Terry and Aunt Pam are looking after me fine, so I don't want you to worry. Terry's even… doing this parenting thing, which is weird. I know he misses you too."

He breathed in, shoulders rising to touch his neck. When he exhaled, it was soft and shuddering, bouncing off his lower lip to tumble back into the quiet.

"I wish you were around. I keep wondering if my life would be different, if I'd be happier. I think I would. I guess I'm never gonna know, though, but I just… I wish you were here," he said. The grave stood still and silent in reply. He tried to smile again and tapped his knuckles gently against his head.

"I'm fine. Still got the titanium plate in as a souvenir. It's not given me superpowers yet, but… this is pretty 'tragic hero backstory,' so… who knows, right?"

Cal let out a short, awkward laugh. Then, unsure what else to do, he stooped down.

"You're not looking so great, though," he said, reaching forward. His fingers teased into the moss, picking it gently and methodically away from the cold stone. His thumb ghosted over the carved headstone, tracing an invisible arc over the engraved letters.

Here lies Jonathan H. Greenwood, loving father and husband.

Cal got back up on his feet and brushed grave dirt from his jeans.

"I, ah, I guess that's all I had to say," he said awkwardly, wiping a hand through his hair. Then, he bowed his head, voice barely above a murmur.

"I miss you, Dad," he said quietly, "I really think I do."

Quiet descended, expected yet still somehow jarring. Cal gestured mutely over his shoulder, took a few steps back, then left without another word.

⁓

The house lay heaped and quiet on the landscape, just like always. He barely noticed the sensations of returning: the gentle *thwsh* of unkempt grass as he crossed the yard, the mottled sound of floorboards near the door. All familiar, and invisibly so.

"Where's Uncle Terry?" he asked, kicking off his shoes in the hallway. Pam took up her seat at the table and plucked the still-smoking cigarette out of her ashtray.

"Oh, I dunno," she said, waving it in the air with a shrug. "Probably still at the station. He's been pretty worked up the last couple days."

"About the road thing?" Cal asked.

"About the road thing," she confirmed, voice low and husky. As she glanced up from the ashtray her look sweetened, in the way it did whenever she wanted to imitate a true-to-life family sitcom.

"So, how are you doing? Speaking of the thing. Or, not. If you don't want," she asked.

"I'm fine," Cal deflected, through a mouthful of potato. Seemingly unsatisfied with the amount of emotional bonding going on, Pam pushed further.

"Was everything alright? Up at Stony Brook?"

"Like I said: it was fine. Emotions were had. Pretty sure I saw a ghost," Cal replied, smiling. "Standard May 13."

"And you promise me you're not just joking to cover something?" Pam insisted skeptically. "Your uncle does that, and I swear, the amount of problems—"

She was cut off by a loud buzzing noise. The family cell phone buzzed on the table, screen flashing. Realizing the time, Cal grimaced and lifted it to his ear, voice already prepped at monotone.

"Hey, Todd."

"*Hey fucknuts, where the hell are you? Your shift started twenty minutes ago,*" asked Todd, his usual drawl made all the worse by the hum of static. Pam's expression soured like milk on a hot day.

"Working!" she said, voice low and harsh, as if she could sneak it under the receiver. "You can't be out on deliveries, there's a wild animal on the loose!"

"Yeah, I know, I know. I'll be there soon," Cal said, putting a finger in his ear. Pam bit her lip and raised her eyebrows, in the way that only middle-aged women seem to know how to do. Incalculable rage and potential wrath, all communicated in a single, bouncing brow.

"*Whatever. Some guy asked for a pizza in advance, get your ass here,*" Todd replied, before hanging up. Cal put the phone down, glanced at the clock, and shoveled a final few heaped mouthfuls of meatloaf into his cheeks. His shift had started a half hour ago, not twenty minutes, but maybe Todd would be so out of his gourd on paint fumes that he wouldn't notice the mistake.

"I gotta go! I have the family cellphone," he said, grabbing his coat. "I'll be safe, back before eight, bye!"

"Cal!" Pam yelled, but he had already darted from the room. The door slammed, and she slumped back into her chair with a defeated tut. Cigarette smoke curled around her like a friendly arm in the cavernously empty house.

That boy was too good, she thought. And try as she might, she couldn't press down the nagging dread that the universe liked to take away good things best.

~

The sky soared overhead, golden hour in full swing. Shaded yet shadowless, stuck fast in time. Cal stood in the square of halogen light outside the pizzeria, squinting at Todd's shaky writing.

"Friendly Fields," he read, repeating it under his breath. That was on the other side of town, way up where the northeastern edge met the foothills. As far as he knew, its only main exports were homemade meth, and those groups of weird kids who threw firecrackers at each other in the school parking lot. He made a mental note to tell his Aunt Pam that the delivery was to somewhere else. Someplace safer, like an old folks' home, or an animal sanctuary. That'd put her nerves to rest.

He checked the straps on the pizza box, before taking a last look at the address. Whoever Howard Triptree was, Cal just hoped he was hungry for pizza and not murdered delivery boy, because if that happened it meant the last person who ever saw him alive was Todd.

Cal put his helmet on, and swiftly pedaled away into the dull coarseness of night.

Friendly Fields had been kept far out from the main town, like quarantined livestock. Instead of buildings and old stumps, it was surrounded by the sighing waves of Pennsylvania state in almost every direction. The locale seemed almost unfairly picturesque, until you reached the chain link fence; from that point it looked like an animal pen, great aluminum cattle hunkering in scattered clusters across the bare mud. That was probably the nicest way of considering it.

Cal slid to a stop by the gate and hid his bike in the undergrowth. Out front, a couple of collisions had knocked pieces off the welcome sign, so it now read "*Welcom t F endl F elds*" in tarnished hot-pink letters. He didn't feel too skittish being out on the road given that Friendly Fields was the only place where, come rain or animal attacks, people would still be out drinking on their porches long into the night.

Number twenty-six lay right at the edge of the park. A poorly attached generator chugged broodingly against the trailer's outer shell, making it look lumpen and deformed. The blinds were closed, and as Cal drew closer, he realized that they'd actually been taped in place, flush against the window. Alarm bells started to clang in the back of his head.

What if this guy actually *was* a murderer?

He sniffed the air. No rotting flesh, he thought. Just the acrid cringe of cigarette smoke mixed with gas. Maybe he was just a meth cook. They never tipped, but at least they always took the pizza quick. Cal got out his phone and flipped the screen up, thumbs jostling against each other as they reached to type on the number pad.

Nine on, one all plugged in and ready just in case. Then, he picked up the pizza again and took a deep breath, trying to take solace in the fact he was completely ready to drop and run. That, and nowhere near cute enough to kidnap.

He rapped on the polyethylene panel, which wobbled in the frame. Immediately, there were the sounds of movement from within. Footsteps, and the occasional bang of something being moved. Cal took a step back as they approached, then came to a stop behind the door.

The guy who answered looked like a post-apocalyptic office worker. His thick-framed glasses were cracked in the corners and held together in several places by tape, strands of slightly too-long hair poking out from underneath his cap.

"What the hell do you want?" he said, voice rattling. Cal gestured nervously to the pizza.

"I, uh… Mister… Triptree?" Cal asked.

"I didn't order any pizza. Go away," the man replied, slamming the door shut. Cal stood there a second, like he couldn't quite tell what had just happened. And then, unexpectedly, there came more noise. The scratch and crack of locks being undone again.

The door swept open again, revealing the ragged man in all of his splendor. Behind him, Cal could see the inside of the trailer was lit up in sickly purple tones by what looked like grow lights. Darting suddenly forward, the ragged man snatched out a hand and wrenched the pizza box from Cal's grip. They made eye contact for a split second as he pulled it back, as if to let the theft sink in, and it was in that long, brief moment, that Cal became aware of another pair of eyes upon him.

They were wide and probing. Barely visible and half-obscured by the man's outstretched arm, the rims ragged and red from crying. A girl's eyes.

Then, the door closed, and she was gone. Slammed out of existence by a polyethylene board.

Cal stood there a moment, stunned. When he turned around and started walking, it was slow, and shuffling. Blank. And then it sped up. A walk. A jog. A run and then, as the gate came into view, a sprint.

He'd seen too much, he thought. In an instant he'd seen it all, remembered it all, like looking at an old picture, she had looked *exactly the same*.

The thick tresses of hair. The little cross necklace, now crooked and sticking to skin soaked with sweat. And the eyes. The big doe eyes, all the clearer without the big plastic glasses and yet made dim by the horrible half-light of the trailer.

It couldn't have been, he thought. But it was. He'd stared into that trailer's guts, if only for a second, and seen something he shouldn't have. Something that shouldn't have been.

As he rode, he fumbled into his pocket, clumsily undoing the 9-1-1 with one hand. He went to the speed dial, nearly falling from his seat as he hastily raised it to his ear.

Ringing. Ringing… And then a click.

"*Hey, you've reached Trevor! Leave a message after the beep, unless you're a body snatcher,*" chirped the answering machine. Cal pressed the receiver close to his lips.

"Trevor!" he called down the line, in between gasps for breath. "Oh my god… Trevor! You were right! There's something really, *really* weird going on! I saw… I just went to Friendly Fields, and…"

He glanced over his shoulder for a second before returning the phone back to his face, cold plastic sticking to his sweat-slicked cheek. When the next few words tumbled out of his mouth, they were fractious and dry.

"Trev," he said, words short and gasped, "I… I think I just saw Leslie O'Neil."

WHO TOOK LESLIE O'NEIL?

AMESVILLE, 1993

She was bleeding. She could feel it, against the raw kiss of steel around her wrist, pooling in hot drops at the end of her fingers.

She didn't feel right. Not just inside, but outside. Everything clung to her, like even the air seemed to know she shouldn't have been there. That she was so fundamentally out of place, her very presence in the trailer made the world seize.

Leslie wished she'd said something. To the boy. He'd seen her, and she'd seen him, and... Maybe it was her all her fault now, for not doing anything. Maybe it had always been her fault. How else could it have happened?

The man slammed the door shut again and smirked at the pizza. He took a slice, and crushed it into his mouth, tossing the box onto the couch with his free hand. A little cheese oozed out onto the upholstery. He didn't seem to care. His name was Wittey, maybe. He'd said it once, what seemed like days ago.

His bloodshot eyes wandered to her as he chewed, making her shrink back. Slowly, he turned around and took out another slice. Then he squatted down and tossed it gently onto the floor in front of her, like he was feeding an animal.

"Go on," he said.

Leslie didn't need telling twice. She snatched forward with her free hand, taking bite after searing bite without pausing for breath. Pushed it as fast as it could go, even if it burnt her tongue. She was so, so hungry.

Wittey watched her, a grimace tugging at his lips.

"Jesus," he said, shaking his head. He then went back to the couch and began fiddling with a bundle of wires. Leslie licked her fingers and let out a rattling gasp of relief. It hurt, but the hunger was gone, at least a little. Now, all that was left was... something. Sadness mixed with regret. She stared at the door, frozen still at the moment of lost opportunity.

She should have said something, she thought. Maybe he would have called the police. The outside world had looked so normal, just like it had done before. She could have run.

"They stopped looking for you, y'know. Nobody's gonna come," said Wittey. Leslie jerked her head around to look at him. He was still far away on the couch. That was good, but the gun was right next to him on the table.

"Don't get me wrong," he went on, "they kept going for a while. I mean, the police didn't, but the town definitely did. Guess eventually they just thought you were dead, or never coming back. Bad luck for you, I guess."

Leslie didn't reply. She wasn't sure how she felt hearing it. Part of her thought that if everything were normal, she would've started crying. But she felt too numb for that now.

"You should talk to me, y'know. I could help you out," Wittey insisted. "Y'know, I'm—I'm a good guy. I ain't gonna hurt you. I could help."

Another pause. Wittey's face contorted into a sudden mask of rage. He jerked forward and grabbed a piece of circuit board off the table.

"Goddammit, say somethin' when I talk to you!" he yelled, hurling it across the room. It shattered loudly against the wall near her face, bursting into a cloud of plastic and metal chips. Leslie screamed and held her head in her hands. Her wrist twisted in the tight metal cuff, and she let out a groan of pain. She could feel it biting into her skin.

Wittey watched what he'd done for a while, before standing up again. Then, he leaned down onto one knee and snatched a hand forward, fingers curling around the steel handcuff.

"That a little tight? Huh?" he said, voice a shudderingly low mutter. He went into his pocket and brought out a key, held between a thumb and forefinger.

"You want me to loosen it up for you, right?" he asked. Leslie nodded, and immediately Wittey leaned in closer, seeming to blot out all the light behind him like a foreboding eclipse. His long, greasy blonde hair stroked against her raised knees as his face closed in, but fear kept her from shuddering. When he spoke again, his voice was hardly above a whisper.

"Then tell me what it was like. When it happened," he said.

She could see herself in his eyes. She looked afraid. But still, no words came.

Then, as if on cue, the door rattled.

Wittey twitched his head towards it like a rat hearing footsteps, and stood up into a strange, loping hunch. He took the gun from the table and glanced through the peephole. Then, he pulled back. There were a flurry of clicks and cracks as he unlocked six or seven chains and latches, then pulled the door open. Cold night air flumed through the doorway, where two shadows loomed.

The first man to enter looked rough. Unkempt and feral, like he'd been sleeping in the woods. The moment he saw her he grinned, and she noticed all of his teeth were almost perfectly yellow. But he was forgotten immediately when the man he was accompanying came in.

She'd never seen someone like him. He was... perfect. All porcelain skin and neat, angular hair. It was almost unsettling. His dull red shirt seemed to pulse between the white suit jacket lapels like a foul, engorged heart, adding only more to the fact that against the dusty disarray of Wittey's trailer, he was almost unreal. Like a hallucination.

"Stay outside, Mister Daisy," he said to the yellow-toothed man. "I'd like not to be disturbed."

Daisy nodded. He took one last look at Leslie, smirked, and then was gone. The door rattled a final time as he closed it behind him.

Wittey lost stature the moment the pale man came in, like a frightened dog when its master comes home. Leslie didn't blame him. When the pale man looked at her, there wasn't any warmth in it. No familiarity. He had eyes like a doll's: sharp and clear, but... unliving. Unfeeling.

He stared an unblinking stare, and smiled a perfect, beautiful smile.

"Hello Mister Wittey. You say she's not talking?" he asked. Wittey nodded.

"I think it must've scrambled her up," he said. The pale man took a few steps forward, eyeing her closely. Then, he laughed. It was gentle and deep, like a dark, underground river.

"She's not brain damaged," he said, picking up the revolver from the coffee table, "she's just frightened, as any little girl would be. Allow me."

Almost involuntarily, Leslie squeezed her eyes shut. Pressed herself up against the wall, as if to disappear through it, and away from harm. But when harm didn't come, hesitantly, she cracked an eyelid open. The pale man was still stood there, but without any motion of coming down for her. Examining.

"She's bleeding," he said, turning to face Wittey. "Uncuff her."

Wittey started as if shocked and rushed over to her. In a matter of moments, he'd fumbled the handcuff open, slipping it from her wrist before retreating quickly back to a corner. The pale man smiled and swept away a pile of electronic debris from the kitchen table. Then, he sat down, and gestured to the chair opposite.

"Please," he begged. Leslie didn't reply, but hurried into the chair nonetheless, trying to rub away the dull ache spreading through her fingers. The pale man seemed to notice and drew himself up a little. Righteous indignation and anger, but with all the aggression surgically removed.

"I apologize for my... *associate's* lack of care. People like him teeter on barbarism whenever the situation becomes too tense," he said. "You must be very frightened. I don't know if Mister Wittey has already made it clear, but I assure you we are in no way associated with the people who took you. Their goals are not ours, and certainly not mine. Right now, I just want to help you. My name is Mister Carnassus."

He laced his fingers together, honeyed tones seeming to lap up and over his knuckles as he spoke.

"Do you know who took you?" he asked. She didn't reply.

"I can't help if you refuse to talk, Leslie. Can you talk?" he asked. Leslie, predictably, didn't. She just sat and stared. Carnassus' lip twitched, and he let out a long exhale through his nose. Calmly, he went into his pocket, and laid a pistol on the table.

"I'm not a bad man, Leslie, but I feel it's only fair to forewarn you; I don't take disagreement well," he said. Leslie gulped, and felt her tongue twitch painfully in her mouth. When her voice came out, it was quiet, and raspy.

"I can talk," she said. Carnassus' smile widened, and he leaned back.

"Good. I'm very pleased," he said. He considered her for another few moments, looking her up and down with his cold doll's eyes. Probing for weaknesses, she thought. And all the while, the gun lay between them, barrel pointed squarely toward her. Always within arm's reach of the white hands laced so civilly on Carnassus' lap.

"Now that we understand each other a bit more clearly, let's talk about you," Carnassus said, after a few moments. "How do you feel?"

"Scared," she replied, surprised at her own honesty. Carnassus' perfect face slid into a mask of empathy, as flawless and deliberate as an illustration.

"I know, Leslie. And while your emotional wellbeing is of concern to me, what I need to know right now regards the more... *profound* parts of your psyche. Are you finding yourself able to think straight? Do you feel your emotions are inappropriate to your situation?" he asked, smiling gently at her.

"No," Leslie said, after a few moments. Carnassus' face curved into what was almost a convincing grin. The doll eyes, however, never became less sharp, or predatory. Never stopped watching.

"Very good. I'm glad to hear it," he said, teeth glistening. "That's extremely helpful. And you've not experienced any irregular heartbeat, or unexplained bleeding?"

"I want to go home," Leslie said, a little grit coming into her voice. Carnassus looked utterly unfazed.

"I know," he repeated.

"When can I go? I don't know anything, I just want to go home," she repeated.

"I'm afraid that's not quite possible right now, Leslie. But maybe if you answer my questions, we can see."

"You can't keep me here," she said, shaking her head. "This is… this is illegal. You're gonna go to jail if you don't let me go."

Carnassus straightened the gun on the table, and sighed. Like he'd just stepped in something.

"We're a little pressed for time. I'd much prefer it if you'd just answer my questions for now," he said.

Leslie stared at him for a second, hands balled to fists in her lap. But what could she do?

"No. Nothing's wrong with me," she said finally, staring down at the grimy table.

"I see," Carnassus answered, smiling widely at her. "Thank you, Leslie. What a help you've been so far."

He turned in his chair to face Wittey, who had since come to loiter by the couch. Began to talk about something. Food. Leslie hardly noticed.

Her eyes flicked upwards. Carnassus' wide back seemed to glow in the light like virgin snow. Her hand came up and over the table, groping out to snatch the heavy steel handle of the gun. The barrel rose, as if guided by a tugging line. It was all just reflex. Just like at the shooting range.

Finger pull. Hammer back.

Click.

Nothing.

Carnassus stopped.

Leslie gritted her teeth, pulling again and again.

Click, click, click.

Slowly, calmly, Carnassus turned to face her again. Leslie felt something terrible boil up in her stomach.

Click.

No. No, no, no, no!

Click.

A hollow sob rippled out of Leslie's belly, and the gun clattered from her grip onto the table. Wittey was staring, wide eyed, but Carnassus' smile was eerily undamaged.

"I'm very sorry, Miss O'Neil," he said, taking the gun. "You seem to be under the impression that I'd leave a loaded gun on the table, and that tells me I obviously haven't made myself clear."

When he next spoke, his voice was soft, and gravelly. Not like a man, but a refined beast.

"Please allow me to correct that impression," he said.

The smile faded. The mask went neutral and expressionless, like a snake about to roll its eyes back into its head and bite. But still his dead gaze focused ever sharper, taking in every detail of her. When he spoke again, his voice was louder. Less charismatic, and more monotone, as if he had finally given up trying to seem anything like a normal human being.

"Call Mister Daisy back in, please," he said. Wittey jolted across the room and pulled open the door, saying something quick and muffled. A few moments later, in came Daisy. Stoic and blank, expressionless in his intent. Somehow, he still wasn't as unnerving as Carnassus, who remained still and staring in his seat. Waiting for the atmosphere to settle to his liking.

"Mister Daisy, do you know how old this girl is?" he asked, not looking away from Leslie.

Daisy shook his head.

"She's sixteen, if you believe it. Looks young for her age, doesn't she?"

"I suppose," replied Daisy. Carnassus *hmmed* in agreement, and then for a few moments there was silence. Just the hum of grow-lights in the back, and the noiseless shriek of tension in the air.

Carnassus waved a hand.

"Break her fingers," he said. Without a pause, Daisy closed in. Leslie let out a whimper, which bloomed out into a panicked scream as he braced her wrist down against the table.

"No! No, please, don't!" she cried, trying to wrench her arm back. His gloved hands wrapped around her index finger and jerked forward. About to pull back, and—

"Wait," Carnassus said, holding up a hand. "I've changed my mind. Shoot her."

Daisy's hand flew from Leslie's wrist to her hair, and she screamed again. With an agonizingly hard pull, he yanked her face back, pistol rising up to her temple.

"In fact," Carnassus interrupted again, leaning back in his chair, "leave her as she was."

Daisy let go, and Leslie fell forward onto the table. Her breath came in juddering, heaving sobs. Carnassus, emotionless stare still unmoved from her, inclined his head towards door.

"Thank you very much, Mister Daisy. Please, resume your duties outside," he said. Without a word, Daisy strode across the room, and disappeared out of the door again. Leslie was still sobbing, but quieter. Less frantically. She was starting to feel the numbness creeping in again. Whatever had made her pick up the gun was gone. All the world now seemed only to be a glint in Carnassus' lifeless eyes.

He laced his fingers again and put them on his lap.

"You need to be aware of one thing, Leslie. If I believed, even for a moment, that someone was looking for you, or that you had a chance of escaping, we wouldn't be sitting here together right now. You would be dead. Anyone who knew you were here would be dead. Mister Daisy would make sure of that."

He smiled, but it was one of horrific promise more than joy.

"You live only because I choose to let you. And I only choose to let you because your being alive means nothing," he said. Then, he rose from his seat, fingers deftly pinching buttons back into place on his jacket. Wittey stirred at the sudden movement and retreated a few inches further into the glum shadows of the trailer. Carnassus moved towards the door before addressing him, calmly and directly.

"Mister Daisy will be back for the machine in six linear hours' time," he said. Wittey's face clouded over with a look of doubt. Or at least, even more so than before.

"And what about her?" he asked, looking over his shoulder at Leslie. Carnassus looked too, gaze now changed. Half human, slowly morphing back into the man he wore in public.

"Nobody's looking, and she can't escape," he said softly. "As long as those two facts remain true, you can do whatever you like."

With that, he opened the door and stepped out of sight.

⁓

Night waxed, and the light waned. After hours of furiously moving between computers and pulling apart circuitry, Wittey disappeared into the other room and—she presumed—to bed. He hadn't tried to speak to her much after Carnassus had left, approaching only to replace the cuff onto her uninjured wrist. Leslie couldn't exactly blame him. Even after Carnassus was long gone, the sheer threat of him lingered. Heavy on the air, like he'd painted blood up the walls. She bit her lip and tried to bury a sob back into her throat. She knew it would be loud, and ugly.

It would all make sense soon, she thought. She'd wake up. She'd be back home, in the right place, at the right... the right...

She couldn't hold it back. The sob burst out of her, strangled and high, before she managed to catch it in her palm, but it was too late. The horrible realizations couldn't be ignored a second longer, and now they were pouring like water from a burst dam.

She wasn't going to go back, she thought. It wasn't a dream, it was all real, and they all thought she was dead. Pa, and Bradley… god, they probably gave her a funeral. And they thought she was gone, forever. Buried underground in the dark.

Leslie pressed her forehead against her knees, face twisting into another muted sob. The dark tightened around her, a pit finally easing closed. She didn't see the little green light wink to life amidst the pile of old debris. But she certainly heard what it said.

"Leslie."

She gave a start and looked up. The room lay still.

"Hello, Leslie," repeated the voice, "there's no need to be afraid. I know you can hear me."

She hugged her legs close and huddled into the corner. But despite her wide-eyed stare, she saw no one.

"H-Hello?" she asked quietly. For a while, there was no response. And then, there came a crackling sound, like a telephone with a bad connection.

"The radio, on the desk. Look for the connection light," said the voice. Leslie's eyes wandered, coming to rest on a tiny, bright shape, which flickered and danced enticingly in the blackness. Instinctively, she tried to move towards it, but came to a sharp and painful stop when the cuff bit hard into her wrist.

Leslie winced. She and it weren't going anywhere.

"I… I can't," she called in hushed tones, "I'm handcuffed."

No response. And then, the radio spoke again.

"There should be a pen with a metal clip within arm's reach of you. Find it," it said. Leslie looked around, hand groping over every surface it could. When her fingers finally fell upon the familiar shape, she felt something bloom in her chest. Hope, and disbelief—but at this point, she didn't care how this person seemed to know it would be there. She could think about that when she was free.

"I assume you've found it by now," the radio went on. "Break off the clip and slide it into the cuff between the locking mechanism and the teeth."

Leslie did so, metal jangling as she strained to shove it inside.

"Now, tighten the cuff as far as you can, then let go," it said. Leslie bit her lip and squeezed the steel band tight. It bit and burned, but the pain kept her sharp. Insistent.

Then, to her surprise, it sprang back. Metal shivered on metal as the teeth slid along the pen clip, and the bracelet fell open. Leslie pulled away and rubbed her wrist, skin visibly raw and pink in the dim light.

Then, cautiously, she climbed to her feet. Craned her head to look around the room, as if it was all going to turn out to be a trick or trial. But it was just her, and the strange, all-seeing radio.

"You should be free about now," it said, crackling. "Now come over to the unit, flick the blue switch on the left, and speak into the handset."

The radio was buried underneath a tangled pile of reclaimed wires. It was a boxy gray thing covered in an array of dials and switches, whose form was made anonymous and incomprehensible by the darkness. After a few moments of searching she found a blue switch, and the handset whined in response. Slowly, she raised it up to her lips, and pressed on the plastic button.

"Hello?" she asked.

"Hello Leslie. It's good to hear from you," said the voice. Leslie turned so that she could watch the bedroom door and cupped the mouthpiece closer to her lips.

"How do you know my name?" she asked, voice shaking. "Do you know where I am? Who is this?"

"My name is Howard. I know exactly where you are. The how isn't important right now—we need to concentrate on the task at hand," replied the radio. Leslie gritted her teeth and let out a small whine of distress.

"I need you to help me. Please, call the police, tell them where I am," she pleaded.

"I can't do that. But I can help you escape, if you listen to everything I say, very carefully."

"How?" Leslie insisted, voice growing urgent. "What do I do?"

"First, I need you to find something inside the trailer. On the living room coffee table, there should be a large, gray box labeled 2-98-0-4."

Leslie put down the receiver and loped across the trailer, hands ghosting over the table as she felt around for the box. She found it in a corner, noticeably clear of any debris, and when she picked it up, it nearly sent her toppling over. There was an unexpected weight to it.

"Okay. I have it," she said, fumbling with the radio mouthpiece as she tried to stop the box crashing awkwardly onto the desk.

"Undo the twist valves on the side and open it. Tell me what you see."

Leslie did so. There was a loud clunk, and what sounded like air escaping. The lid was too heavy for just one set of fingertips and took both hands to lift open. The inside seemed to be lined in heavy metal.

The top opened up, revealing another set of valves, and a glass divider through which papers could be seen. After a moment's hesitation, Leslie opened the panel and picked them up. The papers were handwritten, and covered in red pen, like someone had been furiously editing it. One corner was scarred black and burnt.

"It... looks like an essay, or something," she said, reading aloud. "The Principles of..."

Leslie didn't recognize the word that came next, but she tried her best to work it out.

"Ha-llan-ite...? Hallanite," she said, eyes scanning back to the beginning. "The Principles of Hallanite Resonance, by H. Van Hallan."

"Good, that's the right one. There should be a phonebook by the telephone—circle the third number on page 705. Then, put everything inside the box and re-pressurize the valves."

Leslie did so, hurrying to grab yellow pages and prepare it as needed. As she placed the phonebook inside the box, she noticed the air inside it felt odd. Clinging and unusually still. Heedless, she pulled the lids back into place and re-turned the valves. Inside the walls of the box, she could hear a high-pitched whir, and then a whooshing hiss.

"Okay, now what?" she said.

"Go over to the east window, untape the blinds, and pull them up."

"Why am I doing all this?" Leslie asked, picking her way across the room.

"Just trust me. Everything you're doing right now is vitally important," the voice insisted. Hesitantly, Leslie unpicked the greasy tape holding the blinds in place and tugged on the winch string. The trailer filled with clean, pure moonlight, like rain rushing into a dirty cup.

For the first time in what felt like a lifetime, she saw the outside. Not in the brief moments of an open door, not in her desperate dreams, *right there*. Waiting for her.

It all looks the same, she thought. And yet, unmistakably altered. Aged.

As her eyes adjusted to the low evening light, the shape of a beat-up car faded into view, hunkered down just behind the bend like some waiting animal. The headlights were off, with no sign of the driver.

Not moving from her watching spot, Leslie pulled the radio receiver up off the table, and clicked the button again.

"Is that you? Can you see me?" she asked, eyes scanning over the little hill for movement. Occasionally, she could have sworn she saw something moving in among the branches, and a glassy glint. Or was it just a trick of the light?

"Don't get distracted, Leslie. You need to listen to what I'm about to tell you very carefully. Everything must happen in a very specific way," said the voice. "When you get out of the trailer, you need to take a left at the end of the road. Take the box with you. No matter what happens, keep running until you meet two boys on bikes. Do you follow me so far?"

"Yes," Leslie said. She felt uneasy standing by the window. Like she was being watched.

"After you meet with them, you need to head south down Innsmouth Road about a half mile, alone if you have to. You'll see a flamingo lawn ornament, that'll tell you where the hatch is. Get there by 5 a.m., and once you're inside, don't go back out under any circumstances. Do you understand?"

"Go to the hatch. Don't come out. I understand," she said. Her eyes wandered momentarily upwards, and out onto the dusty nightscape beyond the window.

She saw it again. It was definitely there, the glint of glass in the bushes.

"Leslie?" asked the voice.

"Yes?" she said, looking away again to consider the radio. "I'm still here."

"Good. There's only one last thing you need to do: step back about three feet."

"Okay…" Leslie said, putting down the receiver and stepping back. For a few moments there was silence. Her eyes crawled back up to look at the window, as if expecting someone to be there. But there was nobody. Just the radio.

"I'm very sorry for what you're about to see," it said, "but believe me: he deserves it."

Then, came the screech.

A deafening, electronic wail, flooding out of the speaker with a rising, tinny pitch. Leslie screamed in surprise and clapped her hands to her ears, pain whining in her skull and behind her ears.

Higher. Higher. Higher still, and then with a burst of sparks and belch of smoke, the radio speaker blew. Thick black vapor glooped from a crack in the radio box, crawling over the ceiling like water falling in reverse. Leslie stood there for a few seconds, just staring at it.

At least, for as long as it took her to realize the bedroom door had eased open.

"Deserves what?" asked a voice from the darkness. Leslie froze. Slowly, she turned her head, locking eye to bloodshot eye with Wittey. He loomed like a ragged specter, leant against the hallway wall.

"I… I…" Leslie began, taking a step back. Wittey started moving.

"Who the fuck was that?" he asked, voice rising. "Who the fuck were you talking to?"

Leslie yelped and took another step back. Her foot met an unexpected stop, and the floor slammed up to meet her. Wittey advanced. She crawled backwards, knocking over piles of old parts and magazine towers in a bid to get away from him, only to be stopped by the hard knock of a cabinet against her back. Wittey's eyes tracked sideward. In a jerking swoop, he grabbed a kitchen knife from the block, knuckles white over the plastic grip.

"You're gonna tell me who that was, right now," he said, pointing it towards her as he approached. "Or I fucking swear to god I'll cut you open."

Leslie scrambled back, hand held up to shield herself, and shut her eyes out of reflex. Wittey bore down on her, silhouette breaking through the moonlight.

"Who spoke to you!" he cried, raising the knife. "Who was on the fucking radio!"

What followed was perhaps the saddest part of the story of Sterling Wittey. Not what he did, or what he was. It was the fact he'd never know the answer to the last words he ever spoke, before his head exploded.

The window behind him shattered into pieces, barely masking the wet thud of a bullet squeezing itself through his skull. A chunk of his forehead burst open and Wittey fell immediately, hard and fast with the shock of sudden death.

Leslie sat in place, mouth open. She didn't scream. Didn't know if she could.

There was blood on her face. On her shirt and dripping off her chin. *His* blood. She didn't wipe it away or try to run. She just… sat there. Trying, vainly, to process what had just happened. Outside she heard an engine rev hard, and then the spin of tires passing onto concrete. When she finally climbed to her feet again, the car around the bend was gone.

She dragged the lead box across the room and dropped it by the door, shaking hands prying at the locks. The body lay motionless behind her, head and face nothing more than a dark stain of blood and peeled meat.

She gave it a final look, as long as she could stand, before revulsion welled in her throat and overcame her.

One lock. Then two, three, four. Chains and latches, clicking and scraping to the tune of her frantic, shuddering breath. She grabbed the door. Twisted, pushed, and just like that, she was out and surrounded by open emptiness.

Leslie stumbled forward, catching herself on the side of the rickety stair. She stayed bent over the railing for a minute, just breathing. Trying not to throw up. But no matter how much cold air she gulped, her throat wouldn't unclench.

The night was quiet, as if it hadn't just witnessed the shot. Like she'd turn around and there would be Wittey, alive. With a knife. Ready to skin her alive, or…

She took a deep breath. She needed to go.

Leslie grabbed the box and pulled it into her arms, swaying back and forth to catch the weight as she walked. The grass was wet and scratchy on her legs and tangled round her feet. But steadily, determinedly, she continued. As if pulled by an urgent hook through the ribcage, tugging her forward through the dark night towards safety.

The voice had known, she thought. Maybe it had been him in the car, but even if it wasn't—he'd known Wittey would go in front of the window. He knew she'd be handcuffed. Maybe it really knew she'd be safe, then. The thought kept her pushing through the terror. A dim speck of hope.

Onward, and onward. Through the brush-puckered dirt road, pine needles nipping at the soles of her feet. She didn't see another soul as she loped around the bend, and the road opened up into a concrete yawn. Still she ran, a lone silhouette in the moonlight.

Soon, though, she began to flag. Her half-run became a walk, then a fall. She stumbled, and the box tumbled out of her grip and thudded against the concrete. It didn't hurt. In her little closed off space, all she could hear or feel was her own hoarse breathing. There wasn't anyone out there, she thought. Maybe the voice had been wrong about that.

And then, from somewhere far off, she heard a noise. Voices, and the drone of tires on the dusty road. Leslie lifted her head and peered blearily across the road.

The waxy grin of two bicycle lamps rose to greet her.

BEDSHEETS

AMESVILLE, 1977

The grayness throbbed. Endless, grime-speckled deepness running from floor to wall to ceiling, so uniform it almost pulsed.

Yule felt like he was dreaming. Trapped in a windowed tomb where the glass reflected nothing but the nothingness, kept company only by the sullen tick, tick, tick of time slowly running dry. Perhaps if he closed his eyes and waited, he'd wake up. He'd be in bed, with no missing girls or power cuts to drag him back into the shivering panic.

But the raw sting of cuffs against his wrists told him otherwise.

He just kept replaying the charges in his head, over and over. Kidnapping. Him. A kidnapper.

The interrogation had been so brief that he hardly remembered it; like the memories were second hand. An out-of-body experience, retold to a brain that had just been floating somewhere behind him.

The coffee had tasted flat and lifeless. The man talking to him had prickles where he'd missed with the razor and a band of pale skin on his ring finger.

"You're a soldier," he'd said, looking over the papers for the fifth or sixth time.

"I was," Yule had replied.

"They see some shit, soldiers," he'd said. That part stood out, over the two hours he'd been in there, that stood out the most. They see some shit.

That had tipped him off. Shifted the weight in his gut somehow and marked the moment he realized they were building a silhouette of him. A shooting range target for the newspapers and jury: the ex-soldier, the minimum wage earner, the dangerous black man. He'd not said much after that. He wasn't going to give the recording anything more. Just kept telling them to check the goddamn CCTV, show that he went straight back to work. But that wouldn't happen until morning, so until then he was a suspect.

Or at least, that was what they'd told him.

The cells were cramped, and cold. Relegated to the south side of the building, where the night winds came howling in through the barred windows. At night, the entire row of them seemed to hum and moan in unison. The sound of it just made him feel lonelier.

Maybe that was what they wanted. For him to feel vulnerable. Stick him in the worst cell they had, with the meanest guard, maybe even find more excuses to keep him as long as they wanted to make him pliable. Desperate to escape. Maybe that was why they'd given him the cold cell, with a big iron pipe hanging prominently from the ceiling. After all, they didn't have to interrogate him again if he took the short drop to hell, he thought. The little joke made him smile, even though it really wasn't that funny.

After a few hours, Yule found that if he pressed his forehead against the bar and angled his neck, he could just about see the rest of the police station through the open door. There were a couple of other officers who would walk past once in a while, but the entire station seemed dead. Yule would've thought there'd be more men working with a young girl missing.

But then again, he'd also have thought that they wouldn't put an innocent man in a cell.

From the looks of it, there was only one other person in the building that night who wasn't a cop. And even though he didn't look helpful, from the way he was leaning on the front desk Yule could at least guess he'd be entertaining. Something about him screamed 'avid neighborhood watch member.'

"I want you to put out an arrest warrant," he said loudly, punctuating the final words with a hard jab against the front desk. The police officer looked bemused, and cocked his head forward a little.

"So you *did* see them, Mister Peterson?"

Peterson rolled his eyes, and let out a frustrated, hissing scoff.

"No, I didn't see them—*this* time. But I bet my goddamn life it's that Evans kid, and his asshole friends," he said. "There were hundreds of the damn things, cockroaches, pillbugs, you name it—all of 'em, dead. Stone dead. I reckon the little sickos musta dumped a box fulla them through the attic floorboards, right above me."

The cop wrote something down. Didn't look much like writing, more like he was just scribbling random lines. Then he closed his notebook and put it back in his pocket.

"Look, Mister Peterson, we've got a missing person case right now. We don't have the guys to spare. Maybe we can look at it tomorrow," he said. Mister Peterson's shade of crimson deepened into something more quiet and hateful. Yule could barely hear him when he next spoke.

"Half the town has been out looking for her, and while everybody's singing kumbaya in a fucking field for some runaway, that Evans kid and his gang are organizing! They're using the chaos as a cover!"

"To sneak into your house, and dump insects through your bathroom ceiling," the officer repeated flatly. Peterson slapped a palm to his head.

"Yes! Exactly! That's what I've been telling you!" he said. The officer stared at him for a few seconds before his shoulders slumped. He was tired. A lot more tired than he looked when the conversation had started.

"Look, we'll send some officers round tomorrow. Talk to their parents. Will that make you happy?" he said. Peterson tightened his lips.

"I'll be happy when those little bastards are behind bars," he said, turning to leave. The station doors slammed closed behind him, and the noise bounced across the concrete floor. The cop scoffed under his breath and shook his head, crumpling up the page from his notebook.

Yule smirked, cheek curling into the cold iron pole. That had cheered him up a tiny bit. A moment later, the cop on guard reached forward and rapped the bars with his baton.

"Get back from there. Go to sleep," he said. Yule smiled weakly at him and took a step back.

"Guess you're happy to be on cells, huh?" he asked. The guard considered him with a bloodshot eye and banged the bars again with a little more force.

"Go to sleep," he repeated, as expressive as a brick wall. Yule's smile faded, and he drew back. He pulled his knees up to his chin, and shrank back into the darkness, acutely aware of the temptation to act out; to give in and go along with their script.

But he wasn't going to play that game.

He was going to wait. And wait and wait just as long as it took for him to get out because no matter how hard they wanted shortcuts, they were still cops. Short of planting her body on him they couldn't keep him there forever. They could take his job, take his apartment, none of that mattered. Not really. Yule had seen enough men die young to know that the only important thing was living.

He put his head against the cold wall and stared out the window. Sickly stars stared through the bars, seeming to dance as his breathing rose and fell.

He hoped she was okay. That she'd just run away with some boy or joined the circus. But as much as he wanted to believe it could be that simple, life usually didn't work out that way. Even though he hated to think about it, Leslie O'Neil was either in the trunk of a car, or a foot below the topsoil. The world was a meat grinder, Yule thought, and it didn't have any patience for things that couldn't stand up to the blades. She might have had a gun, but she'd been trusting. Overconfident.

If she'd stopped on the road to talk to him of all people, Yule couldn't say she wouldn't do it again.

He closed his eyes and laid his head against the wall. He could hear cars rumbling outside. Leaves blowing. Crickets chirping. For a while he lay there, imagining he was out there too. Just feeling the wind wash over him. Then he tried to settle into the bed, lying the sheets to one side. Sleep didn't come easy, but eventually, it came.

His dreams were full of dead bugs.

The hours ticked by in silence. Alone on his bed, Yule twisted and turned as visions of the jungle swooped oil-like against the watery drop of high-school memories. His dreams were like that now. Indistinct, and intermingled.

From inside that velvet-thick dreamscape, he wasn't aware of the nervous chatter of a cell door being opened and closed quietly and deliberately. He couldn't hear the muffled *clack, clack, clack* of shoes creeping towards the bed, or the slow crumple of fabric being pulled away.

In truth, it must've been some other sense. The feeling of something predatory drawing close that snapped Yule's eyes open. He sat bolt upright, a gasp held tight in his chest. He didn't see anyone in the cell with him, but then again, he didn't see anything at all.

The entire station was black. Pitch black. The night outside filtered blue through the windows, throwing the barred hallway into a strange and uncanny twist of unfamiliar angles, before terminating in hard blackness beyond. No cars, no crickets. The entire building sounded empty.

But in the deep silence, Yule couldn't shake the feeling he wasn't alone.

Eyes still adjusting to the sudden blackness, he made his way out of bed. His fingers curled around the cold steel bars, wide eyes peering side to side across grazed knuckle skin. The chair opposite the cell now sat empty.

"Hello?" Yule called. His voice was quiet, fading quickly as it passed out of the dusty moonlight.

"Hello?" he repeated, louder. "Anybody?"

The darkness offered no reply.

Yule felt an intense, urgent fear well up in him. Something wasn't right at all. He stood there, frozen in his gripping place, staring hard into the blackness to see what lay beyond. He didn't see the stark white bedsheets come sliding out of the dark behind him, pulled taut into a shining band.

Yule let out a strangled gasp as the fabric tightened over his throat. Soon, though, the surprise gave way to a white flash of panic. His hands clawed and pried upwards, and the fabric bit harder in reply.

Yule croaked and gasped again, struggling for breath. He could feel blood pooling in his face, under his skin. He tried to scream. Nothing came out but a smothered, bubbling sound.

The man behind him pulled again, tighter and tighter. Grunted, like an animal heaving. Yule shoved an elbow down into ribs, and the man let out a pained grunt—but he didn't let up. He was strong, stronger than Yule was. And Yule was fading fast.

His hands grasped up but were knocked away. Fell. He was struggling less now. Fading.

He couldn't breathe.

He... he couldn't...

Hands fell. Legs buckled.

Tighter. Tighter.

Everything felt numb. He needed air, he could feel blood swelling in his lips, fit to burst through his head. Unconsciousness grew like a wriggling red dot in the darkness. Pooling over him.

He couldn't think, it... it was all too close. Too... too dark.

He couldn't...

He...

In the deep, pulsing blackness, he was dimly aware of a sensation. Something familiar brushed up against his fingertips, half made of muscle memory and dancing like Christmas lights as he circled the drain. Instinctively, he grasped forward, and his fingers found a handle. Then, a trigger.

The bang seemed quiet, and far away. So did the scream. It all felt like it was happening somewhere else, but when the hands let go it all came rushing in. Hot and yet searingly cold, the taste of blood and life. Yule fell forward, coughing and panting, hand flying to his neck.

Behind him, he could hear the man groaning, and the dim spatter of blood on tile. Yule looked up, head spinning. When he tried to talk, it hurt. It sounded like pain, felt like pain, but it didn't stop him.

"Help me!" he croaked, rattling the bars. "Somebody, please! Help me!"
The darkness still offered no reply.

He turned onto his back, trying to stay steady on legs gone liquid. The man was crushed into a corner, bloodied bedsheets tangled at his feet. The two looked at each other for a long, brief second, and for a moment, Yule's vision righted itself. In amongst the dark, he saw a flash of navy blue uniform.

That was all he had time to see, before the man pitched forward. A fist slammed hard into the side of Yule's head, and he fell like an unfastened post. The last thing he heard was the throbbing clang of his skull colliding with the bars.

Then, he knew only darkness, and the rhythm of his own pulse beating in his ears.

Sensation.

White hot like a match in the dark. Something probing at his eyelid.

Yule opened his eyes and immediately regretted it. A sharp, shuddering pain shot through his head as unexpected daylight flooded his vision. The man examining him jerked back and held up his gloved hands.

"Hey! Hey, take it easy!" he said, blue palms upturned. "I'm trying to help, you took a nasty fall."

Behind him, a group of maybe three or four cops were stood outside the cell, arms folded. The old cop from the day before was among them.

Yule stared at him, eyes wide and bloodshot.

"A... I took a..." he muttered, looking around the room.

It was pristine. The blood was gone, and so were the bedsheets. The only marks were the ones he'd made, complete with a scabbed trail of blood from where he'd been laid.

"You musta hit your head or something," the medic said, probing around with a piece of gauze. "It's nothing too bad, just a cut near your ear, but you might be concussed."

"You... you don't understand, you..." Yule said, looking up at the police officers. "Somebody came in here last night. Somebody tried to kill me, they tried to strangle me."

"Looks like they didn't do a very good job," said one of the cops, quietly. There was a muffled patter of laughter.

"I'm serious!" Yule shouted, panic overcoming the swelling pain in his head. "Somebody tried to fucking kill me in the middle of the night, that's how this happened!"

"What's wrong with him, Doc?" asked one of the cops. "You sure it's not something worse?"

The medic frowned.

"No, but… even mild head injuries carry some risk of disorientation," he said. Yule slapped his hand away and straightened himself up against the wall.

"I'm telling you," he said, trying to keep his voice steady, "this wasn't an accident. A man attacked me."

"Well, unless it was somebody with a magic video surveillance eraser, my money's on a fall. Somebody get this motherfucker to a hospital," said an officer, stepping forward. It was the one from the interrogation, with the patchy chin and failed marriage tan on his finger. Yule stared at him, and for a brief second, doubt crept in.

Had it really happened? Maybe he had just taken a fall. Dreamed it.

But there was something in the police officer's grip as Yule was helped to his feet. The angle of it maybe, or the way the light hit his uniform. Yule felt his eyes wander downward, where they found something gut-wrenchingly familiar.

Blue uniform. The guy had been wearing a blue uniform.

All at once he shot up and shook his forearm from the officer's grip. The group twitched, moved to lunge at him until his palms flew up and he backed dizzily into the cell a few paces.

"No, I'm fine. I'm alright, I don't need to go to a hospital," he said, wide eyes flicking across the crowd of faces beyond the bars. It could've been any one of them. Did they know? The cop with the patchy face folded his arms, rough stubble twitching above his lips.

"I dunno about turning you loose like this," he said. Yule spoke softly, rasping a little as the words crawled through his bruised throat.

"But… that means I'm free to go? I can leave?" he asked. "You… you got the surveillance tapes?"

The officer nodded.

"Your alibi checks out. You're free to go, but you should see somebody about that head, boy," he replied. Yule edged towards the cell door, the cops on the other side parting but never quite disbanding. They just looked at him.

"Alright. I'll think about that, I just gotta…" Yule said, eyes unconsciously straying to the exit, "…you guys got a phone?"

The patchy faced officer grunted and nodded some ways down the hall. Yule followed his gesture, eyes unconsciously scanning the tile. Looking to see if it seemed cleaner than before, but he hadn't noted it. What did a police station floor usually look like?

"Sir?" asked the officer. Yule snapped out of his daze, wide eyed like a deer in headlights.

"What?"

"I said the phone's just down there," he repeated, pointing. "But I'll tell you now, you skip town and it'll end badly."

Yule looked over his shoulder, exhaled, and nodded.

"Alright," he said, trying to conjure the least fake-looking smile he could. "Thanks. Thanks a lot."

He pressed a final inch and was out of the cell's grip. The urge to bolt leapt in his legs, but he pushed it down. Suppressed it, tried to walk normally, tried to smile. But as he made that long walk down the now bustling hallway, Yule couldn't help but feel his eyes drawn to every stray face that passed him by. Every strange glance, every glare.

Was it just for who he was? Or did they know something?

The phone was in the middle of the lobby, encased in a plastic pillar. He punched in the number, glancing over his shoulder every spare moment just in case. The line was crackly and faint as he raised it to his ear, gaze still scanning the crowd behind him for a threat. Yule barely even noticed when it clicked, and the white noise of breathing appeared on the other side.

"Hello?" asked a voice. Yule clutched the phone to his chin.

"Ornell? Ornell, listen to me, I'm at the police station," he said, voice hushed. "They just let me go, I need you to come get me."

For a few seconds there was no reply. When it came, it was short and simple.

"Alright, man," he said. The line clicked and went dead. Yule held the phone to his ear for a few more seconds before hanging it on the hook again. The bell let out a single, half-hearted ting as he set it down, but he didn't hear it. Yule was already halfway towards the door.

THE DEAD GIRL

AMESVILLE, 1993

"Holy Shit. Ho. Ly. Shit," Trevor said, locking the door. He turned around and stared up the stairs as Cal came wandering down.

"I put her in your sister's room. She's passed out still," Cal said, flexing his shoulder. It was sore from dragging. Trevor raised his hands up to his face, palms gently probing over clammy cheeks.

"Cal, she's Leslie O'Neil, and she's alive, and… and in my sister's room," he said, eyes barely visible between his fingers. Cal came down onto the ground floor and held up a hand.

"Trev. Trevor," he repeated, "don't freak out."

"You found her in a trailer!" he said, voice going deadly quiet as he glanced up the stairs. "And now she's in my house, why is she in my house?"

"Hey. Hey. Trev. Just calm down buddy," he said, pulling him into the living room, "she's completely alive, everything's fine. Your mom's not gonna be back for days, it's all good."

"It is *not* all good, Cal! There's a girl who should be dead up there, and you're acting like it's perfectly fine!" Trevor said, yelling as much as his terrified whisper would allow.

Cal gripped his own hair and closed his eyes, trying to find stillness inside the shifting shadows behind his eyelids.

"Okay. We just have to keep our heads screwed on right now, right? Just… keep calm. Stay constructive," he said. When he opened his eyes,

Trevor was all scrunched up on the couch opposite, like a frightened cartoon bird.

"I'm finding it really hard to feel calm when you're looking at me like that, Trev," said Cal.

"Oh, I'm sorry," Trevor replied breathlessly, "I'll just stay real calm about the *dead girl*."

Then, his face fell, as if a terrible, frightening cold had coiled around his heart. "Oh god. What if she dies here? What do we do? What if they think we're connected?"

"She's not gonna die," Cal replied.

"Well she didn't exactly seem like she was gonna go run a marathon, Cal! You gotta go check on her."

Cal cocked his head back.

"What? Why me, it's your house!" he said.

"You're the one who found her! And you talk to girls! Y'know, sometimes!"

"When?"

"You talked to Ellie Smitt in biology yesterday!"

"Because there was bird shit in her hair, Trev! That's a helluva different thing to seeing if somebody's gonna die!" Cal protested. Trevor screwed up his face, anger and desperation momentarily directionless. Then, suddenly, he rose from his seat and strode across the living room.

"Hey! Where are you going?" Cal called after him, as he disappeared through the door. The sound of drawers being opened and contents shifting called out from the next room. Then a pause, and a slam as a drawer finally closed again.

Trevor came marching back through, eyes fixed straight on Cal. When he saw what Trev was holding in his hand, he couldn't hold back a groan.

"Seriously?" Cal asked.

Trevor slammed the little figurine on the table. The man pointed his warped plastic bow up to the ceiling, half-blind for age and grime.

"I'm calling in my Green Ranger," he said resolutely. Cal shot up to his feet.

"No. No, no, no, you already cashed that shit in when I asked Heather Lockley to the dance for you in seventh grade."

"And she said no!" Trevor replied, brandishing the figure at him. "When we gave each other these, we said we'd get one *successful* favor. That was a sacred pact, Cal."

"We were eight," Cal replied, folding his arms. Trevor let out a huff of frustration and put the figurine back down.

"I broke my collarbone when you called yours in," he argued.

"Yeah, because you had to make it look real when you 'broke the wing mirror on Terry's car.' I just needed you to make it look like it wasn't me, not that you had a death wish!"

Trevor went mute and sat down. But the look of fury never left his face. And then, he just… sat there. Looking at him. Cal shifted in his seat, trying not to look back.

"Would you stop?" he said. Trev jutted out his jaw and hardened his brow.

"Sacred. Pact," he repeated. Cal groaned again and rolled his eyes as if he was having a stroke. Then, he rose from the chair, and snatched the figurine off the table.

"Fine," he said, putting it in his pocket. "Jesus, just take that look off your face."

Trevor's expression lightened immediately into a sweet, smug little smile. Cal could almost chart his slow drop back into panicked reality as it faded.

"I should get a phone. Get ready to call the cops," he muttered, "just in case."

Cal sighed, and began to walk up the stairs. The ranger's little plastic bow dug into his thigh with every step, barely blunted by thin pocket fabric. He hated how much he liked Trevor sometimes, the chubby little bastard.

Julia's room was the first one in the upstairs hallway. Like most of the other bedrooms, it was empty most of the time. Trevor was the youngest of six siblings, some of whom had been packed and gone before Cal had even met him, but for some reason Mrs. Vasquez didn't like letting go: every single one was kept as it had been when they left, even down to the clothes laid out on the bed. Cal always thought it was kind of creepy, like they'd died or something.

He pushed open the bedroom door, wood hissing as it scraped the carpet in a long, slow arc. And then, there she was. Leslie O'Neil. Bloodied and splayed out on the bubblegum-colored covers. She still looked herself, even without the grain of old photograph paper.

Cal moved into the room, slightly crouched. It was only when he found himself a foot away from the bed that he realized he didn't have any idea what to do. Did he turn her over? Check her pulse? He should check her pulse, he thought, leaning forward. But did he do it on her neck? Would that be weird? That was weird. Just go for her wrist.

Cal clamped his fingers against her arm. The skin was clammy and gritty, sweat mixed with dirt.

And he couldn't feel a pulse.

Nothing. He tapped around a little, but still nothing. For a moment, Cal felt a surge of panic up his spine. She was dead, and now there was a dead body in Trevor's house.

Then, Leslie let out a short, hoarse gasp in her sleep, and snapped him from the panic attack before it bloomed. Cal took a deep breath and tried to center himself.

She was covered in dirt, and blood. At first, he'd thought she'd been stabbed or injured. But now, looking at her, he couldn't see a single cut anywhere. Which meant all the blood belonged to somebody else.

He felt something in his stomach shift when he realized. She didn't look like she could kill anybody, he thought. But apparently adrenaline made pregnant women able to lift cars, so he didn't know what it'd do to someone who'd been through…

…*whatever* had happened to her.

As he examined her, he found himself looking for signs. Frost on her hair from being cryogenically frozen, or alien goo, but without actually touching her there wasn't anything he could tell—apart from that, by the looks of it, someone had probably bitten the big one.

His eyes wandered over to the box, still within arm's reach on the dresser. She'd been clinging to it for dear life until the moment she dropped.

Cal looked at Leslie a final time, but she didn't stir. He stalked over to the box and peered through the top but couldn't see through the darkened glass. Maybe Trev would know what it was now he'd calmed down.

Cal put his arms around it and heaved. The unexpected weight knocked the air out of him, and he tottered in place to keep his balance, leaning against the wall as he descended back down the stairs for fear he might slip and break something.

"Trev? She's asleep, but alive," Cal panted, as he reached the bottom. "You should probably take a look at this."

No answer. As he got closer to the living room door, Cal realized he could hear something. The gentle *skrish, skrish* of shifting paper.

He turned the corner and suddenly it was snowing indoors in mid-May.

Paper on the couch, paper on the table, even paper on the floor. Dozens upon dozens of sheets, all covered in scratchy, bullet-pointed writing. Trevor was in the corner, hurriedly pulling more from a cabinet drawer, lit in blue-and-white tones by the flickering glow of the CRT monitor nearby.

"No... Alaskan werewolves... Skynet..." he muttered, quickly scanning each page before, seemingly unsatisfied, throwing it over his shoulder in his hurry for the next. Cal put the box heavily down on the couch and picked one up.

"THE CACKLING FIEND MISTAKES," it said in large lettering at the top, before dropping down a line.

"One. Man opens Cackling Fiend box when it's very clearly not something he should open (Result: death)."

"What the..." Cal muttered, before Trevor interrupted with a loud, triumphant call.

"Got it!" he said, waving a piece of tattered paper over his head, and turning his wide eyes towards Cal. "So she's alive? She's good?"

"Are these your stupid movie cliché lists?" Cal asked. Trevor seemed not to hear him through his muffling cloak of enthusiasm.

"Well this one's *The Woman From Mars*—afraid of water. Did she look like she was afraid of water to you?" he asked, adding the paper to the small pile on the table. He then circled a few with a pen, before going to rifle through the drawers again. Cal looked over one the papers.

"*Girl out of Time, She-Wolves of London, Carrie.*" The running theme wasn't particularly cryptic. Cal couldn't help but laugh.

"Are… you doing what I think you're doing?" he asked.

"I've got all the ones about women, that should be a narrow start," Trevor replied, pointing to the pile. "Did she have like, fur, or something? No objects flying around?"

"I'm not answering that, Trev."

Trevor screwed up his face.

"Why not?" he asked. Cal pointed to the box.

"Just stop having a nervous breakdown for a second and help me with this thing," he said. Trevor narrowed his eyes at the lead-lined box and shook his head.

"Nah, I don't think so," he said, going back to the papers. Cal stood there, dumbfounded.

"You… don't think we should open it?" he asked, feeling out the words like a wall in the dark. Trevor flicked through a few pages and tapped a line.

"Yeah, no. Opening the box never goes well. There's always a killer monster or evil spirit," he said. Cal rolled his eyes again. He'd done it so many times by now it felt like they might go trailing out of his face.

"Sure, Trev. Meanwhile, here in the real world, I'm probably just gonna open the box," he said, getting up.

"Hey, if you wanna go messing around with the weird lead-lined box we found with a crazy runaway, be my guest," Trevor said, grabbing a stapler. "When an alien parasite comes out, I reserve the right to say I told you so."

Cal scoffed, and walked over to the box on the side. He craned to see through the glare on the glass and squinted. No wonder it weighed so damn much, she had a phone book in there.

His fingers lightly clasped over the seals and twisted. There was a loud hiss of escaping air, and Cal recoiled. Trev span around in his chair and they both stared at it for a long, silent second, then at each other.

"Alien parasite. Ten bucks," Trevor said, unblinking. Almost unconsciously, his free hand curled around the stapler like a club. Cal took a step back towards the counter. Cautiously, he undid the second set of seals, and winced at the slightly quieter groan of air rushing in. Up came the thick glass panel.

Cal furrowed his brow. Slowly, he reached forward with a finger, and gave the phonebook a prod. And again, this time sharper. Solid. Phonebook-like, one might say.

He reached in and picked it up. It was completely normal. No arcane scribbles or hidden panels.

"So what is it?" Trevor asked. Cal shrugged, and put it down.

"Just a plain old phonebook," he said, putting it to one side. Then he stopped and frowned.

There was something else in there. What looked like a large manuscript, covered in red pen. He picked it up and looked it over, reading the title aloud.

"The Principles of Hallanite Resonance, by H. Van Hallan," he said, turning to Trevor. "What the hell is Hallanite?"

In place of a reply, there was a furious chatter of fingers upon keys. Click. Silence.

"Nothing," Trevor replied, shrugging. "Search for it doesn't come up with anything."

Cal hummed thoughtfully, flipping the front page open.

It might as well have been in ancient Greek for all that he understood. He flipped through the pages, scanning down for something he might get, but even the pictures were complex. Huge graphs with coded axes, and tables of long, precise electrical voltages and frequencies. The notes in the margins were even more cryptic. The writing was whipping and quick, scribbled hurriedly as soon as an imperfection was found. "Needs work" said one. Another simply read "???" in reference to what was either a typo, or just a very long word Cal didn't know. Others were strange, and even a little ominous.

"Prolonged exposure proved fatal for subjects four through nine" was annotated with "the dog did not die!" in sharp, purposeful letters.

"So what is it?" Trevor asked. Cal shrugged and closed the covers.

"I dunno," he said, "it looks like a scientific report, but… it's kind of weird."

"Weird how? Like, government knows vampires exist weird?" Trevor insisted, turning around. Cal looked back at the red-welted manuscript and shrugged.

"Honestly? I couldn't tell you." Trevor took the manuscript up and flicked through it, face growing more and more confused with every page.

"So? What's it about?" Cal asked.

"I don't know," Trevor replied, shrugging. "There's some stuff on radio frequency, but there's lots of other things too. Biological samples, electrical charts… real high level. I'm talking, like, *beyond* college level."

"So why does *she* have it? And a phonebook?" Cal asked, glancing up the stairs. Trevor's stare hardened, like a soldier from a movie. A man with a mission.

"Lemme check the lists," he said.

Cal went limp in his seat.

"Again? These are movie clichés, they're not gonna help!"

"They're more than that, Cal!" Trevor replied, bustling around for a stapler. "There's real, practical knowledge in these things!"

"What, that we shouldn't light candles around a pentagram?" Cal replied, laying his hands on Trevor's shoulders. "Buddy, this is real life. Not movies, not kid shit. There's a real girl up there, who's in real, actual trouble."

"Yeah," Trevor said, wriggling free, "a girl who went missing years ago and hasn't aged."

Cal didn't reply. Otherwise, he'd have to admit Trevor had a point.

"You know why people tell fairy tales?" Trevor went on, fiddling with the stapler. Cal stifled a groan of frustration and rolled his eyes. Whenever he got like this there was no stopping him.

"No, Trev. Why do people tell fairy tales?" he repeated sarcastically.

"Warnings. For things that'll kill you if you get them wrong even once," Trevor said shortly, clacking a staple into the pile. "Don't go out after dark, don't trust strangers, don't pussy around with fairies—medieval stuff. These things? They're *modern* fairy tales, and the first rule of survival is the second things get weird, call the cops," he said.

In response, there was a shriek of smashing glass behind them. The boys wheeled around just in time to see a pair of feet flying up and out of view, streaked by trails of water flung from a broken cup.

"Shit!" Cal said, giving chase. His shoes crackled over the broken glass as he raced up the stairs, Trevor behind him. The sounds of crashing and scrambled movement came from inside Julia's room, growing louder still as they opened the door.

Leslie was by the window, frantically trying to open the broken latch. She'd dragged the blanket from the bed and knocked a couple things down in her rush across the room. Cal ran in and stopped two feet shy of her, palms up.

"Hey! Hey, it's alright!" he cried. Leslie turned and looked at him with wide, panicked eyes.

"No cops!" she said, shaking her head. "You can't!"

"Calm down, you're safe!" Cal replied, taking a half step forward. Leslie flinched and nearly fell away from the window, propping herself up on the bed. Her head was still shaking, matted hair kicked up into a bristled mass.

"You're not safe," she repeated, voice going quiet. "None of us are safe."

"You stay here, I'm gonna call—"

"No!" Leslie howled, suddenly filled with panicked energy again. She moved to stop him and, instinctively, Cal stood in her way.

"We won't! Just calm it! Nobody's gonna call the cops, as long as you just stop and breathe for a sec!" he said, turning to Trevor. "Will they?"

Trevor lingered in the doorway, wide-eyed. Even though he didn't answer, Cal took the fact he hadn't bolted as agreement. The room went quiet, filled only by the low undertones of Leslie's shallow, frantic breaths.

"See?" Cal said, palms still raised. "We're friendly. We just wanna help you."

Leslie looked at him, shoulders still raised like a hound about to bolt. But then her eyes glanced to the clock, and her breathing slowed. Something in her stilled.

"I…" she said, voice hoarse, "water, please."

"Alright. I'll get you some more water, just don't smash it again," Cal said, taking a few steps back. "You stay with her, Trevor. Make sure she's alright."

"Me? Why me!" Trevor hissed as he passed through the door.

"I took the last turn," Cal replied, going down the stairs before Trevor could protest.

As Cal looked out the windows, he could make out nothing more than his own reflection, made honey-yellow by the lightbulb glow. Beyond that, the nothing waited. Trevor's house floated adrift in the deep, silent trench. There might as well have not been a world out there at all.

They'd call the cops, he thought. In the morning, when she'd calmed down. Or maybe he'd just wait until she inevitably passed out again. Seemed like the preferable option, but it hardly mattered—either way, they'd come, and take her somewhere else. Her, and all the weirdness and fear. Then things would all go back to normal.

Cal never thought he'd be anxious for the familiar turn of the wheel. Right now, though, he missed it more than he'd ever imagined he could. He'd go back there when it was all done with, slip back into routine like he'd never even been gone. Until then, he thought as he rounded the stairs, he'd just keep getting water. That was simple enough and didn't involve touching anybody.

Alone with his thoughts, he almost felt optimistic. He looked up over the sink, and at his own reflection in the kitchen window. They smiled at each other.

And then, they vanished. As suddenly as a candle flame blown out, the reflection disappeared.

Cal froze up. The lights had all gone off again. Silence descended over the darkened house, cut by the sounds of whimpering and footsteps upstairs.

"Cal? She's freaking out!" Trevor called from the landing. Cal put down the beaker and groped through the blackness into the main hall. He looked up, though he really had no way of telling if Trevor was even there.

"What's going on with the lights?" Cal asked.

"How should I know!" Trevor replied, followed by the creak of his considerable bulk shifting nervously in place. "Uh... maybe it was a fuse or something."

"Right. I guess I'll go check the breaker," Cal said. He hadn't made it more than a few steps before Trevor called after him.

"If you hear a weird noise, don't investigate!" he said.

"I've seen movies before, buddy. I know the protocol," Cal replied, moving on through the blackened doorway and into the kitchen.

Without power, the house felt wholly unfamiliar. Even when the lights were off, the ambient hum of wires in the walls usually filled the place with a pleasing, almost welcoming white noise. But now, groping his way across the room, there was only Cal and the silent, foreboding dark.

The door to the back room rattled and whined as Cal swung it open and a wave of cold air washed over him, bringing the smell of the night in with it. He stood there for a few moments, just staring into the darkness. Trying to get his eyes to adjust.

The back room wasn't an original part of the house. It was tacked on, really more of an attached shack than a room. The ceiling was full of gaps, much like the walls, but instead of fresh air they led up into a blackness between where one floor ended and another began.

The fuse box lay on a partition, near the opposite end of the room. It was an old, thick thing. The kind of electronics they made back when they thought it'd have to survive a nuclear war. The panel cover was stiff and let out a high-pitched shriek when Cal finally managed to curl his fingers around it and pull.

He narrowed his eyes, and leaned in. All of the switch labels had been rubbed away by time.

"Jesus," he muttered, reaching forward. Cautiously, he gave the leftmost one a flick.

Click. Nothing.

One down. And another, and another. Each time, the click rang hollow into the enduring dark beyond. By the fourth, Cal was beginning to think it might not be a fuse issue.

He cursed under his breath, and shivered. Cal hadn't realized how cold it was out there. Not just a normal coldness, either. An unfriendly, ushering kind of chill, like a hand leading frantically away from the dark. He hardly noticed the strange, full feeling in his ears, or the brief crackle of static between his shirt and his arm.

But when it came, he heard the sound. Quietly at first, like the soft crack of raindrops somewhere between the floors. And then all at once, it descended: a black blanket of particles dumped through the ceiling gaps, covering him from head to toe. Cal yelped, and ruffled his hair with his hands. It was only as his palm passed briefly into the moonlight that he saw what had fallen on him.

Insects. Dozens upon dozens of dead, twitching insects, legs twisted up and writhing on the floor, and on his clothes, his hands, his hair. A curled up black spider, clinging to the hairs on his arm in an unliving clutch, stared up at him with endless, glassy eyes.

Cal screamed. Shook his limbs, slapped his skin. They came off him in droves, bouncing and tapping on the carpet. Behind him, he heard Trevor yelling as he cannonballed down the stairs, brandishing a broom as if he was going to smite something with it. Cal slapped his forearms a couple more times, a low moan of disgust punctuating his panting, frantic breath. And then, as if in reply, the house hummed.

Cal hissed through his teeth and screwed his eyes shut, a sudden white burst of pain digging tight at the back of his skull. As quickly and suddenly as a woken sleeper, the house sprang back to life, the lights blaring full blast again. Trevor looked down at their feet and cried out, little swarms of dead insects now visible.

"Eurgh!" he cried, batting at the floor with the broom. "What the hell!"

"There's more out back. *Waaay* more, like hundreds," Cal replied, shutting his eyes. All over his skin. Clinging with dead legs. He shook again and tore off his shirt, ruffling out his hair a few more times for good measure. Trevor put his hands on his hips and surveyed the mess in front of him.

"You don't think...?" he began, looking up.

"I think it's fairly safe to label everything weird under 'to do with Leslie' until proven otherwise," Cal croaked, shuddering again. He leapt in place, and then let out a shivering groan. "I need to shower."

He turned to leave. Trevor followed.

"So, what? She kills bugs now?" he asked.

"Well something did, and put about a dozen down my shirt— *urgh*," Cal said, gagging as he closed the shower-room door.

Trevor's shower was big enough to fit three people in, and Cal was only about half sure they'd never tried to. The bathroom was Mrs. Vasquez' pride and joy—she probably poured about as much into Trev's college fund as she had into the plumbing. Way easier to keep a horde squeaky clean if you've got the facilities, Cal thought.

He stood underneath the hot jet of water, rubbing soap over his neck for the umpteenth time. Every time he felt a trembling on his arm hairs he recoiled, but it was getting to the point where scrubbing hurt.

He screwed the valve shut and stepped out of the cubicle. As he went, he caught a look at himself in the misted mirror, all blurry and indistinct. He looked tired, he thought, even as a blob. Or at least, he did until wrenched back to alertness.

A heavy creak sounded on the stairs outside, followed by a light thud. An unexpected loose floorboard, and a scramble to leap away from it.

Cal pulled a towel around his waist and hastily unlocked the bathroom door. At the sound of the latch undoing, there was a flurry of footfalls in reply downstairs. Heavier now. More uneven. As Cal rounded the landing, he heard the sound of more steps in the hall, and the steady click of door locks being undone.

One hand trying to keep the towel in place, Cal followed. Down the stairs. Through the hall. Into the door, then out.

He skidded to a stop on the front porch, bare skin prickling against the frigid night air. Before him, a hunched over figure padded towards the edge of the light. Leslie O'Neil, and her big, leaden box.

"Hey!" he called. She wheeled around and looked up at him, eyes wide. But not with fear this time.

"Don't stop me. I can't stay here," she said, shaking her head. "Believe me, you're not safe."

"I didn't know you could talk in full sentences," Cal said. Leslie frowned.

"It's called shock," she replied, looking over her shoulder. "Look, it's not that I'm not grateful, but I really have to go."

"Where?" Cal insisted.

"Someplace that's safe," she replied. Cal stared at her and chewed his lip. Then, after a few moments, he shrugged.

"Alright," he said, taking a step back towards the house. What started as an instinctive, resistant scowl became an expression of confusion written over Leslie's face, as if on a delay.

"...Really?" she asked.

Cal shrugged again, if only to hide a shiver.

"Yeah. I'll tell Trev the cops came and picked you up. And I won't tell anybody we saw you," he said.

Leslie narrowed her eyes at him.

"Why?" she asked.

Cal squeezed his eyes shut, trying to stay measured despite how tired and freaked out he was.

"You want the honest truth?" he said, rolling around the statement in his mouth like a sour grape. "All of... this. Mysterious missing people, weird science, bugs dying and shit? I don't..."

He paused. Sighed.

"Look, Trevor might have a hard-on for this kinda thing, but I don't. I don't wanna have to worry about whether some unexplained entity is gonna come and kill me if I call the police."

"You have to believe me—"

"That's the thing," Cal cut in, "I do believe you. I mean, look at you. You've been missing for years and you look exactly the same. It's stuff I can't explain, and honestly, I don't want to explain it. If you being around means something is gonna come after us, then maybe it's better if you *do* go your own way."

Leslie stared at him, almost suspiciously.

"...Thanks," she said shortly, as if she didn't know how to respond. Cal didn't reply. He didn't know what to say—or rather, what the right thing to say was. Leslie stared at him for a few seconds more, gave him a nod, and began to move out of the light.

Then, Cal raised a hand.

"Wait."

Leslie stopped. Turned. Cal took a deep breath.

"I have to know one thing," he continued, swallowing the lump in his throat. He knew he couldn't let it go. "What happened to you?"

Leslie didn't answer for a while. She just looked at him, with an expression he couldn't quite decipher. After what seemed an eternity, her eyelids lowered a little, and her lower lip trembled. Could've been from cold, but something told Cal it wasn't.

"All I know for sure is that six hours ago, it was 1977. And…" she said, trailing off. When she next spoke, she didn't sound like she believed herself. Or that she didn't want to.

"…And now it's not," she finished. "Sorry for getting you involved."

With that she walked towards the road and out of the light, becoming nothing more than a blurred silhouette against the cloud-pocked moonlight. Cal watched her go for some time. Heading the wrong way if she wanted to get to town, but still she moved with perfect purpose. Maybe 'somewhere safe' meant as far away from Amesville as possible.

A fresh gust came rolling in, wrapping unwelcomely around his damp skin. He let out a groaning shiver and retreated back inside. After making sure he was adequately alone and the doors were all locked, he laid down on the couch and pulled a blanket over himself. Settled in for a long few hours of ceiling staring.

Seconds. Seconds to minutes. Five minutes, to a dozen, to thirty. He lay there for about an hour, just staring. Trying to will himself to fall away from consciousness, but he couldn't get what Leslie had said out of his head. In truth, he couldn't get any of it out of his head. At about 4 a.m., Cal sat up and glanced defeatedly at the clock face.

It was no good. Now that he was alone in the dark, everything was rattling him more. Everything she'd said.

Sorry for getting you involved.

What the hell was that supposed to mean?

He got up and shuffled his way through into the kitchen. Trevor was still snoring loudly on the chair, showing no signs of stopping. Cal smiled. At least when things got weird, Trev never changed. He could count on that.

He kept the light off, navigating through the room by touch and countertop alone. As the glass filled, Cal stared out of the window absentmindedly. Without the kitchen lights on, he could see all the way through the night, down towards where the town proper started. Shiny little beads of light in the middle of the forests and hills.

And then, at exactly 4:03 a.m. it wasn't.

At first, Cal thought it was some trick of the dark. Then he realized, it *was* the dark. Or rather, a lack of light. In an instant, every electrical light for miles went out. Cal squinted, barely able to make out the silhouettes of distant buildings.

And then the hum began.

Quietly, at first. Hardly even audible. Cal was only aware of it when his skin started to prickle, and a deep, bass throb began to rise in his ears. A sudden sting of static ran between his finger and the metal sink, and he drew back, stung—and all the while, the hum rose. Higher. Louder.

All around him, in the air, in the house, in the ground. A feeling like hooks. First on his skin, and then his joints, his bones. Dragging.

Tearing.

He couldn't even hear the throb of his heart in his ears now. He opened his mouth to cry out, but there was nothing but the hum. All around him. Inside him.

The air became blindingly bright and washed everything away in a searing green flood.

SUNSHINE

AMESVILLE, 1993

Cal opened his eyes. His bedroom was filled with morning light, beaming directly onto his face. He groaned, rubbed his brow, and sat up. Beside the bed, his alarm clock was still ringing through the busted speaker. Nearly 8 a.m. Fantastic.

He lay back down on the pillow, stared at the ceiling and frowned. He felt like he hadn't slept well. Like he'd dreamed something odd, but he couldn't remember what it was.

Downstairs, Pam called his name. Cal yawned and swung his legs over the side of the bed, squinting in the light.

The sun rose over May 11, 1993.

Just like always.

DEVIL, DETAILS

AMESVILLE, 1977

Yule could always tell what kind of situation it was by the way Ornell's tires sounded. Whenever he was mad as hell, he'd jerk the steering whenever he had to turn, and make the rubber screech against the asphalt. For a while, as they drove back from the police station, neither man said a word. The wheels did all the talking for them.

When the car finally rolled to a halt at a stop light, Yule exhaled through pursed lips as if silently whistling. He could feel his moment arriving, like a weight slowly being lowered onto his chest.

"Look man, I know what it looks like," he said, staring straight ahead, "but I swear to y—"

"I know you didn't do nothing," Ornell cut in, shaking his head.

Yule looked at him.

"You... do?" said Yule.

"Man, the hell you think I didn't?" Ornell replied. Then, he exhaled out of his nose, and tapped the steering wheel. "Maybe I believed 'em for a second. Felt like a movie or somethin'."

Yule raised an eyebrow.

"But you don't believe it now?" he insisted.

"Nah, man. Not for more than five minutes or so," he replied, smirking. Silence pervaded as he turned a smooth, low corner. The tension in the car defused itself, like a rubber band with all the snap taken out. Yule hadn't been expecting that.

"I mean I'm not gonna complain, but… why?" he asked. Ornell stared through the windscreen, thick brow tensed. His fingers tapped idly on the wheel for a few seconds before he leaned forward, as if activated.

"You remember when I killed that bird?" he asked, glancing sideways from his view of the road. Yule cocked his head back and furrowed his brow.

"When you… No. I don't remember that. You killed a bird?" he said. Ornell laughed gently and shook his head.

"When we were… I wanna say eleven? Yeah," Ornell insisted, smirking. "We had this one jank-ass crow hurting the crop down on the old peanut farm. So one day we're fuckin' around shooting cans out back, when I hear that lil' bastard crowing. And I said to you 'let's shoot it dead,' right?"

He paused for a moment, and Yule held up his hands.

"Your call, man, I have no idea what you're talking about."

"Well you didn't say nothin' at the time. So I get the pellet gun and find that lil' coal-feather bastard hangin' out on his tree. *Bam*," said Ornell, making a pistol motion with one of his hands. "Right through its evil lil' heart. So I'm whoopin' and cheering, because that shit made me feel like the black John Wayne, but then I turn around and your bald ass was cryin'. Not even makin' a noise, just tearing up and shit."

He laughed again, but his smile softened into something more thoughtful. More serious.

"You didn't do it, man. Not got the heart for it," he said. Then, he smirked. "And that was a bird. A whole-ass girl? Forget about it."

Neither man said anything for a while after that. They didn't even look at each other. Yule sank into his seat and watched the road crawl backwards under the car. Smiled. It wasn't until the next stoplight that Ornell finally broke it.

"You quit smokin' today?" Ornell said, gas station crawling into view. Yule ground his teeth a little, suddenly aware of the finger tapping unconsciously away on his thigh.

"Maybe tomorrow," he replied. They pulled in next to the off-white pumps, beside a scuffed Ford. Ornell went into his pocket, shifting bulk rocking the car as he pulled out his wallet.

"Grab a couple packs, and some appleheads," he said, pushing a few dollars into Yule's palm. "Keep the change."

Yule smiled, trying to make it as genuine as possible, but though the fear of Ornell's judgement was gone he found himself more troubled than ever. As he crossed the gas pumps alone, the thoughts intruded. Someone had tried to kill him, he thought. Actually, really tried to end him.

It hadn't been like that overseas. It felt... anonymous. They weren't just coming after him, they were coming after all of them. Even if they'd been told otherwise, the 'Cong weren't really after their blood. They just wanted the soldiers out.

But nobody had tried to choke him to death.

He caught himself staring at his own reflection in the gas station door. He looked tired. *Couldn't really expect much else*, he thought, pushing his way inside.

The normality of the whole place was jarring. Lit up just like usual, as if it hadn't noticed the murder that almost happened a few blocks away. Yule limped up to the counter and put some notes on the counter.

"Old Golds. Three packs," he rasped, grabbing a pack of candy from the side. The counter clerk obliged, handing over a foil pack in exchange for crumpled notes. Yule felt like he was on autopilot until he turned to go and was confronted by a familiar pair of large eyes.

His hard expression turned into a smile, only half forced.

"Hey, Ollie! How's it hangin'?" he said, a forgotten spark of joy dancing in his chest, pulling stronger than the need for nicotine. Ollie smiled at him and opened his mouth to speak, suggestion of a stammered syllable seeming to bounce noiselessly around the back of his throat. It was deadened, however, by a red-nailed hand on his shoulder.

Yule followed it up, past a slender wrist, to a bony elbow, and finally to a tense, tightly strung neck. Yule had never seen Ollie's mother before.

She was never with him at the arcade, and now, looking at her, he was beginning to get a picture of why.

She had an odd angularity to her. In her squat, thin nose and bleach-blonde tresses, as if she might puncture the air as she walked. She clutched Ollie's shoulder and pulled him partly behind her lime green dress, as if a wild animal were approaching.

Yule's eyes met hers and they narrowed.

At first, Yule thought he recognized that look. The one that shouted the slur of their choice like a car alarm in the back of people's heads. But the longer he looked, the more different it seemed. Somehow more primal than hateful. Fearful, even. The look of a mother with her back to the campfire, waving a knife at approaching wolves.

It told him news traveled fast. That there was still a girl missing, and as far as people knew, he was the only person they'd dragged in the hole for it.

He didn't wait for her to say anything. Yule mumbled something quickly—even *he* wasn't sure what—and made a beeline for the door. The kid at the counter called out to him that he'd forgotten his change, but Yule hardly heard him. He just listened to the hot flush of blood swelling in his ears and the feeling of shame raking at his chest.

As he walked to the car, he found himself hyper-aware of it. The looks from people, across the street or out of windows. Like hearing a song for the first time and noticing it everywhere.

Now he was more than just the town spook, he thought. Now he was something far, far worse.

From the apartment roof, the entire town looked like nothing more than a little raised grid. Pretty much everything he'd ever really known, no bigger than God's bingo sheet, lying in the weeds.

Yule dangled a single leg over the edge, heel lazily tapping against the concrete siding. Cigarette smoke swirled over his nose and lips, twelfth stick slowly burning down to a stub between his fingers.

The details of Leslie O'Neil were slipping from him already, he thought. He wished he'd known to note it all, how she'd looked, how she'd spoken—it was hard not to imagine her as the black-and-white portrait staring up at him from his hands, slightly crinkled by his fingers. He'd found a couple of them stapled to the pole outside his building. Maybe that'd been on purpose.

She'd been sixteen years old. Six-fucking-teen. When Yule was sixteen, he'd been scoring dime bags up by Simpson Creek and playing football. He'd been nothing. He was a kid.

"Why you?" Yule muttered, looking down at the picture. His neck throbbed. "Why me?"

Half the question had already answered itself in his head. Evidence or not, if they'd found him hanging in his cell, that was a confession. Case got closed. Yule died, and Leslie O'Neil… who knew? The thought made him feel nauseous, but he'd already thrown up everything he could. The world felt close and claustrophobic either way.

The police were involved. That, or someone close to the police. Someone with access. And someone who was desperate to pin it all on the perfect wrong man.

He barely stirred as the metal door shrieked some ways across the roof, and familiar, heavy footsteps approached.

"See anythin' interesting?" Ornell asked, standing a few feet behind him.

"Nah. Not much," Yule said, turning around. "What you standing all the way over there for?"

Ornell thumbed the belt on his bathrobe.

"Didn't wanna scare you or nothin'," he said. Yule rolled his eyes and threw his cigarette over the side.

"You think I'm gonna jump?" he asked. Ornell shrugged.

"Well I don't know, man—might be edgy after what happened. I'm an imposing presence," he said, wandering over. He sat down next to Yule, robe flapping limply in the breeze.

Yule teased another cigarette from the packet and offered one to him. He refused it with a meaty palm and went into the pocket of his robe. They lit up in silence, the tickling sting of tobacco mixing with the heavy, waxen pungency of weed.

That was business as usual in hard times. When Ornell's last girlfriend had left him, they'd made it two straight hours in silence, smoking on the roof. They weren't talkers, at least when they weren't drunk. The army had made Yule that way, but he didn't know about Ornell.

Yule took a long draw, and watched the smoke billow out of him and dissolve away.

God's bingo grid, he thought. *That was all it was.*

"So who knows about it?" he asked shortly. Ornell seemed to get the implication, because his entire body sagged.

"I don't know what you're talking about, man," he said.

Yule turned to him, voice harder.

"Who knows, Ornell?" he asked again.

Ornell looked at his knees, ashamed.

"Couple guys at work. And those old ladies that play dominoes outside Bahama Johns," he said, pausing as if he could taste how painful the details were. "Whole town's talkin' about Leslie, lotta people want answers—but I set 'em straight, man! I swear, I told 'em you didn't do it, that they'd let you go."

"Ornell," Yule said, holding up a smoke-strewn hand. "It's alright. I know you did."

He sighed and took another long draw as the world stretched and yawned around them.

"Don't matter much. Released or not, I'd bet I'm the only suspect so far. Folk in this town don't much liking hearing much beyond the first thing they're told."

"It'll blow over, man. I swear, when that girl gets found, they'll forget," Ornell insisted.

"When. Right," Yule muttered, re-lighting the cigarette. Silence reigned as the two men surveyed the town. Yule wasn't sure if Ornell saw the place the same way he did now. He almost hoped he didn't. He breathed out a few more clouds of cigarette smoke, and then inclined his head towards Ornell.

"Do you ever get the feeling something ain't quite right in this town?" he asked. Ornell shrugged and blew smoke out of his nose.

"Sometimes, man. I dunno. Shit's always been kinda fucked," he said, hacking at the end. Yule's expression tightened, as if a fly had just buzzed past his ear.

"No, man, like *weird* weird?" he insisted. Ornell stopped mid puff and cocked his head back into the folds of his neck.

"*Weird* weird?" he repeated slowly.

"Like… unexplainable shit," Yule went, punctuating his thoughts with the burning end of the cigarette. "Like, Roswell kinda stuff."

"You think that girl Leslie got jacked up by ET's and shit?" Ornell asked, nodding. Yule rolled his eyes again.

"It was just an example, man."

"Topic setter. Aight," Ornell said, nodding just as confidently as before. Then, he paused, as if the meaning of the sentence had finally wrapped itself around his psyche. "Wait, I don't think I follow."

"I dunno, Ornell," Yule replied. "Something is just… it ain't sittin' right inside. Things have been happening that I don't think are normal."

"Cops are racist, dude. Ain't exactly breakin' news," Ornell replied, shrugging. Yule frowned.

"It's not just because of the Leslie thing. Some of the stuff that happened before was just…" Yule said, shaking his head. He took another draw, and let it filter out between his teeth.

"Couple days ago, I find out there's some guy from Harvard living under a fake name outside of town. All the radios are all fucked up, all the dogs are goin' missing, and then the police…"

The statement caught a little on his tongue, fingers ghosting around the raw skin on his throat.

"...Well, it seems like they're real into the suppression of evidence right now."

Ornell said nothing, but simply offered him the joint without a word. Yule stubbed out his cigarette and took it.

"I'm telling you, man," he went on, feeling the pot shivers in his ribcage, "somethin' ain't right, in a big way."

"I dunno, Yule. You had one of them 'acutely traumatic experiences' again. Maybe you ain't thinkin' so straight," replied Ornell, a note of concern creeping in. Yule sucked smoke through his teeth and nodded out to the horizon.

"I ain't thinking, I'm seeing. Look," he said, gesturing for Ornell to do the same. "What do you see?"

Ornell shrugged again.

"I dunno. Trees? Buildings?" he said. Yule blew smoke through his nose, and locked eyes with the empty streets below.

"What don't you see?" he continued. Ornell frowned and took back the joint.

"What the hell kinda question is that?"

"Think about it, man," Yule insisted, gesturing sharply to the streets below. "Girl goes missing. Whole town's talking about it, media coverage and everything, what would you expect to see down there, right now?"

A few slow seconds ticked by. And then, like a fearful flower blooming, Ornell's mouth opened, and his eyebrows raised.

"Cop cars," he said, looking back up to Yule. "There's no cop cars. I can't see a single one."

"Me neither. And I've been up here all damn day," Yule replied. He took the joint to its burning end, before pointedly stubbing it out on the concrete. It spat and bristled with cinders as it went to ash on the stone.

"Like I said, something weird is goin' on here, Ornell," Yule replied, staring down the town as if it might pounce. "Leslie O'Neil might be missing, but the cops sure as hell ain't looking for her."

He pressed his hands into the cold concrete and climbed to his feet. A brief sting of fear lit up in Ornell's eyes until Yule took a decided step away from the edge.

"Where you goin'?" he asked. Yule stopped and zipped up his blue denim jacket. With sunset on its deathbed, the night winds were already rising.

"I'm going away for a while, I think. Go see my old man and lay low for a little bit," he said. Ornell turned around, looking like a kid whose birthday had just been canceled.

"For real? How long?" he said. Yule shrugged.

"A week. Maybe two. Cops told me to stay in town, but they can go fuck themselves if they think I'm gonna play it like that," he said, burying his hands in his pockets. Ornell sighed thoughtfully and bounced his heels against the edge of the roof.

"I guess I can't stop you, man," he said. Yule paused by the door and gave Ornell an almost pained look. He felt like he was having to send a beloved family pet to the kennel.

"I won't be gone long. Just 'til all this dies down," he said. Then he paused, and for a moment the world seemed to pause with him. The two of them just looked at each other from across the rooftop, concrete stained a deepening blue as day turned almost unwillingly to night. Yule could feel words dancing on his tongue, barely restrained by something he couldn't quite name.

Something weird is going on, they said, step by terrified dance step. *I can't be here. I can't be involved; not more than I am already.* A moment later they took a hard turn by his teeth, selfish fear twirling itself to something more profound.

I can't be around you, he thought, looking at Ornell. *I can't bring it your way.*

But the words never fell. Whatever held them back was deep, and nameless.

"Two weeks," he repeated, tapping a palm against the door as he descended. "Tops."

It wasn't hard to fit his entire life into a duffle bag. His passport. A pair of shoes. A pistol brought out and put back away twice, finally hidden in a bundle of shirts near the bottom. A reminder that no matter how well things went, they could always get ugly fast.

Yule didn't know if he was going to his dad's place like he'd said. Maybe he would—but he also had enough cash under his mattress for a budget motel. A budget motel somewhere far, far away, with doors that double locked and beds that faced the whole room. Somewhere they hadn't even heard of Leslie O'Neil. Yule paused momentarily when he thought of the name. The smiling face, and the missing poster. Christ, if he thought he had it bad, what had happened to her?

Couldn't think about it for long. Made him feel... he didn't quite know how. Only that it was somewhere north of misery. He had to calm down, he thought, going to the bathroom. It was no good him freaking out, not now, not when escape was so clearly in view.

The shower water bit hard enough to blunt his nerves. Surrounded by steam and white noise, the terror seemed almost illusory, something he'd half imagined. For the first time in what felt like days, Yule let his guard down. Closed his eyes and let it all wash over him. He didn't know how long he spent in that shower, cuts buzzing on his throat and hands. Could've been minutes, or hours.

All that mattered was that at some point, it was cut short by a noise outside. A clatter and a thud, from the entrance hallway. Yule froze, yanked out of his quiet place like a fish on a reel.

"Ornell?" he called, voice barely audible above the shower. He twisted the faucet and the white noise cut out, leaving nothing but the heavy yawn of settling steam behind.

Yule stood in place and listened. No more noises, but he'd definitely heard something.

"Ornell? That you?" he called.

No answer.

"Shit. Shit, shit, shit…" Yule muttered, running over to his bag. The pistol nearly slipped out of his hands when he picked it up, metal slick on his fingers. At the door, he stilled himself. Bent his knees and shifted his weight to the side of his feet. Just like they'd showed him in basic.

Slowly, cautiously, he went forward. Peeked out.

Nobody outside. He pressed on, silently pushing the door open as he went out into the hallway. He could see almost every room of the apartment, and all of them lay still. The only blind place was around the corner from the entrance hallway and front door. Yule swallowed, spit sliding around the hard stone in his throat. Shit. Shit, okay. He could do this. It had been years, but he'd done it before. Just like a reflex.

Around the corner, point, and…

Yule popped out, gun swinging up to both hands. He found it pointing at nothing but a door.

He stopped there a second, as if he didn't believe there was nobody there. Then, he lowered the pistol, and doubled over, letting it clatter out of his shaking hands.

"Jesus H. Christ…" Yule muttered, shaking his head. He'd really thought that was it for a second. He felt like he might throw up.

He straightened back up and adjusted his towel with one hand. For a few moments, the euphoria of safety made him feel light as air. But when he saw what else was in the hallway, he felt himself fall back to earth.

A package. Wrapped in newspaper and secured with brown packing tape, now lying like a lumpy rock on the carpet below the mail slot. Yule considered it for a moment. Looked around, as if it might be a trap. As he reached down to pick it up, he kept the gun ready, just in case.

The package wasn't heavy, but the wrapping made it look huge. He turned it in his hands and found a piece of paper stuck to the front with a safety pin. The message was short, and forceful.

"PLAY ME," it said.

LOOSE THREADS

AMESVILLE, 1993

Cal sat at the table, barely listening to the warble of the kitchen radio. Pam always told him that he had his youth to keep him awake, but he wondered if he'd left it on a bus or something.

He gave a start when Pam loudly dropped her own bowl on the table. She smirked.

"Late night?" she asked. Cal shook his head and returned to his breakfast.

"Didn't sleep well," he said, through a mouthful of cereal. Terry came through and sat down, putting his folded newspaper on the table. Pam kissed him on the cheek and smiled.

"Gracing us with your presence this morning?" she asked. Terry picked up a cigarette and popped it in his mouth.

"You keep talking like that, you might accidentally flatter me," he said, eyes turning to Cal. "Doesn't look like I'm the one that needs cheering up right now."

"He didn't sleep so good," said Pam sympathetically. Terry snorted and gave Cal a nudge with the newspaper.

"You up all night with that new camera, huh?" he said. Cal looked up, brow furrowed.

"New camera…?" he said groggily. "I got that thing days ago."

"Might wanna check your watch, kiddo. Came yesterday evening," said Terry. Cal frowned. Of course it had. He remembered. He'd gotten the camera, gone to bed, and then... here he was.

"Right. Sorry, I'm... really tired," he replied, looking down at his bowl. A single, sad loop of mushy wheat floated on the discolored milk. He felt like he empathized with it, somehow. Terry lit his cigarette and passed the pack back to Pam, still looking at Cal as if planning what to say.

"You, ah... you got anything big at school today, then?" he asked. Cal let out a quiet, fatigued groan, and looked up again.

"Nothing much. Biology test," he replied. Terry let out a *hmph* sound, an awkward half smile on his face. That only lasted until the radio starting shrieking.

All of their heads snapped to it, and Pam nearly fell out of her chair.

"Jesus!" she shouted over the noise. She knocked over her chair as she shot up onto her feet, scrambling across the room. Raised a fist above her head.

Slam.

"*KZZRRTports of KKKKKKTTTZZ*"

And again.

"*KKKKRRRRRRRRRHGT*"

And for a third time, her little fist came down, rattling the box.

"*KKKRRRGGGTTTZZZarge-scale re-development around the Sledmore Plant, which Senator Casey called a 'much needed injection of life into the area.*" Pam grinned and turned around with her palms up.

"Shoulda been a radio engineer," she said, picking her chair back up.

"You mighta broke the damn thing," Terry grumbled, pouring himself some coffee. Pam poked him in the shoulder and tightened up her face.

"Oh no, you don't get to screw me on this—what was it you said? You'd have the TV fixed by when?"

"I told you, I'm gonna fix it later today, after I've taken that old compressor out the fridge," Terry replied, smirking at her. "Maybe I'll just get you to hit it a couple times."

Cal stopped listening to them around there. It felt weird when old people were like that.

He closed his eyes and ran a hand through his hair. His head felt strange. Like he had a headache without the pain, kind of just pressing over part of his brain. He needed a distraction, he thought, zoning into the burble of the radio. The announcer's voice was pleasant and rolling in his ears. Soothing, almost.

"...*traffic flows easing up around 6 p.m.. You're listening to WBLD-FM Sullivan, here's Kenny Lahey with culture and travel.*"

Kenny Lahey, Cal thought. He remembered him; he had a nice voice. Not too loud, or sharp. That'd be nice. Even better, Amesville barely had a culture, so if he just let it wash over him, he wasn't gonna miss much.

"*Thanks Bill,*" said Kenny, audibly moving closer to the mic. "*So let's start this one with a question—who took Leslie O'Neil?*"

Cal perked up a little. Something about the sentence made his head fizz.

"*That's the query posed by a well-known graffiti piece on Amesville's Clarence Street, which has recently come under fire not just from janitors, but from activists. The work, referencing the disappearance of an Amesville schoolgirl in the late seventies, has recently been nominated to be a listed Pennsylvania Historic Attraction; however, spokespeople from the group 'Respect for Victims' have said that Mayor Huntley's recent push to have the graffiti officially recognized by the tourist board is 'offensive and tasteless.' But despite a long campaign to block...*"

Cal wasn't listening anymore. Something in him felt... *urgent*. Like a lit coal right in his gut.

"What happened to Leslie O'Neil?" he asked. Pam and Terry stopped talking and looked at him. He probably seemed more surprised at it than they did.

"She went missing in the seventies. Don't think they ever found who did it," Pam said after a few seconds, matter-of-factly. Then, she nudged Terry, and gave him an eyebrow raise.

"You worked on that case right, hon?" she said. Terry blinked, face completely neutral. As if he hadn't even been asked the question.

"Yeah. Not much though," he said, taking a sip of coffee. Cal leaned forward on his elbows. The coal in his belly glowed brighter, the twinge in his head tighter.

"Yeah, but like—did she die? Nobody ever found her body, right?" he asked. In the second that followed, Cal noticed a strange kind of tension come over the room. Something in the way that Terry paused before he answered, punctuating it with the clink of his cup on the table.

"No. Had a suspect, but nothing ever turned up. Never found her."

"So—"

"I don't much like talking about it, Cal," Terry cut in, voice flat. Cal clamped his jaw shut and sat back into his seat as Terry picked up the paper and scanned over it in silence. Pam gave Cal a sympathetic look, miming a half-hearted 'sorry' across the table. Cal gave her an awkward smile, and looked back at the lonely Wheat-O. Now he just felt like a moron.

"I, uh… I should get my stuff together," he said, pushing the chair out. As he passed, Terry looked up and gave him a half-strained smile.

"Have a good day, kiddo," he said. Cal smiled back.

"Thanks," he replied, quickly moving on. He heard Terry let out a taut breath behind him as he went. *Didn't sound angry at least,* he thought, as he took his bike from out of the hall and slung his bag over his shoulder. Outside, the day was clear and bright, sunlight pouring in from spotless skies.

As he went to push his bike out the door, Cal felt fingers fall onto his shoulder. Pam gave him a squeeze and smiled. The smell of her cheap perfume was kicked up by the breeze and kissed his cheek as it passed.

"Don't worry about your uncle. I think he's just a little sensitive about the whole thing," she said quietly.

"Because they never found her?" Cal said. Pam's lips tightened.

"Never found her," she confirmed, nodding. Her look became far away, and she squeezed his shoulder again a little more sharply. Cal laid his hand on hers and squeezed back. At that, Pam moved to let him out the door and gave him a nod when he turned back.

"Stay safe out there, Cal," she said, waving him off. Cal smiled at her briefly, before mounting the bike and rolling into the street.

As he rode, Cal pulled a sharp left, starting on the little path through to Hope Meadow Park. Sun or not, he needed waking up—and today, just like every day, he felt like flying. Unfortunately, it turned out he was late to a face-to-face meeting with a flung breakfast burrito that morning. Some ten minutes after he left home, Cal found himself walking down the main street, fingers gingerly poking at a blob of pink sauce spattered up his face.

His bike spokes clicked and clanged as he walked it down the sidewalk, morning light turning rose colored against the worn-out buildings on Clarence Street. He'd twisted something up on the chain when he'd fallen, and now it made a dangerous clacking noise whenever he pedaled.

So, he was consigned to a slow move, watching the town go from 'dead' to 'lethargic.' A couple of the stores were open—at least, the ones without boards. Cal looked at them as he passed, trying not to see his own reflection in the window. It wasn't hard: once you reached a certain point, there weren't many windows left to look through.

A soot-blasted old restaurant shut down after a fire and never reopened. Either a coffee shop or copy shop, made unclear by all the missing letters on the sign. On the corner, an old building sagging in between the dry-cleaners and a dusty old hardware shop. The door and windows were boarded over, the remains of an ancient 'for sale' board lying in moss-pocked pieces at its feet, advertising a real estate agency that didn't even exist anymore. The time-stained sign above the entrance read "Joytown Arcade."

That made it seem a little sadder somehow, Cal thought. The fact it had been an arcade. There was some parallel to all the joy leaving town in the last few decades, but Cal was too tired to really think about it. The thought petered to nothing as he turned to go, hands tight on the handlebars.

Then, he stopped.

There was someone across the street. A man, staring at the arcade.

No. Staring at *him*.

The man was old looking, in a wide brimmed hat and an ill-fitting suit. Stood alone on the sidewalk, hands at his side. It took Cal a second to clock the fact that one eye was unblinking and painted on. There wasn't enough face for Cal to really see what his expression was. He could only make out the strange, prosthetic mask which covered half of it.

Cal stared back, unconsciously moving behind his bike frame like a shield. The man lingered. Just staring.

RRRRRING.

Cal yelped, and his hands flew up. His bike frame clattered to the floor as he took a step away from the sudden noise: the sound of a mechanical bell clunking inside a nearby payphone. After a second, Cal took a breath and stilled himself, glancing back across the street. The old man was gone.

RRRRRING.

Cal pulled up his bike, eyes tracking back to the phone. It continued to ring as he walked past it, echoing out into a tinny hiss. Even as he turned the corner towards school, he glanced across the street again, just in case the old man was still there. But Cal was all alone.

Behind him, the phone outside Joytown rang out into the nothing, until finally, unanswered, it died.

⁓

There were still nearly five minutes until first bell, so the hall was as full as it was going to get. Sneakers and high heels scuffed their way over the grimy diamond-tiled floor, on their way from who-knew-where, talking about god-knew-what. None of it really interested Cal—he felt odd. And not just because of the pink sandwich sauce running down his cheek.

He could still feel the dreams in his head from the night before. Not what they'd been, but what they'd felt like. Now that the outlines were gone, it was just hazy strokes of urgency pressing against the inside of his head. Like something screaming, but without words. Just a feeling, and a bad feeling at that.

He wasn't a fan.

Cal laid his head up against the locker door. He waited there for a good few seconds, just relishing the cool press of the metal on his skin. The noise washed over him, like an obscuring tide on a stone. For a few seconds, he wasn't just someone else, he was nothing at all, or... at least, he usually was. Today he could feel something. Something sharp and irritating.

"You lose a fight with a breakfast sandwich again?" came a familiar voice from beside him. Cal gave a start and turned around.

"What?" he asked blearily.

Trevor beamed, moon-faced, and took a fingertip's worth of pink sauce from Cal's cheek.

"Your latest bid in the 'peer cruelty Olympics,'" he said, flicking it away with a slight grimace. Cal's fingers wandered up to his face and sunk into the half-dried sauce streaks.

"Oh, yeah, uh..." Cal said, going back to his locker. "Some asshole in a blue Toyota tagged me on my way here."

"You're lucky you got that internal bike helmet," he said, reaching forward and tapping the back of Cal's head. Cal grunted, and swatted the hand away.

"Would you quit it? And for the hundredth time, it's like a *tenth of an inch* of titanium. Probably wouldn't help much anyway," he muttered, roughly moving some books to one side. Trevor snorted to himself and folded his fat arms.

"Somebody woke up on the dick side of the bed this morning," he said, leaning against a locker. Cal rubbed a hand drearily over his eyes.

"Sorry, I'm just... ugh," he said, pressing his head on the locker again.

"Hit the Mountain Dew a little too hard last night there, champ?" Trevor said, face all curled in mock concern. Cal sighed and pulled his forehead away from the steel, a little squashed oval of sweat peeling away to mark where he'd been. Trevor's enthusiasm seemed undamaged by the blank stare that followed.

"So, some guy on the boards posted up a pic this morning," he said, pausing dramatically, "photo of frickin' dog boy."

"Do you ever wake up in the morning and wonder if you're going nuts?" Cal asked, unzipping his bag.

"Sure. I mean, I keep coming here by choice, for one thing," Trevor replied, gesturing around them. Cal shook his head.

"No, like… *nuts* nuts, like—*Basket Case* nuts," he insisted. Trevor screwed up his face, like he'd been insulted.

"Well, *Basket Case* is some Frank Henlotter bullshit—"

"I'm being serious," Cal interjected, shoving a book into his bag. "I woke up this morning and felt like I'd been awake for days."

"So, I'm assuming that, in your semi-zombified state, you forgot to bring your brand-spanking new camera. Or, you just decided to pound it into dust," Trevor pointed out, nodding at the bag. Cal looked between them for a moment, brow knitted.

"My what?" he said, eyes widening as the realization hit him. "…Shit. I forgot to pack it this morning."

"But you have it, right? It came?" Trevor insisted.

"Yeah, yeah. It did," Cal said, going back to his bag. Trevor raised his eyebrows expectantly.

"…And?"

"Yeah, it works. Zoom and everything," Cal replied, slinging the bag over his shoulder. He felt like he could remember the details clear as day, but… it felt like he was looking at them through a muddied-up lens. Trevor's expression softened, and he took a step back. Considering him.

"Jeez. You're not even freaking out a *little* over this. Maybe you are sick," he said, giving Cal a gentle nudge on the arm. "If you get to the nurse now, you could probably get the whole day off."

Something in Cal lurched back into the present. The urgency of making a decision, maybe. He shook his head and straightened up a little.

"Nah. I'm alright," he said, shaking his head. "They'll probably think it's to do with the whole dead dad thing and make me go to the counselor again."

Trevor smirked, seeming to see the sudden change.

"Your loss," he said, shrugging, "but when you're in a test fifth period, just know you could've gotten out of it."

From its high perch on the wall the school bell wailed, and the stagnant sea of people rippled. Flowed. Then, rushed every which way, into puddles and lakes behind laminate doors. Cal stuck tightly to Trevor's side, like he was a big battering ram.

"I'll grab it tonight after school. We can go film in the woods like we planned," Cal said, trying to be loud enough that Trev could hear. A look of small sadness came over Trevor's face, and he shook his head.

"Ix-nay on the orest-fay. Went past it this morning, there were a ton of guys in vans, looked like construction."

"What, you're afraid of cranes?" Cal asked. Trevor pushed him a little, and he laughed. Now that he wasn't thinking about things as much, Cal felt more and more himself every passing moment. Everything was okay. Normal. Trevor, the movement of the school, the way it all felt. The dreams had all just been little nothings, made to get left behind.

"Mom told me never to play in construction sites. Plus, I dunno if it'd be breaking federal laws, or if we'd get electrocuted, or—"

"I hear you, Trevvy. No forests," Cal replied. They came to a stop outside of room 209, and Trev lingered by the door.

"Still, meet at my place at eight? My mom left pizza money," he said.

"You know it. Although, I should probably be back at my house before midnight. Terry seems kinda cagey today," Cal replied. As they parted ways, Trevor flashed him a hand to the forehead, eyebrows raising as if in some kind of arcane greeting.

"Make sure you come back, traveler," he said. Cal smiled.

"I *never* never come back," he finished. The words came as easy as water tumbling from a spilled glass.

The rest of the day passed and went without much pain. Over hours the feeling of disconnection lessened, and by the time the final bell rang Cal felt just about himself again. The memory of the strange dreams faded from view like a carpet stain.

He went over to Trevor's a while, where he mostly talked about the dog boy, and refused to watch the end of a movie. Now it was well into the night, and Cal found himself lying underneath the covers, staring at the ceiling. He could hear Pam and Terry arguing about something through the floor. Didn't sound heated, just... mad.

He ground his teeth. Tossed. Turned.

Sleep didn't come. It wasn't even the shouting; he just couldn't switch off. The inside of his head felt like it was buzzing, just replaying the day over and over again. Something was off. Askew. But he couldn't tell what.

He sat up and stared at the wall a while.

What if he was going crazy? Like, if the titanium plate in his head had leeched some kind of chemical into his brain, or something. The question circled over and over in his head, sometimes a yes and sometimes a no. The only thing that was clear to him was the fact he wasn't going get to sleep anytime soon.

He swung his bare legs over the side of the bed, cold floorboards sending a tingle through his soles. His steps were quiet, and deliberate. Feet found familiar places in the dark where he knew the boards wouldn't creak; all too many times he'd heard the arguments downstairs stop after a wincing groan of the wood.

He walked over to his desk, bathed in sterile moonlight from the open window. When Cal looked out over the empty fields beyond the house, the landscape was alien and unfamiliar. In a cloudless sky, the usually pale dot was now a beacon in the waxy black, spitting half-shadows down to the ground below in tones of silver and bruise blue.

He stared out the window a while, feeling his thoughts calm. It didn't happen often, he thought, but it looked pretty out there. Serene. Even the black mass of forest seemed more blurred and docile.

Cal's hands ghosted down towards the video camera on the desk. He picked it up, idly flicking switches and opening components. Not really thinking. Part of him hoped doing something with his hands might clear his head. He'd wanted to try the camera out so badly before, but now it felt less important.

What exactly it was less important *than* had eluded him so far. A feeling. Something big, and dense, lurking in the back of his head like an old stone, and all he knew was that he could feel his stomach sink when he thought of the name Leslie O'Neil, or saw the black, squatting silhouette of the Sledmore Plant in the distance. He was lost in thought about them when something drew his gaze back out, and towards the fields outside the house.

There were lights in the wood.

Cal opened the dusty window and leaned forward on the desk. The night wind scratched over his cheeks and down his collar, eager to meet him.

Lights, he thought. There were definitely lights, around Lover's Bend. Not flashlights, though—they were moving too fast. More like car headlights. Who would be dumb enough to drive off-road there?

He tracked them through the darkness, eyes following as they danced and winked in and out of sight.

He looked down at the camera in his hands and knitted his brow. He remembered the seller page had said something about it having an infrared mode. Night vision. He brought it up close to his face, scanning over the bulging side for the right switch. When he found it, he turned the camera over and pulled out the LCD viewing screen. A click of the lever turned the feed from murky to a stark, ghostly white.

He turned it towards the window, leaning out as far as he dared. Even fully zoomed in, he could only just make out the stinging pulse of car headlights in the woods beyond. Still couldn't see what they were after.

And then, the screen just went blank. Or, flickering, sort of. The little LCD readout filled white, with the occasional whisper of blackness slithering through it. It wasn't until the *boom* reached him that Cal looked up and realized what he'd zoomed in on.

Fire. Rising up in a noxious orange cloud from just beyond the edge of the trees, billowing out with a low, growling rumble. For a moment, the night glowed amber, before the cloud fell in and swallowed itself.

Cal kept watching out into the darkness. From the stillness came a second sound. Louder, and clearer. Like a dog howl and bull moose roar, mixed with a deep, throaty screech. Cal centered the camera back on the trees.

Lights. The smell of burning gas. And, faintly, the noise of tires straining against all hope.

Suddenly, a bank of branches on the edge of the wood swelled. Pressed, then burst, like a stuck pimple. A van popped out of the undergrowth, careening as it hit the bare ground.

It drove almost parallel to the house, making desperately for the road. Swerving and ducking.

That wasn't right, Cal thought, feeling the blood rise in his neck. He pulled up the camera and tried to get a bead on it.

What he saw made his stomach go leaden. He looked over the screen. Back. Over. Back again.

To the naked eye, the van looked like it was just wildly turning away from nothing. But on the camera, it looked like something was chasing it.

But it was incomprehensible. A thing, a mass, glowing in the infrared like it was made out of light. Its shuddering bulk twisted as it bounded after the van, body arching and stiffening like a sprinting dog. Even without the camera, he could see signs of it now—huge footsteps punching against the grass, the heat of its breath in the air.

But not the thing itself. Without the camera, it was utterly invisible.

The van tried to veer again, but the thing was too fast. It swung itself into the side, nearly launching the van off its wheels. The vehicle arced and twisted, turning back. The driver must've passed out or worse, because when it finally screamed out of the turn, the thing was bucking and waving. A van without a driver.

It was only as Cal zoomed out a little to follow it that he realized where it was going. Or rather, where it was coming.

A spike of adrenaline burst down his neck. Cal threw down the camera and flung himself towards the door, feet pounding on the floorboards. He could hear his aunt and uncle stop talking downstairs, almost feel them turn their attention upwards to him.

Good. Had to get out.

Had to get their attention. Get out.

"Aunt Pam!" he yelled, scrambling to get to the stairs. "You gotta g—"

He didn't hear his own voice after that. Barely even heard the sound of the van bursting through the wall downstairs, ripping down half the house with it. The stairs gave way beneath his feet and Cal suddenly felt himself become weightless. Fall.

And then, black.

But not for long. Long enough, though. To Cal only a second had passed, but time had other intentions. When he opened his eyes, he thought he'd gone blind. It was only as he felt a tearing sensation in his lungs that he realized the house had filled with smoke.

He coughed again and groped against the wall, limping out into what remained of the hallway. Something was on fire further into the house, but he couldn't tell where. The walls had... it was all gone. The remains of the van were squatting like a monolith in the dust. A man had gone through the windscreen and wasn't moving. Cal couldn't even see Pam or Terry. Didn't know if they...

His mouth tasted bloody. When he coughed, it came out in little droplets. The sound of fire and his own heartbeat filled his ears, life and death thrumming along at each other.

Had to get out, he thought. Had to.

With a cry of effort, Cal dragged himself towards the back door. A smear of blood trailed where he'd been. He fell against the wall, breaths coming in short, painful gasps. His ribs felt all segmented like a bike chain. It hurt.

His head snapped to the side. A noise. Something wooden, cracking and snapping. In the firelit fog, he saw something at the end of the hallway move. But nothing there to move it.

The sound of heaving breath. An unseen head, probing around a doorway. Looking for the van. Looking for him.

Cal let out a silent gasp of terror and grasped at the doorknob. His hand was slick with sweat, and he could barely get a grip on it. Shifting weight groaned from the hallway. Metal shrieking as the van slowly moved aside. A mass, moving closer.

With a cry, Cal gripped on the doorknob with all of his might, all of his weight pressed on the door. It flung open and he fell heavily onto the back porch. It knocked all the wind out of him and sent hot flashes of pain up through his leg and ribs. He groaned and dragged himself forward.

Inch by inch.

Had to get out.

Had to escape.

But it had heard him. And he could hear it moving into the kitchen, towards the back door, the unseen, heaving thing. Cal struggled to his feet. Through the pain, through the burning, forward, *forward*, stumbling but never stopping.

In the moonlit field he looked like a speck. A lone mote of dust, pressing through the bleak, silvery night. The wind made the long grass wave like an ocean, and he felt like he was drowning.

There was a buckling noise as the back door splayed and burst, as something far too large forced its way through. Cal whimpered, trying to go faster. Dragging his broken ankle. Blood on the grass.

Didn't care.

Had to move. Had to go. Had to live.

And then

Ka-thud.

No.

Ka-thud. Ka-thud. Ka-thud.

No, no, no, no, no. Footsteps. Bounding footsteps, picking up speed behind him. Cal turned around and screamed. The grass was moving! The grass was...

Something huge and heavy hit his chest. For a moment there was a blinding, incomprehensible pain. Like lightning writhing in his skin. It was all he felt as his skin burned and his heart stopped in his chest.

The pain lasted only a moment. He wasn't alive to feel the next one pass.

KILLING STRANGERS

SLEDMORE FACILITY, 1993

Mister Daisy had killed maybe eighteen men in his life. Nineteen if you counted accidents, and more if you counted... well, whatever the green light in the hospital had been. It seemed like killing to him. Point was, he'd seen things that would make a normal person go ashen at the thought of it.

Yet even as the number climbed, he found he felt less and less about it. The most he'd get was the occasional flash of passive awe at the way all things seemed to tend toward routine. The sun rose, the world turned, and strangers killed strangers. Differing details, like so many landmarks on the highway, blurred as they passed.

Death moved him little, he thought, but Carnassus and the green light were a whole other thing entirely.

The room beyond the double doors was large and sparse. Decorated enough not to arouse suspicion, but no more. Wooden wall paneling shone dull in dim light, tinged reddish-purple like freshly butchered meat. Low piano music throbbed in bass tones through the air. Even the radio dared not raise its voice.

And there at the other end of the room, he sat. Motionless, like a spider waiting at the edge of a web. From the moment he entered, Daisy felt Carnassus' eyes upon him. Waiting, and watching. Without a word he approached and sat down on the single chair which lay ready on the other side of the desk. Between them, the Eraser Box sat as both reminder and warning.

Carnassus laced his fingers together, dead eyes fixed on Daisy. When he spoke, it was soft and toneless.

"Tell me what happened," he said. Daisy cleared his throat.

"You were right," he replied. "It came back. Right after the flash, just like last time."

"And?" Carnassus said.

"Made its way to the edge of town. I only got there after the police, but it looked like it ran a truck off the road, ripped up a house then disappeared. Driver was dead, as well as a couple adults and a kid. Least, from what I saw," said Daisy. For any other man, the statement may have hung heavy. But even death's suggestion seemed to flatten itself before Carnassus' cold, unfeeling gaze.

"Were there direct witnesses?" he asked, barely missing a beat. Daisy took a moment, then shook his head.

"No. Don't think so anyway."

Carnassus hummed thoughtfully, and it resonated around the room. Overpowered the cowering music, though no more than a whisper. Finally, he unlaced his fingers and straightened up, inward gaze turned outward again.

"Things have escalated. The time machine works as expected, but Leslie O'Neil has failed to re-appear in the right place. And now, this anomaly seems fully recurrent," he said, calmly and slowly. Daisy felt his trigger hand twitch.

"So we deal with her, too," he said. Carnassus shook his head.

"You're failing to see the greater meaning. In the last loop, somebody murdered Mister Wittey with a rifle. Leslie O'Neil escaped with key data, and somehow found her way to a shielded location before we could undo any of it. How does that happen, Mister Daisy?"

"She had help," he said.

"Help that knew where she was. What was going to happen," said Carnassus, eyes narrowing to cold, dead slits. "Help that knows how to keep themselves out of my control."

"So, what are we gonna do about it?" Daisy asked, trying not to make the tension clear in his voice. Carnassus never so much as cracked.

"We escalate in return," he said. "Until both of these problems have been dealt with, assurance must be increased, and security must be guaranteed. Circling the wagons, so to speak."

A white hand fell gently on the cube, fingers tracing its dull edges as he spoke. Calmly, even affectionately, as if it didn't have a belly full of death, or whatever twisted version of death waited in the green light. When he spoke, Carnassus' voice had an oddly warm quality to it, like he was talking about a beloved family pet.

"We'll repeat the same few weeks for a while. People in this town are creatures of habit. It'll be easy to tell who's a threat, with a little observation. The ones whose habits mark them out, I want you to deal with, just like the hunter. Do you understand?" he said. Daisy chewed the inside of his mouth and leaned back in the chair, considering what he'd heard.

"A purge," he confirmed. Carnassus nodded, and his chair sighed as he leaned back.

"If you'd like to put it that way, then yes," he answered. For a moment there was silence. Then, the air changed.

Carnassus' eyes narrowed a little, dead slits homing in on something. He leaned forward again, porcelain brow shadowed by the suggestion of a frown.

"Define your hesitation, Mister Daisy," he instructed. Daisy felt something in his chest twinge. A slip of the face, maybe. Something in his body language. Fuck.

"I'm assuming that circling the wagons means we don't hire extra help," he said, hand ghosting over the cigarette pack in his pocket as he spoke. Carnassus' reply, as always, was immediate and resolute.

"No. There are too many variables already. Bringing in more outside attention risks exposing the entire project," he said. Then he smiled, features twirling effortlessly into something more benevolent. Calming. Even if Daisy knew it was a lie, he'd be damned if it wasn't a good one. "Even if you fail, there are numerous opportunities to undo it."

Daisy considered the notion. The cube he saw on the table, and the great black thing he knew lay below them. Even if it seemed heavy, it was at least familiar. Strangers killing strangers, even if the world had a tendency to turn in the wrong direction.

"Point me where you need me," he said. Carnassus pushed the Eraser Box across the desk, then laced his fingers once more. His expression was blank. Bare, save for an outward face, like an empty building.

"Thank you, Mister Daisy. I will be in contact when your services are needed," he said, gesturing to the door. "Please ensure the live subjects down below are secure before you leave. The next green flash will be deployed in an hour."

"Yes, sir," Daisy replied. He knew that saying any more was meaningless. He left the room and entered the elevator at the end of the hall without stopping. It wasn't until the chrome doors shut behind him that Daisy felt his stomach unclench.

"Jesus," he muttered, patting down his shirt.

Against his better judgment, he found himself starting to miss government work. That had at least made sense. This was more complicated, and 'complicated' didn't suit him.

As he exited the office below, Daisy went into his pocket and pulled out a pack of cigarettes, popping one into his mouth as he reached the second elevator. He lit it and smirked at the familiar feeling of smoke rasping past his dry tongue.

Still, he thought, there were worse places to be than the right side of the green light.

RIGHT MAN, WRONG TIME

AMESVILLE, 1977

The VHS tape sat in the middle of the kitchen table, an intrusion in gray plastic cladding. The front was covered by a luridly colored sticker which said, "Debbie Does Dallas," half scratched away from repeat viewings. Yule stood across from it, just staring. Considering it, and the layers of bubble wrap and aluminum foil it had been wrapped in.

Was he not following something here?

He hiked up his towel and wandered into the living room. The tape clacked as it settled into the VCR, inner mechanics whirring to life. Yule turned on the TV and sat down.

Without any intro or interlude, the screen flurried to life. Tinny, badly balanced trumpets blared out of the speakers as the camera homed in on a group of cheerleaders. As a group of football players ran cheering onto a weirdly empty field, "DEBBIE DOES DALLAS" flew onto the screen in bright red letters.

Yule sat there, confused grimace still etched into his face.

This was just porn. Somebody had just sent him some porn. Was this a threat or something? Or a joke? He twisted around on the sofa and looked around the apartment again.

"Ornell?" he called out, loud enough he might hear him behind the door. "Man, this ain't funny, it's just... weird, and kinda disappointing."

No answer. Yule stared through the apartment for a little while longer, just to put his mind at rest. Make sure he could turn around in the confidence he wasn't being watched. However, after a moment, he realized he couldn't hear the badly acted tape behind him anymore.

Yule turned back around, then stopped. Something wasn't right.

The TV set had gone from moist technicolor to an unsettling, gray-green grain. Upon realizing what now lay upon the screen, his gut yawned.

It was *him*. He was there, right in the middle of the street, stood waiting at the ATM, completely unaware that something was watching him.

The screen filled with static splice-lines and the picture changed. Another grainy video, this time of a building. His building. Onscreen, Ornell's car pulled up to the curb. Yule saw himself stumble out, hurriedly cross the lawn towards the building door, and disappear.

More static. The video changed to a slow crawl on the street, as a shot zoomed in on Yule walking out of a coffee shop.

Static.

Yule standing at the bank.

Static.

Yule driving out of town.

A final burst of white-and-black fuzz. The screen was lit up in sickly night vision tones. At first, Yule couldn't quite make out what he was seeing in the murk. But when he did, it made his veins tighten. A window, *the* window, filmed from outside. Framing the figures of three police officers as they wrestled him to the ground in the living room.

The screen changed a final time. Not to more CCTV footage, but to a washed-out, brightly lit desk. A pad of paper took up most of the screen, the message on it clear and blunt in sharp strokes of black marker.

"THEY'RE WATCHING YOU," it said. The screen lingered on it a few seconds, before a gloved hand peeked in from the bottom of the screen. With a thumb and finger, it pulled away the top sheet, revealing more writing underneath.

"MEET AT EL DORADO GAS STATION IN ONE HOUR."

The hand reappeared and pulled the sheet away to reveal a final message.

"TELL NOBODY," it said. The camera lingered on the pad a few seconds longer, then the screen went dim with static. It crackled and hummed one final time before the picture went back to normal: onscreen, a group of scantily clad girls were hugging, and saying something meaningless.

Yule watched the screen blankly for a moment, before turning off the TV. Then, he sat. Silently and motionlessly. Feeling his stomach swirl around behind his navel like spaghetti on the end of a fork.

The room suddenly felt very close. Yule sat there a minute longer, weighing up his options. But he always knew that he couldn't decide against the dense dread welling in his belly. He glanced at the clock on the wall. Not much time at all. He knew where the El Dorado was, and it wasn't exactly walking distance.

He got up off the sofa, letting the towel fall from him. Didn't notice the cold.

He had to get some clothes.

The El Dorado hadn't been open in about fifteen years. It stood upon the flat, featureless barrens west of town, where fleets of coal vans and lumber trucks used to rattle past on their delivery runs. Once surrounded by trees, now there was nothing left but a pocked sea of stumps.

The place wasn't just off the grid, the grid had upped and moved on completely.

As he wound towards it, Yule couldn't stop thinking about the TV. The sight of himself. Every half mile or so he found himself glancing in the rearview mirror for the telltale glare of tinted windscreens. But nobody followed him, and by the time the El Dorado came into view, he was far enough out of town that they probably weren't going to catch him on CCTV either.

The derelict gas station seemed to lean curiously in as he rolled to a stop in the parking lot. He could make out a couple of other cars, but they were wrecks: rusted metal frames sat on cinderblocks or just squatting on the bare ground, chassis to stone. None of them even had windshields anymore. Rows of old pumps stood watch beneath the sagging outdoor ceiling, which had partially collapsed over the entrance.

He waited there for some time, pressed against the seat to hide his silhouette. But he perked up when he saw a little light come winking out of the undergrowth some feet away.

It was a man on a bicycle. The brakes whined as it juddered to a halt, and Yule heard the guy swearing as he stumbled off it. He looked Yule over for a moment, bike wheels still slowly turning. Then, he began to walk towards the truck.

Hurriedly, Yule grabbed the gun from the passenger's seat. Kept it ready in his lap, just in case. A last scan of the horizon, and he rolled down the window.

"You just keep your distance. I'm armed," he said, voice as low and threatening as he could make it. The figure held up his palms.

"Well, I'm not," he replied, sounding like the kid who forgot his gear for practice. His voice was high and reedy, though Yule couldn't quite make out his face in the dark. He grabbed the gun and wrapped his palm around the handle.

"Who are you?" he asked. The man began to lower his hands, and Yule stuck the pistol through the window.

"A friend! A friend, I'm a friend," the man said, quickly stretching his hands back up high. "I made the videotape."

"Yeah I guessed that," Yule said, not lowering the gun. The man shifted in place a little.

"I'm on your side. You can trust me." he insisted.

"I've had a funny couple days with people who say that. Last one tried to strangle me," Yule replied. He could feel the sweat from his palms condensing on the steel. The man took half a step forward, but it didn't look purposeful. Nerves. This was a guy who wasn't used to having guns pointed at him. Maybe that was a good sign.

"I know," he insisted, voice going a little strained, "about the police. What they were gonna do to you. I'm here to help."

Something in Yule uncoiled. He'd not heard anybody say it out loud before. The implication had been there, but... nobody had said it. He narrowed his eyes at the man, still largely hidden in the sagged shadow of the outdoor ceiling.

"And how'd you find that out? About the police?"

"Digging in the right places. Breaking a lot of workplace ethics," the man said, craning his head around. "We should get somewhere that isn't out in the open."

Yule shook his head and tightened his grip on the gun.

"We're not going anywhere until you prove to me you're not one of them," he said. He wasn't really sure how the guy would do that, but part of him still needed to know. The man thought, and then held up a single finger.

He slowly reached down into his jacket pocket, fingers teasing at something. Yule curled his finger over the trigger. Ready.

Slowly, the man passed something into his mouth, and tightened the grip on his hand. Click. Click.

A little flame sputtered to life for a second, before dying into something glowing and red. The man breathed in, and then exhaled. A cloud of pungent, bitter smoke wafted over Yules face. He scowled and lowered the gun a little.

"Are you honest to god smoking a joint right now?" he asked. The man grunted in agreement, exhaled again, and took it out of his mouth.

"To prove I'm not a cop, or... with the government, or something." He coughed, holding the little glowing stub aloft. "Want some?"

"Stamp that shit out, man," Yule insisted. The man obliged, dropping it to the floor and crushing it beneath his boot.

"See. Now you know I'm not an undercover agent."

"That's bullshit man, undercover cops can do all the reefer they need to. Just take your damn jacket off and turn out your pockets."

Slowly, the man did so. He threw his jacket onto the ground, revealing a grubby white work shirt beneath. When his wallet hit the ground it sounded light. Empty, or close to it. Wasn't much else in his pockets either. Keys. Change. A little pocket knife. When he was done, the man shivered a little and gestured to his possessions on the floor.

"See?" he said. Yule gestured with the gun.

"Now take a couple steps forward, real slow. Lemme get a look at you," he said. The man obliged.

In the moonlight, he looked washed out, almost luminous. Locks of straight blonde hair peeked out beneath his ball cap, along with flecks of what looked like aluminum foil. He was thin and pale, eyes bright but hollow. Like he'd seen something he shouldn't have. Palms were dirty, too. Oil and soot.

Yule narrowed his eyes. Then, slowly, he brought down the pistol. The man smiled and gestured over his shoulder with a thumb.

"My place isn't too far by foot. It's safe, we can talk there. Too dangerous to drive."

Yule clenched his jaw and shot a glance out at the open road. Headlights or not, anybody came out looking for them, there was nowhere to head. Nowhere to turn off neither. Guy had a point.

"If somebody comes and jacks my truck, I'm makin' you pay for it," he said, pocketing the gun as he pushed open the driver's side door. The man smiled and turned, pointing to a haze of light in the distance.

"I'm over at the Friendly Fields trailer park. Temporary arrangement," he said, starting to walk down the road. Yule stayed put, arms folded.

"Call me cautious, but I usually don't go places with people who know my name, but I don't know theirs," he said. The man nodded and held out an oily hand.

"My name's Sterling Wittey," he said.

UNRAVELING

AMESVILLE, 1993

"Well, it's nothing fatal," said the doctor, leaning back from Cal and turning off his flashlight. "Blood pressure's a little high for a kid your age, but all in all you seem healthy."

Terry leaned forward.

"Really? I mean look at him, Doc," he said, gesturing to Cal, "he doesn't look..."

Cal sat mutely in the chair. He'd been like that since they'd reached the doctor's office. Wide eyed and staring at nothing, like he was watching war movies play out on the wall. And that was after the sweating, and the vomiting. Terry hoped he'd gotten it all off his shoes.

The doctor looked at Cal again, unconsciously tapping his pen against the arm of his leather chair.

"Could you go over your symptoms again with me, Cal?" he asked. Cal didn't answer. Terry reached forward and put a hand gently on his shoulder, like he was waking him.

"Answer the doc, kiddo," he said. Cal focused back in on the world, and his stare went from wide and blank to small and nervous.

"I didn't sleep so well," he said, voice quiet. "I feel... weird. Like I shouldn't be here, like everything's wrong. Like it's a dream, but I can't..."

He paused, and took in a long, low breath through his nose.

"I don't feel good," he finished. Then, he went quiet again, focus lingering on the doctor, before inevitably falling through and back to the wall. Guess that was all they were getting. Dr. Thompson knitted his brow in thought, then visibly lightened his face.

"Do you think you could go down the hall to Nurse Castle, and get your details recorded? Height and weight, that kind of thing?"

"Yeah," Cal replied, getting up out of the chair. The door clicked shut, and Terry ran a hand over his scalp.

"So, what is it, Rick? We talking flu, tumors, what?" he asked, voice hoarse with worry.

"Nothing like that, Terry," he said, shaking his head. "He seems perfectly healthy."

"Then why do I get the feeling you mean to tell me something I'm not gonna like?" Terry asked. Dr. Thompson pursed his lips thoughtfully and began idly cleaning his glasses.

"It's obvious something's wrong, but it doesn't seem to be a conventional illness. Physically speaking," he said. Terry leaned forward in his seat and tapped his temple.

"You think it's the thing in his head?" he asked, gut turning. "Like, the plate leeching into his brain, or—"

"Terry," interrupted Dr. Thompson calmly, "it's medical-grade titanium, not lead. Even with significant skull coverage like Cal has, there's no risk of contamination. The body might reject the plate, but if that were the case it would've happened a long time ago."

Terry tightened his lips. Passed his fingers over each other, pushing the tips one by one. He knew he did that when he was nervous, but now it was too ingrained in him to stop.

"So what does that mean?" he asked. Thompson leaned back in his chair.

"I think that Cal's symptoms are certainly worrying. He definitely feels them, that's clear, but strictly speaking, it seems more similar to acute anxiety or a paranoid disorder. Have you noticed any change in Cal's behavior recently?"

Terry interlaced his fingers.

"No," he said, looking at the floor. "Just yesterday he was fine. All excited about this new video camera, or something. Couldn't wait to use it."

"Hmm," Thompson replied. He turned around to the computer at his desk and clacked away at the keys. When a new window popped up, he gestured to it.

"It says here he's got a family history of mental illness? Could you confirm that for me?"

Terry felt something in him drop. In all his wildest dreams, he had never thought he'd be having this conversation. Not again. Not Cal.

"Yeah," he said quietly, "My, ah... my sister, Trish. She's been that way a while. She's in Northwest Psychiatric right now, I think. Near Toledo."

Thompson gave a well-practiced look of sympathetic concern and turned off the computer screen.

"I see. I'm sorry to hear that, but at least it gives us someplace to start," he said, scribbling something down on a pad. "Here's what I'll do—this is a number for a Justina Afolaukis, she's a psychotherapist down in Laporte Township. You call her up, tell her I gave you a recommendation and I'm sure she'd be willing to give you a discounted rate."

He handed Terry the piece of paper, and he considered it.

"Thanks," he said, stuffing it in his pocket. Then, he looked back up at Thompson, and the hard lines of his face softened a little.

"Seriously, Rick. I mean it, seeing Cal on such short notice and everything."

The doctor smiled and put his glasses back on.

"If you want, I could prescribe something in the meantime. A half dose of diazepam, maybe. Something to keep him calm."

Terry held up a hand.

"I, ah... I don't think that's the best idea. I'd rather wait 'til we know exactly what's going on," he said. Thompson nodded, and leaned back in his chair. The two men shared slightly concerned smiles for a moment before either spoke again.

"He's a good kid, Terry. I'm sure it's nothing serious," Thompson insisted, as Terry zipped his coat.

"Yeah," Terry said quietly, "I hope so too."

The car ride home was quiet for the most part. Terry's radio had been spewing static since he started it up that morning, and he figured it wouldn't make for particularly calming background music. The car rolled slowly through the morning light with little noise, Amesville's slowly rousing form crawling by. Cal spent a good part of the journey back staring out of the window, much like he had on the trip there.

By the time they reached Clarence Street, Terry had almost forgotten he was even there. When he spoke it made him jolt, even though it was quiet.

"How many people live in Amesville?" he asked. Terry looked at him quizzically for a second, then craned his head to look around at the streets as he drove.

Empty sidewalks. Boarded up windows, and plastic bags caught in the dead breeze. That was all there was, and really all he remembered it being.

"Not many," he said. There was a pause, and Cal turned from the window to face him. Something about his face unsettled Terry—like he was seeing through him again. The lights were on, it seemed, but Cal wasn't really in there. When he spoke again his voice was soft, and monotone.

"Then why are there so many houses?" he asked.

Terry wasn't quite sure how to answer. What kind of question was that?

"They built a lotta houses in the eighties," he said, turning a corner. "Lot of people left town around then."

"Then how come nobody else moved in?" Cal asked, voice slow and quiet as he turned to look out the window again. "Why are they just empty?"

Terry went to answer, and then stopped. Something in his belly turned. Like the feeling of seeing someone beautiful do something ugly for the first time. As he turned his head a little to look at the town crawling by, he suddenly saw it too. There *were* a lot of empty houses. Row after row, some just in the middle of completely populated neighborhoods. They weren't dusty, or overgrown, just... empty. Little pockets of nothing that he'd just never noticed. They looked lived in, but Terry couldn't remember seeing anyone actually living there.

He slowed the car down a little and coughed into his arm. Tried to take his mind elsewhere, or at least keep it on the road.

"So, the doctor says—"

"That I'm crazy," Cal cut in. "I couldn't find the nurse, so I just kinda waited outside the door."

Terry chewed his lip. Nodded to nothing.

"Right. Well, no, that's not exactly what he said," he said slowly. "He just thinks that maybe this ain't the flu, is all. That it might be somethin' to do with stress." There was a pause. The low rumble of the engine filled the car, and then Terry coughed again. "You got everything squared at school? You're not, ah... getting trouble from any of the other kids?"

Cal shook his head.

"No."

"You and Trevor ain't fightin'? Not got girl troubles—or, or boy troubles, I ain't... uh..." Terry said, trailing off. Cal visibly clenched his jaw and bundled his hoodie in around himself.

"Look, it's none of that stuff," he said. Terry held back a frustrated groan, hiding it in the taut space behind his teeth. Tried to think back to that 'Positive Parenting' book Pam had got him. Something about... criticizing, but not... wait, that was the other way around. Not criticizing, but... aw hell, he didn't remember. Probably wouldn't help anyway, they'd not really had much on 'if your kid goes nuts.'

Terry felt himself twinge internally. That wasn't fair, he thought. Even if he didn't say it.

God, this was stressing him out.

"Well," he said, slowly and methodically, "how about you tell me what you think it is, and we can go from there."

Cal stared through the windshield for a few seconds. When an answer finally appeared, it made Terry's blood run cold.

"Leslie O'Neil," said Cal. Terry felt a wave of nausea come over him. A sudden, hot panic, rising in his shoulders and fingertips like bees in a jar.

"What?" he asked, voice quiet. Cal furrowed his brow, eyes still far away.

"I… I don't know how to explain it," he said, shaking his head. "I feel like… I feel like there's memories I should have that I don't. Or, that I shouldn't have, but I do." His lip trembled slightly, and then he clenched his jaw. "I don't even know who Leslie O'Neil is, but I can't stop thinking about the name. It feels like it's just screaming in my head, and I don't know why, and… and it feels like we're all in danger, all the time and it's all connected to her."

Terry felt his foot shudder on the gas. He was at a loss for words. They'd gone dry and sticky in his throat. The walls of the car suddenly seemed extremely tight.

"Danger? Danger to do with… with Leslie O'Neil? How?" he asked. Cal shook his head, unable to hold back the panicked shudder on his lip.

"I don't know. I don't know but I feel it. In my head, in my thoughts, I…" he said, voice cracking. Terry felt his hands grip tight on the wheel. His heart was doing backflips against his ribcage. God. God, it couldn't be this. Not again. Not after all this time.

"I barely know anything about her, but I feel like I can see her, in my mind. A face, a voice… and that unless I can work out why, we're all going to die," Cal said, eyes going glassy. A breath scampered into his throat, high and stuttered. "Uncle Terry, it feels like the world's ending."

Terry didn't reply. Although it felt like a second, he said nothing for the rest of the car journey. He just stared through the windscreen. Through the road, through everything. Lost somewhere in the internal roar of panic.

He only snapped out of it as his keys rang in the front door lock. He didn't even remember how he'd gotten there, or out of the car, he just felt like he was floating. Suspended in thick, liquid panic.

Oh god, he thought. Not now.

"You, ah… you should get to bed a while, kiddo," he said, pushing his way inside. "Get some rest."

Cal stared at him, wide eyes peeking out from beneath his tangled mess of brown hair.

"I'm not crazy, right?" he asked. Terry took a few deep breaths, holding onto the banister rail for support. He felt like he was going to vomit.

"No," he said, shaking his head. "You're not crazy, I just… I have something I forgot to take care of. You get to your room."

Terry peeled away from the main hallway and up the stairs. Through the bedroom. Into the bathroom. Down. Bowl.

Retch.

Again. Twice more. Nothing much came out; except the beer he'd had that morning. It was a pale, sickly sort of brown foam that splashed and flicked against the ceramic.

Terry craned his head back and gasped for air. Fell to the side, body wedging between the side of the bowl and the sink. He gripped the seat and stared dimly into the wallpaper. A single thought whirled through his head, over and over and over.

It's happening again, he thought. *It's happening again.*

He wasn't surprised. He felt like he should have been, but he'd known this was coming ever since he'd heard somebody had moved back into the old Sledmore building. The second the radios started going haywire, he'd known. And somewhere, deep in the dead of night, as he lay awake in bed, he would imagine what he would do when it arrived. Where he'd go. Who he'd call.

All of that seemed so far away now. He sat down on the bed and opened the drawers.

His hand closed over the gun and drew it out. The steel was still black and shiny, barely used. He laid it in his lap and the wound in his leg throbbed hard, reminding him of a time he once thought far away. He caught his own reflection, warped by the barrel. What was he doing?

Terry picked up the gun and shoved it back into the bottom of the drawer, revulsion rising in his throat. Then he sat back on the bed for a few, tense seconds, before heading into the bathroom again. Fixed his hair. Washed his face.

Maybe it wasn't as bad as he thought. Even with Cal the way he was, maybe things weren't spiraling. Nobody had disappeared, nobody was watching. Maybe it was all just a big mistake.

He stared at himself again, rivulets of cool, clean water running down his face. Breath returning, not searing but warm. And though the dense stone of dread still sat deep in his gut, at least his head had stopped racing.

Answers, he thought. That was what he needed. And he knew the person who could give them to him.

Down the stairs, down by the door. He remembered seeing it, Pam had said something... with a white and green... there.

From a pile of old junk mail, he fished out a little folded pamphlet. Everyone had gotten one; he'd seen people going door to door with them. He took it through to the kitchen and laid it on the table, "*Sledmore Industries and Your Community*" staring in bright type at the ceiling, above a shiny illustration of a power plant working in the woods. He flipped it open and scanned the page. The inside was dense with text, and all kinds of data and statistics, and read at the bottom:

Your views as a resident are incredibly important to the process. If you have something to tell us, please call the number below.

Carefully, he unhooked the phone from the wall, and put it on the table as well. Finally, he grabbed a beer from the fridge, and sat down.

Terry chewed his lip. Moved his eyes between the phone and the pamphlet, slowly keying in the number with a steady click, click, click. The dial tone pulsing on the other end a while, then it stopped.

"*Hello, you've reached the Sledmore Community Team. My name is Mister Doe, how can I help you?*" asked the man on the other end. Terry cleared his throat and sat up straighter in his chair.

"Yeah, hi," he said, "my name's Terry Greenwood, I was Amesville chief of police up until a few years back."

"*And what can I do for you today, Mister Greenwood?*"

"I need to talk to the guy in charge," he said.

"*I'm afraid Mister Carnassus may be difficult to get hold of without a prior appointment.*"

"No, you don't understand," Terry insisted, tapping his hand on the table, "I'm not calling to complain, I need to have a discussion with your boss about an old police matter."

"*What police matter would that be?*" asked the man. Terry froze up a little. He realized he'd not even thought of what he was going to say. How was he supposed to phrase it?

"It, uh… it's about an old missing persons case," he said slowly. "A girl who disappeared a few years back, Leslie O'Neil? I just, ah… well, there's a slim chance there may still be evidence on his land."

There was a long pause. Not even the sounds of typing or breathing on the other end. Terry frowned and moved the receiver a little closer to his ear.

"Hello?" he asked. After a few more seconds of silence, the voice returned.

"*Mister Carnassus has an opening at 5.30 p.m. today,*" it said. Terry blinked a few times, and then checked the clock. Four hours' time. 'Difficult to get hold of" his ass.

"Yeah, that's… that's great, I'll be there," he said, nodding to nobody.

"*If you just come down to the building reception, we'll sign you in.*"

"Sure thing."

"*Thank you for calling, Mister Greenwood,*" said the man. "*We look forward to seeing you.*"

The other end clicked and hung up. Terry slowly lowered the droning handpiece away from his face and laid it back on top of the telephone. He sat there in silence for a second, collecting his thoughts. It was happening, he thought. He was doing something.

Alone in the kitchen, he opened the beer, and chugged it. Went back for another.

It burned, but he needed it. He always needed it.

The parking lot was jarringly symmetrical, all razor-sharp lines and flattened concrete, blotted only by two cars scattered across the span. Terry pulled into a space and stepped out into the cool dusk air, stretching his legs. He felt a little unsteady in his ankles and his stomach, the dim echo of panic still bouncing around his gut.

As he stood, he craned his head to look around. Try as he might, he couldn't see another living soul, even through the windows on the stone tower's face.

Inside, the building was just as empty and still as the outside. The sharp tang of bleach and sickly undertones of lavender mixed into a sterile, gray kind of smell, the same color the walls. The unmanned front desk was lit by a strip of fluorescent light, but the corridors splitting away on either side were completely dark. Terry chewed the inside of his lip and tried to stay frosty. It all seemed odd, and if past experiences had taught him anything, 'odd' was just another word for dangerous.

"Hello, Mister Greenwood," said a voice from behind him. Terry gave a start and wheeled around. A man in a security vest was standing a few feet behind, smiling at him with yellowed teeth. Terry sighed in relief and ran a hand over his head.

"Sorry, you ah… startled me there," he said. The man in the vest took a few steps past him, into the darkened hallway. There was a click somewhere in the ceiling, and the fluorescent strips buzzed to life overhead.

"They're motion activated," said the man, gesturing up to the lights. Terry put his hands in his pockets and tried to summon a smile.

"Everyone clock off early today?" he asked. The yellow-toothed man laughed.

"We're just about to start a big hiring push. Most of this stuff is autonomous anyway," he said, offering a hand. "Mister Daisy, chief of security."

"Pleased to meet you," said Terry, shaking it. "Guess you already know who I am."

"I do," said Daisy, breaking the shake. "Mister Carnassus is expecting you upstairs."

Daisy led him through the building, first one way then another. The place was like a drably decorated maze, Terry thought, looking down hallways as they passed. No people, no signs—just corridor after identical corridor, ducking and weaving over one another. By the time they came to the elevator, Terry was almost worried there wasn't ever going to be an end to it.

Daisy pressed the button and stepped aside, gesturing into the elevator.

"After you," he said. Terry half-smiled at him, and they filed inside. No music played as they ascended, only the deep set whirring of the elevator cables as they wound further and further up the side of the building. The silence made Terry feel nervous.

The elevator doors opened onto a wide hallway, decorated with landscapes. The sterile, lavender-bleach smell persisted, even stronger than it had been in the lobby. At the end, a pair of dark, mahogany doors stood shut. Without a word, Daisy went forward and pushed them open.

The office yawned to meet them. At its center, Carnassus sat with his head down, looking over some documents. It took him a second to notice they were there, his dark eyes flicking up and over the rim of his glasses. He smiled, removed them, then swept the documents aside.

"Mister Greenwood," he said, standing up and offering a hand, "thank you so much for calling."

"Thanks for meeting me so quickly," Terry said, shaking it. Carnassus gestured and he sat down opposite. Daisy took up watch by the door, arms folded. Carnassus smiled and leaned back in his chair, and the well-oiled mechanism didn't so much as creak.

"Can I get you something to drink, Mister Greenwood—or, may I call you Terry?" he asked. Terry shifted in his chair a little. This was all grander than he was expecting, and suddenly he felt very much like a small-town cop again. Except, now he didn't even have the badge.

"Uh, sure," he said, nodding. "Throat's kinda dry, that sounds swell."

Carnassus took two glasses from a side cabinet, along with a small bottle of something amber.

"Macallan Single Malt. Thirty years old, from Scotland," he said, handing Terry a glass. "It's made to be sipped."

Terry smiled and gestured with the glass, as if to indicate he knew jack shit about good whiskey. Carnassus took a cursory sip of his own drink, before putting it to one side.

"So, I understand you want to discuss a missing person with me?" he said. Terry nodded and put down his glass. The whiskey burned a little in his gullet as he did, but it was enough to mask the nerves.

"Yeah. Old missing person's case, old stuff…" he said, looking over his shoulder. "Could we, ah…?"

"Certainly," Carnassus cut in, nodding across the room. "Mister Daisy, if you'd like to wait outside, please."

Daisy nodded and pushed out of the double doors. Carnassus watched him go, then centered his vision sharply back onto Terry.

"Right. How, ah… familiar are you with Amesville, if you don't mind me asking?" Terry asked. Carnassus smiled, showing a brief flash of tooth.

"Very, actually," he said, voice low. "I grew up here. Left around the mid-eighties."

"Right. So, you were around when Leslie O'Neil disappeared," said Terry, nodding. Carnassus' face clouded, and his eyes went back down towards the desk.

"Mm," he hummed in grim agreement. "I remember. Awful thing, what happened to her. Just awful."

"Well, that's what I wanted to talk to you about. It's a cold case now, so I'm alright to share details, but to cut it short no body was ever found," Terry went on, pushing, watching every twitch across Carnassus' perfectly sculpted face. But so far, there had been nothing. Behind his interlaced fingers, his face was the picture of genuineness.

"And what's the significance of that to me?" he asked. Terry shook his head.

"Well, some of our leads suggested she might be somewhere near the grounds here," he said. Carnassus thought on it a moment.

"I see," he said, nodding slowly, "and with all the development going on, you think we might find something?"

"Not for sure, but…" Terry said, injecting a slightly dramatic pause. "Well, there's a possibility."

"I should hate to think," Carnassus replied, nodding in concerned agreement. Terry smiled, and this time it was genuine. It was like being an officer again, teasing out openings and looking for information—he'd only had to do it a couple times in Amesville, but it was goddamn thrilling every time. Made him feel like he was in control. He could stop things.

Time to push, he thought. Seize the opportunity.

"Well, y'know, with the amount of construction work going on, there was always a chance," he said, matching Carnassus' stare. "You ever consider starting out someplace a little newer?"

Carnassus smiled. When he spoke it was almost practiced, like he was addressing a crowd.

"I think real change has to come from normal people. Normal communities, like Amesville. Innovating energy isn't enough, it's got to be available to everybody, from the ground up."

A little glint of tooth broke through his lips. When he next spoke his voice was almost a purr.

"If we can succeed in Amesville, we can do it anywhere in the U.S. And after that, who knows?"

"Yeah," Terry insisted, nodding, "but, why here? I mean, this place can't exactly have been top of the list, there's plenty of vacant land nearby that wouldn't need redeveloping—if I remember correct, this place wasn't even a power plant, it—"

"Was a radio factory," Carnassus cut in, "I'm aware. Excuse me if I'm wrong, Terry, but I feel like you're trying to insinuate something."

Terry stopped. Took another, decidedly longer sip of his drink, and felt the buzz grow in the side of his head. When he put it down, it was heavier than he expected it to be.

"Look, I can't get into the details," he said, running a hand clumsily through his hair, "but this building is… there's been a lot of things happened here. Things that the police were involved with."

"That *you* were involved with," Carnassus probed. Terry shook his head. It felt odd. Warm, and foggy.

How strong had that whiskey been?

"Wasn't just me. There were others, it was… I can't talk about it," he said, eyelids blinking blearily. Carnassus leaned forward, imposing himself like a fever dream.

"Who?" he asked softly. "What were their names?"

Terry went silent. Something wasn't right. This wasn't right at all, he felt… he didn't feel…

"I should… should go," he said, voice now a low, burbling drawl.

He tried to stand, but his legs gave out. He fell hard back into the chair, hands twisting underneath his own weight. His right thumb bent backwards and gave a short, sharp snap that sounded like it should've hurt. But he could barely feel it. It just felt like… pressure.

"What have you done to me?" he slurred, rolling a little in the chair. Mr. Carnassus sat back and stared at him. Like a child, watching a fly crawl around with its wings pulled off.

"Something mild," he said, lips curling at the edges. "Enough to keep you lucid. Though, I think someone was drinking before this, weren't they?"

He smiled. His eyes had gone all cold and dead, like a snake's. As if they might suddenly roll back into his head as his jaw unhinged. There wasn't an ounce of warmth in them, just… nothing.

"Mister Daisy," he said, eyes still fixed almost hungrily on Terry. "I think Mister Greenwood is feeling unwell after his drink. Please bring something to wake him up a little—and a wheelchair."

The reply came back tinny, and barely decipherable. Terry's eyes rolled a little in his head. Everything sounded muffled, and far away.

"You can't do this, you can't…" Terry slurred, trying to shake his eyes back into focusing. He could barely even feel the spit rolling down the corner of his lip. A little cold, sharp light came into Carnassus' eyes, predatory gaze never swaying from what it saw. Basking in it.

"You must think I have no idea what I'm doing here," he said, voice purring. "That's good."

Terry tried to move and failed. He gave a little twist and jerk in the chair, the globule of spit bursting into a stream down his cheek. Carnassus followed it down his face, disgust and fascination mixing to a blackened nothing behind his eyes.

"That was The Branch's mistake, I think. Trying to parlay, trying to make a deal with you. To reason with you. They thought money and safety would keep you tame, and yet here you are selling them down the river to a man you know nothing about. But I don't make mistakes, Terry—and you feel free to hold me to that."

Behind him, Terry heard the double doors swing open. The low, heart-like thud, thud, thud of heavy boots behind him. Carnassus looked up and nodded to someone Terry couldn't see.

Then came the pain. Cold sharpness as something punctured his throat. Something ran into his veins, down his shoulders, up his jaw. With every second he became more aware of it. The blurred dizziness cleared, edges and light becoming so sharp it was almost painful. Flies, buzzing behind his eardrums.

He felt wired, but still, his body wouldn't move. Carnassus cocked his head like he was watching a wingless fly wriggle around on the table.

"There," he said, smiling. "Do you feel more awake?"

"Why? Why are you... doing this?" Terry gasped. His lips were less numb, but pain was starting to creep up his neck where Daisy had syringed him. Carnassus' eyes glinted, like two dead stars in hollow space.

"I want you to tell me everything you know about Leslie O'Neil," he said. Terry tried to screw up his face in disgust, but it came out more as a strange twitch.

"I don't know anything about her," he drawled, shaking his head, "I swear. We just... we got told not to look for her. We got told to pin it on somebody, that's all we knew, but after that... they didn't... they didn't ask us to—"

"Do you know where she is?" Carnassus cut in. Terry shook his head, eyes wide.

"No, I swear. We never knew what happened, we just..."

Through the haze, shame wrenched hard in his gut. He could feel tears burning at the corner of his eye. He'd imagined what he'd say when someone found out, knew what he'd done. He'd rehearsed the line a hundred times in his head, but never said it.

"...we just did what we were told to," he said, shaking his head.

Carnassus' smile faded. In fact, all of his expression did. As if the words had struck something he didn't expect them to. The only thing left on his face was an awful, perfect neutral mask, and nestled inside were just two dark, empty holes. Devoid of life, devoid of empathy.

Seeing, but not feeling. Knowing, but not understanding. But after a few seconds, something curdled in the empty space.

Disgust.

His eyes flicked up to an unseen Daisy, and he nodded sharply downwards.

"Check him," he said, moving away from the desk. Suddenly Terry's vision arced up to the ceiling as hands clamped around his head, yanking it upright. He writhed gently in the chair as Daisy's thickly gloved fingers wrenched his mouth open and pulled his lips apart. Daisy grunted and looked up at Carnassus.

"He's got fillings. It won't take," he said, letting go. The shadow of Carnassus' face loomed over him, blocking the light. His voice was light, almost human, but his face betrayed nothing.

"Mister Greenwood doesn't look well, even after his medicine. Maybe a walk would perk him up," he said. Daisy pulled Terry roughly from his seat and sat him in the wheelchair. He wheezed, and rolled a little in the fabric seat, barely able to move.

The trip down the hallway rolled by in a haze of bright lights and steel doors, and then down. Down, and down and down—from where to where, he couldn't tell, but he knew. The feeling of the earth swallowing them up, elevator by elevator, until they were so deep you could hear the concrete hum.

When he finally began to come back, he realized they'd been stopped for some time. But as the blur tightened into visible shapes, somehow it all seemed to make less sense.

They were in a vast, underground space. Gray, vaulted ceilings lit up with stark white floodlights, black metal girders crisscrossing in maddening, unfollowable patterns from wall to wall. Huge glass cubes sat in rows, connected to the tangle above by umbilical-looking electrical cables.

And the noise. The low, primal roar of electricity and motors, copper thrum and steel whine, all mixed together into a wall of sound so thick it was almost visible. He could feel it, soaking into the floor and walls, deeper and vaster than the untouched earth beneath it.

Daisy was looking over some machinery nearby. Carnassus stood with his back to them both, hands on his hips. Just looking over it all.

Terry tried to breathe. Tried to contain himself. He had to escape, but... he couldn't. He couldn't move his legs—hell, he could barely even speak. He tried a few times to simply rise from the chair, but his leaden limbs didn't budge.

Oh god, he thought. *What have I done? What have I done?*

He let out a despairing groan, and let his head fall a little to the side. At first, he didn't quite understand what he was looking at. It was only as he saw his own eyes, made faded and dark by the thick smoked glass, that

Terry realized he was staring at his own reflection. They had stopped him next to one of the cubes, close enough that, at any other time, he could've reached out and touched it.

He squinted. Something was moving, behind the glass. A dark, shifting shape, huddled in the back corner. It looked like it was rocking back and forth, and yet stayed in the same place.

There was a flash of light. A roaring crackle. Electricity danced inside the enclosure, illuminating it in sharp lightning tones. Terry screamed.

It was a kind of man shape, but wrong. *All* wrong. A dozen gaping, misshapen jaws sprouted from a head bulbous with eyes, tangle of arms waving and clawing below.

But the most horrifying thing about it was, he wasn't even sure what it was. A ghostly aura of itself, seeming to twist and form grotesquely. But every few seconds, parts hardened. Became flesh, then faded, then became flesh again, making it seem to grow and wither at the same time. Sometimes, the entire thing seemed just to flicker and blink in and out of being entirely.

It was unthinkable. Impossible.

As soon as Terry screamed, the creature reacted. Its head jerked a little and suddenly the body was alive, twitching towards the glass panel. There was a loud, muffled bang as it slammed itself against the wall. Over, and over, and over again.

To the side of him, someone laughed gently. Almost musically. Carnassus walked over to the side of the cube, and laid a perfect white hand against the glass, the impossible thing still thudding against it.

"Horrible, aren't they?" he asked, eyes following the massive body as it crawled across the enclosure. Then his dead gaze turned to Terry, immobile and vulnerable in the chair.

"I'd have done that to you, if you didn't have all those fillings in your head," he said, smiling as he tapped the side of his jaw. "The process interacts... *strangely*, with metal. It's quite spectacular."

Terry turned to look back into the now-darkened cube. The hulking shape was back in the corner, as barely visible as before. Rocking in place, without moving.

"What is it?" he asked, voice trembling. Carnassus' smirk bloomed into a strange smile. Happiness without happiness.

"A living mistake. Countless instances of one entity, all trying to inhabit the same place in spacetime," he replied, joyless wonder focused on a column of lightning which crackled up from the rolling aura. "An endless well of paradox static, ready for harvesting."

Daisy returned from the side and glanced at Terry.

"System's all hooked up," he said, taking the handles of the wheelchair. But then, Carnassus moved towards Terry. Daisy let go, his gloved hands replaced by Carnassus' own long white fingers. He turned the chair and began to slowly push it further and further into the cavern.

"You can't do this to me," said Terry, shaking his head. "You can't. People know I'm here."

"I'd stop trying to cast threats, and focus on appeasing me, Terry," Carnassus replied, pulling the chair to a halt. They had stopped beside what looked like a large metal slab on the ground. Or at least, it seemed that way until Daisy pulled a lever. With a grinding screech, the slab receded. Terry finally knew what he was looking at.

A pit. A bare cube of empty space walled almost entirely by titanium. Sat beside it, Terry suddenly felt his own weight. The fall was nearly eight feet down. Carnassus leaned down, sculpted lips hissing just shy of Terry's ear. His voice was barely above a whisper when he spoke.

"Tell me everything you know about Leslie O'Neil?" he said. Terry felt his gut seize a little.

"No," he whispered, shaking his head, "I... I c-can't, I..."

There was a quiet, wet *schlick* as Carnassus' lips parted to smile. He straightened back up, and carefully, slowly, wrapped his hands around the wheelchair handles.

"That's all, then," he said. Before Terry could process it, the chair jerked forward. The seat tipped and for a brief moment, he was weightless. Just floating limply in the middle of nothing.

And then the floor. He collided with a bang and felt all the breath go out of him. One arm was twisted up funny beneath him, but he couldn't feel anything in it. With a gasp of surprise and fear, Terry summoned all of his strength and turned himself onto his back. He looked up, just in time to see the metal lid close tight above him.

Then, darkness.

Nothing but darkness. The sound of his own panicked breathing.

Oh god, oh god, wait—a noise. A noise in the blackness, a sort of hum. A whir, like wires being filled with electricity. And… something appearing. Softly, at first. Wriggling and glowing like a long, thin worm in the nothing.

And then it grew. And grew, stronger and brighter, tracing out a hollow square above him. With growing horror, Terry realized that he was seeing something start to bleed through a hatch in the ceiling.

He opened his mouth to shout as the hatch slid open. Green unlight blasted over him. Into him. Through him.

The feeling of a thousand hooks. Blackness turning to colors outside of time and space. To Terry, it lasted seconds, minutes even, but it didn't. It only seemed that way.

In truth, it happened faster than the sound of his scream could travel. Faster than he could think, even breathe.

And then, nothing. No sound, no feeling. Only the unlight, pulsing and swelling from its growing place behind the metal grate. And then, it faded too. The hatch clicked and swung back to seal it away, and the metal lid of the pit slid open. Light flooded into the dark space.

But Terry Greenwood was gone.

FLAMINGO

AMESVILLE, 1993

Tick. Tick. Tick. Tick.

Second falling over second. Clicking then fading as another crested to fill the space. Cal sat at the table, staring into his empty cereal bowl. How the ceramic curved and dipped in its own hollow shadow. All perfect and white.

He gave a start as Pam set down her own.

"Late night?" she asked. Cal looked up at her, snapping suddenly back into reality.

"What?" he replied. Pam smiled and took a puff of her cigarette, sitting down on the only other chair.

"You look a little… spacey. You want a coffee?" she asked. Cal blinked a few times, as if the sentence didn't quite make sense. He shook his head, even though that made it swim.

"Nah, no, I'm good. I don't think…" he said, standing up. Then, he stopped, his eyes fixed on the clock.

Something was welling in the back of his head. A feeling. Like… he'd done this before. Déjà vu, but stronger. And it wasn't going away. The clock hand danced in circles on the wall.

Tick. Tick. Tick.

Falling. Folding. Over and over again.

The feeling in the back of his head grew. A kind of red pressure, boiling and urgent. His hands were shaking, everything felt close and tight against him. He reached up to grab the cereal box and it crashed onto the countertop with a loud rattle, spilling little multicolored fragments over the plastic. Pam looked up from her coffee, framed by steam.

"Are you alright?" she asked, long fingernails clicking on the mug. Cal ran a hand over his brow, reaping the cold sweat. His eyes darted back and forth over the counter, bouncing off the colored specks. They all looked the same. Repeating. Over and over.

He felt sick. He felt like he'd been sick for a long time, but yesterday he'd been fine. But it felt like he…

"Cal?" said Pam, getting up out of her chair a little. Cal heard the chair legs squeak and flinched.

"I'm okay, I'm fine, I just feel kind of unsteady," he insisted, wiping his forehead again. "I… Could Uncle Terry drive me to school?"

Pam got out of her seat and began to walk towards him, hands gently falling over his shoulders. She smirked.

"Sure," she said, pulling him slowly away from the counter, "and then your Uncle Walt can clean the yard, and Uncle Hester can give me a foot massage."

Cal pulled away from her, nearly stumbling. He caught himself on the table and turned to face her again. It suddenly felt hard to breathe.

"What?" he asked. The red pressure grew. Swelled, into something like radio static.

Pam gave him a strange look and shrugged slowly at him. It made her bangled wrists jangle and ring like little ceramic bells. They sounded strange. Atonal.

"Who's Uncle Terry?" she asked. Cal stared at her. He didn't know for how long.

Tick. Tick. Tick.

Folding and falling. Sinking, then repeating.

Over and over.

Pam came forward and put her hands back on his shoulders, guiding him a little more forcefully into a chair. Her little smirk had been washed away by concern. It made her look old. Or, older.

"You don't look like you're feeling so good, kid," she said, looking him over. Cal stared at her, wide eyed. He felt like something was venting through his veins, into his throat. Cold heat. Something like panic, but worse.

"How do you know my mom?" he asked, voice small and raspy. Pam jerked back a little, like the question had physically and painfully collided with her. For a moment she didn't reply, mouth open in a confused little 'o.' When she finally did, there was something almost wounded about it.

"You don't sound so good, either," she said, rising to go. "I'm gonna call in an appointment, you wait here—"

"Why am I here?" Cal asked, grabbing her arm. "How do you know her? How do you know my mom, Pam?"

Pam stared at him. She didn't pull her arm away—he couldn't grip it tight enough to hurt.

"I was there when you were born," she said, giving him a slightly pleading smile. "I know you don't remember, but... but I helped your mom after the crash, and—"

"How did you meet? Why do you know her?" he insisted. The glimmer of hurt in Pam's eyes turned to something less sharp. Confusion. For a moment her gaze darted away to the floor, face locked into a puzzled, almost alarmed expression, like she noticed the weirdness too. But then, as if snapping back to role, her eyes lifted again. She pressed her wrinkled knuckles against Cal's forehead.

"Honey, you've got a fever. You're delirious," she said, getting up. "I'm gonna give Doctor Thompson a call, alright? You get into bed."

She said something else after that, but Cal didn't hear. The red pressure welled in his ears, through his throat. Hot and urgent, growing and tugging. He only realized she'd stopped talking when she pulled away and went to the phone.

All Cal knew was that his legs led him across the hall. Through the front door, without a word. Something told him it didn't matter if he said anything. Did anything.

As he walked down through the yard, he could feel the world jarring against him. He didn't feel sick anymore, he felt awake, vividly aware now that something wasn't wrong with him—but that something was horribly, horribly wrong with everything else.

He saw it everywhere. On the empty road, the feeling that something else should have passed him. House upon house with nobody inside, no car out front, and no signs of life. Like everyone inside had just disappeared off the face of the earth.

Cal felt like it had always been that way, he remembered it and yet he didn't. He felt like for the first time he was seeing clearly. He could finally make out the growing empty spaces in between.

And all the time, the black shape of the Sledmore Power Plant stalked in the distance, like a hunched beast. Watching the town from afar, never moving from its place on the horizon. Cal stopped at the corner and watched it a while, swollen white plumes boiling and rupturing up into the sky from stocky cooling towers.

He moved through the quiet streets, feeling like a loose penny in a dryer. For a while, as his path took him down the hill through Hope Meadow Park and back towards the main road, there was silence. He didn't see another person out in the streets – not that he expected to.

Even past the park, the paved strip past the old obelisk was completely empty. The only spectator to his passing was the statue, stood blackened and worn by time, a single question announcing itself to no one in white spray paint.

Who took Leslie O'Neil? he repeated in his head, as he stopped to look at it. The question itself filled him with dread and somehow, he didn't think it was a coincidence. Made him think about trailer parks.

RRRRRING.

Cal turned his head. A rattling bell echoed down the street, crying from outside the old arcade.

RRRRRING.

Something in his chest tugged, like the feeling of seeing light in the dark. He moved towards it, the bell seeming to grow louder and more urgent the closer he got.

RRRRRING.

He stopped beside it and took a deep breath. Reached for the phone and raised the receiver up to his ear, suddenly aware of his own shallow, nervous breathing. Silence waited on the other end.

"Hello?" he asked. For a moment nobody replied. He was close to taking the phone away from his ear when he heard the muffled sounds of movement on the other side. Cal held a breath in his chest and instinctively looked around. The street was still empty.

"Hello?" he repeated, a little more loudly. This time, he barely finished the word before someone replied.

"Head south on the Innsmouth Road. Don't stop until you see the flamingo," it said, shortly and sharply. Cal opened his mouth to reply but was met with the clack of the receiver going down on the other end.

He stood there for a few moments, stock still, the receiver still pressed tight against his ear.

It had been a girl's voice. Someone his age. But in the end, he thought, it didn't really matter if he knew the voice or not. It sounded familiar, and that was enough. Or at least, he felt like it was. He tried not to think about how little sense it made, it seemed counter intuitive; sense had obviously made an early turn off the road before it reached town.

He took a deep breath and tried to calm the whirling ball of nerves in his belly. Despite how much he wanted it to be otherwise, this was all too big for him to handle by himself.

He punched in the next number without looking, falling back on muscle memory. As the other end of the line rang, Cal checked his watch. It was early enough that he wouldn't have left home.

The other end rang out into the automated voicemail. Always did that. Telemarketers, or something. The line ran to an atonal beep, and Cal cleared his throat.

"Trevor, it's Cal. Pick up the phone," he said, looking over his shoulder again at the empty street. "Come on, come on, come on…"

"Why are you calling me?" came a voice on the other end. Cal turned back to face the booth and cupped a hand over the receiver.

"Trev, listen to me—I'm not gonna be at school today, but I need you to meet me by the gates at lunch," he said, voice low. He could almost hear Trevor squirming nervously on the other end.

"What? Why? Why aren't you in school?" he asked. Cal looked over his shoulder again and clenched his jaw.

"I'll explain when I see you, okay?" Cal replied.

"…Okay," Trevor agreed hesitantly. Cal didn't expect him to say otherwise. Trev had a nervous disposition, but he was at least consistent when it came to attendance.

"Alright. I'll see you then," Cal said. He hung the receiver back into its cradle with a plastic-toned clack. He was suddenly alone again in the empty quiet. He turned around to survey the street one last time. Nobody around, even if he felt like there should have been.

He'd seen a half-faced man here before. Some day out of time.

Shoulders hunched over, Cal put his hands in his pockets and turned back around towards the house. His step was hurried but deadened. A kind of loping half run.

The pressure persisted.

⁓

He didn't remember the crash. Not really. But he felt it. In the road, in the air. In the dark spiral of tree limbs, weaving together into a living tunnel. And it wasn't just Cal, either—most people avoided taking it, even though it was one of the few roads out of town that actually connected to a highway at the end.

Something had just never been quite right about that road. People always said it was the blind turns and dark spans where the trees had eaten up the lights, but now Cal thought it might be more than that.

Beside him, Trevor shifted nervously behind his own bike handles. He looked over his shoulder, left hand rising to wipe beads of sweat from his tan brow.

"How far are we going?" he asked, turning back to Cal. "I don't know how long I can stay out. I can't be late for fifth period."

"I don't know, Trev. Until we see a flamingo."

"Like a real, living flamingo?"

"Maybe. I don't know," Cal replied, still staring into the yawning tunnel. Trevor pursed his lips and looked gravely down the road, bike rattling as he dragged it behind him.

"Dude, what's going on? Why weren't you at school?" he said. Cal shrugged and leaned a little more heavily on his bike frame.

"Pam thinks I'm sick. Or going nuts."

"Is she wrong?"

"If I answer that honestly, you'll think I'm going nuts too."

"I already think you're going nuts," said Trevor, planting his tires a little more firmly into the dust. Cal smiled a little, eyes falling back towards the tunnel of trees.

"I guess that's a start," he said. Something in the back of his skull pulled him out of the middle distance and firmly back into his own head. "I think something strange is going on. Like... like we've been living the same day over and over again."

Trevor considered it for a second, and then nodded.

"You're right," he said, turning his bike handles around. "I definitely think you're nuts."

"Wait, where are you going?" Cal asked, turning around to face him. Trevor let out a frustrated hiss through his teeth.

"I'm going to school, Cal! Where you should be going too, instead of chasing flamingos down the highway!" he said, putting his feet on the pedals.

"Trevor, I'm going. I have to, I'm telling you—something isn't right!" he insisted. Trevor sighed frustratedly and turned his feet on the pedals.

"Alright, but I'm gonna tell Pam, and she's gonna bust your ass for it," he called, as the wheels began to roll. Cal let go of his bike, frame clattering loudly as it fell onto the baking concrete.

"Trevor! Trev, goddammit, come back!" he yelled, running to keep up with him. "Trevor!"

"I'm not listening!" Trevor called back, lazily picking up speed. Cal broke into a run, legs already aching with every impact against the blacktop. He couldn't go for long. He was tired. It was only as his determination began to give out that something occurred to him. The red pressure turned clear and solid. A memory, more than a thought.

"Dog boy!" he yelled at the top of his lungs. "Dammit, Trevor! Dog! Boy!"

The statement echoed down the empty road, undercut by the sound of tires skidding to a halt on concrete. Trevor stopped and turned around, face curled in confusion.

"What?" he asked. Cal doubled over for a moment, gasping for breath.

"The… the goddamn… ugh, the dog boy, you know? On those stupid forums you go on," he panted, gesticulating wildly as if it might make it seem less strung out. "You were gonna tell me about it this morning. You saw it like an hour ago."

Trevor stared at him.

"How did you know that?" he asked. Cal looked up and wiped some sweat from his brow.

"I told you," he said. "We've lived today already, I remember it."

Trevor looked him over for a few seconds more. Then, he turned his bike sideways to face Cal, half-astride it like an unimpressive chubby cowboy.

"That's bullcrap," he said. "I probably told you about it before."

"How did I know you were gonna talk about it today, though?" Cal insisted. Trevor thought for a few more seconds. His expression softened into something more curious. Skeptical.

"What color underwear am I wearing right now?" he asked. Cal glowered at him.

– 200 –

"Why would I know that, Trev?" he replied. Trevor shrugged, which made his bike quiver beneath him.

"I dunno," he said. "Seeing if you're a mind reader or something."

"Look, would you just come with me? For like, ten minutes? Just to see if I'm right, if there's something down there."

"A flamingo," Trevor replied flatly.

"Right," Cal said, only realizing how stupid it sounded when he said it aloud. "A… flamingo."

Trevor thought for a final few seconds, and then let out a long, exasperated groan. If his voice hadn't been so high pitched, it might have been dramatic.

"Ten minutes," he said, turning his bike around. "After that I'm turning around."

Cal swung his leg over the saddle as Trevor came up beside him, the two slowly beginning to pick up speed away from town. As they went, Trevor gave Cal a pointed look.

"And I'm only doing this because you got lucky with the dog boy thing. And because having a precog friend would kick ass," he said. Without a word more, they pushed forward.

Cal remembered it all being more lost and winding. In his dreams, Innsmouth Road was a curving, serpentine thing. Cutting through hills and black patches of undergrowth like a scalpel path, all blind turns and darkness. He tried not to think about that night on May 13. About how they were probably following the same path his dad's car had. The buzzing in his skull was enough of a distraction.

They had been going for some time when Trevor fell back parallel with him. His face was streaked with sweat, which had soaked into his collar.

"We've definitely been going longer than ten minutes, dude!" he panted, bike shaking a little. "We should really turn back!"

"Not yet!" Cal insisted, speeding up a little. Even though it made his sweat start flowing again, Trevor managed to keep pace.

"Cal! C'mon, you said!"

"Just a couple more—" Cal began, eyes flicking from Trevor to the road ahead. Something in his brain nagged almost painfully.

He slammed the brakes, friction squeal bouncing against the tunnel of trees. Trevor yelped and hurriedly came to a stop too, near enough leaping off his bike as it toppled into a skid.

"Jeez, dude! Warn me next time, I coulda broke my leg or something!" he said, reflexively wiping his hands on his shirt. Cal, still astride his bike, nodded into the undergrowth.

"Trev," he said. "Look."

The boys peered into the undergrowth. It was a solid mass of bristling green, eating away at the side of the road. But nestled in between the leaves was something different: artificial, neon pink. As their eyes tracked it from the exposed wing, they found the perfect curve of a plastic neck, a beady eye, a slender beak. Cal pulled his bike to the side of the road and walked towards it, brushing branches away from it with his bare hands. Then, he took a few steps back.

It was a plastic lawn flamingo. Just stuck there, right by the side of the road. Trevor walked up beside him, hands on his hips.

"Seriously?" he said, turning to look at Cal. Cal shrugged, and looked back at the flamingo. It was streaked with old rain and dew, but it didn't look old. It had been out there a week, tops. Next to it lay a small beaten track, almost entirely hidden by the grass. He tried to follow it with his eyes, but it become more obscure the further it went, before disappearing entirely.

"It's a marker, there's a path," he said, stepping forward again. Trevor shook his head and took a step back towards his bike.

"C'mon man," he said. "It's been way more than ten. I gotta go, I'm gonna be late."

Cal stared at him for a few seconds. Then, he shrugged in mock defeat.

"Fine," he said, taking a step into the undergrowth. "But when it turns out I got murdered after you left me out here, and you go to hell for abandoning your friend, that's all on you."

He heard Trevor let out a little frustrated noise, like a sputtering kettle.

"Cal, wait up!" he called, running after him. "Cal!"

The path through the undergrowth wound away from the road, into the dense and silent part of the wood. The track was dimpled with clumps of black weeds and crumpled shoots. Fat, green fronds of grass grew like a dense wall either side of it, occasionally drooping inquisitively forward to stroke Cal's cheek as he passed.

After what felt like three hundred feet or so, the green walls suddenly gave way. Cal pushed into a large clearing and ground to a stop, eyes fixed on what lay at its center. The sound of Trevor following him filled the empty space, and then echoed into silence. That told him they'd both clocked the same thing.

A hatch. Made of what looked like solid steel, all misty and tarnished from wind and weather. The top was latched shut by a wheel lock, and it looked sturdy enough to survive a bomb blast or two. Or maybe, Cal thought, something more profound than that.

He took a few steps forward, before Trevor called out to him.

"Whoa, whoa, whoa, what are you doing!" he said, reaching out as if to stop him, a few seconds too late. Cal pointed to the hatch.

"I was going to check that out, Trev, what else was I going to do?"

"Are you kidding me right now? Seriously?" Trevor asked, walking forward. "That is like *the* first mistake they make in every movie."

Cal tilted his head back in exasperation.

"Seriously?" he asked.

"You open the hatch, you get eaten, or even worse, *I* get eaten."

"Nothing's gonna eat you, buddy. It's a hatch, not an alien spaceship."

"What if it's a prepper?" Trevor retorted sharply. Cal screwed up his face.

"A what?"

"A prepper. Y'know, people who think the world's ending, and put themselves in bunkers. What if they murder us for finding their spot?" he said, as Cal slung his backpack onto the floor. He produced a flashlight, matches, pocketknife, all of them stuffed into his pockets. Trevor hovered beside him, looking on nervously.

"What's all that for?" he asked.

"Contingencies," Cal replied, standing up straight again. "You wanna be lookout?"

Trevor blanched a little and looked around the clearing.

"I don't know if I wanna be out here alone, man. What if the prepper comes back? He'll find me first," he said. Cal tossed him a flashlight, which he fumbled, dropped, and hastily picked up.

"Welcome to the exploration team, then," Cal said.

"But—"

"Your mom's out of town, Trevvy. When they call to say you were absent, just delete the message. Now come on," Cal said, reaching down to grip the lock wheel. Trevor looked like he wanted to protest but couldn't think of anything that could argue with him.

Cal strained and heaved against the wheel. After a few seconds of wrenching it gave a start, broken from its weathered sticking place. It opened with a soft groan, and the smell of dry, purified air muttered out of the gap.

Inside lay darkness. Their flashlights danced down the long entry shaft and against a bare concrete floor below. A metal ladder ran all the way down, rungs gone brown with rust. Cal eased himself over the edge, the soft sound of his shoes and hands against the ladder echoing and morphing in the unseen places below. All the while, Trevor stared down at him, face half worry and half wonder.

The feeling of his foot hitting solid ground was jarring. Cal froze at the bottom of the ladder, flashlight still clamped between his teeth. He wasn't claustrophobic, but the feeling of being surrounded by the bunker, all closed in by the underground darkness... it made the hairs on his arms bristle. The feeling that anything could be waiting down here for him.

What waited below was, in fact, a chamber with a low ceiling. At one end, another wheel lock door stood tightly shut. Cal looked up and raised an arm to shield his eyes from Trevor's flashlight beam.

"Are you coming down or what?" he asked.

"Right. Yeah, I can do that. Uh…" he said, awkwardly looking for somewhere to put his flashlight. He stuffed it into a pocket and crouched down, leg feeling gingerly around for the first step like a fat antenna. Rung by rung, he clumsily made his way down.

"Not too bad, right?" Cal said encouragingly. Trevor looked around, going a little pale.

"This might be the creepiest place I've ever been in my life."

"I know," Cal replied, gesturing to the door. "Let's go further."

He took a step towards the door, and then froze. The room went from black to a scabbed, dark red as lights on the wall suddenly blared to life.

A klaxon roared and bounced around the tiny room, underscored by the grinding of something moving in the walls. Trevor screamed and made for the ladder, but by the time he made it to the first rung it was too late. With a loud clang, the hatch above them swung shut and locked tight.

The klaxon stopped, and the two boys looked at each other, wide eyed with panic.

"Cal!" Trevor cried, still clinging to the ladder. Before the rest of the sentence could come, there was a new noise. Cal stumbled away from the door, falling against the opposite wall.

The door swung open. Light flooded in, bright and fluorescent. A figure, stood ready in the doorway, held up a shotgun shape.

They lowered it.

"Oh," she said, "you showed up this time."

Cal felt a hard breath uncoil in his chest. Eyes adjusted, he could now see the person clearly.

It was a girl. About his age, maybe a little older. Her clothes were faded, and dirty, thick brown hair awkwardly hacked into a matted bob. The moment Cal saw her, he knew who she was. He'd met her before, he thought. In a dream.

"…Leslie?" he asked, voice cracking. Leslie let the gun hang at her side, and her stance shifted. Became a little more exasperated.

"Would you get up?" she said, gesturing with the barrel. Trevor stepped away from the ladder and held up a shaking finger, eyes wide.

"You're… from the news," he said, looking at Cal. "Is she…?"

"Yes, Trevor. It's me, Leslie O'Neil. Time travel is real, and we're all trapped by a maniac. Now get in," she replied. A moment after the last word left her mouth, Trevor's eyes rolled back a little. He did a sort of stumble-run a few steps and then doubled over. He let out an ugly retch, and there was the sound of something liquid hitting the concrete.

"Oh, shit," Cal said quietly. Leslie didn't seem as concerned.

"He does that almost every time. He'll be fine," she said, gesturing with the gun again. "Now come on already. I don't know how good the shielding is out there."

Trevor straightened up and wiped his mouth. He looked dazed. With a final look at one another, the two boys began to walk, following Leslie as she turned back towards the corridor behind her.

Down, and into the bunker they went.

THE PLACID ISLE OF IGNORANCE

AMESVILLE, 1977

"You've not got any electronics on you, right?" asked Wittey, closing the trailer door. Yule gave him a withering look.

"No, man, I left my payphone in my other jacket," he said, wincing as the crumpled foil hat scratched against his scalp. "Do we really gotta wear these?"

"Never hurts. Buddy of mine says it helps block thought-based bugging," Wittey replied matter-of-factly. He went over to the kitchen nook and took two glasses from the cabinet, judiciously filling them with something that looked cheap and smelled cheaper. As Wittey came over and handed him one, the sharp tang of nail polish wafted up from the tumbler.

"You'll want some of that. Helps get rid of the cognitive dissonance a little, when the curtain gets pulled away, so to speak," he said. Yule considered it a moment, twitched his nose, and then looked back up.

"Man, what the hell are you even talking about?" he said, putting the glass down. "I just wanna know who's watching me, and what that's gotta do with you in the first place."

To his surprise, instead of being taken aback, Wittey smiled. He gestured with the lit cigarette between his fingers and nodded.

"Right approach. You shouldn't trust me; you don't even know me. Kinda shit that's gonna keep you alive," he said. "I work at a security firm, Shelley and Sons. You ever heard of 'em?"

Yule's eyes flicked around the trailer. First to the knives at the nearby kitchen counter, the hammer on top of the toolbox, and the gun on the coffee table. Then, to a branded pair of grubby overalls on the back of a chair. At least that part of the story checked out.

"Nah," he said finally.

"Don't blame you," Wittey replied, wiping his lips, "before about six months ago, nobody had, they didn't exist. Hired me and about ten other guys on startup."

"So it's a new local business," Yule replied, unimpressed. Plausible explanations were starting to form uncomfortably in his head. 'Creepy CCTV operator with tapes of him' sounded less like science fiction, and more like an episode of *Columbo*. He shifted, the gun reassuringly present against his hip. Wittey took a drag on the cigarette.

"A new local business with enough money to offer dozens of below-cost installations," he said, voice lowering. "All the ones in public places have monitoring feeds in our office and the police station. Except that a month ago, stuff started disappearing."

Yule felt something tingle on his skin. A familiar, unknown fear.

"Disappearing?" he asked. Wittey nodded.

"Spliced out," he said, a satisfied smile coming over his features, "but I'm ahead of them. See I make backups sometimes, y'know? Just in case of interference operations, outside agents..."

He pointed with two fingers, glowing cigarette aimed almost accusingly at the ceiling.

"It's all you. At the bank, going down the street... I didn't really get it until last night," he said. "I watched the feed, saw 'em take you away to the station. It hits 1:20 a.m., and then... *fwoosh*."

He sketched the shape of an explosion with his hands.

"Everything goes. In the office, in the station. Everywhere. No record of either operator terminating it, neither." He leaned forward, voice no more than a whisper wreathed with tobacco smoke. "Outside of the biggest coincidence in history, the only way all those cameras got turned off was if some third party has access. And I'd wager something happened to you that night, right? In the police station?"

Uneasy weight shifted against Yule's ribs, like a giant sitting on his chest. The mention of it made him feel like he was going to leap from the seat, like panic setting in. He could still remember it, the moment before he'd woken up. When the pain had been a red, wriggling dot in the dark.

"Yeah," he said, rasp in his throat a reminder. "Somebody tried to kill me."

Wittey nodded, as if that was what he'd expected to hear.

"Sorry," he said, taking another drink. "Sounds about right, though. Somebody has a vested interest in seeing you go down, and nobody being able to prove involvement. Might be the same people I'm trying to dig stuff up about, and I goddamn bet it's whoever took that Leslie kid."

"And who exactly is that?"

"I've got theories. We just have to do a little digging and you can remove yourself from all this," Wittey insisted. Yule frowned at him.

"And what if I just decide to remove myself in the traditional, get-in-my-car-and-drive-away sense?" he said, looking at the door. Wittey went to his feet, as if a loaded grenade had just been thrown at his feet.

"You really don't want to do that," he said, holding up his free hand. "Look, I get it, this all sounds crazy. But if you walk out that door, they're gonna kill you. Sooner or later."

"They already tried once. Didn't go so well," said Yule. Wittey shook his head, a sort of fog coming over his look. The dull sheen of animal fear.

"It doesn't work like that. You don't get it; these guys are like the boogeyman. The second this all dies down and everyone takes their eyes off you? They drag you under the bed, and nobody ever sees you again," he said, voice low. "You said it yourself. Somebody tried to kill you in police custody, and now somebody's covering it up. Just like they're trying to cover up that girl disappearing. If they think you know something, which you obviously do, they're not just gonna let you go. They're gonna wait until nobody's looking and put a bullet in your head."

Yule sat in his seat, motionless. All of a sudden, he felt as if he wasn't even there at all, like he was viewing everything from a quiet, faraway place. Empty roads circled in his head. The sight of that girl's smile, without a care. How it looked mottled and empty in the black-and-white copy.

Yule set his jaw. Things had been unexplainable for so long, maybe he was just desperate for answers. True or not, this was a hell of a lot better than nothing. And if the police weren't looking, what hope was there for Leslie if he didn't do something?

If not him, then who?

"Alright," he said. He thought there'd be more, but there wasn't. Seemed like enough for Wittey, who smiled and downed the rest of his drink before reaching across the coffee table, newly emptied palm outstretched.

"Welcome to the revolution," he said.

"Not filling me with confidence, man, gotta be honest," Yule replied, going to take the hand anyway. He was surprised when Wittey forced a drink back into his grip instead.

"Through here," he said, "you're gonna need that."

By the time Yule realized he was holding something, Wittey had started towards a door near the end of the trailer, up on a raised level that he supposed counted as a second floor.

The room beyond was even smaller, shadows made uneasy by piles of unknown debris. In one corner, a cot bed sat covered in documents and photographs, crowded at one side by beer cans. The windows were, like everywhere else, taped shut, one blocked entirely by a large corkboard. Its contents were indistinct and hard to make out in the dark, but when Wittey flicked the light, Yule wished he hadn't.

He took an unconscious step back, face to face with the blurry photo of a dead body. Bloody, eyes vacant and mouth agape.

"What the fuck, man?" he said, almost reflexively. He tore his eyes away to look at Wittey, who didn't seem freaked out enough to calm him down.

"Eileen Vick from Wright, Wyoming. Somebody killed her a few years back, two shots to the chest. Police ruled it suicide," he said, shaking his head. "What a waste, right?"

"Great story—why do you got a picture of it?" Yule insisted, glancing nervously at it again. That drink in his hand wasn't looking too shabby anymore. Wittey gestured to the photograph, then turned his gaze to the other things affixed around it.

"It's evidence. Everything on this board is," he said, eyes flicking from object to object as if seeing them for the first time. "Evidence of *them*."

"So they don't even have a name?" Yule asked. Wittey shook his head.

"They do. I've only ever seen it a handful of times, usually written down by people who aren't around to answer questions," he said. "They're called The Branch."

Yule cocked his head back.

"The Branch?" he said.

"I don't know who they're associated with, but they're obviously associated with somebody. Funds, and everything. We're talking mass cover-ups, fake companies, murders. Over state borders, too," Wittey said. Yule noted a strange, fearful tremor in his voice the more he spoke about them. Made him believe what he was saying a little more, but definitely didn't make him feel any calmer.

"So, what do they do?" he asked, glancing nervously at the board again. "Why'd they try to kill me, why take some little girl?"

"I don't know that, either. Trafficking, maybe? Or, human test subjects—"

"Y'know what?" Yule interrupted, holding up a hand. "I think I'm asking questions I don't want answers to right now. And you should know from the outset, I'm not interested in shooting nobody, or touching dead bodies. I've already gotten implicated in enough as it is."

"No. Nothing like that. Strictly information gathering, with some light breaking and entering, maybe," Wittey said in a tone that was probably meant to be reassuring. Yule felt his blood pressure rising again and took a drink. The chemical sting was numbing, at least.

"Define *light* breaking and entering," he replied, keeping his eyes averted from the body board.

"Nothing huge. A hatch. Maybe a grate on the way," Wittey said, going over to one side of the room. From a pile, he pulled a large, crumpled map and laid it out on the bed. "About the same time we were hired to do installs, a big excavation crew was coming off a project near the Sledmore Radio Factory."

He tapped the map, gesturing to a large red "X" nestled in the hills.

"Right here? There's some kinda maintenance entrance. I've been there myself, brand new, man-sized," he said. "All you'd need to do is go in, see what it leads to. Maybe get some pictures."

"If it's so easy then why haven't you done it already?"

"Y'know, I feel like for a guy who's supposedly on board with this, you're doubting a lot of what I'm trying to tell you," Wittey said, taking a pointedly large drink. Yule clenched his jaw and pinched the bridge of his nose.

"Look, you gotta understand: a man tried to strangle me the other day. I'm kind of on edge. So when some guy tells me I gotta go into a secret tunnel in the woods, I'm not exactly eager to jump on that train."

"I don't see how any of this is going to work if you don't trust me."

"I just gotta know what you stand to gain," Yule said, voice steady. "Even the Vietcong got paychecks. I got literal skin in the game, but I don't know what *you're* all about yet."

Wittey scoffed and took a long drag of the cigarette.

"That's like asking a bunny rabbit why it's against snares," he said, gesturing with the burning tip of the cigarette. "I'm against these sons-of-bitches because they're a threat to the American way of life. These... whatever they are, they've just up and decided democracy doesn't work for them. And unless true citizens, true patriots do something about it—" He gestured sharply at the board. "—Eileen Vick from Wright, Wyoming. Police ruled it suicide," he said, pointedly.

Yule stared at him, squinting to make out details in the dimness. Nostrils flaring. Jaw set, and eyes wide. Crazy, he thought. Definitely crazy, but he wasn't lying. He'd imagined that'd make him feel better, and in a way it did. It just also made him feel worse in about a hundred others.

"You're not exactly a calming presence, but it seems like you believe in what you're saying," he said, folding his arms. Wittey smiled at him and nodded, like a half-excited dog.

"More than anything."

"But if we're gonna work together, I want a couple ground rules," Yule continued, putting down his drink. "First off, you're not allowed to drive my car. Second, if we're gonna jump into this shit, we're not coming out 'til we know exactly what happened to Leslie O'Neil."

"That might be difficult," Wittey replied, but Yule shook his head.

"Don't care, man. Police aren't looking for her, just like they wouldn't look much for me. Somebody's gotta take care of people like that. Not gonna compromise," he said firmly. "And third, I'm not going into some covert ops sewer hole without protective gear. A gas mask, industrial gloves, all of it. Could be anything down there."

Wittey smiled and flicked the dying stub of his cigarette into the carpet, where it twisted and died like a stepped-on worm.

"I already thought of that part," he said, walking to the closet door.

THE DEFINITION OF INSANITY

THE BUNKER, 1993

The stag almost looked alive. Had its neck not been at a precise right angle, it would have looked as if it was just sleeping at an odd tilt between the operating theater chairs, horns artfully puncturing the seat covers. It couldn't have been there more than a few days.

Everything else around it was ancient in comparison. Mold and moss grew in fat, slender strips over the old chairs and tables, moisture seeping silently inside through a long, thin crack in the high ceiling.

Cal's eyes pulled back into close focus, movement gliding in his peripherals; a wisp of steam, rising from a towel-clad glass beaker. Something brown and sweet smelling swirled against the rim as it was held up to him.

"His name's Buck," said Leslie, handing him the beaker. Cal looked at it, frowned, and looked back up.

"The drink?" he asked. Leslie nodded through the murky window.

"The deer," she said, "that's his name. Falls in through the crack in the roof every fifth day, if the loop makes it back that far. Done it nearly twenty times."

She glanced up thoughtfully at the tear in the ceiling. Like she was lost somewhere behind her eyes.

"Bad luck, I guess," she said, eyes tracking suddenly back down to the floor. "Just big enough to fall through, small enough not to notice, going up through half a mile of rock... Million to one chance. Happening over, and over and over again."

Cal considered what she said for a second. His grip on the hand towel tightened.

"I don't really know how to respond to that," he said. Leslie smirked, like she'd been told an old joke.

"Yeah. I know," she said. Cal gave her a weak smile and took a sip. The thin, sugary taste of instant hot cocoa and way too much water prickled over his tongue. Satisfied, Leslie turned around and walked back to the other side of the room.

The little atrium felt tighter than it was, owing mostly to the squat ceiling and dim lights. To one side, there was a makeshift kitchen consisting mostly of canned food, bottles of water and a Bunsen burner. On the other, piles of old clothes and bags, pockets turned inside out. She'd left all the money on top, like an inverted wishing well.

Trevor was sat on one of the upturned benches, clutching his own beaker. He looked pale and sweaty. Cal counted him vomiting twice, but he'd not had his eyes on him the whole time. Maybe he'd wandered out in between bursts of asking Leslie if she was real or not.

Leslie didn't seem to mind. It was like she was used to it.

She took a sip of her drink and sat down against the desk in the corner. For a few moments, there was nothing but the dull whir of the bunker beneath them, before the silence grew too heavy to bear.

"You guys usually have questions, so... I could just answer 'em right now, if you want," she said, eyes flicking between the two boys. Cal set his jaw.

"Usually?" he asked. The red pressure in his head was pulsing again. Dream images, trying to press themselves into reality. A scowl flickered over Leslie's face. Annoyance, or... just discomfort. It was hard to tell.

"We've done this before. A lot. The whole town's been looping through the same two weeks over and over again," she said, glancing down at a piece of paper on the desk. "Forty-three times, actually. You probably half-remember some of them, on account of the whole titanium skull plate thing."

"So how long is that?" Cal asked, voice quiet and shuddering. Leslie's face fell a little, and when she looked over at him again, there was genuine sadness in her eyes. She cleared her throat and raised her own beaker to take another drink.

"Seventy-eight days, real time. Give or take a few," she said quietly. The number hit Cal like a sledgehammer, ringing ears and all. He stared at the floor for a couple of seconds, mouth open. Trevor stood up, and jerkily put his beaker on the bench.

"Where are you—"

"I think I'm gonna thr… oh god. I think I'm gonna…" he muttered, before hurriedly loping over to the bathroom. The sound of something spattering against the chemical toilet's plastic bowl tapped out through the metal hallway. Cal was surprised he had anything left in him to throw up.

The beaker burnt his hands, but he felt numb to it. All he could feel was the deep desire for it not to be true, ringing in his bones. Whirring in his head. But it didn't feel like a lie. He felt like he remembered it wasn't.

That was the worst part, he thought. Couldn't even disbelieve her for one, happy second.

"And we always come here?" he said, slowly and measuredly, as if his heart wasn't threatening to leap up through his throat. Leslie shook her head.

"Not always. You didn't answer much at first, let alone show, but… as things started to get worse, you turned up a lot more. Went from about once every week to every other day."

Cal felt something twinge in his belly. Familiar yet sharp and venomous. Fear without a name.

"What do you mean, as things got worse?" he said, looking up. Leslie's face fell, eyes lowered.

"Big things are harder to forget than little ones," she said. "The more big things happened, the more you showed up. So you being here tells me that something big just happened again."

Cal took a deep, sharp breath through his teeth.

It was all true, he thought. He wasn't nuts, he… they were all traveling through time.

Time travel.

Time.

Travel.

The phrase repeated over and over in his head, circling like an invisible vulture. The words made sense, but they didn't. Couldn't.

Time travel.

He stared through her. In his shaking hand, the cocoa slopped and ran over the rim in fat globules, leaving pink heat welts across his fingers. He didn't care. He could barely feel it.

"So, what? We're all just repeating the same couple days over and over again, forever?" he said.

"Not forever. We're going to find a way out. That's what we're doing here," Leslie replied. "So unless you've got any burning questions, we should probably get to it."

Cal sat staring at the floor, insides churning. He felt simultaneously like a weight had been lifted off his chest and swung right into his gut. He wasn't going crazy. It was memories, half-forgotten feelings.

Like the feeling of dying. The feeling of something giant and invisible burning through him.

"There's something else out there," he said, looking up. "I don't even know how to describe it, like a living *wrongness*. What is that?"

Leslie's lip twitched.

"Sounds like a Volatile," she said, crossing her arms. Cal cocked his head and she grunted, rubbing her brow. "Sorry. It's hard keeping track of what you know and what you don't."

"Yeah, I definitely don't know what one of those is," Cal replied. It sounded about right though, he thought, trying to ignore dim memories of charred skin. Leslie nodded.

"They're what happen when you try and make a time traveler who doesn't need a machine. Except, they never turned out right, they just keep trying to endlessly recur over themselves. I think. There was a paper

I got in the trailer, but it's... fuck, it's really, *really* complicated," she said, sighing.

"Can it get us in here? The Volatile?" Cal insisted. Leslie shook her head.

"No. Or at least it hasn't so far. We can probably ignore it for now," she replied. Cal widened his eyes and threw a hand towards the entrance.

"So we're not gonna do *anything* about the giant monster?" he said. Leslie's flat expression flattened further and she drew herself up, authoritative silhouette seeming to fill her corner of the room.

"I don't mean to freak you out, but a Volatile running around isn't exactly topping the danger scale right now. But it's something for the list, at least. Might explain a couple things."

Cal furrowed his brow.

"The list?" he asked. Leslie stood up and gestured to a door across the room.

"Like I said," she replied, "there might be a way out of this. But it's not exactly stepping out dressed in sequins."

⁓

The back room was full of consoles and machinery, some weakly blinking on the ghost of a long-dead charge. The only bright one sat in a corner, running off a noisy backup battery. According to Leslie, it detected whenever there was a 'green flash,' and time jumped back. Cal hadn't asked much more after that.

Leslie sat amidst a pile of boxes, Van Hallan's thick manuscript always within arm's reach. She would periodically pick it up, flick to one of the many dog-eared pages, and then scribble something down. Behind her, a map of town was rolled out on an old bench, covered in pen marks and circles.

Over the next half hour, Leslie asked dozens of questions. At first, she mostly just referred to the map, quizzing him on what areas of town were empty. After that, the questions got stranger. She asked him if any insects had died en masse. Whether he'd seen strangers in town he didn't recognize or remembered people that didn't exist. That part had taken considerably longer, but when the subject of his uncle had come up, it was almost troublingly succinct.

"What kind of person was he?" Leslie had asked. It had taken Cal a while to answer, partly on account of the stone in his throat.

"He was a good guy," he said. Leslie sighed gently through her nose.

"I meant more in terms of his role. What did he do?"

"Oh. Right. He was a cop, back in the seventies and eighties," Cal replied quietly. At that point, Leslie looked up from the notes, and put a hand on his shoulder.

"Sorry," she said. He'd smiled and nodded. Informally accepted the pity, like he was used to. They didn't say anything about him after that.

After the questions finished, there was a long, increasingly agitated silence. Leslie marked things down, double- and triple-checked places on the map. Eventually, she let out a hiss of frustration, and let her pencil drop.

"Problem?" Cal asked. Leslie chewed her lip and gestured halfheartedly to the map.

"It doesn't make sense," she said. "I don't see anything."

Cal cocked his head.

"See any what?" he asked. Leslie reached over and pulled the map up for him to see, a fine plume of dust rising in its wake.

It was Amesville, circa late seventies, mapped out in grayscale. However, huge swathes of it were scribbling out or covered in large black crosses. Half of the streets were covered in notes like "Deer acting strangely" or "Man with half a face." The landscape seeming almost sick with it, like a spreading rash in random patches. Cal's eyes instinctively wandered down to his own house. It was simply labeled "Accident."

Leslie gestured to the map again and shook it a little, like it had misbehaved.

"I thought there'd be a pattern or something. Like we could see what Carnassus was doing, but there's... *nothing*," she said. Cal narrowed his eyes in disbelief.

"Wait, Carnassus? The energy plant guy, *that* Carnassus?" he said. Leslie clicked her tongue against her teeth impatiently.

"Yeah. He's the one with the time machine," she said offhandedly, looking back to the map. "Guess this isn't one of the times you know that. Should've checked."

Cal squinted once more at the map, as if he could see in a few seconds what she'd missed over months. But she was right—a cluster of houses here, an old road there, strange events just scattered around town without rhyme or reason.

"I don't see anything either," he said. Leslie put the map back down and rubbed her temples, eyes squeezed shut.

"We just have to think," she said, brow furrowing, "what do we know? What's happened recently?"

"All I remember clearly right now is Uncle Terry. Or... the fact he's not here anymore," Cal replied, sifting through what he could remember for something that might help. "He was on the police force when you disappeared. That's something, right?"

Leslie opened her eyes and perked up a little.

"He ever tell you anything about it?" she asked. Cal shook his head.

"Didn't like to," he replied.

"What about the arcade?" came a voice from behind them. As Cal turned to see Trevor leaning against the doorway, he found himself surprised at the unfamiliarity of him

Not in a bad way. An unexpected way, like the feeling of reaching out for a wall in the dark and finding nothing. Cal had expected him to shake, or at least look pale. But in the dim light of the back room, he seemed almost normal. His voice was muted but measured. If it hadn't been for his loud Hawaiian shirt, he would've looked more like a man than a teenage kid.

"The arcade?" Leslie repeated, eyes straying to the upper portion of the map. "Joytown?"

For a second her features softened. Something bright appeared in her stare, the dim shadow of a smile alight on her cheeks.

"I used to take my brother there," she muttered, as if it were something involuntary. Reflexive and blurted, like throwing up. No sooner had the words left her mouth, though, the glow faded. Receded into something more at the mercy of reality. Something with weight.

"Have we ever gone in before?" Trevor asked.

"I don't think so," she replied, still staring at the map, but now with an expression closer to hate. Cal noticed her eyes had drifted over to the Sledmore Plant.

"What's so special about the arcade?" he asked, looking back up. Trevor came closer and pointed to the map.

"There's six payphones in Amesville. Leslie got told to call a specific payphone, the one outside the arcade," he said. Cal wrinkled his nose.

"Maybe it's in the same place so I'll always see it," he replied. Trevor shook his head and pointed to the map again.

"But there's another payphone on the way from your house to school. And two *more* nearby. Why call that specific payphone, every single time, outside that specific building?" he said, looking up at Leslie. "And, it's the same arcade where Yule Lincoln worked. It's already connected."

Leslie frowned.

"Yule Lincoln? What's any of this got to do with him?" she said. Trevor looked awkwardly at his feet.

"Well, I mean...he was the one who kidnapped you. Or at least, everyone thought he did."

Leslie looked up at him, eyebrows raised. It was the first time that Cal had seen her look close to shocked about anything.

"What? No, he...he caught me cutting school, the day I..." she said, shaking her head. "He didn't have anything to do with it. What happened to him?"

Trevor shrugged.

"I don't know. My mom just used to tell me not to go in there, because everyone said that was where he hid your…" he said, trailing off as he realized where the sentence would terminate. He coughed and shook his shoulders, as if the pause was on purpose.

"They never charged him. Don't know what happened to him after that, she never said," he finished. Cal felt something light up in his head. A connection.

"Uncle Terry probably worked on that case," he said, looking between them. "I bet that's why he disappeared; he knew something."

"That's a lot of coincidences for one place," Leslie said, shooting Trevor a look. "You might actually be onto something, Trevor."

She took some paper up from her notes and wrote down a quick, spidery paragraph.

"You guys should probably try and get there before sundown," she said, not looking up. "Green flash usually happens after dark. It's not flared up for about sixteen hours, so we're probably due another any time."

Cal stood up, hand flying first to his forehead and then out, as if to slap away the suggestion.

"Wait a damn second," he said, looking between them, "we're just gonna go? Just like that?"

"Time pretty literally isn't on our side here," said Leslie.

"But we don't even know if anything's going to be in there. What if we get erased too?" Cal argued, turning to Trevor. But this time, his look wasn't returned. Trevor's brow furrowed, and he stood his ground.

"I'm with Leslie. I think we should go," he said. Cal's face fell.

"Trev—"

"I'll never see my mom again, Cal," Trevor cut in, a quaver of weakness creeping into his voice for the first time. "If we don't figure out what's going on, she's never gonna come back. What else are we supposed to do?"

Cal felt something in him go still and dead. The part that had been hoping they wouldn't need to go. After a line like that, he couldn't think of a reason not to that didn't make his ribcage shiver with guilt. He hung his head.

"So what happens if a green flash happens while we're out there?" he asked, quietly.

"You'll get reset. Maybe to yesterday, maybe a couple hours ago. Then I guess you'll come back again," Leslie answered. Cal stood up sharply, knowing his legs would refuse if he thought too much about it. He could feel himself getting more afraid, even as he tried to stop it. Like his body just knew.

"Let's go, then," he said.

The instructions from Leslie were brief, and well-rehearsed. Look for anything out of place. Don't draw attention. Come back when you're done. Even the goodbye was short and to-the-point.

He should've asked how she was, he thought. Maybe he'd done that before. Either way, as he stood alone in the dying glow of the day, Cal found it difficult to think of anything except the danger he was in. A kind soul might've called it survival instinct, but everyone else would probably have skewed towards cowardice. He didn't care.

With the sound of wheezing behind him, Trevor crawled over the concrete lip of the pit, and stood up. For a few moments, Cal felt him standing a few feet behind. Just… looking at him.

"We should get going," he said, starting to walk.

"Wait," Trevor replied, trying to catch him up. Cal kept walking.

"What, Trev?" he asked, slowing just before he broke the tall grass. Trevor gave him a thoughtful look and took a deep breath in through his nostrils.

"I'm scared too," he said. Cal stopped, and turned.

"I dunno about scared—I'm fucking terrified," he said, rubbing his hands over his face. "I mean, Christ, Trev, what are we even doing?"

"Saving the day," Trevor replied. He smiled, aware of how cheesy it sounded. Cal gave him an exasperated look.

"This isn't a movie," he muttered. Trevor took a few steps forward, grass rippling under his sneakers. He went shoulder to shoulder with Cal, staring out at the same honey-yellow patch of dusk. Night was falling on Amesville, and now they both knew what came with it.

Trev nudged him gently with an elbow.

"Hey, at least this kind of means we're the heroes, right? The only ones who can make a difference against the big, bad evil guy," he said. "Just… promise you won't leave me behind, alright?"

Cal laid a hand on his shoulder, eyes still focused straight ahead.

"I won't," he promised. "No matter what happens."

He gripped Trevor's shoulder a little tighter, and then let go.

"Guess we'd better go be heroes then, huh?" he said, pushing back into the undergrowth.

"We've done this forty times, apparently," Trevor replied, following. "Maybe we already are."

PREY REFLEX

AMESVILLE, 1993

He always wondered if it was real. The *feeling of being watched* thing.

Always looked that way on the nature documentaries. When they showed angelic little gazelles grazing, they always seemed to know when something was waiting in the tall grass.

Daisy sipped his coffee without looking down. He couldn't exactly taste that it was burnt—he hadn't tasted anything for about eight years—but he could feel it. A kind of blood-like, metallic sensation as it washed over his tongue.

His eyes tracked them down the road, hardly ever blinking. Watched as they retrieved their bikes, talking and looking around the whole time. They couldn't see him, parked off in the trees—and they certainly didn't feel his jaundiced stare. Guess that was a key difference between humans and gazelles.

Slowly, the two boys set off back towards town, and out of sight. Daisy kept his eyes trained on their point of departure as he raised a boxy cellphone to his lips, gloved thumb stroking the well-worn speed dial button.

Silence greeted him on the other end, and he knew not to wait for a "hello." Just to get on with it.

"You were right, the cop's kid is involved too. Even brought a friend with him," he said, taking a sip of coffee. "You want me to take care of it?"

The answer was quick, and purposeful.

"No. See where they're going first. There might be more." There was a brief pause as wheels imperceptibly whirred in Carnassus' thoughts. Weights and variables. What he could afford to lose, and what he couldn't. "After that," he finished, "the game is yours. Keep me informed."

The line clicked and went dead. Daisy let the phone drop from his ear and tossed it lazily back into the glove compartment. He liked that about Carnassus: even if the guy did freak him the fuck out, he was efficient. Never liked to say more than he needed to, at least in private. For a guy with all the time in the world, he was always in a hell of a hurry.

Daisy smiled to himself as he drained his coffee, tossing the cup out of the open window as he pulled the car up and onto the road again.

He'd drive slow, he thought. It wasn't like they had anywhere to run.

SLUICE

AMESVILLE, 1977

The rubber suit was a size too small, and the way it squeaked with every movement made Yule think it wasn't designed for extended wear. Wittey, driving surprisingly well for all the liquor in him, hadn't said a word since they left the trailer. As they passed onto a rural road, he opened the glovebox, and put something in Yule's lap.

"You'll need this camera. Careful, it was expensive," Wittey said, taking a hand off the wheel to drag on his cigarette. "When you're done, just go back out the way you came in. I'll be waiting for you directly north. Head straight up for about ten minutes until you hit the pine barrens, you'll see me. Job done."

"And what do we do then?" Yule said, examining the camera.

"Expose them, man. Get pictures, evidence, that kinda shit," he said, shrugging. "After that, we leak it out. Get it all over the news, give 'em no place to hide."

"Right. That sounds good," Yule said, nodding. His gut didn't agree.

As he caught sight of himself in the rearview, it was like looking at another person. Someone who was breathing fast, sweating a little. Who had this look in his eye like he was going to do something stupid. Anxiety pooled dense and hot at the base of his skull, searing yet icy cold: like sinking into deep water, and seeing the shoreline of normality shrink to nothing on the horizon.

There wasn't any coming back from this, he thought. If he did this then it was admitting it was all true. The government, kidnappings, arranged murders… He closed his eyes, gut roiling. Tried to think about something else, something that could center him.

A picture of a girl with long brown hair, tacked to the sea of evidence. She'd had a rifle, but she'd been cocky about it. She had a brother and a father and a life. She'd treated him just like anybody else and now she was gone. From where he was sat, there was only one person in the beat-up Camaro who both knew where she might be and had the strength to help. Yule set his jaw. Something clear bounced in his head, a light in the fog that made his insides feel solid and ordered again.

If not me, it asked, *then who?*

He held the thought in his mind and took a deep breath in through his nose, drawing the cold somewhere deep into him. When he breathed out, he could almost feel the heat and panic coming out of him. Purging out like poison carried on his breath.

Looked like it was still all him. Maybe it always had been.

The car rolled to a stop somewhere just off the road. Wittey cracked his door, and the cabin lit itself in sulking tones, barely better than the night darkness beyond.

"It's over there. Maybe two hundred, three hundred feet," he said, breathing heavily for nerves. "It's red. You'll be able to see it."

"Alright."

"You nervous?"

"Yeah," Yule answered. He wanted to say something funny, but the fear made it difficult to think of anything. Wittey took a last drag and threw his cigarette through the open car door, free hand patting on Yule's shoulder.

"Good. That'll keep you alive," he said, putting his hands back on the wheel. "Remember: go north. Pine barrens."

"Right. Thanks," Yule replied. He sat there for a moment, deciding whether the goodbye should've been more emotional. Wittey might be the last person he ever saw, Yule thought—but he sorely hoped he wasn't.

Without another word, he pushed open the door, and squeaked out into the dark undergrowth beyond. Behind him, the car tilted and whirred slowly back to the road, sound fading to nothing in the blackness. After that, Yule was alone.

Without a flashlight, it was almost impossible to make out anything but the blank mass of darkness before him. However, as his eyes adjusted, he found certain angles of familiarity in the moonlight. The signs of Wittey's recent footsteps, cutting a trail through the dewy undergrowth. In an odd way, it made Yule feel better knowing he hadn't been lying about being there before.

The path wound through the trees like a shoelace dragged through bike spokes. Yule went slowly, trying not to listen to the sounds of his own body made deafening by the close quiet. The slick whisper of his soles on wet grass. His heart, thudding somewhere between his throat and his ears. The sound of saliva, popping and slapping against the inside of his mouth.

Now that it lay in almost every direction, the dark seemed less predatory and more disorientating. Dreamlike. When the trees closed in and the moonlight disappeared, it was easy to forget he was moving forward at all. Up could have been down, left could have been right. Yule tried not to think about it too much. If he did, he quickly found himself losing his sense of balance.

Night wound on. The path led ever forward. Soon Yule found himself doubting there was even a hatch at all, before the undergrowth broke before him. The night unfurled its wings in milky starlight tones, scene arrayed clearly beneath.

A little stone hollow sat beneath the sky, a crack in the black landscape. Thin, ragged trees grew in clumps by the side, lit red by a cylindrical bulb bolted to the side of a concrete pillar. At its feet lay the hatch, almost predatory in its stillness; a solid, sturdy-looking thing with a heavy-duty wheel lock on top. Dying grass melted into a ring of trampled dirt around its rim, accumulated filth muffling Yule's cautious approach.

It's real, he thought, staring at it. And with it, everything else felt a lot more real, too. The fear became paralyzing as he stood by its edge, wanting to look around for danger but unable to take his eyes off it. But even more terrible was the realization some seconds later: there was nothing in the wood but him and the hatch. Nothing between him and it, no birds, no insects, no noise. Just the hollow, and him. It had all gone as silent as the grave.

With a final glance over his shoulder, he reached down and heaved at the wheel. With a shrill cry it came loose, spinning on the ill-disturbed bolt inside. Heels dug into the dirt, Yule lifted the heavy cover, and the metal hatch yawned open.

Immediately, he recoiled.

The smell was unlike anything he'd ever encountered. The dull reek of rot and antiseptic, clotted together and wrapped in ozone. He took a step back and gagged, hand flying up to his mouth. Inside, he could hear something trickling. He unclipped the flashlight from his belt and shone it through the hole, revealing a slow-moving stream of reddish liquid, which gurgled gently below.

The flashlight also revealed the shape of a metal rung, affixed to the inner wall. That at least told him it was meant to get a person inside, but…

He looked back and forth, as if some way out might present itself. But it didn't.

He tried to swallow the stone in his throat. He couldn't be the guy who let a kid die because of a sensitive nose. He just had to… go for it. Not think. He could hold his breath the whole way down, right? As he lowered himself below the lip of the earth, he knew he was going to find something troubling down there—he could just dimly hope it'd show up sooner rather than later.

When he landed, thick liquid hugged up around his calves. He tried to ignore the sickening warmth of it and focus on the path in front of him: a solitary electric light waited upstream about two hundred feet away, the only point of brightness in the greasy dark.

Slowly, Yule lowered his flashlight. The beam hit something shiny in the water, and Yule clamped his teeth together in an attempt to silence a surprised scream.

It was an eye. Bright blue and fogged by death, floating nestled in a furry socket. Little by little the flashlight revealed the rest of the dead animal, drifting just below the surface. It was so decayed that Yule couldn't even tell what species it was.

As if to claw back his attention, the sluice tunnel shrieked. Ahead of him, metal ground on metal, and a square of bright light appeared some ways ahead. Yule looked up just in time to see something dog-shaped drop from above and disappear below the surface of the water with a splash. The tunnel screeched shut once more, and the light disappeared. Now there was only Yule, the electric light, and what he now realized was a river of corpses.

He stood there for a few moments, frozen. A hundred negative sensations fought to do their instinctive work. Disgust, fear, anger; to retch, to flee.

And yet he did nothing. Didn't even breathe, for fear of letting the smell of it in.

But he had to go forward, he thought. Into realization, and the sublime terror that came with knowing what his situation was. Knowing that now he believed what Wittey had told him and was too far in to go back.

Slowly, his legs sloshed forward. The sensation of old bones curiously poking against his suit felt like blows from a metal pipe, running up through his body in waves of goosebumps. But he continued, never looking, holding his breath, limbs pulled forward only by cold mental resolve. He'd done it before, in the rotten marshes and killing fields. It all came back like nausea in his muscles. He tried not to shake and failed—but it barely disturbed the scabbed surface of the river.

Inch by inch. A stride seemed a mile. But gently, silently, he advanced.

The way was shut by some kind of gate at the other end. The newest body floated motionless beside it, turned lazily as if sleeping. But that illusion only lasted until he saw what lay below its hips: a pile of twisted up, half-formed legs and limbs exploding outwards from seedbeds of flesh. He'd never seen anything like it before.

"What the fuck…" he muttered, taking a step back. He didn't know if it was a blessing or curse when something diverted his attention. What he thought was the buzzing of his own nerves got stronger, and deeper. With growing horror, he realized the tunnel was vibrating around him. A light came on above the gate, pulsing red. Metal ground on metal again, and the sluice gate eased itself apart.

Water was flooding in. Driving the filth further down.

Yule always marveled at how simply thoughts came at times like that. When terror became so white hot, the truly thinking part of him just couldn't comprehend it anymore. The body took over, unconscious parts working in perfect harmony towards one goal: live.

Eyes turned. Saw a new hatch, an exit, a slat of light at one side indicating which way it opened. Hands on the rung, now on the lid, heaving. He didn't hear the grinding of the tunnel yawn, the roar of filthy water. It was only as he dragged himself up and over the lip that he felt in control of himself again, shocked back to waking thought by the unexpected coldness of tile against his cheek.

He lay there for a second, acclimatizing to sensation again. The roar of water was quieter now, replaced by the atonal shout of dogs barking. The room he was in was lit a sterile white, bright enough to be blinding after a short journey through the sluice pipe.

With a groan, Yule pulled himself to his feet. His vision was hazy and blurred, but as his senses sharpened, he came to realize he was surrounded by banks of cages, stacked up like maze walls. The room was entirely tiled white, floor to ceiling, the only blemish a smear of viscera from where he'd fallen.

And all around him, dark animal shapes cowered. Half the cages were inhabited, not that you'd know it; the denizens pressed themselves into the corners away from him; silent, broken and pitiful. If he'd had the time, or a brain unclouded by the syrupy fog of adrenaline, Yule would have been horrified; but he wasn't sure whether his place beyond the wire mesh was any better than theirs.

Breath hard and heavy, Yule dropped to a knee beside an empty cage, and peered around its edge.

Beyond, the room opened up into a larger floorspace. Beyond the enclosures the space was mostly bare, save for steel work surfaces and a collection of safety posters. Close by, a large wheeled table stood waiting, covered almost entirely by a large white sheet. Two doors stood on different walls, though where they led was a mystery.

No other people, though. That was the important part, he thought, taking a picture before hanging the camera back around his neck.

Quickly and quietly, Yule emerged from his hiding place. The terror of discovery had given way to something deeper, and less definable. The base, animal feeling that he was somewhere he was never meant to go. What exactly was happening in that somewhere was even less clear.

His eyes wandered over the walls, to one of the posters above a sink.

It was minimal: stark black type against a white background, announcing itself with bare, unquestionable authority.

"IS A SUBJECT SUITABLE FOR TIER 3 DISPOSAL?" it asked, *"REMEMBER O.P.E.N."*

Below, the word "Open" was spelled down the side, with smaller type sprouting limb-like from each letter.

*Originally from test site area. Properly decontaminated. **Eighty pounds or less. Non-human remains.***

Yule stared at the final word, stunned. Then, as if in shock-induced autopilot, he raised the camera and took a picture. What the *fuck* was going on here?

Glancing around for answers, his eyes soon fell on a box. Or rather, two boxes: one on the wall next to him, and a smaller one on the table nearby.

The smaller one was squat and leaden gray, with a tumorous bump on one side, sat on top of a large, unmarked manila folder. The one on the wall, however, had brighter plumage: A red warning sticker which forcefully declared, "TEMPORAL EMERGENCY SUPPLIES." With a final look around, Yule turned to a supply locker, and opened it.

Inside, a couple of helmets sat on the shelf, like the kind military police wear. Below, a pile of folded plastic bags labeled *"For Use In Flood"* sat in neat, ready squares.

Yule reached forward and picked up a helmet. It was oddly heavy, like it was full of something dense inside. He stuffed it into one of the clear plastic bags, before turning his attention across the room, and to the cube on the table. Yule grunted a little as he picked it up, surprised by the weight. He tried not to speculate on what it was.

Seemed like a good strategy, by his metric. Like how they'd taught him to listen for things during an episode, just concentrating on the way things felt. The concrete stuff. Heaviness, texture. So far it had done an admirable job at stemming the heavy, horrified feeling in his gut. Just get in, and get out, he thought. No need to think about it.

Like most strategies, it could only last so long.

With shaking fingers, he dropped the heavy cube in the bag, and opened the folder it had been sat upon.

"ERASER UNIT SAFETY," it said in bold print at the top. Heart in his throat, Yules forced his eyes further down to the stark black-and-white text below.

Always make sure to review your safety equipment before use of Hallanite equipment. If a titanium-lined helmet is unavailable in the field, several layers of aluminum foil can mitigate the worst effects of temporal amnesia.

Down.

The Eraser Unit contains exactly 5 lbs. of Xenosubstance S-130 ("Hallanite"). Exposure to even small amounts of low-voltage S-130 radiation can cause Chimeric Ageing Syndrome, as well as significant deformity.

Yule was reading so fast now that every second word seemed to jump. Down. Further and further.

It couldn't be.

Be sure to stand at least ten feet away from subjects during the Erasure Procedure. To ensure the subject is properly erased, cycle the power supply at intervals of ten seconds. Follow up any emergency field procedures with questioning, to determine if the subject has been completely removed from the linear flow of time.

Yule dropped the paper. It landed with a hollow slap on the table, pages fluttering back to the front page.

There was no word he knew to describe it. The feeling of being overwhelmingly tiny. Even down in the bunker, he felt the vastness yawning all around him. The hugeness of it all.

Time… they were going to… they…

A wall of noise broke his stupor. Something clanked far away, and the animals answered: roiling and shaking in their cages as footsteps approached.

Shit.

Shit.

No time to think.

Just had to move, had to act.

Bag still in hand, Yule dived to the floor and towards the metal table. With an audible snap, the camera strap broke as it snagged between him and the leg, falling into his lap as he desperately dragged himself behind the sheet.

He curled in tight. Held his breath. Listened.

A door opened somewhere, and footsteps entered. Voices in the middle of conversation, completely unaware of his presence mere feet away.

"…not saying it's a lost cause, I just think bio-propelled time travel is less promising than using the machines," said one, a woman with a low, smoky voice. Her companion snorted and put something down with a clatter.

"Just because you prefer lab animals to human beings doesn't mean we all do, Indira," he said. The woman's footsteps stopped.

"Human beings can at least rationalize why things are happening to them. They can even deserve it," she said, to the gentle clicking of fingernails stroking a cage door. "Animals can do neither."

The man let out a deep, exasperated sigh.

"I'm not gonna argue about this again. Whether we're using a machine, or trying to make something move by itself, mortality rates mean human-only testing is out of the question," he said, harshly underlining. "No matter how we go about it, time travel is messy. You know that."

The woman's footsteps clacked across the room, followed by the sound of another door opening. At once, even underneath the white sheet, Yule felt the air change. Like a heavy hum, so deep he couldn't even hear it.

"So you're telling me *that* seems more viable than machine-based time travel?" she said. "Even if it is, that poor dog doesn't deserve it."

The man sighed again and audibly leaned against something.

"Dogs don't output three megawatts of energy, and dogs don't need to be kept stable by dampeners. Whatever that thing is now, it's sure as hell not a dog," he said. The woman huffed and walked back across the room.

"She has a name," she remarked, passing dangerously close to the covered table. Yule clenched his jaw as he saw a pair of black kitten heels appear in the slit of space between sheet and floor, barely an inch away from him. The man snorted derisively.

"I'm not calling it Jemima. It's a test subject, I'm not exactly on a first-name basis with the human ones."

And then, a moment of silence.

"Oh my god," said the man.

Yule's heart seized.

Fuck.

Fuck, they knew he was there. What was he going to do? Maybe he could make it to the pipe. Maybe he'd run, maybe if he just *went for it,* he could get right out of here, right now, just sprint his way out of the nightmare like—

"Stenson must've already taken the eraser cube back downstairs," groaned the man, to the tune of something clattering again. "Christ, my feet are already killing me as it is."

The woman chuckled to herself. The kitten heels moved out of Yule's sightline and away, clacking across the room with newfound vigor.

"Re-route funding to human testing, maybe they can buy you chairs," she said. The man gave her a sarcastic laugh, before following her back across the room. The door handle creaked as someone put their hand upon it and pulled.

Creak. Click.

Silence.

Yule let out a gasp and fell out from behind the sheet, struggling to scramble to his feet amid laden arms. After a few ragged, centering breaths, he looked around. The room was largely the way it was before, except for one key detail: one of the doors now stood ajar.

Despite himself, Yule froze. As much as his body cried out to flee, something compelled him to stay. They'd been talking about something in that room, he thought. A poisonous curiosity was in him now: a primal, unknowable feeling that something terrible and important lay close.

Step by step, he moved towards the door. As he approached, the air pressed harder around him, carrying a low, asymmetrical crackle of electricity on the deaf hum. Quietly, Yule pressed his shoulder against the white wood, and pushed.

The room beyond was large and bare, just like the former. The ceiling boiled with coils of wire and metal plates, running to places unknown through holes in the wall. Two thirds of the space was cut off by a large, seamless plate of thick glass, reinforced at the sides with black steel. But Yule wasn't looking at that.

He didn't scream. In the moment, it was like he forgot how. The camera dropped from his hand and quietly went to pieces on the floor.

There was no model in his mind for it. No comparison to beast nor man nor monster, a living void of knowing maybe twelve or fifteen feet long. Motionless it shifted, flickering back and forth between being and not: a hundred dog-like jaws twitched, sedated upon a huge steel platform; sickly strings of electricity rippled across it's skin, lighting the room in flashes.

Yule's heart raced. He could almost feel his pupils dilating, his jaw clenching, his stomach rolling, as if every single inch of his body rejected what he saw. The room seemed to spin, close inward then outward, a thousand insect legs of horror scratching at his head from the inside.

Then, the creature moved. An unguessable limb reared up and split, peeling like overripe fruit. A single, awful noise shook the glass: a braying, sucking sound, caught horrifically between a human gurgle and an animal roar.

And in reply, the room exploded. The dogs in the cages were all up on their feet. Barking, whining, gnashing their teeth against the sides of their cages as the one thing they had left to fear made itself known.

That was all Yule could take. He never made the decision to run, it was dictated to him by the very base of his being. The urgent, mindless need to flee, rubber-clad feet screeching on the tile as he tore towards the exit.

His legs hit the sluice with a heavy splash, though now the waters lay clearer. The stench of decay remained, but it didn't stop him gasping. And though nothing pursued him through that rotten out-vein, it felt like an escape. A desperate push through nausea and panic, to free himself from the jaws of the tunnel and flee.

He could barely fathom what he had seen. But he knew even that was far, far too much.

The rungs were slick beneath his hand, ascent made jerky and slow by the bag clenched in his fist. The fumes of the place made his head spin, peripherals darken, a feeling of blood-colored fire seething in every fiber. Yule knew that if it got worse, he would just go limp. Pass out, maybe.

Not now, he thought. Please, not now, not here. He was so close.

A screech. A give. The wheel turned and the hatch opened, and with a last, desperate groan of pain, Yule hauled himself up the final rungs and over the lip of the pit, struggling up with his shoulders like a land-drowning fish.

He lay there for a few moments, just letting his body drink air. Then, with a groan he climbed to his feet and, unexpected even to himself, ran. Hard and fast, like he had all the energy in the world. Even though he was out, his thoughts remained down there in the tunnel. That was what propelled him forward, to go north. Putting anxious distance between him and the sleeping form of the bunker.

Deep beneath his feet, the bunker thought of him, too. At least, in its own unliving way. Dead dreams, signaled only by the steady blink of a silent alarm, throbbing red inside the supply cabinet far below.

The run to the barrens was mercifully short. He stumbled often, slowing down to a crawl by the time the trees ended. Once or twice, Wittey's dim headlights flashed in the dark like firebugs, guiding him out of the forest and into the strange, flattened landscape of the old pine grove.

Once, it had been a cluster of dark, tall trees. But now, it looked like a hastily shaved face. A long, dark stream burbled through the dirt, cut deep and thick. Beyond, the land seized and undulated into a squat hill, overlooking the river. Atop it stood the Camaro, waiting.

Slowly he ascended, good hand pushing against his knee for extra force. Every step, the cube banged against his thigh, and clanked against the helmet inside the bag. When he finally crested the hill, Wittey was stood some ways away by the car.

"You made it," he said, offering him a smoke. Yule stopped and doubled over, shaking his head.

"You were right, they... shit..." he panted, looking up. "Something really, *really* fucked up is going on in there."

"You get pictures? Where's the camera—"

"It broke, it doesn't matter. You gotta listen to me," Yule insisted, wide eyes locking with Wittey's. "They're doing something to do with time travel. There's a lab, and animals and something I don't even know what the fuck to call."

Wittey's eyes widened, and his jaw went slack.

"What? How?" he asked, voice gone hoarse with urgency. "What did you get?"

Yule held up the bag, which clunked a little.

"These," he said. "Some notes, and… well, I don't know how it does it but something that erases people too. Listen, man, I don't know if they knew I was there, but we gotta get the fuck outta dodge. Somewhere safe."

"Good idea," Wittey replied, holding out a hand, "give me the bag, I'll start up the car."

"I'll throw it in the backseat," Yule replied, rounding the hood. But Wittey didn't move, almost insistently so.

"It can't go in the backseat. No space," he said. "I'll put it in the trunk, just hand it over."

"I'm already here, man, just get in the…" Yule replied, glancing down to the passenger side door. It all seemed to hit him at once through the adrenaline haze, like an oncoming train he didn't hear coming.

Fresh dirt on the tires, like it'd just doubled back from somewhere. Wittey's reflection in the wing mirror, hand reaching slowly and deliberately beneath his jacket. The dark outlines of bags piled high on every seat but the driver's side. No room for another person.

"You mother-fucker," Yule muttered, taking a step back. Beside him there was a soft, metallic click. The sound of a hammer teased back by a thumb.

"It's nothing personal, man," Wittey said.

"Oh yeah? Well it feels *real* personal, given that you're personally pointing a goddamn gun at me," Yule replied, teeth gritted.

"Just give me the bag, Yule. I don't want to kill you," Wittey said. Yule stood his ground, plastic bundle still clutched to his chest.

"You're probably right about that. I don't think that's gonna stop you, though," he said, slowly turning around. "If I'm honest, I'd say the only reason you haven't done it already is because you don't wanna damage whatever's in here."

Wittey stood before him, silhouetted by moonlight. He held the gun limply at the hip, like someone from an old noir movie. In the half-light Yule could see his face was almost expressionless—and yet somehow, incalculably ugly.

"You plan to do this the whole time? When you were telling me all that bullshit about freedom fighting, you were just imagining putting a bullet in my back?" Yule insisted, taking a tentative half step back. No gun, he thought. No ride. He didn't know what was gonna come after stalling, but the only other option was dying in a rubber suit. Wittey's expression changed to one of fear, veiled barely by frustration. The gun barrel waved in the air as he spoke.

"You don't get it. You just don't get it; this is bigger than you. It's bigger than me, I can't risk a leak. I can't."

"If it's bigger than *you*, how come *I'm* the one with a gun pointed at me?" Yule replied. Another half step back, but this time too obviously. Wittey's hand flew up, arm straight and pistol hovering ready to fire. Yule froze up.

"Come on, man. Just put down the gun," he pleaded, slowly and deliberately. "I'll give you the bag, and I won't tell a goddamn soul. Nobody."

Wittey shook his head, gun still poised.

"I reckon you wouldn't. But it doesn't matter. You went into their territory; they've probably got your face on a dozen cameras by now. Hell, you were already on their radar when we met, you've been dead from the goddamn start. I need to *live*—and to do that, I gotta make sure they can't be led back to me, even if they torture you."

Yule gritted his teeth. This didn't feel good. This wasn't going in his direction. The thoughts weren't coming out, they were all tangled together, deadened in the blur of barely suppressed panic.

"You talk an awful lot for a guy who's out to shoot somebody," he said, slurring a little. He didn't know if it was the right thing to say or not. Maybe the realistic part of him knew it didn't matter. Wittey's finger tensed visibly against the trigger, and Yule closed his eyes.

He always hoped in his last moments he'd be alright with passing on. But all he found himself doing was hoping for a miracle before the gunshot rippled through his quiet, blind space. Maybe he wished too hard, because when a noise finally came it didn't herald death—somehow, it sounded worse.

"Shit," Wittey said.

Yule opened his eyes. The gun hung at Wittey's side, pointed towards the floor. His eyes were fixed on something in the distance, no longer glassy with the promise of grim work. Now, they were locked firmly in the present, and terrified for it.

Yule turned his head to see what he was looking at, and his blood ran cold.

Headlights. Nearly a dozen of them, dancing in the darkness of the trees. And, to Yule's horror, getting closer by the second. Wittey skittered towards the driver's side door like a frightened rat and flung it open, gun abandoned on the bare ground. Yule just stood there. Stunned. Like he was watching a storm blow in. It was only as the truck engine roared to life beside him that he realized he wasn't dreaming. And by then, the fleet of black trucks was already at the bottom of the hill.

The dozen seconds that followed seemed to take minutes through the adrenaline lens. Yule turned, lungs already flooding with air. A single thought throbbed through his brain. Primal, and simple.

Drop it, he thought, eyes locked on the bag. *That's what they want. You don't need it—you just have to run.*

As if answering by itself, his good hand flew out to the side. Fingers unclenched, plastic grazing against his palm as the bag tore itself away from him.

And then, it was gone. Arced away over the lip of the hill, and down into the dark stream below. Yule never heard it hit the water, but then again, he couldn't hear anything. He was already running.

Thundering down the hill, not knowing where he intended to go. Feet pounding, lungs burning. Engines behind him. Voices. Flashlights cast his own shadow in front of him as he found flat ground, bobbing in time with pursuing feet, chasing down after him through the tree line and into the dark. As Yule burst through the undergrowth, he felt electrified. As if he was seeing and hearing everything at once, like a spooked deer. But the truth was, when the shot that felled him finally came, he didn't even know it had happened.

All he felt was the pain. A sting, and the sensation of something cold sticking into his back. Not a bullet, though: a needle. As its payload spread through his bloodstream, his legs quickly went from underneath him like a knife through the ribs, unexpected and sharp. He collided face-first with the ground as he fell, cheek smashing against rocky dirt.

After that, he didn't see anything at all though the chemical haze. Not the men in their black vans, dragging him through the pine barrens. Not the dark water, thick and gurgling, as it ran blind through the bends of the wood. And not the strange, semi-translucent shape of a plastic bag, surfacing like a pale, dead jellyfish.

Floating down the river, for all the night to see.

METAMORPHOSIS

AMESVILLE, 1977

He wondered how it remembered. They said it did at school, even when it was just goo, somewhere between caterpillar and butterfly. Ollie smiled, stroking the side of the chrysalis with a cautious forefinger. He could almost imagine all the little thoughts bouncing around inside it, like they were swimming in Jell-O. Part of him hoped the goo remembered what it felt like to be a caterpillar, once it had become something beautiful. It seemed sad, otherwise.

He straightened up, eyes straining to fix on the pale blue shape in the bushes. Around him, the night was quiet and warm. No wind stirred the trees or waved the grass, and the only noise was the gentle buzz of crickets, and the burbling of the stream beside him.

He took a deep breath in through his nose and smiled to himself.

The world was quiet, out here. Safe, and tranquil.

"T... T-t..." he muttered under his breath, tongue leaping of its own accord. "T-tranquil."

He was getting better. Day by day. Maybe he'd show Yule in the arcade how he was doing, how he could say almost all the names of the games now. That'd be good, he thought. He hadn't seen him in a while.

He walked along the river awhile, beaten-up sneakers bending on the slick rocks. The moon was high in the sky now, throwing silver half-light down on the landscape. The entire night had a taut, electric feeling in it, which pulsed and pulled in the stillness. Like something exciting was about to happen.

He felt safe, there in the night. Unseen, and unheeded. The darkness stretched around him like a pair of shielding arms, obscuring his little form amidst the leaping shadows. Here, he thought, nobody could touch him. His palm gingerly ghosted over the big, finger-shaped bruises on his upper arm.

Nobody.

As he reached the bend in the river, Ollie paused. The night purred with the clack and bang of engines, rattling from somewhere far away. He looked around. Not afraid, just curious. There wasn't any way to drive into the little valley behind the house. The only ways in were through the back fence or down the stream.

Ollie turned towards it and squinted at the dark surface of the water, looking for glimmers of moonlight caught in the flow. But something else caught his attention.

It was floating. All slippery and water-washed, waving with the current against an outcrop of rocks. Ollie frowned. For a moment, it seemed the limp silhouette of something white and slimy dragging itself from the murk, but another moment in the moonlight showed its true, less fantastical form: a plastic bag, weighed down by something submerged below the surface. He drew a little closer.

Someone had tied the top closed. Tight, too—enough to trap a lot of air. There must be something inside, he thought, picking through the rocks towards it. Like a message in a bottle, or a smuggler's treasure. Maybe, he considered with rising excitement, it was meant for him.

He reached the edge of the burbling water and leaned down. Teetered over the lip, face scrunched with the effort of keeping his balance as he reached. Leaning, on his toes, a little further... he could just hook a finger...

His weight shifted. There was a sickening lurch as his foot slid down into nothing and for a moment, the moonlit sky whirled around him. Then came the cold.

The stream wasn't deep. Rather, just deep enough. His back never hit the bottom, but the surface never left his sight, whirling above him. And all around him, water. Dark and formless, dragging him deeper and further away from the world above. But that was just until the need for air and the rush of water up his nostrils sent Ollie kicking upward.

He surfaced with an almost surprised gasp, treading water towards the bank. In one hand, he clutched the wet snout of the plastic bag in a triumphant fist.

When he finally hit solid ground again, he put the bag down and looked himself over. He was soaked from buttons to bones in stream water. Now, the night wind felt bitter on his damp skin. If Ma saw him in this condition, she'd… well, she wouldn't do much. She'd probably not say a word to him for a whole day. That was bad enough. Between the sudden discomfort and pronounced fear of his mother's wrath, Ollie almost forgot about the plastic bag. Lying deflated, almost dejectedly on the floor by his feet.

But his bounty was not forgotten for long. Not after he opened it, to see what lay inside.

His eyes widened. Brightened.

It was a helmet. A heavy one, too. Like the kind that army officers would wear but rounder and newer, all black and shiny. He reached inside and grabbed it, letting the rest fall a short way to the floor as he put it on his head.

It was far too big and slipped over his forehead even when it was buckled, but Ollie didn't care. He looked like a spaceman, he thought. A Martian policeman. He gave the helmet a sharp rap with his knuckles, delighting in the fact his head didn't feel it.

But the chill wind rose to remind him where he was. It was late, he thought. He should get home. Something in him tugged him away too, a kind of childish urgency. The innocent fear that whoever the bag belonged to might come back and take away his new toy.

He picked up the bag and adjusted the helmet. Before him, the land rose in an ill-kept tangle of trees and vines, ending in the unseen back fence somewhere beyond.

Like a moth in the dark, Ollie flitted away from the moonlit space and out of sight.

The hole in the fence was just bigger than he was. Hidden by a thick curtain of creepers that had erupted over the wall some years before. Most of the yard was like that past the hard, concrete patio, and by night it was almost solidly black. But Ollie liked the dark. It was a place where being little and observant was a good thing, like a mouse between the walls. As he ranged back towards the house with his treasures in tow, his big eyes flicked towards the upstairs window.

Unlit. Ma hadn't gone to bed yet, he thought. She wouldn't have come to check on him. If he could just make it back upstairs, he'd be home free.

With wet hands, it was even easier to slide the glass back door open with a flattened palm. Slowly and deliberately, so there was little more than the sliding chatter of plastic on plastic. It was so quiet, in fact, that when a noise finally came Ollie nearly cried out in surprise. But then, if he had, his yell would've had company

It was high and fast. More of a choked shout than a scream, terminating suddenly as something in the kitchen shifted against the counter. Ollie knew what that sound meant, and it made his heart shudder.

He froze without meaning to. The world suddenly felt tight. Small.

Ollie could hear him, too. In there, with her. Breathing in heavy, rumbling bursts. The sound was shaped like him. Hulking and filthy with hair. Warm and foul like a dog's breath.

He was an animal, Ollie thought. And he had to get away from him.

He kicked off his shoes at the door and padded forward, wet socks making a soft *pffsht* noise against the bare boards. He was quiet, he thought. Small, like a little mouse. He could make it to the stairs, turn the corner, and get away from…

Him.

He was stood in the kitchen doorway. Vast shadow filling the frame, blocking out the light. And now, Pa's eyes were fixed on Ollie. Wide with silent, white-ringed fury. Behind him, Ma leaned up against the kitchen counter, holding her face in her hands.

Ollie gulped. Tried to breathe past the stone in his throat.

"I-I w… w-was j… j-j…"

"Living room," Pa rumbled. "Now."

Pa's bulk shifted towards him, and Ollie flinched. Did as he was told and ran down the hall into the living room.

The television buzzed quietly in the corner, until Pa turned it off with a meaty paw. The remains of a TV dinner and some scotch were left out on a folding table, pushed aside when someone had gotten out of the chair. Ollie could imagine why.

He hated the noise of it worst of all. How the cries just stopped like that after he hit her. That was the part he could never get out of his head. And now he was going to get it, too.

Pa sat down in the armchair like a reclining gorilla, fists knotted up against his lap. Ollie hovered by the doorway, until his father sharply gestured to the sofa.

"Sit," he said, glowering, "and take that shit off."

After a moment of confusion, Ollie remembered he was still wearing the helmet. With hurried, clumsy fingers he unbuckled the strap and set them both down behind the sofa. Hidden, as if that might make Pa forget about them.

Then he sat. Shrunken, as if he might just slip between the couch cushions and hide. For a few moments, neither of them spoke. Pa just stared with bloodshot, bleary eyes. Ollie knew when he was about to speak, because he seemed to take a few practice breaths first. Little belches of hot, stinking breath, as if he was revving up.

He'd not been this drunk in a long time. That was bad.

"Your ma got a call from school today," he growled, brow hardening, "some teacher, sayin' you said some other kids were pickin' on you. That right?"

Ollie nodded, and Pa let out a low rumble.

"Look at me," he said. Ollie pulled his eyes up, cautiously meeting his father's across the room. He nodded again.

"Y-yes," he said.

"Paul Brennan. That the kid? An' don't you lie."

Ollie nodded, not breaking eye contact. Pa rolled back into the seat a little, eyes burning and glassy. An old silverback, staring through zoo glass and seeing nothing.

"Mm. Paul Brennan," he grunted after a few seconds. "He's Harper Brennan's boy. Met him while I was out at Stilgoe's. Says his boy's been suspended because of you."

"He c-called me a f-f—"

"Shut your mouth when I'm talking to you!" Pa yelled, lunging forward in his seat. Ollie's jaw snapped closed, and he flinched. A moment of tension fluttered between them.

And then, Pa leaned back. But the fury never left his stare, or the throbbing veins in his neck.

"I work with Harper," he said, "he's a decent man. And he's real hurt by what you done to his boy, Ollie. Real hurt."

"B-but I—"

"He's gonna get held back a year. And that means Harper's got another year to wait for full-time help on the farm. He's thinkin' of pullin' Paul outta school entirely. All because you *told* on him," Pa finished.

Ollie's jaw dropped a little. He didn't know how to reply.

"W-what was I s-suh-supposed to do?" he asked quietly. Pa rumbled deeply through his nose and settled into his chair, like he'd just been asked the dumbest question on earth.

"You shoulda knocked his jaw. Fought him, for Christ's sake, made sure he didn't do it again. Then the school woulda gone to me an' Harper, and we'd have known it was just boys bein' boys."

"But it wasn't! He p-punched me and c-c-alled me a fa-f-faggot! He d-does it every day, he g-gets all his f-f-riends t-to as well!" Ollie protested, voice raising without him meaning to. Pa responded like an angry hound, rising a little on his hackles.

"And he's gonna keep doin' it, until you act like a man and stand up for yourself!" he said, one hand slamming down on the chair's arm. For a moment, the act cleared the fury from him. Replaced it with tired frustration, deep and glowering like old coals. Pa rumbled again, crackling and deep like a low fire.

"Look, we live in a community, son. And when you act, you gotta think of the community first. Harper cutting back his business means higher grocery prices. Somethin' like Paul Brennan getting pulled back hurts the whole town—and if you're the one who tells on him, that's your fault. And I tell you what, too: ain't nobody gonna respect you until you start solvin' your own problems instead of cryin' to whoever's in charge."

He leaned forward, elbows on his knees. The acrid stench of whiskey rolled off him and wafted through the air. A reminder, and a warning.

"Your ma's been coddlin' you. Going in with all that touchy-feely speech therapy stuff. But she knows she's not meant to do that anymore. It stops now."

Ollie's eyes widened. He tried to speak, to express the yawning shock in his belly, but nothing came out. Just air, like a fish drowning on land. Pa grunted and leaned back again.

"It's clear to me you ain't gonna improve unless you stop relyin' on other people to solve your problems. Now on, you're gonna grow some balls and speak properly, you understand? No more waiting for some shrink to make you better—you do it yourself. And tomorrow, you're gonna march straight into that principal's office, and tell 'em Paul Brennan didn't do nothin' wrong," he said.

For a moment, Ollie was frozen in his seat. As if his body was preparing itself for whatever reaction was coming next.

What came was a sob. From somewhere deep in his gut. He didn't mean to—it just spilt out of his mouth, followed by another, and another. Ollie felt a few fat tears well at his eyes and break free, rolling down his cheek like hot marbles. They distorted his vision and turned everything wavy, like he was under the river again.

That was probably why he didn't see the smack coming.

It was hard and sharp, an open palm thudding over his cheek. He saw the obscuring teardrops tear themselves from his face, flung by the sudden motion, and drop in an arc to the floor below.

His ears rung. The sudden, intense distress had been replaced by something numb. Disbelief, and yet somehow the feeling he had been expecting it since he'd sat down.

"I'm s-suh-sorry," he said quietly. "I don't und-d—"

In a single, well-practiced movement, Pa withdrew his hand, and formed it into an accusatory finger.

"Stop that," he said, voice hard, "right this goddamn second. *Men* don't cry."

Ollie remained silent, staring straight ahead. He felt like he was dreaming. A hand slowly raised up to feel the bright, hot patch on his cheek. When his fingers felt up against it, it burned. Pa scowled, taking his silence as another invitation to berate him.

"You gotta shape up, Ollie. I fought in 'Nam—if I acted the way you did in boot camp, they'd beat the shit outta me. And I'd have deserved it," he said, shaking his head. Then, he suddenly came forward, hand stretching out and clamping onto Ollie's shoulder.

"You gotta…" he said, before trailing off. He frowned, bleary eyes tracking away from Ollie's, and down towards his palm. As he raised it up and towards the light, it glistened. Like a wet stone.

Confusion came into his face for a second. Then it slid into anger again.

"Why are your clothes soaking wet?" he asked, voice low. Ollie went white.

"I-I fell. In the b-bathroom," he said, voice no higher than a whisper. For a moment, he could see the anger curdle to rage in Pa's lumpen face.

"You been out to that creek again," he said, voice low and monotone. Ollie shook his head feverishly.

"N-no! I fell—"

"That where you found that shit?" Pa interrupted, burning stare dropping towards the bag on the floor. Ollie kept shaking his head, clinging to the lie for dear life.

"No!" he repeated, "I p-p-puh-p-promise!"

Pa stood up out of his chair, slowly. Deliberately. His nostrils flared once, and he raised a finger at the helmet.

"Put it on," he said.

"What?"

"I said put it on!" Pa yelled, voice filling the room. Ollie leaped from the sofa and near enough landed on his belly, scrambling towards the discarded helmet. He clumsily put it on, still sliding over his head with every movement. Once it was affixed, Ollie stood facing the door out of the living room. Too scared to turn around.

But when Pa told him to, he did. Just like always.

He stood about a foot away, huge form filling Ollie's view. His hands were hung limp and ready by his side, one already balled into a fist. Clenching and unclenching, like he was warming it up. Even if he couldn't see it, Ollie could feel his gaze on him. Hard, and furious.

"How dare you lie to me in my own house," he said, voice dripping with slurred fury. "You little lyin' bastard, sittin' there, cryin' your eyes out, when just now!"

Smack. A blow against the side of the helmet, so hard it knocked Ollie off his feet. Even with the metal in between him and Pa's fist, it made his ears ring. He toppled, landing on the floor in a heap.

He simply stared, stunned again. In that moment, all the pain and panic receded. Sucked away for a second like the tide around his ankles. All Ollie found he could think about was the fact Pa hadn't ever hit him that hard before.

"Get up," Pa said, arms back down and ready. Ollie obeyed.

This time, the strike came without a word. Harder, overhand, like he was swinging a hammer. Ollie stayed on his feet, but barely. His vision was blurring a little. He felt nauseous.

Pa took a step back, reeling a little from the force of his own punch. He let out a ragged, wet breath, spittle dancing between his lips.

"Don't you ever fuckin' lie to me, boy. You wear a fake face and I swear to the Lord Jesus Christ almighty I'll smack it straight offa you!"

Another strike. And another and another, punctuating the last three words with force. Pa's fist rained down on the helmet again and again, until finally Ollie fell down.

He didn't feel much at all. He couldn't even hear whatever Pa was screaming at him.

It was only a few seconds after that he became aware of himself lying on the floor. The helmet lay askew on his painful, pulsing head. His ears were still ringing too bad to hear, but he could still see. The red of Pa's blood, dripping off his knuckles and onto the carpet. Crimson dancing amongst light spots in his peripherals.

His eyes slid down to the dull, translucent white of the plastic bag, warning label visible inside.

"Warning, danger of death," it said. Ollie felt something in his belly turn. It called and he answered, drawing it in close to his curled-up form. He had no idea what it was. What it did.

"Get up," said Pa.

But he trusted it. Trusted what it promised.

Death.

"*Get up!*" Pa yelled, dragging Ollie to his feet by the shirt.

His fingers unhinged the safety clasp. Curled around the metal catch.

Behind him, the slithering sound of Pa removing his belt filled the room. He was saying something, but Ollie couldn't hear. Not for ringing, but for the sound of thunder. The electric whine of something never felt before. Like he was flooded with the night, numb and safe and impossibly dark.

In secret, guilty dreams, Ollie had wondered what he'd say. But when the time finally came, he didn't say a word. Didn't need to. The feeling was enough.

He turned around, box held at chest height. Pa's eyes narrowed for a second, dimly considering Ollie's hands on the catch. That was all he got, before Ollie's delicate fingers pulled sharply upward, and the hatch opened.

Light. Thick and sickly green, which flooded from the gap in the box and blasted the room in blinding brightness. The smell of ozone filled the air, crackling and whining. Ollie gritted his teeth and held the box up further, as if it were a shield. He could feel it rattling, heating up in his hands, burning—but he held on.

And he never looked away. Not for a second, not even when the light stung his eyes. From deep down inside of him came the unnameable thing he could no longer deny—he wanted the monster dead, he wanted Pa dead. And he would watch him die, just to make sure.

From the center of the light he writhed. Clothes sputtering and burning away from his body in gouts of flame. He dropped his belt, which uncoiled on the floor.

Pa held up his hands. It looked like he screamed, but the whining of the box was too loud to tell. For a single second, his eyes locked with Ollie's, all of the anger having fled from them. The look of dominance, the look of rage without a direction, all gone.

Now there was only fear. Fear of death, fear of pain. An animal's fear.

The box smoked and crackled. The light grew to its apex, and then, just like that, Pa was gone. Just... *gone*. As if pulled apart by a thousand hooks and made into nothing. With a cry, Ollie pushed the latch back down. The box closed, and the light receded.

He fell to his hands and knees, letting it drop and bounce under the couch. Behind his eyes, he could see the throbs of his headache in red vein lines. It felt strange, too. Like something on the surface of it was tingling.

All that remained of Pa was his belt buckle, which sat half-melted on the floor. Slowly, Ollie crept forward and picked it up, as if to confirm he wasn't dreaming.

He... Had he really...?

Without thinking, Ollie stashed the buckle under the couch along with the box, and then crawled back to the bag. The only thing left inside was a thick stack of documents. Feverishly, he pored over it. Looking for any sign, any explanation of what he had done.

"Ollie? Ollie, honey?" came his mother's voice, strangely high and carefree. "Is everything alright, I can smell smoke."

Ollie quickly shoved the bag and the helmet under the couch, scrambling to hide them away before his mother came in. As she rounded the door, a renewed stab of fear went through him. What would she do? What would she say, when she came into the living room and found Pa was gone?

Smiling. She was actually smiling, holding a hand over her eye but *smiling*. It quickly turned to a look of concern when she saw him on the floor but Ollie swore he saw it like sunspots for seconds afterwards.

"Sweetheart?" she said, rushing over to him. "What happened? You look dazed."

Ollie paused for a moment, stunned. Then, he nodded. Tried to smile.

"I'm f-fine," he said, as if he could barely believe it himself. Her hands came down to feel through his hair, checking for cuts and bruises. Tender, but purposeful. She looked down at him, one eye nestled in bright purple bruising. Ollie knitted his brow, despite the fact it made his head hurt.

"Ma," he asked, "how'd you d-do that? What happened t-to your eye?"

Ma's hand went up to her own face, as if she'd forgotten all about it. Her eyebrows raised, and she flashed him a quick, almost embarrassed smile.

"Gosh, I… Well I don't remember," she said, examining it in the wall mirror. "I must've walked into a doorframe. God, I wonder what the girls are gonna say about it tomorrow."

She turned back around.

"Could you go get mommy some ice?" she said. Ollie nodded and went out into the hallway without protest. He felt like he was floating. Like everything wasn't real, the feel of the freezer door, the sensation of air on his face. But… it was. It was all real, he'd really done it, he'd…

His fingers tightened on the ice. Cold. Numbing.

They were safe. Finally safe.

He walked back into the room, marveling now at how large it seemed. Ma was sat on the couch, directly above the box and the helmet. Completely unaware, just holding her beautiful face. As he watched her, Ollie felt himself smiling. Grinning, even.

He didn't quite know the emotions yet. Hadn't given them name or form in his thoughts. All Ollie knew was that there was no joy in him, and yet, he had never felt so happy as he held out the bag.

"Here," he said. Ma took it and pressed it on her eye with a relieved sigh.

"You're such a good boy," she cooed.

"I think we have some frozen peas as well, if the ice doesn't work," Ollie said, looking over the room again. It was all so vast. So clean now. Like his stink had all been washed away. As he finished his sentence, Ma's head perked up. Her smirk bloomed into a smile, and her good eye fell warmly on him.

"Ollie," she said. "You didn't stutter once."

Ollie smiled back at her. He hadn't even thought of that. He nodded and sat down.

"I didn't," he said. Ma reached forward and ran her fingers through his hair. Teasing at the thick black locks, not seeming to mind the fact it was still wet. He could feel the warmth spreading from her palms and onto his skin.

But he found it didn't reach further than that. He felt all cold inside, like the dark stream.

And it felt good.

"I knew your hard work at speech therapy would pay off. I'm so proud of you," she said. Her hands came down to cup his cheeks, raising his forehead to her lips.

"You are a little wonder, Oliver Carnassus," she said.

POLYBIUS

AMESVILLE, 1993

Trevor thought it looked like a haunted wreck. Cal thought it was more of a slasher movie set. The only thing they could agree on, stood out in the unwinding light, was that neither of them wanted to go in.

"Do you think we should've brought a weapon?" Trevor asked, feet firmly planted on the sidewalk.

"It's an abandoned arcade, Trev. I don't think we're gonna get hurled into a gunfight," Cal replied, still not moving.

"But still, we should have something right? Like a knife, or a spear."

"Because I bet the spear store is still open," Cal replied, going forward to try the door handle. It only rattled in the frame, locked fast.

"Well, there goes one plan," he said, turning to face Trevor—only to find he wasn't there. He was maybe a few feet to the left, squinting down the alleyway.

"Trev?" Cal said flatly. Trevor didn't move, glancing at him quickly before returning to his squint.

"I think there's a side door, down there," he said, nodding. Cal went to stand beside him, focusing on the spot Trevor's eyes were trained on.

He was right. Down at the end of the narrow alley, half hidden in a drift of garbage bags, was a sliver of cracked white paint. And beside it, between wood and doorframe, lay a thin strip of solid blackness. A way inside.

"Nice one, eagle eye," Cal said, moving towards it. The entire alleyway was adrift with ancient garbage bags, spread like withered black snowballs across the slimy concrete. Together they picked their way through, tossing bags aside to mine the drift. After a few minutes, the door was clear enough to pull open a little.

Cal wrapped his fingers around the edge and tugged. The hinges whined and seized halfway through its swing, but there was enough room to squeeze through. Cal peeked around the lip of the door, and into the dark.

The inside of Joytown smelt exactly how Cal had expected it to—but that wasn't exactly good. It was a stale, almost unexplainable scent: the heavy dullness of wet carpet and tobacco stains, lathered with the stinging tang of animal droppings, mildew and ammonia. Rows upon rows of dark, unpowered arcade machines stood like black obelisks in the gloom, patterned with dirt and dust.

But there was something else there, too. Something familiar, yet out of place. The feeling of electricity, tingling behind the wall of musk and decay. The briefest hint of ozone in the air.

"We should get a move on, otherwise it's back to square one," he said, shuddering. "What are we meant to be looking for?"

Trevor ran a hand over the nearest machine and examined the thick black layer of dust which came up clinging to his palm.

"I don't know," he said, hurriedly wiping it on his jeans. Cal frowned.

"Trev, you were the one who said the building was a clue, what do you mean you don't know?" he asked. Trevor's hands flew up in an exaggerated shrug.

"I dunno! I guess we look for something weird and… not right," he said, appraising the gloomy maze of cabinets that stretched into the darker, more solid parts of the building. Cal glanced back over his shoulder, towards a door behind the counter.

"I'll check over there. You take the cabinets," he said, gesturing further in. "You're basically half computer, maybe you'll find something."

As if in response, Trevor's wandering hand jerked back with a high-pitched snap as part of a cabinet's plastic cladding came away in his grip.

"Something tells me most of these aren't gonna be working," he said, wandering into the standing mass. Cal felt a brief flutter of anxiety as he passed out of sight. The longer they stayed, the more he found himself feeling that something wasn't quite right.

The office was unlocked, and the entrance swung open with a creaking whine. Nothing barred it on the other side except for cobwebs. Cal kept the door wide open, partially for what little light shone through, and partially because he feared not having an immediate escape route.

A battered old desk squatted next to a rusted filing cabinet in the center of the room. As Cal drew closer, he could make out the shape of an ashtray, this time piled high with cigarette butts like a confused mountain peak, spilling onto piles of faded paper strewn across the rest of the wooden top. Receipts, it looked like. Earnings and expenditures, the former of which seemed abysmally small by the end. It was almost a relief to see it had closed for normal reasons, rather than death or mysterious disappearance. Joytown hadn't been killed by time travel, just home gaming systems.

Cal turned his head towards the filing cabinet, drawers askew. With a strained pull, the top drawer came loose, screeching against the rusted rail as it opened up.

Inside, papers sat in quiet rows between plastic dividers. They were organized by year, stretching back to 1972. Cal flicked through them with his fingers, scanning over the text. They mostly looked the same as what he'd found on the desks. Earnings and expenditures. A story of success and failure told through the uninterested narrative of digits and dollar signs.

His fingers danced across the rows. His eyes fell on the section labeled "1977" in grubby handwriting. Even if he was expecting nothing, it didn't hurt to check.

Lazily, his index finger slid over each of the documents in turn.

Earnings and expenses. Earnings and expenses. And then, like a bolt from the blue, something distinctly out of place. Something weird.

"*Ordr Form,*" it said in messy, hand-typed letters, "*Howard Triptree.*" What lay below didn't look standard, either—judging from the spelling mistakes, the owner had drafted it up himself. "*Dlivry of one (1) arcade csbinet SERIAL: P-003,*" followed by a name box. Cal mouthed it out to himself.

"Po-ly-bius," he said. As he finished, another sound came worming its way into the room. Trevor.

"Cal?" he said, voice quiet and thin. "I think I found something."

Forms still clutched in his hands, Cal made his way quickly across the room and back out into the main lobby. Trevor was stood some ways into the maze of machines, almost at the back wall. At first Cal couldn't see what he was looking at, but as he pressed further in, he saw flashes.

Something huge and pale, occasionally peeking through the gaps between the machines. But when he finally came to Trevor's side and saw it in full, he still wasn't quite sure what he was looking at.

It was something big, and boxy. Covered up in a thick, yellowing dust sheet from top to bottom, it sat almost flush against the old wall, suggesting nothing of what lay beneath save for three black cables which emerged to fit into the wall and floor like probing tendrils.

Trevor was stood a few feet away from it. As if it might bite.

"What do you think it is?" he asked. Cal took a hesitant step towards it. The monolith thing stood stock still, waiting.

"I guess we better find out," he said. Half to Trevor, and half to himself. Cloth kissed his fingers. Wrapped. Pulled.

In a single motion the sheet sighed into a pile on the floor. What lay beneath offered no answers; only more questions.

It was an arcade machine: pristine in comparison to the dark, mold-speckled monoliths stood in watch around them, swooping plastic still neon bright. Cal's eyes were drawn up towards the hard-edged, space-age writing slapped across the top, mirrored in his mind in ink and paper tones: "Polybius."

Trevor gave him a nudge. Cal glared at him.

"What? Why not you?" he asked.

"You're the one with the tin head, you look at it," Trevor replied, taking a step back. "I'll keep watch over here. Far, far away from it."

With a breath held tightly in his belly, Cal made his move. At first, he just sort of looked at it, hoping a second sweep of the flashlight might reveal something he missed.

Yet now that he understood the outlines, he realized the cabinet didn't look normal at all. It was all asymmetrical in an oddly organic, troubling kind of way. One that made something in his spine crawl. Parts had obviously been added later and hastily covered up, not to mention the thick cables running from the base to places unknown.

Cal brought up the yellowed papers and squinted.

"This got sent out to Howard Triptree… why is it back here?" he muttered, his hand ghosting over the control board. It had been torn out and replaced with an array of switches and dials, all tuned to specific ranges and states. Like they'd been left that way on purpose, or whoever used it last hadn't had time to reset.

"How do you turn these things on?" he asked. Trevor let out a small, awkward whine through the corner of his mouth, and shuffled in place.

"I dunno, Cal, I really feel like we should leave this alone. At least talk to Leslie about it first."

"And what if we get flashed back before we can, Trev?" Cal replied, going to his hands and knees. His fingertips traced down to a switch near the bottom and clicked.

A hum ran through the soles of his shoes. The feeling of something under the floor spinning up. The entire arcade seemed to disappear entirely into blackness, drowned out by the isolated bubble of cathode ray light.

And then, it flickered. Alternated between dead and alive every couple of seconds, barely holding onto life. Cal's eyes were drawn to a hole punched through the upper corner of the screen, bleeding cracks. Writing appeared onscreen. Occasionally it would glitch as the screen died, lines of uniform code leaping into fragment lines before reverting.

"Trev, come look at this," Cal hissed, creeping forward. The lack of a reply didn't cross his mind as strange. All he saw was the writing, hung upon the blinking screen.

Even when he got close enough to see it, Cal didn't understand. It was random gibberish, mashed together in sets of brackets and dots. He saw a few things like "frequency" in there, but what exactly they meant wasn't clear. The only thing he really understood was the last line, so familiar from a hundred nights spent playing text adventure games.

>Y/N?

Yes or no. Yes or no to *what?*

"Trev, get over here," he repeated, slightly louder. For a few seconds, there was no answer from the blackness behind him.

"He'll be over in a minute," replied a voice. But not Trevor's.

Cal wheeled around, heart flying into his throat. Two silhouettes slid out from the dark, like the blackness itself sprouting shape.

Trevor entered first, whimpering. Then a long arm slithered into view, curled tight around his neck, which bloomed into a man shape, ushering Trevor forward into the light. When he spoke, his yellow teeth shone golden in the CRT glow.

"Step away from it," he said. Cal didn't move, even though he wanted to. His knees felt like they'd collapse under him if he stopped supporting himself on the cabinet. And yet, something in him bubbled. Bristled and reared, like a cornered rat.

"Let him go, and I will," he said, though his voice carried little threat. The yellow-toothed man smiled, but it was more mildly surprised than happy.

"I feel like it's only fair to be straight with you," he said, bringing up a pistol. "All you're doing right now is haggling your way down from head shot to gut shot."

His thumb rasped slowly back on the hammer. Beside it, Trevor let out a little whimper. His wide eyes had been focused on Cal since he'd come into the light. The two stared at each other for a moment. Caught. Like they were floating in a wave they knew was going to crash into the shore.

Cal tried desperately to think straight through the liquid whine of panic in his ears. With a single, shaking step, he went forward. Palms up, and eyes wide. The yellow-toothed man turned the gun back towards Trevor's throat, and nodded to the cabinet.

"Who told you about the time machine? How'd you find it?" he said.

Cal froze.

"The time machine…" he muttered, tempted to look back but held in place by the soundless threat of noise and death. Something odd bloomed in his heart. Like excitement, but grimmer. His mind's eye cast itself behind him, and at the question looming onscreen.

Yes or no, asked the time machine.

"I don't know what you mean," he said. Trevor's eyes widened in silent terror, but the yellow-toothed man hardly reacted.

"You make a single move and I'll blow your friend's throat out," he said.

Cal clenched his jaw. Tried to straighten up a little, fingers feeling ever so slowly up towards the keyboard, space mapped out in his muscle memory. But his eyes never left Trevor's, not for a second, no matter how painful the confusion in his face was. What else could he do?

"Survival" asked the time machine. "Yes or no?"

Trevor's sobs of fear had gone quiet, drowned in the widened pleading of his eyes. Every fiber of his being, every terrified nerve called out to his friend in the dark.

Please, they said, *don't.*

Cal liked to think his eyes said he was sorry. Or that he was terrified, or that he knew what he'd promised. That they weren't out of time.

All the time in the world, asked the machine. Yes, or no?

He never heard the gun fire. He saw the moment it came up as he tore his eyes from Trevor, hand coming down heavy on what he prayed was the right key.

Or, maybe he did, and mistook it for the crackling roar that rose up in his ears. The feeling of a hundred thousand hooks ran over every inch of him, like twine was threaded through every atom, yanking in a different direction. Pulling him apart, pulling everything apart, the very fabric of him ripping and bursting unknown colors in a cascade. Reversing, now falling, now breaking apart all at the same time, before finally it clapped against itself, harder than Cal had ever felt.

The universe cascaded inwards. Air filled his lungs. Solid ground, and gasping breath.

DEEPER STILL

THE BUNKER, 1977

Swing. Swing. Swing.

Lights passed overhead.

Like pulses.

Swing. Swing. Swing.

Were they moving?

Was he moving?

It came in stops and starts. Lots of ceilings. Sleep, then ceilings, and someone in his mouth. Prying his teeth with latex gloved hands. More ceilings.

A van. A car, maybe. Concrete, and then…

Swing. Swing.

Glare.

He'd stopped.

At first the white haze threatened to drag him back to black again. He didn't fight it. But this time, it only tugged. Jostled his nervous system like a bad guest on the way out.

His thoughts started to solidify. He became aware of the glaring light watching above him, and a shadow cast by some unseen figure at his head. The walls were made of concrete and dark, reflected glass. The sound of metal scraping on something filled the room.

He could hear the figure moving.

Yule squeezed his eyes shut and clenched his jaw. His clothes were rustling. He could barely feel it, but he could hear. They were reaching down and moving his sleeve. Were they injecting him? Oh god, were they executing him?

He let out an unwilling yelp of fear as the tugging on his wrist got harder. And then, he stopped. Something was loosening. And then again on the other. Footsteps. A button being pressed, metal on metal, then... silence. Yule opened his eyes and looked down. Unconsciously, his right palm rose to be examined. Just up in the air, like it was greeting him.

They'd undone the straps. Yule sat up, and immediately regretted it.

He swung his legs over the side of the trolley and doubled over, and a PA system crackled to life in the opposite corner of the room. The voice on the other end was calm, and flat. Like an airport announcement.

"Approach the object with your hands held above your head. Any attempts to interact with the object prior to instruction will result in stoppage with lethal force."

As if to punctuate the end of the sentence, there was an electrical click. A dim green light turned on at the other end of the room, revealing something he hadn't even thought to expect. But then again, he didn't know what exactly to make of it, either.

It was a machine, but that was about all he could tell. A black, unsettling mass of struts and cables bolted to the wall like a fat spider. A thick plastic shield covered almost all of it, with only a single bare button on the control panel accessible through a circular opening.

Yule raised his hands and began to walk. When he had gotten a couple feet away, another command came.

"Slowly lower your right hand and press the red button."

Something hummed beneath the floor. The sound of so much electricity being pumped into something that it made the air seize with invisible tension. Was it all going into the machine?

Yule stood considering it for what was obviously too long.

"Slowly lower your right hand, and press the button," it repeated, still monotone. "Failure to comply will result in stoppage with lethal force."

Yule felt his hand twitch in reply. The part of him that usually tried to figure a way out just... didn't. Like it had all been switched off. There just wasn't anything left. He'd failed.

He hadn't found Leslie, he thought. And now, whatever was happening, he knew he was probably never going to find her. He'd never make it back to Ornell. Never smoke on the roof again, never have coffee at Stilgoe's.

He'd failed, he thought. What else was he supposed to do, he thought, pressing the plastic button.

A burst of light. The sound of something deafening sprung up around him as the world disappeared. Impossible colors. Unthinkable angles and shapes danced in the slow cascade of the world around him.

Vicious. Primal. So loud it felt like the very sound of it would force him apart.

The feeling of a thousand hooks in every atom.

Pain.

Light.

And then, a floor. Or at least, the expectation of one rising to meet him as he fell. What Yule found instead was a bed, and *then* a floor.

He slammed into the covers and let out a cry of surprise, before bouncing down to hit the ground. Air punched out of his ribs; he lay there. Not breathing, not moving, not even daring to think.

Just waiting. Listening.

He could hear crickets. The dry crack of cicadas hitting thin aluminum walls. From somewhere above him, there was the sound of something whirring, low electrical tones slowly spinning down into something dulcet and deep.

He could smell ozone, he thought.

That was never good, but he was alive to smell it. Exactly *where* was a different question. Yule strained, and tried to move, but every breath felt like an uphill battle.

With a grunt, he grabbed at the side of the bed and dragged himself to his feet. But as soon as he was at the apex, he dropped. Fell to his knees, weighted by exhaustion.

With a frustrated, defiant gasp, he lifted his head. Tried to look around and assess the situation, guided by the animal instinct to bolt but limited by the thinness of his own breath.

He was panicking. Nothing made sense, first he was… *somewhere*, now *here*. Somewhere unknown. His heart thudded. Sweat ran down his neck, hot and clinging like a sickly layer of anxiety on his skin.

Couldn't panic. You panicked, you died, even back home. They'd taught him how to stay calm, a lifetime ago. Naming things. Things he could see, things he could hear. That was it, that was all he had to do.

He was in a room, he thought. Smaller than the one before. Less secure, like a bedroom. Judging by the hollow sound of his own footsteps, that small room wasn't on a foundation, either.

Warehouse? No. Smaller.

A trailer.

What could he smell? Gasoline. Fumes from a large, boxy generator idling in the corner. It was connected to… to something. A mass of wire and cable tangled in strange angles around a steel globe. Had he… had he come through it? What was it?

Yule gritted his teeth. Shook his head. Didn't matter, didn't have to be specific. Just had to keep himself thinking. Thinking was living.

Maybe he'd really traveled through time. Or maybe he was dying, and this was all the final credit roll of a dying brain. He couldn't really tell.

God, it felt like he was suffocating.

His head turned towards the door. Fingers clenched on the filthy bed-clothes. No matter where he was or what condition he was in, there was still only one truth he could see: that nobody stood between him and the door. Had to start somewhere.

With a sudden upsurge, Yule tried to stand again. As soon as he straightened up, he toppled forward, collapsing heavily into the doorframe. A corner slammed against his temple, and as he slid to his knees, something hot seeped into his eyebrow.

He leaned against the door for what seemed minutes, gasping. His head was swimming. He felt like his lungs were on fire, everything was on fire. But the simple truth remained that it was keep going or die. Just like then, and just like now.

He stumbled into the hallway wall, barely able to catch himself. When the wall unexpectedly gave way to an open living room, his legs did too.

His eyes drifted upwards. In the bright patches of moonlight, he could see a hand. Curled up and twisted all the wrong way, like someone had fallen over. He soon found that 'falling over' was the nice way of putting it.

Somebody had near enough blown half of the guy's head off, whoever it was. A dark pool of blood had spread beneath the remains, with footprints leading out of it all the way to the lazily swinging back door.

For a while, he felt as if all he could see were the footprints. They were thin and patterned with zigzags, like from the kind of sneakers his kid cousins would wear. The kind Leslie O'Neil might've worn. By the time he realized what he was fooling himself into hoping, it was too late. The hope was already there.

That, and a strange feeling of unfairness. If they *were* hers, that meant he'd come close. Followed her into that realm of madness, pushed himself right to the edge, and still missed by an inch. If he'd had the strength to go on a little faster, the footsteps said, maybe he'd have found her. Brought her back, cleared his name. Made all the world right again.

But he couldn't. And that was okay. It wasn't like there was anything he could be expected to do about it—something in the slowing drum of his heart told him that he was going to die here, whether he got up or not. He didn't like it, but at least he could accept it.

And yet, when a shadow appeared at the door, he still made to stand. Even if he barely made it an inch, at least he could go out knowing he wasn't a quitter. It was better than his last thoughts being about sneakers.

The back door was now wide open, propped up behind the figure, now half-entered into the trailer. It looked like an old man wearing a threadbare white linen suit. As Yule steadied himself, he realized that one staring eye was painted on, sat unblinking over a prosthetic face mask. He didn't say anything to him. He didn't have the breath. He just stood there, shaking. Staring.

The man in the white suit looked him over with his one good eye. Sniffed the air, and grimaced.

"You just get here?" he asked, voice rasping. Yule nodded. The half-faced man grunted, went into his pocket, and pulled out a crumpled piece of paper. He scanned over it whilst Yule watched in silence. Then he grunted again. Put the paper back in his pocket.

As if in response, the inside of the trailer flashed as a pair of headlights swung by in the distance. The man glanced at the window and grimaced again. It was hard to tell exactly what it meant with only half a face to go on. The other side remained calm, and unblinking.

The half-faced man reached out a hand and grabbed Yule's sleeve, one good eye staring hawkishly into his own.

"We should get you to the car," he said, supporting Yule on his shoulder. Yule nodded, as if he had a choice in where he got dragged. He could barely stay on his feet.

He gave the crumpled body one last look as they circled the blood pool. Then, they were out into the cold night air, Yule stumbling for every aided step. The half-faced man was surprisingly strong for his age, though by the time they had made it down the steps into the backyard, he was winded too. The sharp sound of slammed car doors echoed over the trailer, urging them on.

The sea of tall grass hit them in a rolling wave. Still the half-faced man persisted, pulling them forward into the blind undergrowth. Faintly, Yule could hear footsteps crunching towards the trailer behind them. Searching for them. About to try the locked door or see the shattered window. Find the dead man inside.

After a few minutes, the grass ended as abruptly as it began. Out on the flat land, they both stopped, doubled over. Yule felt like he was on the verge of passing out.

"I... I can't..." he gasped, hands on his knees. The half-faced man spat and took a ragged breath into his belly.

"Don't die here," he said, pointing wearily across the field. "At least make it to the car. You can die there if you want."

Yule let out a low rattle that wished it was a groan. Why did he always have to have a choice? With slightly renewed vigor, they made across the moonlit field, towards the car. Yule glanced behind them as they went. It didn't look like they were being followed—he couldn't even see the trailer park anymore.

But for some reason, the half-faced man looked more worried now that they were out in the open dark. His breathing was sharp and caught, and every few yards he would crane his head to stare into the undergrowth around the side of the wide clearing. Like he was looking for something. Or, fearing it. If he'd had the spare breath Yule might have asked him why, but part of him was grateful he couldn't find out the answer.

When they reached the car, the half-faced man helped crumple Yule into the passenger seat. He sprawled, head lolling over the back of the headrest. Almost immediately, the half-faced man took up a plastic breathing mask and pulled the elastic strap over Yule's head. A translucent tube ran from it into a small gray canister wedged awkwardly between the driver and passenger sides.

"Lie there and keep breathing," the man said, pulling the elastic behind Yule's ears. As he leaned away again Yule nodded and parted his numb lips. With what felt like the last of his energy, he took a long, deep breath.

The canister let out a low hiss, and something pure washed down Yule's throat. It felt good. Like breathing. Like *living*. The taste of everything in the world being handed back to him. He took another breath, and another and another, gulping it down hungrily to fill his starving lungs. He felt like a line drawing being colored in.

The half-faced man hadn't waited to see if it worked or not. After Yule had taken his first gulp, he'd rounded the car and eased himself into the driver's seat while hurriedly searching his own pockets.

Now that Yule could think straight, he looked around. The car was a mess—loose piles of paper sat in a drift on the backseat, beside boxy-looking equipment with exposed wires. A few strange little dials sat glued to the dashboard, occasionally blinking, or shifting numbers. They looked homemade.

With a jingle, the half-faced man fished out the car keys.

"We should get back to the house," he said. Yule couldn't quite tell if the guy was talking to him, or to himself. Regardless, the half-faced man turned the key in the ignition and the engine crackled to life, soon settling into a lopsided purr. The grass in front of them blazed for a moment with grimy light as the headlamps blinked to life and were just as quickly switched off.

Slowly, cautiously, the car gained momentum. They crawled forwards, though in the dark the car seemed not to move at all. Without the land-scape as a reference, the only motion Yule could detect was the lurch in his stomach as they turned, which made it feel like the car was just sway-ing in place. The feeling lasted until the black shrubland surrounding them burst into open road.

They rolled to a stop and, wordlessly, the half-faced man leaned over, unhooked the oxygen mask from Yule's head, and pressed it to his own face. He took a few ragged breaths, before exhaling and giving it back. As Yule re-affixed it to his face, the half-faced man's eyes lingered on him. Then he turned back to the road, pressed a foot down on the gas, and the engine growled.

"Welcome to the future," he said, as the car began to move again. "My name's Howard."

Yule didn't reply. The guy probably knew his name already, and even if he didn't, it hardly mattered. It wouldn't change where he was, he thought, staring out of the window at the night beyond.

It all looked the same, he thought. But it felt *off*. Like he'd known he was somewhere else well before he'd been told, like the whole damn world was a sweater one size too small.

That was about when it hit him. Something that felt like it had been waiting since the tunnel—a vast, terrifying weight suspended on a string that felt tantalizingly close to breaking. When it fell, it hit him like a ton of bricks.

Time travel.

Yule felt his heart rate spike. Breathing became strained again as his body raced to catch up with his nerves. He'd traveled through time. Time travel was real, it existed, and he'd—

Oh god.

He'd traveled through time.

His hands shook. His entire body felt like it wanted to bolt, run somewhere, anywhere. But no matter where he went, he'd still be here. In…

His eyes widened. What year was it? He didn't even know what year he was in. Was his apartment gone? What about his father? Christ, what if Ornell was dead, what if they were all gone?

What if everything was gone?

He felt blood rush into his face. The urge to faint rolled into his throat like a pulling tide, but he struggled against it. Tried to breathe. He strained his eyes open, forcing himself to look at the road and confront the world he feared so much to be in.

But as the town swallowed them up, he found the empty stores and darkened stoops looked the same by night. That was a small comfort, and even when the car finally rolled to a stop by the curb, he couldn't quite put a finger on what had changed. If anything *had* really changed.

But he definitely still felt it.

Howard sat rigidly in his seat. Waiting, or thinking. Maybe both.

"When you get out, put the back of your right hand on your left cheek, and cross your left leg over the right when you stand up," he said.

"Why do I—" Yule began, in vain. Before he could finish Howard got out of the car and hurried around to wait on the passenger side. Yule laid his head against the rest for a second, and sighed. Pulled his hand up against his cheek, popped the door, and swung his legs around the seat. Left over right. Feet on the ground, head ducked awkwardly under the frame.

"Why do I nnnnee…" he began, moving to stand. He didn't get any further than that, before all the blood rushed out of his head. A breath stopped, half caught in his throat.

The drop came without challenge. His awkwardly twisted legs unfurled beneath him, body coiling limply onto the grassy verge. His cheek bounced on his knuckles, inches away from a concrete blackout. Driven by momentum and positioning he rolled onto his back, arms splayed and eyes up.

Passing out was really starting to get old, he thought, as he passed out.

~

Time went strangely in the unconscious space. Minutes became days became minutes again, leaving him drifting. Blurred.

Sometimes he was back in the jungle. In the wet heat, struggling and bleeding into dirty water. Other times he was in the bunker. Strapped to a platform. Burning.

But even in his half-lucid state, he knew nothing compared to the fear of waking up. Truly waking, and seeing enough to cement the reality he was in. When the feverish grip of sleep dragged him back under again, he was almost happy for it.

It went that way for days. Or at least, that was the limit of what he could tell. Might have been weeks. All Yule knew was that when he was finally able to breathe again, his body acted before his head could.

His eyes snapped open. Ceiling arced as he sat bolt upright, a motion practiced and honed through a hundred sleepless nights.

The smell of heavy cleaning chemicals and burnt plastic filled his head. The sound of something pumping, and wheezing. Like gas. And then a foul, cloying kind of undertone to the air. An organic stink, all sticky and searing. It was with mild horror that Yule realized it was him—him and the bed, although by now they were sharing a smell. Sweat and blood, and something acidic soaked in with unwashed cotton.

He flinched and swung his legs up over the bed. The apartment swung and drifted as he tried to focus in on it, dark shapes barely enough for his gaze to latch onto.

The room was small and cluttered, windows shuttered and taped over. Wires, like a bundle of throbbing nerves, split out to follow where the ceiling met the walls. A generator chugged broodily in an unseen corner, pushing an acid twinkle of gasoline into the already heavy air. The only true light in the room came from a desk lamp at one end. The dirty lens cast grease-toned shadows over the desk and illuminated piles of newspaper clippings beneath.

Step by painful step, Yule pulled himself up from the bed and across the room, IV stand wheels chirruping. It felt like trying to ice skate uphill—when he reached the desk, he had to fall forward onto it for support. Catch his breath. Every step was one wrong move away from him French-kissing the floorboards.

How long had he been in that bed?

Balanced on his elbows, he clumsily picked at the paper. Local news stories, or reports of weird stuff from elsewhere. Lights in Nevada. A mermaid sighting in Oregon. A few piles in, his heart sank: the only reasonable reaction to unexpectedly seeing one's face in print.

It was a grainy black-and-white picture, his driving ID photo blown up to blurred proportions. Next to it, the headline read, "*Local Man Missing Following Police Investigation.*"

Yule mouthed a string of curse words, noise never quite making it out. His eyes scanned down to the faded print, his heart sinking with every word.

Police are appealing for information as to the whereabouts of 28-year-old Ulysses Lincoln, in connection with the disappearance of Amesville teen Leslie O'Neil. He is not believed to be armed, but the public are urged not to approach him.

If you have any information, please contact the Amesville Gazette on 717-555-0161, or the Amesville Police Dept.

And that was it. The rest of the page was taken up by a long story about Leslie O'Neil. His eyes drew back towards the blurred, scowling figure on the page.

It didn't look like him. Not with his brow set and his lips falling into a natural scowl. That wasn't the person he saw in the mirror or passing by store windows. Somewhere in the back of his mind, something reflexively turned. The part that had to rationalize why he didn't walk out at night or linger too long near nice cars.

They could have used any other picture, he thought, but that was the one they wanted. Because that guy was the one they imagined him as. Not a hero, or a concerned citizen, or even just a good guy. Just 'that spook.'

And nothing he'd done had changed it.

There wasn't a word in the English language to describe it. The walls of reality falling in, and by some perverse miracle, failing to take him with them. He was alive, yet somehow worse than dead. Trapped and surrounded by loneliness without end. Living, but undone.

"It's not light reading," said a voice from the side. Yule didn't turn his head to look at them. He just hung his head down low. Eyes barely open, lips hardly moving when he spoke.

"Do they still think it was me?" he asked flatly. Howard didn't audibly move from the doorway, but the low gasp of an oxygen mask slithered in with him, punctuating the silence with a short, sharp hiss.

"You probably already know the answer to that question," he said, wheels creaking as he stepped into the room. Yule inclined his head a little to see Howard and the oxygen rig he was dragging behind him. He wandered over slowly. Tired, like the old half of his face suggested.

"Nothing mattered. None of it," Yule said, a little edge rattling into his voice. Howard took another furtive suck of oxygen.

"You're still alive. That should matter."

"And what kind of life is it?" Yule said, letting his hand fall heavily on the photo. "Everyone thinks I'm a murderer. Leslie O'Neil never got found... god fucking *damn*."

He grimaced and swiped the documents from the table. They fluttered to the ground like dead, flat snow. Howard coughed and wiped his brow with a handkerchief, parking his old bones on a plastic chair in the corner.

"You're wrong about the second part," he said flatly. Yule looked up. "What?"

"About Leslie. I know where she is," Howard went on, almost casually. "I can take you to her, if you prove you're not a threat."

Yule looked up at him, jaw agape. Had he not felt like hammered shit, he might have lunged across the room at the old man. But now all he could do was stare.

"Where is she?" he asked. Howard shook his head.

"Safe. Or, as safe as anyone could hope to be in this town. But her situation is precarious: if you prove to be the kind of person who's in the habit of making wrong moves, I doubt you'll be of help to her."

Yule tensed his legs and stood upright, trying not to stagger. Weakly, his hands balled into fists.

"And what are you gonna do if I just decide to go look for her myself?" he asked. Howard shrugged.

"Nothing. Even in your condition, you could probably beat it out of me. That's the only way you'll get it before the time is right," he said. "Correct me if I'm wrong, though, but you don't seem like the kind of guy who tortures the elderly."

"So what? I'm supposed to just sit still?" Yule insisted. Howard's smirk faded, as his thoughts turned visibly back towards reality.

"The situation is sensitive. One wrong move, and everything gets lost."

"And you think I'm gonna make a wrong move," Yule said, more a bitter statement than a question. Howard didn't answer, instead bringing the oxygen mask up to his face again. He took a deep breath and heaved, pulling himself out of the chair and onto his feet. Then he turned his good eye towards Yule, gaze steely and resigned.

"I think you have the choice to the wrong thing, or the right thing. And until you understand the real stakes here, I can't say for sure which one you'll choose," he said. Yule grunted quietly and bowed his head. He was starting to get tired of intrigue.

"So, what? I gotta do a test?" he said.

"No. Right now, you're going to rest, and eat. I'm no kidnapper," Howard replied, buttoning his jacket. "All I ask is that in a few hours, you let me show you something. In return, I'll tell you where Miss O'Neil is, and how to find her."

"And after that?" Yule asked.

"That's really up to you," Howard replied.

Yule considered the offer for a moment. Even though he felt the fire go out of him, his hackles were still up. It hadn't been long enough since his moonlit dance at gunpoint to trust anyone completely.

But the compulsion in his chest remained. A memento, really. The only remnant of a life he barely remembered living.

If not me, it asked, *then who?*

Yule lifted his head and straightened himself up on the IV stand. He didn't say a word—he had neither the energy nor inclination. The action itself said enough, as he climbed back into the bed, back laid cooperatively up against the headboard. Howard gave him a grim, determined smile, and began to wheel the oxygen tank out of the room.

"I hope you like soup," he said, disappearing down the hall. "It's all I've got."

THE OPERATOR

THE BUNKER, 1977

In the deep gray hum, Cal felt weightless. Like the concrete walls weren't even there, and that he and the steel table were just pieces of dust, floating. He hardly remembered what happened after he hit the floor. Alarms. Hands on him. And now here he was, handcuffed to a table in an anonymous gray room. No idea how long, or exactly where.

Just him, the table, and Trevor's name replaying silently on his lips, over and over again.

He'd done it, right? He'd gone back to somewhere, but... what if he'd gone forward? Either way he'd left Trevor behind, he'd left him with the yellow-toothed man, and...

Cal set his jaw. The terrible realization he'd done something stupid dawned like cold water dumped over his shoulders. Even if he had gone back far enough to save Trevor, he was handcuffed to a table somewhere he didn't recognize, barely able to stand. Some rescue mission.

The thoughts replayed over and over in a never-tiring whirl. By the time an outside noise came, Cal had almost forgotten he'd ever been anywhere but the room at all. Maybe it was designed that way.

The door whined as unseen hands turned the handle, and Cal sat bolt upright. This was it, wasn't it? The moment he had to escape.

He could rush them, but he was cuffed. He could spit, or bite or bluff. In the moments it took for the door to open, a hundred plans seemed to flash through Cal's head, each less effective than the last. But to his eternal shame, not even one sprang to mind when a person finally appeared.

The man who entered was old and seemed to loom despite his short stature. Light flashed across his spectacles as he quickly and quietly crossed the room, sitting in the chair opposite with surprising speed. Cal opened his mouth out of reflex, but the man spoke before he could form a question.

"Were you sent here on purpose?" he asked. His voice wasn't how Cal expected either. Urgent, almost scared. Cal shook his head.

"No, I—" he rasped, but the man cut him off with a hand.

"Then you must listen to me carefully. There is not much time," he interrupted, putting something purposefully on the table. It looked like half of a crumpled foil gum wrapper.

"You must ball this up and push it tightly into one of your back molars. Like a filling. Quickly now," he insisted, pushing it towards him. Cal, unsure of any other option, balled it up tight and jammed it painfully into the center of his back tooth. As he did so, the man didn't stop speaking, except to glance nervously at his watch.

"You've come here at a bad time. I can get you out, but it will not be pleasant or easy. You must do exactly as I tell you," he went on, glancing momentarily over his shoulder. "In exactly three minutes, something that looks like a man is going to come in here and ask you questions. You must tell him as little as you possibly can, but you cannot lie to him. Simply omit. Do not make anything up. You need only last five minutes, and then you are to wait where they put you until I come for you. Do you understand?"

Cal opened his mouth to speak but was hit with the sudden terror that the foil would fall out of his teeth. He nodded instead, and the man lifted himself from the chair, hurrying back towards the exit.

"You must keep your head, and trust me," he said, card reader beeping as he swiped his ID through the slot. "I will be back for you."

With that the door swung open, then closed. The only reminder the man had ever been there at all was the tap of his shoes, before they too faded away, and Cal found himself surrounded by endless, boundless gray once more. A gentle jingle slithered through the room. The sound of his wrists shaking in the cuffs.

The next few minutes stretched into fearful miles. He didn't hear the approaching footsteps of the second man over his own panic. The sound of the handle lightly turning made Cal jump in the seat, almost deafening in the humming silence. The only indication the man was physically there at all was a soft *tap, tap* as he drew closer, light footsteps barely stirring the surface of the floor. He said nothing as he entered the room, his clean, pressed black suit and tie suggesting nothing of his purpose there. The only thing distinctive about him were the large black sunglasses he wore, despite a lack of sunlight, which gave him a strangely insect-like appearance.

As he sat, the man laced his fingers carefully on the table, his back arrow straight. For a few moments, neither party said anything. The only face Cal could read was his own, reflected and distorted by the glassy black lenses.

Then, after what seemed like an age, the man in the black suit smiled. It wasn't a pleasant smile. Not just forced but unnatural, as if someone was pulling hooks attached to his cheeks.

"This one is Operator Parker. What is your name?" he asked. Something about the man's voice unsettled Cal too: it was generic, so generic that he'd almost forgotten what it sounded like by the moment the sentence finished. Cal didn't reply for a few seconds, trying to remember all that he had been told before.

"Cal," he rasped. The reply was quick and monotone.

"Were you sent here by The Branch?"

"No."

"Do you know how you came to be here?" Thomas Parker insisted.

"No," Cal repeated. Then, he did something. He didn't know what— maybe it was a twitch of his cheek, or the unthinking flight of an eye from side to side as he watched thoughts bounce in his inner vision. Whatever it was, it was a mistake. Silently, Thomas Parker clasped the plastic arm of his sunglasses, and folded them neatly on the steel table. When he looked up again and opened his eyes, Cal had to suppress a surprised scream.

His eyes were all wrong. Cold and icy blue, pupils like tiny, twitching black pinheads, too sharp and too alive to be natural. Every moment they seemed focused on something new, jumping side to side as they darted skin-crawlingly over each detail of Cal's face. They were so transfixing that Cal hardly noticed as Thomas Parker's hand reached into his pocket and put something on the table. A little black box.

"This one is designed to detect lies," he said, taking off the lid. "It will ask you the previous question again, and this time you will tell it the truth. If you refuse, this one is designated to administer medication."

Calmly, and without ceremony, he placed the content of the box on the table: a stainless steel syringe. There was no telling what was inside, only that the casing was well polished, and the needle glinted hungrily in the light.

"Again," Thomas Parker said, "do you know how you came to be here?"

Cal strained his jaw. The answer lay on the tip of his tongue, but now suddenly he seemed unable to think of it. He realized he had barely thought of the unthinkable fact yet, and even now in the grip of extreme terror, he could feel the crushing weight of its expanding shadow above him.

"I traveled through time," he replied. Thomas Parker's eyes twitched and bounced in their sockets, but his hands remained still, satisfaction noted only by another question and the lack of a needle sting.

"How did you come to do that?" he asked. That was more open, Cal thought. A distraction, but an opportunity as well.

"By accident," he replied. At first, he felt almost accomplished in the little un-truth. But all hope faded as Thomas Parker leaned forward, his awful, wrong eyes leaping from detail to detail, unceasingly alive.

"But an accident you intended. You are not surprised by the outcome," he said, piece by slow piece, as if reading a book. "How did you gain the means to travel through time?"

Cal stuttered, taken a little aback. He leaned back hard, inching the chair as far as it would go from the pale-eyed creature before him.

"I found it. We didn't know what it was," he said. His stomach yawned wide as he realized his mistake, tongue stumbling over itself to correct the fatal error. "I didn't know what it was."

But it was too late. The one shining word must've been like a beacon. Thomas Parker's eyes stopped dead in their sockets, intently focused.

"We," Thomas Parker repeated. "You were not alone? Tell us the names of the person or persons who were with you."

Cal sat there, stunned. The question hit him like a ton of bricks to the chest.

There wasn't a way he could omit the answer without lying. No way of getting out of it without jumping under the bus or throwing Trevor under it as well. And yet somehow, despite everything at stake, the answer jumped out of his mouth long before the decision was set in his mind. Even if his brain was distracted, his body couldn't ignore the constant nerve reminder of the green ranger's bow, nestled against the side of his leg.

The figurine was more than the sum of its beaten, plastic parts. More than even the single, juvenile promise they'd made on it. *One free favor*, as if every day of their friendship hadn't paid for a hundred in advance. The longer Cal thought of it, the more it made him want to weep.

He'd promised to keep him safe. And even if Trevor wasn't around, the plastic curves of the figurine were all too real in reminder.

"No," he said. The word bounced around the little room, and for a moment even Thomas Parker seemed taken aback. Cal was probably more surprised than he was, sitting there openmouthed with horror at his own uncontrollable morality.

"We will ask one more time," Thomas Parker repeated, monotone as ever. "What was the name of the person or persons you were with?"

Slowly, agonizingly, Cal shook his head.

"No," he said again. A few moments of silence passed as the two stared at each other from across the steel table. Simple statement, simple outcome.

As calmly and gently as moving the chair, Thomas Parker picked up the syringe and rose from his seat. His gloved fingers creaked as they gracefully crawled into sticking place over the handle, needle rising like a scorpion barb. Cal yelped, instincts in full blast. He tried to stand and back away, but his hands were cuffed to the table. The unexpected jerk sent him flying sideways off the chair, which clattered loudly against the wall.

An iron grip dragged Cal to his feet, vision filled by the horrific, twitching eyes of Thomas Parker. The needle inched curiously towards Cal's throat.

Then, he screamed. Like he'd forgotten how up until then and had only just realized. Long and desperate, so loud that neither of them seemed to hear the screech of the door opening.

"Christ!" came an unfamiliar voice. "Doctor Van Hallan, get in here!"

"Wait, no don't touch him! Don't touch it," said another, much more familiar. "Give me the notebook!"

His footsteps thundered across the room towards them. Cal cried out again as the needle tip slowly and methodically wormed its way into his neck, pain glassy and sharp. Thomas Parker didn't react at all. Not until the older man spoke again.

"Train. Daffodil. Phoneline. Ashtray. Two, five, nine, six, four. Now stop, Operator Parker!" he said. The effect was instant. Thomas Parker froze, as if every muscle in his body had just been mechanically halted. He retracted the needle from Cal's skin, unknown contents still inside the syringe, and let go of him. Cal dropped immediately, panting and sweating. His loathsome eyes unfocused, Parker stepped back into the corner of the room, where he loomed like a silent nightmare.

Cal gasped with pain, half suspended by the handcuffs and half lying on the floor. Everything felt misted over with barely faded panic. But he wasn't all gone, not by a longshot. *Van Hallan* said something in the back of his head. That was the guy. He'd heard the assistant say his name, it was him, the one who started *everything*.

The unknown assistant rushed over and pulled Cal up onto his feet, cuffs straining on his wrist. Van Hallan rounded the table, scowling at the wild-eyed creature in the corner.

"What have I said? What have I told both you and upper management a hundred times?" he said, punctuating each word with a slap of backhand to palm. "You cannot leave an Operator alone with someone. How many times do I need to repeat that?"

"There must've been a mistake downstairs. He must've been sent up ahead of schedule, I'm sorry, Doctor—"

"Enough," Van Hallan cut in. "We cannot waste any more time."

Cal stared, openmouthed. The man before him was not the one who had come to warn him. This one was steelier, harder. Perhaps even a little cruel. The glimmer of fear and empathy had been glazed over with something deliberate, he thought. Still there, but purposefully deadened.

Van Hallan turned to Thomas Parker and inhaled deeply through his nose.

"Is this boy a Branch subject, or a known foreign agent?" he asked. Thomas Parker smiled his invisible-hooked smile.

"No, Doctor Van Hallan. He is neither," he replied, monotone as ever. Van Hallan exhaled loudly and gestured to Cal, not even looking at him.

"You heard him, he's not one of ours. Check him," he said. The other man paused, hands still holding Cal fast.

"Are you sure we shouldn't let the interrogation go on?" he asked. Van Hallan scowled and pinched the bridge of his nose. He took up the syringe and Cal flinched, only for him to shake it gently next to his ear. He grimaced visibly and put it back down.

"There's likely enough sodium pentothal in that syringe to kill a child. If the Operator couldn't account for the fact children are more likely to lie, I hardly think they prepared the equipment to reflect that either. We'll interrogate him with normal staff once today's testing is done, I don't want him down here until then," he said, voice hard and cold. "Check his dental work."

With that, Cal's head was wrenched back, mouth open to the light. The other man peered over him, then tutted.

"Looks like we've got contaminants. Back molar, big one too."

"Then he cannot be volatilized. Put him in one of the upper herding sheds, there's stock in there right now," Van Hallan replied. Cal stared at him, halfway between impressed and aghast, but Van Hallan expertly avoided his gaze. He swept around the room, pausing at the door to glance at Cal, if only for a half second. Then, his gaze snapped back to his balding assistant.

"Are you waiting for something? Get him up there. Call Ops if you need to," he said. Then he waited, but only for receipt of his order. As soon as the other man nodded, he was gone, calmly and steadily on into the invisible spaces beyond.

Cal watched him go, numbed. The sound of the other man radioing for assistance sounded muffled, like it was coming through a wall of hand soap. The sounds and feelings of movement hardly touched him in his far, retreated place.

~

He didn't know whether he slept or not. Without sight, it was hard to tell. It could have just as easily been minutes or hours. The cell was pitch black, completely unlit and clad on all sides with brushed black metal. In the blind space it was just him, and his thoughts.

They were mostly of Trevor, and guilt. Unseen, the sharp reminder of the green ranger in his pocket was ever present and un-ignorable.

Now more than ever, he felt as if he'd left him. Jumped off the ship to float adrift in the dark. Timeless and directionless, trusting somebody he didn't even know to save his life. But what other choice did he have? Whether he understood why or not, Van Hallan was the only way out. The only way to make it right, somehow, some way. He'd give his life for that, it was the least he could do—Trevor probably would've done twice as much, if the universe had let him. Fuck, he probably already had.

But he could go back, he thought. Time travel existed; he'd done it. He would just... go and stop it all before it ever happened. Hire somebody with a gun and an eye scar to shoot Carnassus when he was a teenager. He'd save Trevor, and Leslie, and... an uncle. Somebody he half remembered... but god, it was fading. The face had already gone to imagined lines in his head.

He'd save them too. Just as long as he got out, from... wherever he was.

Ever on the darkness stretched. Ever round the thoughts repeated, until they seemed as much part of the room as the dull hum of underground walls. The thud of his own heartbeat in his ears. Or was it?

Cal sat up. Waited.

Not his heart. It wasn't rhythmic, and it wasn't coming from inside him. He could barely hear it at all, but he could *feel* it, coming from somewhere else, running through the floor and up his legs. Slowly, he leaned down and pressed his ear against the cold metal floor. The bang of something thrashing down in the deep, like the concrete was twitching. A heart attack, some place below.

Suddenly, the room lit red.

In the walls valves awoke, flooded with electric blood. When the alarms sounded, it filled Cal's head like wet, agonizing sand. He fell to the floor, hand clapped over his ears. The electrical klaxon wavered, muffled by his palms, turning to something that sounded like words. Groaning, he took one hand away, still wincing at the noise.

"...gency alert. Lakota Falls Protocol in effect," a woman's voice repeated, steady as a drum but muffled by the walls. "All personnel report immediately to evacuation points within five minutes. This is an emergency alert..."

Outside, footsteps thundered. Voices echoed. Somewhere below there was a deep rumble, and the pop of gunfire. Adrenaline fuzzing in his veins,

Cal climbed unsteadily to his feet. Shifted weight on the balls of his feet, just waiting for something to happen.

As if in answer, the door opened, and the sounds of chaos burst through. Van Hallan circled the door and pressed himself against the wall, wide eyes fixed on the hallway. Cal went towards him, trying to yell over the alarm.

"What's goi—" he began.

"Shh! Sh!" Van Hallan hissed, holding up a finger to his lips. A moment later, a column of people came running past the door, flanked by men in black body armor shouting orders over the noise. Cal saw automatic rifles bobbing in their hands, but only in the moment captured by the doorframe. Another second later, and they were gone.

Van Hallan waited a moment more, chest heaving and rising as he listened out for the dying sounds of company. Then, he threw himself from the wall, beckoning Cal with a shaking hand.

"This way!" he cried, voice crackling as he tried to call over the alarm. "We must go! Do not stop for anything!"

Before Cal could respond, he was moving again. Cal surged forward, carried on a winding adrenaline turbine. The smoky air stung his throat and scratched at his lungs with every frantic breath, twisting and turning through the concrete maze in pursuit.

Gunfire pounded drum-like, growing closer and louder as they pressed deeper inside. But by the time it seemed to reach its deafening apex, it slowed. Sputtered and lost beat as one by one, the guns began to fall silent. It wasn't until Cal started seeing bodies that he knew what that meant.

The first ones were in side hallways. Slumped into corners or splayed out over the floor, hazy and dreamlike in the smoke. Most of them were wearing orange prison jumpsuits, corpses crumpled up in the open doorways of cells. It almost looked like they were sleeping, save for the dark puddles beneath them. But further in, the scenes began to change. More bodies, more people—and not just prisoners. People in white coats, and even a few in black security uniforms.

They didn't look the way they did in movies. There was no artful framing or colored emphasis. They were just there, just the same as a cup or a table. A corpse, with a whole world still working around it. Somehow that just made it worse.

And yet, Van Hallan never stopped. Never even slowed, like he couldn't see it. For the most part, the fear of losing sight of him was enough to make Cal obey. But when he heard an unfamiliar voice, something instinctive in him ground his heels into the floor.

"This way!" it yelled, some ways down the hall. Footsteps drummed around a corner. Van Hallan looked around for cover, but there was no way out. Just the hall, and the doors. Frantic, he took off his white coat, dropped to a knee and began to furiously scrub it on the bloodied floor. Before Cal could ask what he was doing, he rose up again and thrust it hard into his chest.

"Put that over you and lie face down," he said, getting down to one knee near the wall. "Pretend to be dead."

Cal didn't need telling twice. He dropped, draping the red-smeared coat over himself like a blanket, obscuring most of his form. On the floor the air was clearer, but it took every ounce of will to stay still against the prickle of smoke in his lungs, and the crackle of fear on his neck.

The footsteps rounded the corner. A group, three or more. Cal couldn't see them, and he didn't dare move to try. Unseen, somebody slammed their hand against the walls.

"Keep moving!" a man ordered, the first voice Cal had heard.

"We can't!" said one, coughing.

"What about the others? They're still down there, we have to go back! We can't jus—" chimed in another, before all of them were silenced by the sound of a forceful slap.

"If they're still down there, they're dead," came the reply. A few more seconds of furtive silence followed, underscored by the steady hum of electrical fires.

"But," said one of the group weakly, feet hissing against the floor as they shuffled in place. "The bodies, we should... shouldn't we?"

A pair of rubberized soles thundered up the hallway and came to a stop a few inches away from his head. Cal felt his heart leap into his throat, and he held his breath.

The boots stayed still, and Cal couldn't tell if the owner was looking at him or not. He was suddenly aware of the need to cough, to splutter and shake the smoke out of his lungs after what seemed like an eternity of shallow breaths.

"Don't bother. We count the dead at evac, but we're not gonna get there unless you people start running," the voice said eventually, moving away. Someone let out a low grunt of frustration.

"Those are some of the smartest people in the country down there, we can't just leave them!" argued one, sole squeaking as they took a step forward. The man with the heavy boots let out a low, unimpressed grunt.

"There's plenty of dead geniuses. We go to the evac points," he said.

"Fuck this! Fuck it, I'm going back!" came the reply, and the sound of feet beginning to move away. "I'm not leaving Ted behind, I—"

BANG.

Somebody screamed, half surprise and half fear. A moment later there was a muffled, meaty thud as a body hit the floor. Then, nothing. The silent sound of reality setting in. The heavy boots began to move down the hallway again, voice calling over the alarm.

"I'll say it one last time—anybody who wants to live, come with me. You try and go back or slow us down, I'm authorized to put you with Doctor Kasprek down there."

"Oh my god, you… you son of a bitch, you—"

"Like I said, plenty of dead geniuses. Unless you want to add to the pile, start running," he replied, heavy boots clunking down the hall. "Five minutes until quarantine, move!"

The footsteps gathered and shifted, gaining unsure speed until eventually they were nothing but echoes on the steel. Immediately, Cal heard Van Hallan splutter and hack, dragging himself up against the wall. Without speaking they began to run again, all the while trying to ignore the new body on the floor. Even as it passed out of sight, Cal could feel it, just lying there. Sickeningly real.

They eventually ground to a stop in a large concrete vestibule. When Cal caught up to Van Hallan, he was doubled over and hacking violently. Cal joined him, painful splutters rippling up through his ribs. His chest felt like it was on fire.

"Shouldn't we be going the other way?" he asked, panting between words. Van Hallan shook his head and wordlessly mouthed something, unable to get a breath. He jerkily raised his inhaler to his mouth and hammered away at the button.

"No. We can't. They'll check the staff, we'd be discovered," he gasped, pointing to a door across the hall. "Our way out is in the test lab, but we must hurry. We *must* stay ahead of Jemima."

"What's Jemima?" Cal asked. Van Hallan swallowed, and his eyes went hard with fear. Without answering, he began descending the stairs. Cal followed, squinting to see in the unlit gloom. At first, only the solid square of light through the door lit his way from behind. Beyond that, it was almost pitch black, save for dim emergency strips on the walls.

As they went, every so often Cal would think he saw something moving on the ceiling above their heads, but as his eyes adjusted, he realized it was smoke. A thick, undulating cable of it, slithering up against the concrete towards the upstairs door. For a while, that was the only thing that seemed to be in there with them. Bitter and choking, but silent. At least, for a while.

But soon, a sound rose up the stairs to meet them as they descended. Like the slow, burbling thud of blood behind eardrums, or a thousand marbles hitting a steel funnel. Little by little, filling the tunnel like floodwater, until they were surrounded by it.

When they reached the bottom, the stairs terminated in a short, doorless hallway. Beyond it, a long, steel walkway stood suspended over a long drop, wreathed in smoke from beneath. Above it, every lightbulb was blown out—and yet, Cal realized as they entered, he could see perfectly. It was only as their ragged footfalls hit the gangway that he saw why.

Below them, instead of a far-away floor, there was only a glow. A seething, screaming sea.

Volatiles. Dozens of them, contorting and crawling around in the space beneath the walkway. The air above them buzzed with light and static, their arms up and outstretched like howling seaweed.

But there was something else down there. Something bigger, pounding against the walls, invisibly taking up space. Stalking and roaring, wreathed in electricity like a funeral shroud.

Cal felt his palms go slick on the handrails as he realized what it was. The thing from the woods, that was it. Thirty feet away, right below him, and he could hear it. Burbling and bellowing, louder and louder as the lights around it swelled ever brighter.

Cal was suddenly aware he'd stopped moving. That his legs had frozen, that the gentle bounce of the walkway made him feel sick. Like if he took another step he'd fall, and fall and fall until they got him, until they had him, until…

Van Hallan's hand wrapped around Cal's shirt and pulled. The walkway juddered and bounced as Cal stumbled the last few feet and fell through the open doorway. A moment later, he was being dragged up by the collar, catching a last glance of the seething nightmare below before finally the door slammed shut behind them.

Van Hallan wheezed and coughed, feeling at his pocket for an inhaler which was no longer there. As the realization set in, he let his head fall back. Gulped in air like a beached fish.

"We're nearly there… we must… must go on." He coughed, gesturing weakly down the hallway. "Through… there."

Cal looked up. The hallway was ruined, panels and wires hung in sparking banners across the ceiling. A thick, threatening blanket of smoke boiled above their heads like an inverted river, coiling out of the large open door at the other side. Step by painful step they approached, Cal half-dragging Van Hallan alongside him.

As they passed through, Cal noticed an empty medical gurney laid on its side by the entrance, straps burnt open. What had happened here?

The space beyond was in complete disarray. One half of the room was paneled with cracked mirrored glass, the other completely in fragments. Behind it, an array of chairs sat in a viewing station lay scattered on the floor. But what immediately caught Cal's attention was the thing on the far side: a black mass of cables and supports which seemed to grow out of the wall like a tumor, all machine parts and rubber cladding. Much of the front was covered by a thick, plastic shield, with just one opening over a single button. Below that, a light pulsed faintly.

Van Hallan pointed through the shattered glass, towards a dimly lit box in the corner of the viewing room.

"There, the console... press... press the yellow button," he wheezed, shuffling towards the plastic shield. "Set it to preset zero."

Cal did so, sliding cautiously over spikes of silver glass still stuck in the frame. The console beyond was utilitarian and grim, a welded steel box with a screen and a keyboard interface. As he clicked through the screen, most of what he saw was jargon. Only the preset numbers seemed to make sense, even if what they filled the monitor with didn't.

And all the while, the sound of the Volatiles persisted. Over the alarm drone, banging and howling like hornets in a can, and the invisible thing loudest of all. Growing ever louder, like it was climbing upwards somehow. The only small relief was the female announcer's voice, which seemed to cut sharply through the background noise by design.

"This is an emergency alert. Lakota Falls Protocol in effect," it repeated, calmly and clearly. Cal didn't have time to wonder what it meant. He punched in the preset and scrambled back into the main room, where Van Hallan steadied himself breathlessly against the time machine.

Cal was halfway across the room when a loud, metallic WHUD stopped him in his tracks. It sounded again, and then twice more, faster. Something big was at the door at the end of the hall—and even worse, it sounded like it was getting through.

"Don't," came a weak voice from behind him, barely audible. Cal turned in place, still feeling every bass thud of the unseen mass on the door, to see Van Hallan beckoning him with a limp hand.

"It doesn't matter now, whatever is out there," he said. "Come close to me."

His eyes met with Cal's through the low emergency light, and something in them made him approach. Forget the death and danger all around them and press over those final steps. Maybe it was a lack of fear in them. A sincerity. With a shaking palm, Cal took Van Hallan's hand.

The button click was inaudible above the alarm. But that was soon drowned out by the roar of the universe, turning in ways it shouldn't. In a moment out of time, the bunker peeled away around them, lost in the infinite, screaming shift.

Cal felt himself come apart. A thousand hooks tore outwards, then dragged them all together again like the clapping hand of God. As quickly as he went to pieces, the roar spat him back out into the jarring churn of the world: the sensation of gravity pulling his bones downward, of air pressure pressing against his skin. The grip of nausea in his belly.

He fell to his knees. Around him the air unseized itself to the hot, spitting sound of sparks on plastic.

He looked up to find himself surrounded by concrete walls, but not those of the tunnel. It looked like a garage. The floor was covered with stacks of car batteries, hooked up to the object beside him. Cal narrowed his eyes but said nothing. He wasn't quite sure if he was seeing it right.

It was an arcade machine. No, not just an arcade machine, *the* arcade machine. The one he'd used at the arcade, what felt like only a lifetime ago. The same tarnished Polybius logo, the same soot stains, even the spider-webbed crack on the screen. It flickered for a moment then died, as a final spurt of sparks erupted from the cables.

For a moment it all felt strangely calm. Even the sounds of their re-entry seemed like little ripples in a still pond. As Cal stood up, he felt like he hadn't moved at all. Out of the endless quiet came the noise of labored breathing, and a drawer opening. Cal turned to see Van Hallan, lying pathetically between a cabinet and the floor, puffing weakly at a spare inhaler. His eyes widened when they met Cal's, and his lips formed a single, shaking shape as he tried to speak.

"S-safe," he gasped, taking another few puffs. "Three… three minutes before. Cannot stay."

The sentence kept going in weak intervals, but Cal wasn't listening. He couldn't even hear it. He just started walking, like his body was on disbelieving autopilot. Out of the garage and down the hallway, following moonlight into what looked like a kitchen. He stopped just shy of the counter, hands calmly and gently gripping the side.

Then he leaned forward and retched. It hit the marble countertop and missed the sink by a good few inches, looking like gray grease in the dark. He pushed another few times until the tension in his stomach was gone, and the room fell quiet again. His head was spinning.

Slowly, he raised his eyes.

From its vantage point on the hill, the house saw for miles. A sea of trees stood silent, stretched in half shadows. No wind blew. No clouds crept across the moonlit sky, milky sea of stars motionless and uncaring from their perch far above. From the kitchen window, Cal saw the world hold its breath, waiting for something explosive to uncoil in its chest. And somewhere below, loudly and chaotically, the bunker dreamed its final, dead dream. With nothing more than the chirp of an electronic tone, unheard and unseen, it awoke.

A column of fire erupted into the night. The forest convulsed as vast swathes of ground shifted, collapsing in on themselves in a spray of dust and concrete which choked out the moonlight and shattered the window he watched through.

A final plume of flame and gray ash sprayed up like a closing curtain, carried on the tunnel's last breath. The night lay speckled with the sound of debris and the last echoing boom of falling dirt. Cal stared numbly out at the dust field, hands still clutching the side of the counter. Try as he might, he couldn't look away. Like the hugeness of it had locked his neck into place.

He could only watch with growing horror as the dust cleared, revealing movement within. Something huge, shifting.

At first it seemed like some sort of great worm, writhing and wriggling its way out of a pile of dust. But then came the limbs. Even at a distance Cal could make them out, pulling a great, indeterminable body out from the wreckage. The electricity around it was so bright, it all seemed to be made of molten glass.

Crawling from the dead womb of the earth, Jemima birthed itself out into the cold night, form painfully bright against the darkness. Its head arched up towards the dusty moon, and a reverberating, wet screech cracked the air. In those last milliseconds, the thing seemed to shine so brightly that it disappeared entirely.

And then, it was gone. In a blinding green flash the form disappeared, leaving nothing but the sound of thunder in its wake. Cal stared at the point it had last been, mouth agape.

The air was awake with the smell of burning. Jemima's howl—the terrible scream of the volatile—echoed to slow death somewhere in the fallen trees. The sound of one thing ending, and something even worse beginning.

THE SWEET RELEASE

AMESVILLE, 1993

The air in 1993 felt just about the same. Less choked up with God knew what. Cars somehow sounded higher pitched, too. Lighter. As Yule stepped out of Howard's, he realized it was those little things which made the world seem all tilted up. Wrong.

Maybe he was dreaming. But he'd never felt like hammered shit in a dream before, and he sure as hell felt like it now.

Triptree grunted as he heaved himself up out of the driver's seat and closed the door. As he rounded the car, he cast his good eye out across the road, checking for something. Yule looked around too, markedly more nervous, and put his hands in his pockets.

"Man, I don't know how it is now," he said, "but I go hanging around suburban neighborhoods after dark, things might not go so well for me."

Howard stopped beside him, smiled with half his face.

"Won't be here long. Just need to see one thing, over there," he said, nodding towards a building. Yule screwed up his face.

"We're breaking into a house?"

"No. Just taking a look, in through the front window," Howard replied, walking across the empty road towards it. Yule tensed up his shoulders and screwed up his face.

"Sure," he muttered, walking with his hands still firmly pushed into his pockets, "we'll look through the front. That's way less creepy."

Each house on the quiet street was more or less the same. Identikit suburban hideaways, all arrayed in neat lines down the cul-de-sac road. The only way to tell them apart was the lawn decorations—or, if you were lucky, a different paint job. But that seldom ever happened in places like this: they had a pretty specific character, and usually that character didn't include people like Yule being nearby.

He crouched down low to follow Howard onto the front lawn, ducking down for cover next to a bush. Then, he crept to the front bay windows, obscured by a thick curtain in all but one spot, which glowed with a strip of warm, orange light.

"Take a look," Howard said, pointing to the gap. Yule paused for a second, on the verge of refusing. But then, with a final glance around to make sure they couldn't be seen, Yule popped his head up, and peeked through the gap in the curtains.

A little girl sat on an old brown sofa, scribbling something on a page. Almost looked half familiar, but Yule knew he'd never seen her before. He internally winced and turned back, ducking a little to keep his head out of view.

"There's just a kid in there, man. What the fuck?" he said, voice strained.

"Just wait. Watch," Howard replied, unwavering. Yule rolled his eyes and glanced back up again, watching the scene as un-creepily as he could. And then, something in him twisted. A figure entered the room, tall and rotund, wearing a frayed old purple bathrobe. One Yule knew very well, yet at the same time, felt a complete stranger.

Ornell. It was Ornell, older, a little grayer—but it was him.

Yule could hardly hear what they were saying, but he could make out the tone and feel of his voice: that familiar, warm crackle of laughter whenever he said something he knew would get a rise. The kid came forward and gave him a weak slap on the arm. His smile only widened. Yule had never seen him look that happy before.

Yule stared, mouth agape. He felt... he didn't know how he felt. Whatever it was, there wasn't a word in the English language for it.

"Adelaide," Howard said, a little way behind him. "Addy, I think, but I'm not sure. She's four years old."

"He's got a kid…" Yule muttered to himself, eyes still not straying from the scene unfolding. Ornell sitting on the couch. Kicking up his feet on a footstool that looked like it had been used a hundred thousand times. Pointing and smiling at whatever his kid… God, his *kid*.

"I looked him up while you were unconscious. Thought you might want to see him," Howard said from beside him. Yule tried to think of a reply, but only one took precedence.

"Is he alright?" he asked, resisting the urge to put a palm to the glass.

"As well as anyone else in this town could hope. Divorced a few years ago. Cancer scare a couple years before that. But he owns a repair shop in town, got out of lumber before it all went south."

Yule smiled and laughed despite himself.

"Lumber artist went legit," he said, shaking his head. And for a second, a familiar feeling of warmth blossomed in his chest. Through the window, he could hear Ornell laughing again. Just like they always did.

Used to.

The smile faded, and Yule turned back around. His mouth was open, but nothing came out: he had a thousand questions, all churning to be let out at once. And yet the longer he thought about it, only one stood out. He could tell by the way it made him feel nauseous with despair.

"Why are you showing me this?" he asked. Howard's gaze never wavered.

"I could talk to you for hours about how dangerous time travel is. But I know you don't care about that," he said, voice low and quiet. "This isn't about the universe, or humanity. This is about the people we hold dear. It's as simple as that."

Yule wiped his eyes and looked up. The non-prosthetic half of Howard's face almost looked sympathetic, beneath the cragged wrinkles. Though, after a few moments, a heaviness came over it. Yule took a deep breath, fingers unconsciously digging at the soil.

"They're in danger too, right?" he said, nodding. "Just like everybody else?"

Howard grimly chewed his lip and adjusted his hat.

"Just like everybody else," he said grimly. Then, he grunted and straightened up, stretching his limbs. "That's all I had. You're free to do what you want now."

Yule stared at him, not leaving the ground.

"Whatever I want?" he repeated. Howard shrugged.

"You want to knock on that front door and get your life back? To take the girl and leave? I can't stop you. We've already covered that."

"So what's the catch?" Yule asked. Howard exhaled through his nose and took a final glance back to the window.

"If you choose not to help me save these people, you know exactly who you're letting go," he said. The sentence settled in Yule's stomach like a hot iron. Even if he didn't like it, he knew the half-faced old bastard had him.

"That's low, man," he said.

"There are no low blows now," Howard insisted, buttoning his jacket. "When this is all over, we can deal with the mess, but currently, all that matters is whether you're willing to help me or not."

Yule let out a taut breath and laid his head up against the wall. The stars looked the same, he thought. That was a comfort.

"What would I have to do?" he asked, eyes never moving from the points of light.

"You were in the military. You've held a gun, right?" Howard asked. The question snapped Yule back down to earth again, called by the twinge of old fear flaring in his gut.

"You need me to shoot somebody?" he asked quietly.

"Not unless they shoot me first. Then yeah, maybe," Howard replied, "You're more of a distraction. You just have to draw attention away until I can get a good, clean shot on him."

Yule tensed and untensed his jaw, chewing over the implication.

He could still feel Ornell, through the wall. Living, breathing. And try as the jungle might to suck his thoughts back into its hot wet grip, it couldn't quite catch him. Like Ornell was a glimmering thread of safety in the claustrophobic yet boundless rooms of his fear.

"Alright," Yule relented, getting up. "I'm not looking to get killed by nobody, but...whatever's going on here, I'll help. Can't say I'm a good shot, but I'll help."

Howard gave him a surprisingly genuine smile and checked his watch. His face hardened a little.

"We don't have much time," he said, making immediately back across the lawn. Yule caught up to him, the gentle jog still sapping him more than it should have.

"Well where the hell are we goin' now?" he asked.

"I'll explain everything in the car," Howard replied, pressing keys into Yule's hand. "You drive."

Yule stopped dead, considering the object in his palm with disbelief.

"Me? Why am I driving, I don't even know where we're going," he said. Howard opened up the passenger side door.

"Trust me," he said, sitting down, "you do."

~

The arcade sat dark and still. Dry ozone streaked the air like a slap to the face. The only sound in the empty space was the kid, whimpering and gasping.

Daisy felt like he should have been more moved. Affected. Surprised by the sound and light, or even a little awed by the sheer fact he'd just seen time travel. But he wasn't. His corner of the universe was just as solid and blind as it had always been.

Business as usual. Strangers killing strangers.

His grip slackened and the kid fell forward, landing in a crumpled heap on the ground. He immediately turned and tried to scramble, but

Daisy already had the gun on him. The second the kid saw it, he froze. Tensed up as if the barrel's gaze pressed with a crushing weight.

"Where'd he go?" Daisy asked. The kid's lip juddered up and down silently, like a broken ventriloquist dummy. Daisy visibly adjusted his grip on the pistol, enough to make it chatter hungrily. The kid yelped and shook his head.

"I d-don't know," he said. "I s-swear, I don't... I—"

Daisy cut him off with a raised hand. He unhooked the radio from his belt, and he raised it to his lips.

"This is Daisy. There's been a development," he said. When the answer came, it was just as measured and toneless as ever.

"Go ahead."

Daisy sniffed, and the sting of ozone rattled against the back of his throat.

"I think we've found another time machine," he said. "One kid de-rezzed himself, but I don't know where he's gone. Might just show back up in the system."

"Do you still have the other?" Carnassus asked, not skipping a beat. Daisy glanced at the kid cowering on the floor.

"Yeah," he replied. "Says he doesn't know where the other kid went."

"Find out as much as you can from him now. His name, and home address. Don't use the eraser," Carnassus replied coolly. "After the next reset, we can pick him up and start anew. For now, shoot him when you're finished."

For a second, Daisy didn't reply. He stood and waited, letting the feeling wash over him. It was odd.

It happened sometimes. A little moment where he was sure he could feel *something*. The prick of a deformed conscience, too weak to make itself law in his head. Fear of evil. Guilt, and admonishment. At times like this the pull was almost as it should have been, as if the feelings were close enough to touch.

But it always went. Pulled away like a sheet by the wind, the moment Daisy's brain caught up with itself, and remembered he felt nothing.

"Understood," he said. The other end of the radio cut out. Looked like they were done.

Now, it was just him and the kid. Alone at last.

He moved, and the kid yelped. Began to scramble, until the gun came up again. Then he went quiet, just like they always did. Even the suggestion of violence was enough to tranquilize most people, unless they'd been hardened to it. This kid looked soft as new silk.

"Please," the kid muttered, holding up an arm like it could shield gunfire, "don't hurt me."

Daisy put the radio on his belt and held out a hand.

"Gimme your wallet," he said. The kid retrieved it, and held it up in a shaking palm, not daring to take his eyes from the pistol. Daisy snatched it away and unfolded the nylon panels, thumbing through the cards inside until he found what he needed.

ID card, with a little photo. Name and address printed neatly on the side. Daisy squinted, committing as much of it as he could to memory. Then he stowed the plastic card into a jacket pocket and returned his gaze to the kid.

"Okay, Trevor," he said, voice low and calm. "This is now officially a negotiation. You know what one of those is?"

Trevor nodded, not even breathing. Daisy hummed thoughtfully and stowed the gun back in its holster. His eyes swept around the room, looking for something. A tool that was less effective than the gun, but more effective than his hands.

That something turned out to be screwdriver shaped. Old and worn, metal surface puckered with acne-like rust. That'd do just fine.

"I'm not gonna lie to you," he said, picking it up. "It's mostly negotiating whether you end up in a little pain, or a lot."

He bent down onto one knee, so he could see himself reflected in Trevor's wide, watery eyes. Daisy felt as if something should be turning in him, but in truth, it was a lot like staring at a chair, or a piece of meat. Though it yelped and spoke, Daisy couldn't quite *feel* it was a human being.

Even when it bled.

Trevor didn't make a noise when the screwdriver pressed into his face. Terror kept him silent, kept his gaze trained, even as the blade began to etch a line down his cheek.

Satisfied, Daisy took the screwdriver away and held it up between them. Trevor's eyes blearily followed a droplet of red as it crawled down towards the handle. It was the shock that did it, Daisy thought. Fear beyond fear.

"That was for telling me you didn't know anything. And that's how this negotiation is gonna go," Daisy said, wiping the screwdriver clean on Trevor's outstretched leg. "One strike, I'll put this thing through your thigh. Two, I'll put it through your cheek, and your fingers. And three strikes?"

He let the tip of the screwdriver dip slightly, point fixed on Trevor's eye. Daisy heard him take in a short, horrified gasp, and hold it fast in his belly.

"I think you get it," Daisy finished, lowering the screwdriver again. For a moment, nothing in the room moved. Tension held taut. When Daisy spoke, his voice was quiet and rasping. Almost soft.

"Who told you about the time machine?" he asked. Trevor's head shook gently, mouth hanging open.

"I... I don't know who they were. They called on a payphone," he said. Daisy's face betrayed nothing, as if he was utterly disinterested.

"What were you going to do with it?" he said.

"I... we weren't, we d-didn't know it was here," Trevor replied, stumbling over his own tongue. Daisy turned the screwdriver in his hands.

"Do you know where Leslie O'Neil is?" he asked.

"No," Trevor said, voice quiet. Daisy smirked. That was a lie if he'd ever seen one before—tense neck, clenched hands and everything. With a practiced motion, he reached into his pocket and pulled out a pack of cigarettes.

"Three for three, kid," he said, lighting one. "Can't say I didn't warn you, but... I guess that's how it is."

He put the lighter away and held up the screwdriver. Trevor shook his head, brief tremor of deception washed away by fresh, frantic terror. He held up an arm and tried to scramble away on his back, mouth opening and closing like a hooked fish.

"No, n-no! Don't! Don't!" he cried as Daisy closed in.

The screaming didn't bother him.

He raised the screwdriver.

Stopped.

Narrowed his eyes.

Noise, he thought. Not the only noise.

He dropped the screwdriver and wheeled around, hand flying to the pistol at his hip.

~

Yule yelled and dropped down to one knee. He only heard the first pop of gunfire before his ears started ringing. He fell back behind an arcade cabinet, bullets cracking against the plastic siding.

One whizzed past his temple and buried itself in a rotten wall. He felt himself curse under his breath but couldn't hear it. Just the whistling pop of powder burning.

He grunted and twisted around behind a machine, barely avoiding another hail of gunfire. Lost in the haze, Yule pressed his shoulder against an arcade cabinet. Gritted his teeth and heaved. The machine groaned and toppled, smashing into another and another like heavy dominoes. The guy with yellow teeth leaped out of the way, hitting the ground in an awkward roll.

Something in Yule's gut twisted. A forgotten instinct trained into him hard enough that it had never quite gone away. The feeling of seeing an opening. Against himself, he raised up the pistol, one eye squinted. For a moment he lost track of himself. Let in the wet heat, and the smell of burning.

But his hands couldn't go with him. The sights danced and swayed in, grip shaking uncontrollably. With growing horror, Yule realized he couldn't get a bead. He just couldn't keep his hands steady.

BANG.

Yule's gun discharged, bullet whizzing somewhere into the floor. The yellow-toothed man's own weapon came up, and Yule threw himself back, not knowing where the leap would take him. An unexpected machine sat on the ground behind him, catching his heels as he fell. His head smacked hard against the ground, and when he came back up everything was blurred.

In the muffled, shaking pain, he saw a shape emerging on the other side. Somewhere, trained instinct gripped him again. His hand came up in a wide arc, and floatily squeezed off a shot.

The shape clutched its gut. Stumbled, nearly falling over the cabinet as one leg gave out, arm swinging downwards. That was all Yule saw before the hard, black shape of the man's pistol collided sharply with his face, hurled at full force across the room.

With a roar of effort the yellow-toothed man stumbled forward, fist cutting up through the air and into Yule's stomach. Then his throat, his face. Over, and over again, blow after blow. With each collision Yule saw his vision go a little redder. The world trembled and darkened, like he was shutting off. He felt his nose crunch. His ears swell, his eyes close, and yet the bloodied knuckles kept coming.

They only stopped when the yellow-toothed man nearly fell to the ground himself, utterly breathless. For a few long seconds neither of them moved. Then, the man grunted, and bared his decayed teeth.

Jerkily, he climbed back to his feet, one hand fumbling in a pocket. With a series of pained half gasps, he pulled a cigarette up from his jacket and popped it in his mouth, as if it was the water of life. As he lit it, his entire body shuddered, and bent around the deep wound in his belly.

Smoke weaved in and out of his lips, face carved into an agonized grimace. His shaking thumb teased back the pistol hammer, pointed straight at Yule's head.

"Bad play," he grunted.

Yule didn't hear what he said after that. A fresh pop of gunfire lit the room, and at first he assumed that was it. The last sound he ever heard, echoing after him as he died.

But it wasn't. To his surprise, as Yule opened his eyes, he found that he was still very much alive. Still breathing, and still in pain. But alive—and in nowhere near as much pain as the yellow-toothed man. At first, Yule thought nothing had happened to him. He was just... stood there, stock still.

That was until he dropped his gun, hand rising slowly and stiffly towards the gaping hole in his throat. As his fingers touched the edge of it, he let out an odd, sucking gasp, and wafts of milky smoke sputtered out from his neck. Then, it turned to blood.

He dropped to the floor. Convulsed a little. Then, went still.

Howard emerged from out of the shadows, white linen suit oddly stark in the gloom. He gave a quick glance to the body and then rushed over, dropping to a knee next to Yule. At first, Yule couldn't hear what he was saying, like they were on different sides of water. But as his hearing began to pop back in, it came out clear as day.

"Dammit, *where is he?*" he asked. Yule spat out a little blood.

"*Go in and distract him?*" he coughed, "Motherfucker this dude nearly beat my damn face off, where the hell were you?!"

"Where is he, Yule?"

"You're standing on him," Yule replied nodding to the body. The non-prosthetic half of Howard's face curled into a frustrated clench.

"Not him-!" he began. He was interrupted by a sharp, pronounced sob from somewhere behind them. Immediately he was up and on his feet, sweeping out of Yule's field of vision.

Trevor clutched his hands over his face. He'd never seen a person die before. He couldn't take his eyes off the corpse, just... lying there.

When he saw the half-faced man approaching, something in him flared. Panic, maybe. He yelped and tried to crawl out from the table he was hidden under, only to find solid wall behind him. As the man closed in, he held up his hands, bloodied palms outstretched.

"No! No, don't! Please!" he screamed, voice cracking. The half-faced man held up his own gloved palms and stopped dead, like he'd been expecting a very different reaction.

"It's okay," he said. "I'm not going to hurt you. I'm here to help."

For a moment it looked like he was going to take an involuntary step forward. There was a kind of sharp focus in his one good eye, a determination. But he caught himself midway and moved backwards again.

Trevor felt his jaw judder.

"I... I..." he said, unable to get the words out. He just kept looking at the body, looking at the blood... and thinking about Cal. The panic flared, and another fat sob rolled out of his gut. The half-faced man looked pained, and slowly descended onto one knee.

"It's alright," the man repeated, a smile cracking his features a little. "Trevor, it's okay."

"It's n-not. It isn't... my friend—I don't know where he's gone."

"He's safe," said the half-faced man, hands still up. Trevor took a few gasping breaths, like a fish on land. For what felt like the first time, he considered the man before him. Looked him over, in all of his strange, half-formed slant.

"Who are you?" he asked. "Where's Cal?"

For a few seconds, neither of them moved. The question hung between them, the few feet of space both infinitely far, and oddly close. Though the eerie prosthetic stared blindly and unblinkingly off to one side, half-faced man never took his one living eye off Trevor, even as his hand pulled away the mask.

Trevor's eyes widened, and the man smiled.

"I *never* never come back," he said.

THE SUM OF ALL EVILS

NORTHWEST OF TOWN, 1977

The machine gurgled and popped, before a pile of mushy ice dropped almost spitefully into the box. Cal winced and hauled it onto the floor, slush already half-melted. He plunged his bare foot into the ice and gritted his molars. Stinging shock gave way to painless cold. A sigh rolled off his chest. For a brief second he forgot where he was—when he was—and just *stood*.

Feeling.

The warmth of the afternoon sun on his shoulders and the slow creep of numbness growing in his leg.

The motel parking lot was empty, except for the crookedly parked rental truck in the nearest spot to the door. The Polybius machine sat in the bed, wrapped in a tarp and belted securely in place. Two suitcases waited in the backseat, covered by an old cartoon-print blanket they'd found by the side of the road. Neither of them were his.

Somewhere in the distance, smoke was rising. Helicopter shapes circled like flies, dancing slowly around the black column. Radio said it had been a sinkhole, and how it was miraculous nobody was hurt. Van Hallan had turned it off after that and spent the remainder of the long drive out in silence. Cal hadn't been in a position to refuse, he barely remembered anything after seeing the explosion.

They couldn't go back into town. He at least knew that.

A cold wind threw up goosebumps on his arms. Cal took his foot from the ice and turned away from the horizon. Didn't take the box with him as he loped away back to the motel room: there was nobody around to care either way. That was probably by design.

As he opened the motel room door, he made eye contact with himself, reflected in a large mirror that Van Hallan had pulled from the bathroom and angled at the wall. With it, there wasn't an inch of the room he couldn't see from his desk in the corner.

He looked up at Cal expectantly as he entered, fingers curled over a map of someplace. Cal loudly dropped his coat at the door, almost an act of defiance against the thoughtful quiet.

"I didn't see anybody. Not even on the road," he said, shutting the door behind him. "Before you ask."

Van Hallan ran a palm over his liver-spotted forehead, dancing with the glitter of sweat. When he looked back up, his eyes were dark and dim. A man who was tired, but still knew he had far to go.

"You must have many questions," he said. Cal folded his arms, not moving from his place by the door.

"A few," he said. The yawning moment that followed seemed to last minutes. A second, suspended in the golden glow of the afternoon heat, perfect and bright. But Cal could feel the fact he didn't belong there. Every atom of him felt like it was sticking and straining against the air like tugged Velcro. A hundred questions swirled in his head, but when they found their way into words, he discovered his mind was still back in the parking lot.

"Why an arcade machine?" he asked. Van Hallan snorted gently, but there was little joy in it.

"The internal circuitry lent itself to the design. Buying a secondhand machine set off fewer alarms than military-grade electrical supplies."

Cal chewed his lip. Some gate in his head opened and his thoughts turned to darker things. Things that pressed in his throat like a swollen stone.

"What happened? Last night, what did I see? Where even the hell am I?" he asked. The memory of the bodies, jarringly mundane in their sprawling places, danced behind his eyes. He could still hear the alarm ringing somewhere in his ears. Hadn't been able to sleep for it.

Van Hallan took in a long, bracing breath. It emerged weaker and more defeated than what had gone in.

"The year is 1977. Your coming here was a terrible accident of fate, had you arrived any other time than that night, I..." he said, trailing off a moment before setting his jaw. "What you saw was an act of sabotage. *My* act of sabotage. The experiments going on in that facility could not continue, there was no other way."

"No other way than *what?*" Cal insisted, hands flying up. "You still haven't answered my question. *What did I see?* Where was I? What were those... *things?*"

Van Hallan went quiet. Eyes down at the table, he lifted a shaking hand to his spectacles and placed them lightly down by the map. His entire body stiffened up, as if preparing to lift a dead weight from his chest which had hung there longer than he cared to remember.

"What you saw was the end of Project Lilac," he said, eyes still not daring to leave the table. "It was a series of experiments into time travel, conducted in complete secrecy and outside of conventional ethics. Our main objective was to research an element that appeared some years ago in Nevada, to achieve whatever we could, given unlimited resources. Test subjects, funds, facilities... all provided, as long as we attained results in return."

"So you experimented on people," Cal replied flatly. Mutely, Van Hallan nodded.

"Criminals, at first. From Holmesburg Prison, in Philadelphia. Career killers and rapists. Subjects we could feel had gone beyond the protection of morality. By the time they started adding more offenders, most of us had convinced ourselves we didn't need to ask anymore. Didn't need to question why so many looked homeless, or young," he said. Cal stared, halfway between curiosity and revulsion. Van Hallan met his gaze, eyes sagging. Sorrowful. And tired—more tired than Cal had ever seen some-body look before. But he could only feel *so* bad for him, given the circum-stances.

"So, what? You turned all of them into those... electric things?" he said, trying not to let flashes of blinking flesh creep into his mind's eye.

"Volatiles? Some. Not all," Van Hallan muttered, jaw clenching. "They began as mistakes. The failed results of trying to make time travel-ers who didn't need machines, past and future instances of the same crea-ture try to inhabit the same location in spacetime. The instances clash against each other like infinite balloons being rubbed on carpet. We were still working out a way to stabilize or put them down when The Branch realized their potential as a power source and ordered production of more."

"The Branch? Are they the government or something?" Cal asked in-sistently. Van Hallan's expression darkened again. His hand twitched and curled on the table, as if even considering the answer made his spirit wither inside him.

"They have access to the United States government, but they're some-thing separate. Something *other*. Never any names, never faces, only The Branch and the Operators. Always with resources, always with more men and more money. And other projects."

Cal felt a chill creep up his arm.

"Other projects?" he asked.

"Dozens more. Maybe hundreds, all just like this one," Van Hallan replied, voice hard with fearful intent. "All I know for certain is that you *must* stay away from them, no matter the cost. Never let them know your name, never let yourself come to their attention. The Branch is death and suffering incarnate, and they do not tolerate rivals."

The statement hung in the air like the smell of wet paint. Cal felt a shiver run briefly up his forearm, before a hot flush of resentment and fear pushed it back down.

"So why the change of heart?" he pushed, voice cracking. "If they're so dangerous, and you're so willing to help them, why risk it?"

Van Hallan exhaled slowly and closed his eyes. For a moment his body seemed to lift in its seat, years melting in his memory.

"During the war, my father designed weapons—guided missiles, meant for allied cities. He was not a monster, my father, he was a genius, just... in the right place, at the wrong time. A time when evil disguised itself as progress," he said, a refrain of shame quietening his voice. "When I was a boy, I asked him how he came to know what he was doing was wrong. He told me that one day he realized that he could no longer count how many weapons he had made on his fingers. He said that in that moment, he realized how much death he had created, that his hands had crafted more evil than the sum of themselves."

He paused, and the weight returned to him twofold. His voice was rasped and shameful, directed mostly to the faux pine table.

"One day, three months ago, I tried to recall how many human beings had died since the project began. To measure my hands against their actions, just like my father had," he said. The final words seemed bitter and clinging, as if they couldn't bring themselves to leave his lips. "But I'd lost count."

He stopped a moment to sigh, or something close to it. More exhausted and hopeless, like the air going out of a stamped-on bag. He rubbed his eyes and put his glasses back on, dark eyes brought back into focus.

"From then on, I obstructed as best I could. Lied, liberally. Told them that time travel could do things I knew it couldn't, coaxed them into chasing false theories. All until I found some way to wipe the slate clean," he said.

"You have a time machine, why don't you just go back and fix it?" Cal asked. Van Hallan smiled, but there was no joy in it.

"One of many lies I told," he said quietly. "Time simply does not work that way. There is no way for an event to exist stably in multiple instances—if it was possible to change the past, we would not be here talking about it. We would not have even met. It would have been solved from the very beginning, and neither of us would know it."

Cal frowned, and took a step forward despite himself.

"That's not..." he said, shaking his head as if to free the torrent waiting in his gut. "That can't be right. In my time, somebody *is* changing the past. Over and over again, there's a green flash, and... and I remember it, because of a plate in my head, and he's *erasing peop*—"

"I promise you," Van Hallan cut in, "changing the past is impossible. I've tried. Tried harder than I care to admit, but it simply cannot be done."

Then, he paused. An idea lit somewhere behind his eyes, and he leaned forward, voice hushed.

"*Erasing*, you say?" he asked.

"Right," Cal replied, nodding. Van Hallan hummed in agreement, and though it was no more joyful, his expression lightened a little.

"I believe our problems are connected, but not the same. Some weeks ago, a sample of Hallanite was stolen. The Branch believed they caught the man involved, but if things are as you say, they obviously do not find the sample before it resurfaces."

"How do you know it's not them? These Branch guys?" Cal asked. Van Hallan snorted gently and shook his head.

"If The Branch were still involved in your time, there would be no indication. No faces or forms: only a shapeless force, moving against you. The ability to identify even one of the men responsible tells me it's amateurs by comparison," he said, the ghost of a smile tracing on his lips, "And even The Branch would have realized that the past cannot truly be altered, and that 'Eraser Boxes' don't erase people at all."

Cal felt his face flush. His entire body tensed, as if he'd been hit by a bolt of lightning, all the directionless anger flashed out to bare, searing disbelief.

"What?" he asked, voice hardly above a whisper. Van Hallan locked eyes with him.

"As I said, the past cannot be changed. Things cannot be erased, simply moved. That is universal principle: what is true for the time machine is true for the Eraser Box," he said, taking a piece of paper from the side, gesturing with a pencil to the empty seat. "Please. Let me explain."

Despite himself, Cal sat. Didn't even question it. He felt numb. With a shaking hand, Van Hallan drew a large black dot at one end of the paper.

"Hallanite is a hyperlinear substance; connected and resonating with itself, no matter where in time it is, almost like magnetism. When two pieces are given adequate charge at a precisely matching electromagnetic frequency…"

Another big, black dot was scribbled onto the crumpled surface. Then, Van Hallan traced a jagged line between them.

"…the pull between two points becomes so strong that it creates a direct tunnel between them, through spacetime. Put something or someone in that field, and they'll get pulled into one end and pushed out the other. The more power you put into the reaction, the stronger the pull. Right now, we can pull just enough power from the grid to make a basic gate, but your situation is something different. Obviously, by your time, technological development has allowed the pouring of so much energy into the reaction, that whoever has the time machine has access to phenomena that are otherwise purely theoretical to men of this era."

He traced a few hard black lines between the points on the paper.

"Our calculations tell us that at a certain level of power, the pull becomes so strong that both points of the gate try and move towards each other—but they cannot. They are specific, discrete points in time, they cannot be altered. But the space that time occupies can move. If power is maintained."

Slowly, he creased the paper in an "s" shape, until the second circle was overlaid onto the first, following the line all the way.

"It folds in over itself. The past is superimposed over the present, with all the physical particles moved back to the same place. Time travel, but one step to the left, so to speak."

Van Hallan looked up expectantly, as if it was simple. Cal shook his head, halfway between frustrated confusion and unexpected, terrifying hope.

"I… I don't get it. How does that mean nobody got erased?" he asked. Van Hallan's gaze never wavered.

"Universal principle," he repeated, looking back down at the paper. "The Eraser Box is much like a time machine. It works by the same function: a piece of Hallanite is charged, the reaction occurs, and the subject is pulled through an entry point. But then, the connection intentionally fails. The Eraser provides enough electricity to start the reaction, but not to send a subject all the way through to the other side."

The pencil loped slowly away from the first black circle and stopped dead. Then, it traced a dotted line upward, into the empty space around the drawings.

"The subject is left in between, adjacent to time. Waiting for a big enough pull to send them through a gate. Not erased, simply in transit."

"But why does everyone forget them?" Cal asked, half out of fear that it all wasn't true. But what other chance did he have than to believe?

Van Hallan thought for a moment, tapping a finger on his thigh. When he finally spoke it was gentle yet firm, utterly in his element. Enveloped by facts.

"When a normal creature travels through time, every instance of them throughout time is re-ordered. Put back down in place according to the new model of where it ends. Their footprint in time is built to this new point from the ground up, like rebuilding a house," he said. "In terms of whether this is reversible, without a re-entry point, there is no end to be built to. But if provided with an exit point and a large enough attractive charge, theoretically, both they and the memory of them would return."

Cal felt as if he'd stuck a fork in a socket. He leaped up onto his feet, chair clattering loudly behind him. His hands flew to the side of his face as if he might scream but he said nothing, simply stood and stared, mouth agape in a silent, surprised shout of joy.

"They... they can come back? I can save them, I can bring them all back?" he shouted, grinning. He rounded the table closer to Van Hallan, insistent with energy. "We could do it now. Take the time machine from the truck, there's still some of that green stuff in it right?"

Immediately, Van Hallan's face fell, like a dropped stone.

"The time machine is broken," he said, shaking his head. Cal, unaware of how rasped his voice had become, didn't relent. He ran a hand through his hair, eyes scampering in thought around the room as he paced.

"Well, that's alright. That's okay. Because it doesn't *matter* how soon I go back, if I can't change the past. I'll just… wait for you to fix it, then work out a way to do the big flash back in my time."

"You don't understand."

"No, *you* don't understand," Cal insisted, not angry but forceful. "I've got to save somebody. A *lot* of somebodies. And I can do it, I won't screw it up, I swear. I can wait for you to do whatever you have to do to get it working again, hell I'll even get a job. But I *have* to get back."

He turned. All too late, the veil of excitement was pulled away, and he felt the atmosphere in the room. Chill, and tight, like ice on a puddle. Van Hallan sat at the other end, staring mutely at the table again. His head shook as if to underscore something said, but for a few moments no noise came from his opening and closing mouth. When they did, the sentence was dry and almost pleading.

"I can't do that," he said.

"What do you mean?" Cal replied, smile not quite faded. As if there was some hope left that it was only a misunderstanding. Van Hallan bowed his head again.

"There is no way to send you back," he repeated. "I'm sorry, but it just can't be done."

Cal felt the sides of his mouth tense up, pulling it into a disbelieving smirk. He laughed, despite himself, and shook his head.

"What? How is that even possible, there's a time machine right here."

"It doesn't work that way," Van Hallan said, voice suddenly fortified again by shameful fact. "Even if we had enough power, this machine is just an entry point. There would have to be a corresponding machine on the other end to receive you."

Cal's disbelieving smile faded. Became something more hard-edged, that tasted like panic rising in his throat. The feeling of invisible walls closing in.

"So send me to one of the ones from my time. It's literally the same time machine, the same one, I can tell you the date," he said. Van Hallan's brow hardened.

"And can you tell me the time? Down to the minute, down to the second? The co-ordinates of the machine?" he asked. "Time travel is a precision science, attempting to do it outside of a highly controlled lab environment is playing with fire. And even if we had all the information, *that* machine was meant to be disposable. Now that its job is done, the mechanisms are broken beyond repair. The fact it even brought you here at all is a million-to-one miracle."

Cal froze. His eyes stared widely at nothing, still shaking his head gently from side to side, as if his refusal to believe might still change anything.

"No," he muttered, voice cracking, "no, no this… this isn't how it's meant to go. You have to send me—I don't care how dangerous it is, you have to. I promised Trevor, I promised him… I promised I wouldn't…"

Van Hallan didn't move. A stone, straining against the ocean before it. His voice was grim and hollow, but it didn't show any sign of budging.

"Even if I could amass the power needed without being caught, there's no guarantee you'd exit in the right place. Overshoot your mark, and the best-case scenario is that you arrive in the hands of either The Branch, or whoever is in control of the machines in 1993, and even the odds of that being successful are suicidal, unless they knew you would be coming." He ran a hand over his glistening brow, herding sweat into his thinning hairline. A shaking hand toyed with his glasses, easing the rim back across his nose.

"You cannot know how sorry I am, Cal. I wish you could have found out an easier way. I had hoped to discuss it on the road to Boonestown," he finished. Cal mouthed the words back to him, as if they didn't make sense.

"Boones… Boonestown?" he muttered, as if he'd forgotten what language they were speaking.

He couldn't go back, he thought. He was trapped. Trevor was…

"Yes. Boonestown, Nevada. The xenosubstance first made landfall in the desert near there, eight years ago," Van Hallan went on, gesturing to the map. "For now we will hide there. Watch, to make sure no more has arrived. But when things are less dangerous, we can—"

He was interrupted by the sound of the door flying open, and the sound of feet flying across the threshold. Van Hallan leaped out of his seat at the sound, wildly turning to find its source. All he saw as he turned was a silhouette disappearing through the door, and then out of sight. His eyes widened.

"Cal!" he yelled, loud enough that his throat burned. "Wait!"

But he was gone.

⁓

The road thudded underfoot. He didn't look for cars.

Didn't know where he was running. Didn't care. His body was doing it by itself, as if he could run from the pain if he went fast enough. Gulping breaths emerged as frantic sobs, bursting through the undergrowth, through the trees.

But no matter how far he ran he couldn't get away from it. Panic and pain gained on his heels. The need to sob finally tipped past his ability to breathe and he toppled forward, limp with anguish. He hit the ground hard and curled up in a heap, fingers clutched painfully at his hair.

It was all over, he thought. That was it.

He'd failed.

It didn't matter that he'd tried, it didn't matter that he could help. He'd done it, he had the answers, he could go and save Trevor and yet somehow, some way, he *couldn't*. Trevor was going to die, and he was going to die all by himself, alone in that horrible, awful place, fuck. Fuck, fuck, *fuck*.

He dragged the little ranger figurine out into his palm and clutched it hard against his chest, rocking gently back and forth against it on the floor.

"I'm sorry. I'm so sorry, I'm sorry…" he muttered, face awash with hot, stinging tears. "Trev, I'm so… god I'm sorry, I'm sorry…"

He sobbed again, stomach cramping with the effort. One hand still pinned to his chest, he rolled onto his hands and knees, fat teardrops turning to glistening spots in the indifferent afternoon light. He brought the figurine up but could only bear to look at it for a half second before sobs racked him again. He leaned forward and pressed it against his forehead, not caring for the hard stab of plastic.

"I'm sorry," he repeated. "I'm so sorry."

He stayed that way for some time. Felt like he couldn't move, grief sitting on his back like a steel weight. It felt like dying. Like mourning. Like *failing*. For a while, that was all he could perceive: the buzz of shame and pain in his ears, without even the energy to cry out for it.

It was only after twenty minutes of silence that he finally keyed into his environment. The sound of birds and running water. He lifted his head, and met his own gaze staring back at him. It looked hollow and rotted out.

He was closer to the side of the stream than he'd thought, barely an inch. It ran through untamed woodland in both directions, humming dolefully as it murmured over stones and around corners. Cal stared into it for some time, motionless, like a stunned animal. He felt like he was just stopped there: like time had bent a final time around him, trapping him in that silent bubble of grief forever. Mourning for the life he'd lost in a button press.

But time didn't stand still. Nothing ever really did, he thought, as something fluttered in his upper vision. Frayed nerves still wary, Cal's vision flicked upwards as the urge to move jumped in his spine. But it was nothing.

Just a leaf. Spinning as it climbed down towards the water.

Cal watched its path down. His eyes darted down to the waiting water and caught his own reflection down below, and for a moment he hardly recognized himself. He hadn't seen his own face... well, it had been so long he didn't even remember. He stared at it, waiting for the feeling of unfamiliarity to fade.

But it didn't. Not entirely.

Cal narrowed his eyes, fingers rising to trace across one side of his face. It looked wrong. Paler. A set of crow's feet swooped away from his reddened eye; cheek pitted with the beginning of a smile line. He sucked in a breath when he realized the hand on that side was jagged with raised blue veins, skin taut and dry, that the entire left side of his body felt weak.

He looked older. He *was* older. All up one side of him, like a temporal sunburn.

All at once, the grief fell away. Realization washed over him in bright flashes, half-forgotten memories clicking together like freed gears. Howard Triptree, and the arcade. Leslie and the pizza order. The man with half a face. The past was set and always had been, right from the very beginning.

He'd wait forever to help Trevor, he thought. He'd known that from the start. And a few decades was something less than forever.

Silently, Cal stood up. Wiped a wet trail from his cheek as he looked out over the scene. Then, he turned back the way he came, and began to walk.

~

The wind blew gently across the asphalt. The tarp on the machine fluttered, and the motel parking lot stood firm and mostly empty, just as it had before.

The door to the room was still ajar, though a flurry of movement came from inside when Cal disturbed it. It eased open to reveal Van Hallan, layered in a hat, heavy jacket and scarf, pawing for a pair of sunglasses on the table. He froze when Cal's shadow broke the late afternoon light.

For a few moments, the silence persisted. The two stared at each other from opposite sides of the room, completely still. Then, slowly, Van Hallan removed the scarf.

"I was going to come looking for you," he said. Cal stepped inside the room and closed the door behind him, gaze still fixed. He stopped a few feet away from Van Hallan and folded his arms, voice hard and flat.

"Howard Triptree," he said. "Who is he?"

Van Hallan paused, as if he hadn't expected the question.

"Nobody. A collection of investments, bank accounts and forged credentials. I made him when I first began the project, a fake identity with no man attached. Through Howard, I could buy materials that Henning Van Hallan never could without setting off alarm bells. A man alive on paper, but nothing more."

"Well, maybe I need to make him real."

"No, he must stay—if Howard Triptree were to suddenly show up in Nevada, The Branch would descend faster than I could run."

"I know. He stays here in Amesville until 1993. I don't know what happens to him after that," Cal replied. "All I know is that by then, he's real. He's real, he's got half a face, and he's me."

For a moment, Van Hallan's mouth hung open, as if he couldn't quite understand what was being said. But slowly, his eyes tracked to the side of Cal's head, purposefully placed in the harsh glare of blind-filtered sunlight.

"My god," he said, wandering forward. "How could I not have noticed—"

His hand came up to touch the wrinkles, but Cal slapped it away. Van Hallan stepped back with a start, as if woken suddenly. His face lost none of its surprised despair, but Cal didn't reciprocate, choosing only to stand firm and set his jaw.

"It's to do with time travel, right? The face?" he asked. Van Hallan nodded.

"Chimeric Ageing Syndrome. Likely developed on your trip back here," he said, unconsciously tracing over his own wizened cheek. "It happens sometimes, especially on unstable lines, the body isn't put back correctly. Parts age faster than others. It could just be skin level, but without a full examination, I couldn't say for sure."

Cal chewed the inside of his cheek. Past couldn't change, he thought. Whatever it was, however bad it got, he knew he lived through it. At least, for long enough.

"It doesn't matter. I live, I know that. Do you still have all of Triptree's things? The bank stuff, the money?" Cal asked. Van Hallan pointed to a small suitcase, propped up in the corner.

"All there. I intended to burn it when we were out of state," he said. Cal shook his head.

"There's no 'we' in this. Not after you get in that car and go wherever you're going," he replied. "All I know is that I stay here, and I get old, and ugly, and I wait. It's like you said: if you already know it's gonna happen, it doesn't change."

Van Hallan was silent for what seemed an age. Chewing the proposition over in his head, as if he had any choice in the matter. Or, just letting it sink in.

"I'm so, so sorry, Cal," he said. Felt like he meant to say more, but he didn't.

"I know," Cal replied. "That's why the time machine has to stay here with me too."

At that, the life came back into Van Hallan. He crossed his hands sharply in the air and shook his head so suddenly that his glasses nearly flew off.

"No. Categorically no, that cannot happen. The time machine must be destroyed, along with the Hallanite inside of it. Of all places, it cannot remain here."

"It has to," Cal replied forcefully. "And it will. I know it will, *you* know it will, because it brought me back here. I know that by 1993, that time machine is still in Amesville, and you aren't. Whether or not you accept that doesn't matter. It's either here because you leave it, or here despite you trying to stop me."

The implication hung heavy. Heavier than any bullet, the inescapable promise of a future already divined. Van Hallan closed his eyes and sighed, shoulders slumping. What little fight was left in him had gone.

"There are two sets of keys in the briefcase. A small van, and a house back in town, on Claremont Street," he said quietly. "There's adequate space for the machine inside."

Cal went over to the corner of the room and picked up the bag, surprisingly weighty for its small size. He took it over to the dresser and clicked the lid open, revealing stacks of plastic-sleeved papers and documents inside. Three or four sets of keys clattered onto the faux wood, skittering to sleep in circle patterns. He thumbed through them, then clicked it shut again.

"When are you going?" he asked, sitting back down at the table. Van Hallan looked ruefully over to what sparse possessions he had managed to grab before fleeing. Photographs, mostly. No spare clothes or even a toothbrush. Just photographs from the mantle.

"When you ran, I made preparations to leave as soon as possible. Just in case," he said.

"Alright," Cal replied. They said no more than that. Even if Cal had questions, somehow that felt like the sum of it. Slowly, Van Hallan began to gather his things. Rolled up the map, moved the boxes by the door. All the while Cal sat in the rickety chair, staring at the wall. Not thinking of anything, just adjusting.

He was the guy who waited now. Guess he'd have to get used to it.

By the time it was all done with, the sun had run itself ragged on the horizon. Twilight oozed through cracks in the window blinds, dripping orange on the yellowed walls. Van Hallan lingered by the open door, truck idling quietly some ways across the parking lot. Cal still hadn't moved.

"I shall be going, then," Van Hallan said. "I will leave the machine here. You should come back for it as soon as you can."

Cal nodded, but said nothing. Van Hallan began to turn away towards the sunset, ready to ride away and never be seen again. But he was stopped by the sound of chair legs scraping on dry wood, and a tentative step across the old floorboards.

"I'm gonna come find you, when it's all over," he said. Something in Van Hallan's expression lightened unexpectedly. Relief, almost.

"I do not expect to be here by 1993," he said, as if the thought pleased him more than he wanted to admit.

"Then I'll find where you get buried. And I'm gonna find out every-thing you did while I was waiting here," Cal asserted, brow hardening. "Even if you die on the road out of here, somebody's gonna know every good and evil thing you ever did, for better or worse. I want you to know that."

Van Hallan took a deep breath in through his nose.

"Somebody already does. And I cannot get away from him, either," he said, putting his hand on his hat. Van Hallan gave Cal something south of a smile.

"Good luck, Cal. I'm sorry," he said. The door clicked shut, and he disappeared from sight. All that remained of him in the short minutes that followed was the sound of his footsteps on the gravel-strewn parking lot surface, followed by the low burble of the rental truck fading out into the quiet without so much as slowing.

And just like that, Cal was alone. He ran his hand through his hair again and tried to ignore the pit growing in his belly. His fingers crept into his pocket a final time, clasping gently around the sharp plastic angles of the green ranger. Carefully, as if it were made of glass, he placed it on the table in front of him and rested his chin on his arms so they were roughly eye level. A lone beam of sunlight wormed through one of the crooked blinds, like a spotlight.

Ever so gently, Cal ran his index finger over the plastic base, and took a deep breath through his nose. When he spoke, his voice was barely above a whisper.

"I'm coming, Trev," he said. "Slowly, but I'm coming."

DAMAGED GOODS

AMESVILLE, 1993

The backseat of the car was covered in crumpled notes, now occasionally spattered with blood. Yule laid across them, hunched up into a corner with his hand over his nose. Every pothole made his ears ring and his eyes hurt.

But somehow, he didn't mind. It sounded crazy, even in his head, but the pain felt like a reminder he wasn't dreaming. Or dead. No matter how much pain he was in, that was enough to make it all worth it. Just about. Either way, he still wouldn't have traded places with anyone else in that car: somehow, their situation seemed even less desirable than his.

Every so often, Howard would shift in the driver's seat, gaze snatched away from the road, prosthetic eye bobbing like a pendulum. Eventually, the kid in the passenger seat noticed too.

"What are you doing?" he asked.

'Howard' coughed, and returned his eyes to the road again, pulling a hard corner.

"Sorry. I'm trying really hard not to be weird about it, but it's been a while," he said. After a few more seconds of wordless driving, he turned his head again.

"You know it's me, right? Like, you believe me?" Howard asked.

The kid didn't reply, and Yule felt himself wince, awkwardness hitting him like a second-hand pile of bricks. Howard let out a long, rattling sigh through his nose, then put a hand in his pocket.

"Here," he said, holding out whatever it was across the little aisle. The kid took it and looked at it somewhere that Yule couldn't see. But somehow, he could feel the air in the car change. A little something that shook out the dusty malaise, signaled by small breaths and unhunched shoulders.

He was getting pretty good at this whole detective thing, Yule thought. Even after getting the shit kicked out of him. Though, without X-ray vision, he couldn't work out what it was they were looking at.

"All that time?" asked the kid, looking away from his hands.

"Made a promise," 'Howard' replied, shrugging. "Seemed like a good way to remember it. And it blows breaking your collarbone out the goddamn water."

Trevor stared, eyes wide with a mix of wonder and crushing, newfound sadness.

"What happened to you, Cal?" he asked. Yule guessed that was the old guy's actual name. Damn sight weirder than 'Howard'.

"It's a long story. Longer for me than you, I guess," Cal replied. "But I met him, Trev. Henning Van Hallan, the guy from the scientific paper. He told me about everything—time travel, Volatiles, the green rocks, all of it."

"Yeah, but what happened to you?" Trevor insisted. Cal grunted in recognition and gestured to his face.

"Chimeric Ageing Syndrome. It's not fatal, I think. At least, not so far."

Yule sat upright, far too quickly. Regret immediately spilled out in a sea of stars at his peripherals.

"Hey, wait a goddamn second," he grunted, clutching his temple, "is that gonna happen to me?"

Trevor turned to look at him, almost surprised. Like he'd forgotten Yule was there. Cal just grunted and chuckled under his breath.

"Probably not. You might find some wrinkles in places you didn't expect them, but... you should be alright. Mine was a special case. As it turns out, a lucky trip through a jury-rigged, broken time machine isn't exactly lab conditions," he said. Trevor turned back around in his seat for a moment before settling back into place.

"Who's that?" he asked, voice lowered as if Yule wouldn't be able to hear him.

"His name's Yule. You can trust him, we have something he wants," Cal replied. The car juddered as it rolled onto a dirt track off the road, before cluttering to a stop in the trees. Cal checked his watch and chewed his lip in thought, eyes occasionally darting up as if to see something half-remembered.

"Alright," he said finally. "Trevor, you go ahead to the bunker, tell Leslie we're coming. I'll help Yule. Should have about five minutes or so."

"Until what?" Yule asked.

"Something you don't wanna waste time having explained to you. Let's go," Cal said, shouldering open the driver's side door. Yule crawled out into the cold night, lips and nostrils stinging. As he stumbled forward Cal came to catch him, grunting a little under the weight.

"You alright?" Cal asked. Yule sniffed, winced, and spat a dark glob of blood into the grass.

"Just ruminating on why I'm always the one that gets hit," he said, nodding towards the hole in the ground. "That, and the sinking feeling you're gonna haul my ass down there."

"Afraid so," Cal replied. They walked across the clearing, stunted and limping, through the silver-toned darkness. Their voices barely carried into the nightscape, eaten up almost entirely by the trees, but as much as Yule wanted to feel like it was finally a moment of quiet, something in him knew better. A newly trained instinct to feel the tingling heaviness of static in the air.

He got onto his hands and knees, easing himself over the side of the hatch. A boiling sting of fear ran up his ribs as he crested the lip of the earth and the air deadened, surrounded on all sides by the black press of iron and rivets.

But he was there, at least. That kept him going, even if he was terrified. But the push to move was beyond his will alone. He found himself at the bottom, paralyzed, like his body refused to take another step further into danger. It took something unexpected to jolt him out of his own head.

"You're new," said a voice from his side.

Yule opened his eyes and turned his head. When he saw her, it was like a punch to the gut, like it shouldn't have been possible.

Leslie O'Neil just stood there. Ragged and short-haired, but still the same. No trumpets or fanfares, no parade: just the dull hum of air vents and the smell of industrial bleach. Yule didn't even think about saying something. He just froze, like a rabbit in headlights. Leslie gave him the kind of look you'd give clothes you don't remember buying.

"Have we met before?" she asked. Yule opened his mouth to reply. Wretched.

Then came the vomit.

~

The cleanup was quick, and quiet. Yule didn't ask why Leslie had the exact supplies by the door to do it, but lo and behold she did. When he was done emptying his gut, Yule felt like he should've said something—but he hadn't. He'd just mumbled something and stalked away, watching from a corner as Leslie talked to Cal. Just staring.

What did he even say? How does a person even break the ice like that? "Hi, I threw my life away to find you," seemed a little too intense, and, "Hi, I'm Yule," just seemed like an anticlimax. Maybe he'd get lucky, and the whole bunker would collapse over their heads before a good chance came up.

He winced and wiped some blood from his temple. He just thought he'd be happier about it. But now, looking over his own sweaty palms, Yule only felt wave after wave of internal dread wash through him. Gnawing in place of relief, insisting he had only looked for her to clear his own name and save his own skin. Even worse, that maybe it hadn't even been worth it, regardless of his motivations.

Across the room, Cal said something to Leslie, and she turned to look round at Yule. His heart leaped into his throat, but the look was short-lived. Leslie sat down at a small table, and Cal beckoned the others to follow. Silently, they assembled, and after a few moments of furtive silence, Cal cleared his throat.

"I'm not gonna waste any of our time with a speech," he said, "we all know why we're here. Tonight, we're ending this. All of it."

"How?" said Leslie, leaning forward. Cal rolled a thought around his mouth, and grimaced.

"You want the short explanation, or the long one?" he asked.

"I want the one where we all find out what the hell is going on," she replied. "You seem to have all the answers here."

Cal furrowed his brow and ran a hand through his hair.

"The long and short of it is that a man's got a time machine, and we have to get rid of it."

"How are we supposed to get to the thing if he can just loop back time?" Leslie pointed out, folding her arms. "There's nothing to stop him using it the second we show up."

Cal didn't answer immediately. Instead, his eyes wandered visibly up and over Leslie's shoulder, and towards the window far behind. She turned to see what he was looking at, and then twisted back around, brow furrowed.

"You're kidding, right?" she asked.

"The old tunnels lead directly into the space underneath the factory. Most of them collapsed shut when the place was quarantined, but no bombs went off on the other side of that surgical theater," he said, voice low. "We can use it to quietly make our way into the factory space and disable the power somehow. Without electricity Carnassus' machine might as well be an expensive paperweight. We'll be able to move in without being stopped."

"And what do we do when we move in?" Trevor asked. Everyone's eyes strayed to the gun slung over Leslie's back, implication heavy. Cal chewed the notion around his cracked lips and hummed thoughtfully.

"Maybe. That comes after, or during if it has to. But that's not what the second part of the plan is about. It's about bringing people back from the dead: everyone who got erased is alive. And we can get them back," he said.

The sentence settled like cold sweat over the table.

"What?" Trevor asked, voice quiet. Cal took a moment, as if to shake the weight of the statement off his shoulders.

"I talked to Van Hallan about it, a long time ago. Phenomenon's badly named, they're not erased, just traveling, I guess. They need a big enough attractive force to pull them back in. Mother of all resets, so to speak."

"But there's already no power when we move in," said Yule.

"We've got an invisible friend for that," Cal replied. Leslie screwed up her face.

"Wait, I'm confused. Who's invisible?" she asked. Trevor leaned over, as if he was passing lunchroom gossip.

"Big monster dog," he said.

"Sure," Leslie replied, shrugging. "Why not."

"Jemima was an escape route. A living battery full of Hallanite, designed to carry it off into the void where nobody could get at it," Cal continued. "Like every other Volatile, she's electromagnetically active, but she's also saturated with the green stuff. Van Hallan meant for her to jump into the in-between space and take it all with her, but she's got her own natural pull. He didn't count on the fact that any time a Hallanite reaction occurs—time travel, reset, whatever—she piggybacks onto it and re-enters. She's only here until her natural electricity charges up enough to push her back through a gate."

"But how does…" Yule began, before the pieces connected in his head. He flushed, and he held up a finger. "Oh no. Wait a goddamn second, no. No, no, no. That thing from the lab back in '77? That's not a battery, that's suicide."

"It's also the only option we have," Cal argued. "None of us even have to be near her. There's a straight track of road off Innsmouth towards the facility—all we have to do is get something going along it with this strapped to the top."

With that, he hauled a large cylindrical container onto the table. It let out a dull, dense *clud* as it hit the bench, ominous and black.

"More of the green stuff?" Yule asked.

"Just enough, salvaged from the Polybius machine. When it's got a little juice in it, this stuff lets out enough high-frequency noise to drive animals insane. Coupled with the pull from the Hallanite and the dog's natural urge to chase things, she's not gonna be able to resist," Cal said, patting the heavy cylinder. "Once she's in range of the factory, this unit'll turn off, and she'll get attracted to the active piece in the time machine. If the power's gunned to max, and the process is waiting for a kick, the second she comes within sparking range it should set off one hell of a reset."

There was a brief pause as everyone at the table, including Cal, reflected on what he'd said. The dull hum of the vents and the slowly ticking heartbeat of electricity below the floor seemed to rise up around them and wrap the cold implication of danger in stifling white noise.

Cal took off his hat and ran a hand through his hair, one side full and black, the other wisped with white.

"I don't really know what to tell all of you. It's gonna be dangerous, *really* dangerous—but apart from the people in this room, I'm not sure if anybody else in the world is even aware this is happening. Like it or not, somebody has to help, and those somebodies are us. Now, I only planned to ne—"

"I'll do it," Leslie cut in, voice hard. Everyone at the table turned to look at her, sat there with her arms folded and gaze stony. Cal let out a low, gravelly hum.

"You have to be sure. This isn't something to be taken lightly," he said. Leslie's brow hardened to the point of sharpness.

"Like I said," she repeated, "I'll do it. I want to."

Cal let his gaze linger on her for a moment before he nodded. His good eye wandered back towards the surgical theater window, fingers tapping out a noiseless tune on the table.

"You reckon you can use that shotgun if it came to it?" he asked. Leslie nodded, and Cal turned towards Yule. He held up his hands, as if in surrender, and slumped a little further onto the bench.

"You know my deal," he said, shrugging. "I'm in. Don't think much more needs to be said about it."

Cal nodded, and put his hands on the table.

"That settles it then. We'll wait for—"

"I want to help too," came a quiet voice from the side. They all turned slowly to see Trevor, straight backed and hard browed, almost defiant in his determination. Cal considered him with near disbelief for a second, before shaking his head.

"No," he said. "Not if I can help it, out of the question."

"Why? I want to help. I can do something!" Trevor insisted. Cal leaned forward; his good eye was wide with something more vulnerable than anger. Yule couldn't exactly tell what it was—somehow, he knew he'd never felt something like it before.

"I can't lose you, Trevor. I waited for so long to keep you safe, I can't just throw you away. Not for nothing, I just got you back," he said. For a moment Trevor's resolve seemed to waver. But then, he took a deep breath in through his nose, and drew himself up once more.

"That's why you of all people should realize that I've got just as much to lose as anybody else. I have to help. And if you don't let me, I'm gonna end up doing something stupid," he said. For a few seconds, the tension in the room was taut enough to sting. Then, Cal sighed deeply, and pinched the bridge of his nose.

"Dammit, Trev, why today of all days do you suddenly decide to be brave?" he muttered, before opening his eyes again. His hands traced a hard, authoritative line through the air as he spoke. "Look, you can help, but you're gonna be far away from danger, alright? And if danger arrives, you book it the hell out of there. You promise me that, right now."

"I will. Promise," Trevor replied. Cal, satisfied but not quite happy, slid back into his position on the bench. With a final, bracing breath, he lifted his heavy head and surveyed the group, one by one.

"We wait for the next green flash. When that happens, Yule and Leslie will go into the tunnel and make their way north towards Sledmore. When you're there, you find where the power supply is, and you destroy it by any means necessary. After that, get out of there," he said, eye darting between them. "Understood?"

They nodded, Leslie more sharply than Yule. Anything more than a gentle bob made his jaw feel like it was gonna fall off. Cal nodded, eyes misting over as his thoughts left the room.

"Good. You should all take what little sleep you can get. From this moment on, we could start up at any time," he said, standing up. Leslie smirked.

"Aren't you gonna say dismissed, or something?" she asked. Cal laughed, but it was low and joyless.

"Dismissed," he muttered, walking over to look at the consoles. The remainder looked between themselves in silence, just letting the cold feeling of responsibility soak into them. Yule cleared his throat, if only to break the silence.

"I'm guessing I can't book myself a room with a bathroom or something, right?" he said.

Silence descended quickly down there, below the skin of the earth. When something finally jolted him from his half-slumber, it could just have easily been a dropped pin.

Clack. Chnk. Ca-Chnk. Clack.

Yule opened his eyes. The sound bounced all around him in the dark, not threatening but disorientating. Like a tiny little moth, fluttering quickly from tile to tile. Yule turned his head a little and waited.

Clack. Chnk. Ca-Chnk.

There it was again. Not in the room with him as he'd feared, but from somewhere down the metal hallway. The reverb made it sound distorted and strange, but it was nearby. His hand unconsciously groped for the pistol as he rose to his feet. Yule didn't know if he'd be able to use it and hoped he wouldn't have to find out.

He pivoted around the doorframe, eyes wide and darting. But the hallway lay in the same sleeping disarray it had when he'd turned in—the only difference being the bright light emanating out from three doors down.

Yule edged a little further and peered through the doorway. When he saw what was inside, he untensed his jaw, put the pistol in his pocket, and took an intentionally loud step forward. Leslie hardly stirred from her position.

The room was long, with a low ceiling. The sides were piled up with desks and boxes, cleared to form a tight, unobstructed line of space from one side to the other. Leslie stood at the nearest end, feet planted in a wide stance, head cocked. The shotgun nestled in the crook of her shoulder.

For a moment, he watched her. Frozen there, like a moment in time. *Click.*

The hammer met an empty chamber and tutted. Leslie lowered the gun.

"You know, most people do that when it's loaded," Yule said.

"Tried it. Way too loud," she replied, eyes fixed on the wall. She brought the shotgun up again. *Click.* Tut.

Yule walked further into the room and squinted. The opposite wall was flecked with peppercorn-black impact marks. They were centered around what looked like a crude outline of a man's silhouette, drawn in sharpie on the off-white treated steel.

"Anyone in particular?" he asked, nodding to the silhouette. Leslie's lip curled into a momentary grimace, before falling again. She wandered over to the side of the room and dropped to one knee.

"Yeah, actually," she said, putting the shotgun on the floor. She gestured to it and gave him a half-smile. "Not a fan of guns, right?"

Yule knitted up his brow and leaned against the wall, arms folded. He didn't really know what else to do with his hands, otherwise.

"Had to become a little more comfortable with them recently," he said. "So I guess that means you remember me?"

"I do now. It's hard thinking about it, but Cal told me all about what you did, why you were here, and I guess it just clicked. You were the guy with the truck."

"The truck you painted up with a deer, in a move that cost me fifty bucks," Yule pointed out. "Not that I'm bitter or nothing."

At that, Leslie smirked. Yule smirked too, and for a brief moment they were caught in something that felt normal. Like it could have been anywhere, a grocery store, the street—somewhere that wasn't a bunker. But it only lasted as long as the echoing knock of pressure above the ceiling allowed, and pretty soon the smiles faded.

"I'm sorry for what happened to you," Leslie said. Yule exhaled through his nose and nodded, unsure of how to respond.

"Yeah," he said eventually. "You too."

"I guess you probably want to know, right? I mean, you came all this way. Seems cruel to keep it a mystery," Leslie said, sitting down on the floor. Yule shrugged.

"Probably something similar to what happened to me, I'd bet. You don't wanna talk about it, I've at least got a reference. But I won't pretend like I'm not curious," he replied. A few seconds passed in fluorescent-tinged gloom. Leslie sighed.

"It's weird. I don't even know if I don't like talking about it or not," she said, drawing her knees up to her chin. "It's hard remembering."

Yule felt something both comfortably familiar and fearful mix in his gut. Something in the way she sat, the far-off stare. The unmistakable twitch of a finger, or the shake of a leg which should have been still. He knew how she felt, he thought. And he wouldn't wish that on anybody.

"You mind if I sit next to you?" he asked. Leslie nodded, and Yule obliged. The floor beside her was cold, but he'd get used to it. They sat there for a while without talking, just staring at the wall. The black-flecked silhouette loomed up the wall, unfazed and unmoved by the shot in its belly.

"You thinking about home?" he asked. Leslie shook her head, and Yule laughed softly to himself. "Shot in the dark, I guess."

"I'd give anything to be thinking about it though," Leslie said quietly. "My bed. School. Stupid little stuff like that."

"I hear that. Me, I could use a nice cold beer right about now."

"Not some reefer?" Leslie asked. She smirked, not needing to see Yule's surprised expression to know how he looked. "I remember that too, y'know."

"See, if I felt like you were gonna snitch on me, maybe I might not have come looking for you," Yule said, chuckling. He laid his head against the wall and felt the dull hum of the bunker mutter through his throbbing skull. A gentle reminder of the not-so-gentle beating he'd been dealt.

"It's hard," he said. "I might not know exactly what it's been like for you, but I at least know that, no matter what it was, coming out the other side is always hard as hell."

"Yeah," Leslie said softly. He gave her a light bump with his shoulder.

"You get through it, though. Somehow, some way, you get through it. As long as you can just keep putting one foot in front of the other, eventually the clouds break. Just gotta wait it out."

Leslie gave him a weak smile and met his gaze over the tops of her knees.

"So how much of that is actually true, and how much of that was just to make me feel better?" she asked. Yule smiled back at her, and then turned his gaze back to the opposite wall. Like he could see something better than the bare metal, somewhere beyond.

"However much turns out that way, I guess," he said. There was a pause for a second as something in the room dropped. Pretense, maybe. A shield. Maybe both.

"They got me in the woods. I was walking, and I saw two guys come out of a hatch. Then they grabbed me," said Leslie, voice low. "Never even fired a shot."

"I guess we're just peas in a pod, huh?" Yule replied. "I didn't so much as get a single slug in before they got me. Guess everybody's got a plan 'til they get a needle in their neck."

"I won't make the same mistake twice," Leslie insisted, her voice suddenly hard and edged. She sat up, eyes flicking to the shotgun as if to remind her that it was there. Yule frowned.

"Correct me if I'm wrong here, but it looks like you're in a real hurry to kill somebody," he said.

"Not somebody. Just *him*," Leslie replied, final syllable spat out like something sour. Her eyes fixed on the jagged silhouette across the room, fingers tense. Yule felt something inside of himself twinge.

"I get it," he said slowly, "but—"

"Don't give me any of the moral crap. All that stuff about being just as bad as them, I don't care. Not him. He's barely even human," Leslie said, hard gaze now squarely on him. Yule didn't fully relax until her stare was away from the shotgun, and his pulse could finally stop racing. He held up his palms and nodded.

"I get it," he said. Leslie frowned.

"You do?"

Yule shrugged and laid back against the wall again.

"Look, I'm gonna be honest with you, I'm not a philosophy person. Some maniac's erasing people, putting people's lives in danger, maybe he's better off in the ground. So maybe you're right."

He inclined his head a little, so that their eyes were locked.

"All I know is, it'll change you. Not in a moral way, but in a way you gotta live with. When you pull that trigger, it's not like stamping on a bug or scratching an itch: it's agreeing to wake up every day, knowing you took a life. Knowing that you'll always be somebody who killed somebody. You think that's worth wiping this guy off the face of the earth, then I can't tell you that you're wrong. But if you're gonna make that trade, you've gotta know what you're putting up in return."

The last sentence settled ghostlike on the steel floor. Leslie stared at the wall, silently taking stock of what she'd heard. Yule could almost hear the gears turning.

"You too?" she asked.

"Vietnam. More than a couple," Yule replied, nodding. Above them, the bunker rumbled and creaked as slumbering earth stirred in the night. Leslie wrapped her arms around her knees again. Her eyes never left the shape of the silhouette on the opposite wall.

"If it's what'll stop all the nightmares about him? Maybe it is worth it. I don't know," she said. Yule went to nudge her again. Paused. Then, his arm came up around her, and gently tightened. She felt cold.

"You're alright. Might not feel like it, but you're alright," he said.

"Thanks," Leslie replied, voice crackling slightly as she pressed ever so slightly against his embrace. Yule smiled.

"You're welcome."

"No," Leslie insisted, looking up at him, "I mean it, for... I dunno, for coming looking for me. You didn't have to, but you did, so... thanks."

Yule snorted a little and nodded.

"Guess I didn't, did I?" he said.

They spoke no more after that. Didn't need to—all that needed to be said had run dry, leaving only the stolid rumble of the bunker to fill the space. Yule laid his head back and let his eyes fall upward, towards a night sky imagined blindly somewhere above. Some things never changed, he thought.

Soldier or civilian, he always found himself on somebody else's time.

HATCHET

AMESVILLE, 1993

Carnassus had never run there. He couldn't. He'd been slow and clumsy with his own body, and running only made that fact even clearer, advertising his weakness to everyone who saw him. But on nights like this one, there had always been the temptation.

Now, sat alone on the bench, he knew that he had to stay still. The anglerfish floating in the black expanse, the spider waiting motionless at the edge of its web—in the general order of things, prey kept moving, predators waited.

And wait he did. Alone, with the bag.

It sat within arm's reach, squat and boxy, zipper flipped up and ready. Every crease of the fabric asked a question of him, and what lay inside.

Tones of red and blue mixed to bruise colors on the grass as the police cars raced past on the road behind him. Going to the arcade, he imagined. After all, Daisy had never called back, and he knew exactly what that meant. It didn't matter—he'd be back. Time travel made everything seem so tedious that way. Even death was a matter of scheduling.

The sirens lowered out as they flew into the distance, heading for the other side of town. His thoughts lingered briefly towards his own car, parked a short distance behind at the curb.

Then, they became focused on the jogger.

They appeared in his peripherals like a fly, bouncing steadily on the lit path as they made their way towards him. A male. Older, with thin wrists and a reddened face. Hard gait, but weakness behind it.

Carnassus' hand reached over to the bag and tugged the zip, hand a moment from entering…

Then he stopped. Listened.

The footsteps changed. Slowed to the tune of clacking gravel. His fingers pulled back on the zip, closing the bag as a shadow fell upon him. Carnassus looked up, and the jogger gave him a red-cheeked smile, hands planted on his knees for support.

"Nice… night. You mind… if I… rest here a while?" he panted, nodding to the empty space on the bench. Carnassus stared at him for a second, before the reflex to mask himself kicked in. He brightened his eyes and smiled.

"Not at all," he said, shifting over with his hand still on the bag. "Please, take a seat."

The jogger obliged, hitting the bench with a loud groan of relief. He sat against the backrest and raised his head up to the sky, blowing out puffs of foggy air like a coal-fired train. Carnassus looked at him as long as he thought he could get away with, and then averted his gaze.

"You look like you're thinking about something," came a voice, unexpectedly. Carnassus stopped and looked back at the jogger. He was just… staring at him. Looking at him as if he understood what he was seeing. He hadn't expected that.

"How do you mean?" Carnassus asked. The jogger smiled back at him and let out a gasped chuckle.

"Well I mean, I'm crazy enough to be out here in running gear," he said, pointing, "but it's not so often you see a guy sitting alone in a park at ten in the evening, wearing a fancy suit. Figure you've got some thinking to do—used to do the same, back when I had to wear a suit every day."

Carnassus smiled, lips pantomiming the way they had a thousand times before.

"Looks like you've got me all figured out," he said. The jogger held up his hands and leaned back into the bench.

"I don't mean to pry none. A guy's business is his own, I just remember that whenever I was in that kinda situation, I wished I had somebody to talk to," he said. Carnassus smirked, and this time only most of it was fake.

"I really don't think there's anything you could say that would help me," he said, thumb and forefinger kissing over the zipper. Silently, slowly, he began to pull it back. The jogger didn't notice. He just let out a short, sharp little chuckle, and laced his fingers over the rise and fall of his belly.

"Try me. I reckon I know part ways already," he said. Carnassus stopped, hand frozen on the bag's clasp. For a bare second his face flashed with stony, defiant ire, a boot being challenged by an insect. He was half turned away, face obscured, but still coldly noted his own failure to stop the mask slipping.

"Oh?" he asked, consciously pushing back to personable neutrality. The jogger nodded and fixed his eyes out on the horizon as if to maintain the casual distance between strangers.

"Personal troubles," he said. "Like I said, I've been there. A lot."

Carnassus paused. Slowly, his hand fell away from the bag, and back onto his lap. He didn't reply for a few seconds.

"Yes," Carnassus repeated, despite himself. "Yes, I suppose you could say that."

For another few seconds, they didn't talk. Carnassus felt odd. Like he had something aching inside his gut that he'd never noticed until now. Colder than panic, but hotter than fear. His thoughts turned to the time machine bolted to the wall. His electrical muse, demanding and tormentingly beautiful.

"There's a woman," he said, "that I've been in love with… it feels like all my life. Since I was a kid. My entire life is built around her, doing what she needs me to do, things I know only I can do for her, but…"

He trailed off, half-shocked at the anxiety welling in his ribcage. The jogger let out a thoughtful little hum, which made the white whiskers on his lip shiver.

"But now something's changed. Right?" he said knowingly. Carnassus sighed, momentarily tuning into the whining echo of police sirens in the far distance. Leaving them all alone.

"I try to go back and fix everything that goes wrong, but I feel as if I'm climbing a ladder that's unraveling beneath my feet. Just trying to keep pace or I'll fall," he said.

"You ever thought of leaving her?" asked the jogger. Carnassus chuckled joylessly and shook his head.

"No," he replied. "Not an option. She's my life, without her… nothing means anything. That isn't the problem."

"So what is?" said the jogger. Carnassus leaned back against the bench and felt the anonymous rise and fall of the seat against his gloved fingertips. As the wind died down and the trees fell still at the border, night draped its warm jaws over them.

"Recently, I find myself asking questions that I don't know the answers to. The situation is suggesting I'm going to have to do things I've never done before, but I can't guarantee whether I'll even be able to do them. What if I was capable enough to do everything that she asked of me in the past, but this is my limit?" he said.

"So you're afraid," the jogger said. Carnassus considered it for a moment, letting the word slowly sink in. Then, he took a deep breath, and inclined his head.

"Yes," he said, nodding. "I suppose I am."

"You look like a smart guy. You don't need me telling you that it's okay to be afraid."

"I know. At least, in my head, I know it. And yet, I find myself hesitating even to test myself. If that fear makes me hesitate when the time actually comes to act…" Carnassus said, shaking his head gently as he trailed off.

Another silence pervaded. The jogger twiddled his thumbs, neon-clad feet twined over each other as he thought. When he spoke, the question was bare, but benign. Like he already knew the answer.

"Do you love her?" he asked. Carnassus' eyes never left the blank darkness of the middle distance.

"Sometimes, I think she's the only thing I've ever loved," he said. The jogger let out a happy sigh and sat up.

"There's your answer, I guess," he said. "There's fear, and there's love. In my experience, you can always ignore one for the other. Guess you get lucky enough to consciously make the choice."

Carnassus drew in a breath through his nose, the smell of sleeping trees prickling in his nostrils. It felt good. Invigorating.

"I think you're right," he said. The jogger smiled and stretched his arms.

"Guess I must be," he said, grunting, "still, that's just my two cents. Can't say if it solves your problem outright, but... that's how it is."

Carnassus chuckled.

"So do you do this to everyone you meet?" he asked.

"Just the ones that look like they could use it," the jogger replied. Then, he shook his legs and fumbled with his headphones, slipping the band back over his bald patch. "Anyways—shouldn't pry any more than I'm welcome. Sounds like you've got enough on your hands already."

Carnassus turned to him, and for the first time, gave him a look that felt genuine. It had been so long since the last, Carnassus had almost forgotten what it felt like.

"Thank you," he said. The jogger smiled, clapping a sweaty palm lightly on Carnassus' shoulder. And for a second, Carnassus felt it. As if he'd never realized the physicality of another human being, that they were actually there. And for a fleeting moment, it felt fine, good even. An unspoken craving, satisfied.

"Just remember, you're not alone out there," he said. "Might feel like it sometimes, but you're just like everybody else."

Carnassus froze. Something dropped inside his belly.

"Excuse me?" he asked, turning to look at the jogger, who just kept smiling.

"I'm just saying, nobody's that much different. Everyone goes through stuff," he repeated. Carnassus just stared. The fleeting moment had gone, blown away like leaves in a cold, nauseating wind. He felt himself plunge back into the frigid, unseen space, barely aware he had ever crawled out. The world narrowed. Quietly, and without ceremony, his fingers found the zipper again.

"Right," he echoed, his voice flat. "Just like you."

"Exactly," the jogger confirmed, standing up. He looked away, up and down the path, shaking out his fingers and shifting in place.

"Well, enough yabberin' on," he said, moving to look back at the bench. "I should let—"

The sentence never finished. He never heard the bag being undone, or the rasp of glove on the plastic handle as Carnassus' fingers wrapped gently around it.

All he heard was the whistle of the hatchet head as it whirled up towards him and thudded just below his ear. One of the headphone wires fell from the set, severed immediately by the impact. His eyes widened. A hand came up to touch the ax blade, as if he couldn't believe what it was.

Carnassus grunted and gritted his teeth as the swing became a pull. The blade wrenched itself out with a wet *thwuck*, and the jogger fell as if swooning. But Carnassus didn't stop, couldn't stop, for now the question was at hand and the answer was in its proving.

He fell upon him, bearing down like a mad dog as he heaved the hatchet into him, over and over and over. With a final grunt of fury and effort, he raised the hatchet above his head and brought it down, hard.

The jogger's feet juddered. Twitched. A wet gasp bubbled out of him, and finally he fell still.

Carnassus stood up again and stumbled back a little. All the muscles in his upper body ached, half burnt out by the hormone rush of violence. He panted, eyes flicking up and down the body, taking as much of it in as he could. Memorizing and quantifying.

He'd never killed somebody before. Not really, not without the box. Not with his own two hands. He had never feared the moment of action, but he feared what came after. The risk of never recovering from the opiate taste of death and becoming a slave to it like Mr. Daisy.

But as the haze lifted, he found he felt… nothing. The static buzz of adrenaline faded, and in its place, he didn't find rage, or regret or even happiness. The body, and the man it had once been, were little more than scenery. His hand came up to his face and wiped his brow, taking a red smear with it. Carnassus considered it for a moment, before realizing he was sprayed up and down with the stuff.

He smiled.

Nothing at all. He felt no change, no trepidation. Just the familiar, insistent coldness running through him, like the world was nothing more than turning water. Without fanfare, the question faded from his mind. Not only answered but satisfied. With a jerk, he pulled the hatchet from the jogger's head and took a few steps closer to the edge of the darkness, like he was communing with it. The night seemed to unfurl before him now, driven on by his will to open like a flower.

He could feel them. Somewhere, out there. The people who were struggling against him, slowly closing in as asset after asset fell. But now, it mattered less.

Because now, he knew that even if matters fell solely to him, he could do it. Without hesitation or intoxication, no matter who they were or what was available to him. He could kill like an animal and think like a man.

He smiled.

All the worse for them, he thought, walking back to the car.

04:01

AMESVILLE, 1993

A faraway electric whine woke Yule from fitful sleep, just in time to hear the ringing approach of shoes on steel. As he sat up, the door to the room swung open, filled with Cal's silhouette.

"We just had a green flash," he said, quickly and calmly. "Time to go."

Before Yule could reply, the door swung shut again, and the sound of Cal's feet thundered down the hallway. He heard him knock on Leslie's door, and offer the same message.

He groaned, hand rubbing away at the jungle still drumming in his head. His hands groped blindly in the dark for his belt and gun before he finally stood upright in the dark. Waited there a minute, just letting time pass. Feeling his fingers wiggle and his weight shift.

Game time, he thought.

In the atrium, Leslie stood wiping down the barrel of her shotgun, slung ready around her shoulder. Cal was in the corner, hunched over something.

"...through to the biolab division, and—Yule? Good, get a coffee. I was just telling Leslie what your plan of attack is," he said, standing fully upright. He heaved two large red jerricans up onto the side, and hurriedly began wiping away some gasoline that had spilled on his jacket.

"So what are we looking at?" Yule asked, taking a cup of coffee from the side. Or at least, he hoped it was coffee—usually you didn't drink it out of a conical flask. Leslie nodded to the window on the other side of the room: below it, a tangled rope of knotted up lab coats and overalls sat coiled against the steel wall like a fat worm.

"We're going in through there," she said.

"Once you're past the surgery theater, you'll need to head down the adjacent hallway to the biological study wing. Should be a red line going towards it on the floor in the corner," Cal continued. "The place was re-inforced to stop it releasing samples following a collapse. If there's anywhere in the tunnels that's likely to still be standing, it's there."

"Wait a second," Yule cut in. "What do you mean is *likely* to be standing? You haven't checked any of this out?"

"Site was too hot for years. By the time The Branch stopped being interested in it, I already had a few things on my hands," Cal retorted, gesturing around the room. Yule groaned under his breath, masking his grimace with a cursory sip of coffee. Going into unknown territory, with shaky information and little help—this was feeling way too much like the army again.

"Alright. So if this place is still standing, what do we do then?" he asked. Cal shook one of the jerricans, which sloshed merrily.

"There should be an emergency generator in the Sledmore biolabs. Fuel it up, and all the power doors will unseal themselves and you'll have access to a maintenance tunnel terminating just inside the factory space. Once you're inside, find anything that looks like it's generating a lot of power, and destroy it."

"We got anything that might help with that? I'm not sure how much guns are gonna do for destruction of property," replied Yule. Cal smiled, and shook the jerrycans again.

"That's what the second can's for," he said. The acrid tang of gasoline wafted around the room, an insistent reminder of the trials to come. Cal reached into his pocket and handed Yule a little digital watch.

"Put that on. I've synchronized them, Leslie's got one too," he said, painted eye deathly still. "Now you gotta listen closely to me here: no matter what happens down there, you need to have the power off by exactly 4:50 a.m. Four five zero, you understand?"

"Right," Yule replied, strapping the watch over his wrist. Cal nodded, jumpy with nervous energy.

"Good," he insisted. "Four-fifty, no matter what. Otherwise we're sunk."

Leslie checked her shotgun and slung it around her shoulder, before looking over to the two of them.

"So, we good to go or what?" she asked, voice breathy with barely contained fear. The fact she wasn't a crumbling mess right now told Yule the kid was tough as nails—as if he needed any more reminding of the fact. He adjusted the pistol in his belt and swigged away the last of the coffee.

"No time like the present, right?" he said. Cal handed him a gas canister and gave him a look of solidarity. Or at least, half of one—the other side of his face stayed synthetically and characteristically unmoving.

"Give 'em hell," he said. "And the second you're done, get the fuck out of there. It's liable to get messy."

Leslie wandered over to the window and looked at Cal. He nodded, and without hesitation she swung the butt of her shotgun into the glass. There was a loud shattering sound as squared pieces of safety glass flung themselves into the black drop beyond, presence proven only by a soft chiming as they hit the ground below. Leslie reached down and unfurled the makeshift rope over the edge.

"Looks like it goes all the way to the bottom," Leslie said, peering over. She cleared away more glass with her boot and swung her leg over the side, knuckles white on the makeshift line. Her eyes met with Cal's, hard and glistening with determined fear.

"Stay safe," she said.

"You too," he replied, and with that, she was gone. Slipped over the silent precipice into the darkness below, existence suggested only by the sound of the rope tightening and bouncing with her weight. Yule tried to swallow the stone in his throat and slid his belt through the jerrycan handle. It sloshed against his hip as he went towards the window and peered over.

In the dark, he could see Leslie's shape moving faintly down below. He slipped a sweaty hand over the rope and leaned against the open exit.

"Remember what I said," Cal repeated to him. "Get in, get out."

"Right," Yule said, cautiously tugging on the line. He really hoped this kid knew her knots. He eased himself over the lip of the drop and gave a start as his weight yanked downwards, only to stop dead as the rope strained.

His heart thudded behind his eardrums. Just keep breathing, he thought, just keep gripping. One hand below the other, feet ever so lightly padding against the wall. Just like boot camp, descending the knotted rope. It seemed to go on forever, so long that he even began to nervously question whether he was moving at all. When his feet finally found the ground, it felt like a jolt of electricity running up his heel.

He gasped and let go, stumbling back a few steps. Looked down at the ground, as if to check it was really there, and then back up again. Looked like a much longer drop from down below. Yule couldn't tell if that made him feel proud, or more like a rat in a trap.

The smell down here didn't fill him with confidence either. The sharp tinge of ozone and the wet stink of decay were warning signs that things were about to go sideways. He forced a bracing sigh through his teeth and shook out his shoulders. *Still*, he thought, *luck loved an optimist, right?*

"You coming?" came a voice from behind him. Yule jumped and turned around to see Leslie staring bemusedly at him.

"Dammit, don't sneak up on me like that. Coulda shot you or something," Yule said, voice low. Even barely above a whisper, it carried in the concrete tomb, skittering on the walls and gliding above his head. Made him nervous.

"Yeah. Looked like it," Leslie replied, half smiling. It faded as she turned to look across the operating theater, to the blown-out windows on the other side. Yule turned and stood beside her, so that only a sliver of air separated their shoulders. Close enough that she could feel him there.

"Come on," he said.

As they walked, Yule turned his eyes towards the emergency exit, high and unlit atop a flight of stairs. Darkened windows and doorless doorways betrayed nothing of what lay beyond, and each footstep disturbed the ancient earth beneath them. The stairwell muttered and scratched at itself as they ascended, struggling against the bolts which bound it to the wall. But it held all the way up to the door, which opened without resistance, yawning into the embrace of open darkness.

The room beyond was barely visible, dominated by a rectangle of pure black space at the far end: an open doorway that marked the bounds between the world above, and what lay sleeping beneath. Yule had never seen darkness like it: true dark, endless and boundless, carnivorous purpose clear in every formless inch of it. Beckoning him to enter the dead tangle of the bunker, and never be seen again.

As Yule saw Leslie step towards it, he felt the sudden need to call out to her. To warn her of this thing she didn't see, the mouth she was about to walk into. But the fear of the darkness kept him quiet. As if the sound of his voice might wake something.

It only gave him the energy to follow. Follow, and feel the light fall away from him as he too passed below the archway, and the blackness swallowed them whole.

The hallway beyond was cramped and littered with things half seen. Rock or bone, lichen or blood, the colorless circle of electric light gave no clue. All that stood out in the wash of gray and brown was a faded red line, pressed against the edge of the floor like it was trying to hide. As they pressed further, he focused razorlike upon it, as if he feared it would suddenly flit away like a disturbed fish and leave them stranded down there. It was just better to consider the line than the darkness. Even as it led them further away from the light.

Some ways in, Yule felt something in his chest seize. His body reacting before his mind did, at something behind him. He spun around, flashlight dancing against the dusty blackness. Behind him, he heard Leslie stop, and his own shadow leapt forward as she turned her flashlight on him.

"What's wrong?" she asked, voice carrying even in a whisper.

"I heard something," Yule replied. And he had, hadn't he? A dragging sound, like someone pulling meat over a dusty floor. He'd heard it, he was sure, but the darkness yielded nothing. And now, even with his own breath stilled in his belly, he couldn't hear it anymore. Just the dull rumble of the earth sleeping above them.

Christ. Not even a hundred meters in and the dark was already making him go nuts.

"We shouldn't stop. Sorry," he said, turning around. "Time check?"

Silence for a moment.

"Four nineteen."

Yule turned and aimed his flashlight down the hall, and their footsteps began again. He still couldn't help listening out for the sound though, stealing glances over his shoulder every few feet.

They continued on until the entrance lay far behind them. The line swooped and dove around corners to escape them, occasionally obscured by rubble but never quite leaving their sight. By the time it entered its final curve, the bunker was all around them, deep in every direction. It terminated at a set of large glass doors, encased in chipped white metal. A large sign read "S01" above the entryway, guarding the boundary between the bare concrete tunnel, and the white-tiled science division beyond.

Within, all was still. In the dark tomb of the S01, silence reigned. Yule and Leslie gave each other a half-visible glance as they stood at the threshold, bound by fearful recognition that they'd both been here before, and that neither wanted to return.

"What's the time?" he asked. The reply was monotone, and quiet.

"Four twenty-six."

A moment later, Yule felt Leslie's fingers close over his wrist, slowly, and tightly. Without a word, he squeezed back. They stood there for a moment, clasped together. It was hard to know who was gripping tighter, and even harder to tell who summoned the bravery to pull them across.

Deeper inside, the air was heavy. Clenched. The smell of slow rot was overtaken by a hiss of antiseptic and ozone, pounded into submission by the weighty scent of chemicals. As they passed, Yule tried to look in through some of the doors, but the glass was misty, and the rooms lay blacker than black. The only suggestion they were in that terrible place came a few minutes in when the corridor opened up into a central room.

Or, rather, a central kennel. There were corridors of them, stacked from floor to ceiling in welded towers, some open and others shut. In the center of the room lay a steel operating table, surrounded by space—as if the cages themselves had huddled in terror away from it. Yule stopped beside it a moment and looked around. Without a sign to point the way, it was impossible to know which way was the right one.

"Time check," he whispered. For a few seconds there was no reply, and when one came it was quiet and strained with fear.

"Yule?" Leslie said. He turned around, pointing his flashlight at her. She was pressed up against the table, hands frozen against the lip of the steel surface. Her eyes were fixed on something down one of the cage hallways, unblinking. As Yule approached, he went to lift the flashlight towards what she was looking at. Leslie's hand flew up before he could, shaking a little.

"No," she whispered, voice like a tautly pulled string. "Turn it off."

Before Yule could reply, he was cut off by something. A gentle, rhythmic gasping, like the wet slap and crackle of tar-bound lungs. He clicked the button on his flashlight and waited for the pure darkness to descend. But it didn't.

Something was glowing. From where he was, he could see it through the cages, winking squares of blue light twinkling somewhere on the other side. He padded beside Leslie to see what it was and felt a gasp catch solid in his throat.

He couldn't quite tell what he was looking at. A man shape but not, all stretched with distorted proportions. Its silhouette lit up at odd intervals with a sickly blue light, illuminating impossible angles and rolling flesh. It flickered in place, groaning gently like a tree in the wind.

And as Yule's eyes adjusted, to his horror, he saw that it wasn't alone. Another sat hunched up against the cages, rocking back and forth, hissing to itself. A third on the floor looked dead, until the lights revealed its long, shifting limbs swaying back and forth against the tiles like it was feeling out for something.

A sinking feeling in his gut told him he'd seen something like this before. A long time ago, on the wrong side of a sluice pipe.

Leslie pushed against his arm, nodding in the direction of the other door. She didn't need to say anything, because the message was pretty clear from the force behind her palm: *get the fuck out, now.*

Yule held his breath, half-groping in the blackness until he felt the raised steel of the exit under his fingertips.

When they were out, he let out a long gasp and clicked his flashlight on again, swinging it wildly around in the fear that there were more out in the hallway. But once more, they were alone.

"What the fuck were those?" Yule whispered, looking over his shoulder.

"Volatiles. They——" Leslie began. Yule turned back to her, shaking his head.

"All I need to know is whether they'll rip our shit up if we go near 'em. Will they?" he asked.

Leslie nodded, eyes flicking nervously back to the kennel room. Yule took a deep breath through his nose and tried to calm the screech of panic scratching at his neck. The military blinders descended, more welcome than usual.

"Then I don't need to know anything else. Not here, not right now," he said, turning the flashlight down the hallway. "We gotta get our asses outta here."

The beam ran over a tarnished map on the wall, and Yule felt something in his gut relax. Though, not by much: he had to actively ignore the bloodstained fingerprints at the map's edge. That seemed to be the way of things now: a moment of respite in return for two moments of terror.

Couldn't have just been a kidnapped girl, he thought. *Couldn't have just busted into some guy's trailer with a gun and solved the whole thing, no—for some reason it had to all be neck injections and time travel.*

"We can get where we need to be through the furnace room here. What's the time?" he asked.

"Four thirty-one," Leslie replied, though her voice was so quiet and strained Yule almost didn't hear. He chewed his lip.

They had time, he thought. They were close, they could do it.

Without a word they flitted away with a final fearful glance towards the kennel room. As they moved, Yule could feel his eyes rolling from corner to black corner, constantly scanning. His hands itched unconsciously over his exposed forearms, as if the darkness was something swarming and far too close.

It felt different, knowing they weren't alone down there.

He knew they had come to some new place by the smell. Subtle at first, but mounting with every step they took, the vibrating sting of old antiseptic being overtaken by the heavy prickle of ash and smoke on the walls.

The doorway was barred by a set of plastic sheets which stirred as they approached, like the bunker's dead feelers twitching.

The space within was wide, its low ceiling puckered by a series of vents. Beside them, reinforced walls split open at intervals like gaping iron mouths, throats blackened to near invisibility in the dark. Conveyors, now still, led into the furnaces—long enough, Yule realized, to hold a human body. The thought made his stomach turn, but not as much as what the flashlight found in the corners of the room.

Clothes. Some folded neatly in piles, but most not. Prison jumpsuits faded to a sickly salmon color, heaped in drifts on the far side of room, threadbare woolen hats and weather-stained jackets spread amongst them like stones in the snow. Homeless clothes, he thought. Those were homeless clothes.

He turned his eyes up and away from the pile. No more, he thought. He couldn't. He gave the pile a final glance as they left the room, checking the shadows.

But still, they were alone.

The generator room was tiny in comparison to the wide, dead space of the furnace. The floor was inset into the ground, with a small flight of stairs leading into the bed of it. The walls were lined with windows, showing only the face of pure blackness beyond. The generator squatted on the far side, sown to the walls with pipe and cable. Leslie put down her gas canister and gestured for Yule's, gaze trained on the generator's rusted face.

"You used one of these before?" Yule whispered, glancing over his shoulder again. Nothing had followed them, or at least it seemed that way.

"My family had a big one when we lived on a farm. Looks similar." Leslie replied, unscrewing the plastic cap. She went to work, checking switches and hunting for hatches on the machine's dead face. Yule stood guard and checked his watch.

4:35 a.m.

Everything was fine, he thought. It looked like they'd make it and yet, something didn't feel right at all. A feeling in his gut that his brain hadn't quite gotten yet, telling him, insisting that despite their escape, there was still something deadly wrong.

Gas splattered gently behind him as Leslie upturned the canister into the fuel intake.

Sweat dripped down Yule's brow. His hand gripped the gun tightly now, drawing it up into the air. Like a curtain being drawn from a stage, the feeling of danger revealed its face, a terrible realization clotting from the swirl of images. A lot of clothes, he thought, but not a lot of ashes— so where had all their owners gone?

Yule's eye flicked up to one of the large windows, just in time to see a little glow from somewhere within. A fleck of electricity bounced over rolling skin.

"Oh shit," he said, voice barely above a whisper.

The generator spluttered and churned. Lights pinged to life. And then, the screaming began.

They were at the windows. Volatiles, dozens of them, pressed up against the glass in rows, flailing and screeching.

The two of them stood there, paralyzed. Yule didn't think of anything, didn't stir, he just… stared. Openmouthed, like he'd forgotten how to cry out. Across the room, a twisted limb came crashing through a window. The sound of breaking glass was like a shock of cold water, jolting them awake enough to scream.

Yule looked over to the power doors at the other side of the room, wide-eyed.

"Go!" he cried. "Run!"

The tunnel seemed to bend around him, distorted by his own movement and the flood of adrenal noise over his brain. The sound of the screeching things blended into a fog, carrying up behind them like a bloody smelling wind as they sprinted through the maintenance tunnel.

Volatiles were all around them now. Everywhere, breaking through. Shambling up tight corridors as they passed, fully lit and wailing, hunting for the source of the light and sound. Behind him, he heard more windows shattering. The thud of bodies dragging themselves through the broken glass, up to their feet, running. Chasing.

Oh god, where had Cal said to go? Fuck, fuck, fuck, *fuck*, where had he said? Was there something he'd forgotten, what if they'd passed it? What if they were lost, what if they were running deeper? And now the bunker was alive, horribly alive, hungering, screeching and gnawing at its own insides to get them.

And there were more, ever more: beating against doors, pulling them open, roaring and gibbering as the shambling horde grew.

Another corner. A set of stairs, and then a door. A sturdy door, one made of steel and rivets. With a cry Yule got behind it and pushed. The metal slab slammed shut, guts whining as he screwed the bulkhead into place.

Even when it closed, he could still hear them on the other side, beating against the metal with their misshapen, shifting limbs and bent-over bodies. He stepped away and let out a groan of terror as he saw the metal begin to flex at the sides.

They were getting through. The door wasn't going to stop them. He took a step back and nearly tripped, heel caught on what felt like a railing. Stumbling, he turned his face to see what had nearly felled him.

A hatch. Inset into the floor, covered with cobwebs. *The way out.*

His heart leaped into his throat. He looked up to see Leslie pressed up against the wall, her mouth open and her hands clutching at the shotgun. Jolted from the noiseless space of realization, it took him a moment to realize she was screaming. He dropped and grabbed the locking wheel, knees banging hard against the metal floor.

"Leslie! Come on!" he yelled, pulling on it with all his might. Behind him, the door boomed again. A few screws clattered to the floor, and the sound of the horde grew louder. Unseen, Leslie cried out again.

"They're gonna follow us through!" she screamed. "We can't!"

With a grunt, Yule pulled the hatch open. The movement disturbed a ceiling tile underneath, which fell with a loud crack on the ground some feet below. Yule stood and grabbed Leslie by the shoulders, shaking her.

"Jump down!" he said.

"What about—"

"Jump, dammit!" Yule insisted, examining her quickly as he pulled her towards the hatch. Gas canister on her belt. Gun. Watch. She had everything, he thought. That was what mattered. Made pliable by the panic, Leslie dropped to her knees and slid through the hole in the floor, falling awkwardly into the tunnel below. She looked up at him, face still ashen with terror.

"Yule!"

"It's four forty," he yelled. "Go! You have to keep going! Remember what we're here to do, just go!"

Before she could reply, he slammed the hatch shut and pulled the locking wheel back in place, the bright light from below replaced with dull red panic. He could still hear her, over the horde, over the hum of the bunker, down below. Calling his name.

Yule had always wondered what making a decision like that would feel like. Whether it would happen in a second, like jumping on a grenade. Whether he'd always known this was how it was going to go. But now, here, with it actually happening? He just felt like he was wasting valuable time.

He stood but didn't face the door. He was afraid that if he looked at them, he'd lose his nerve. Try to get out of the death sentence he'd spent all of five seconds considering, and what then?

The hatch room terminated in another open hallway, which stretched out into tunnels unknown. He began to walk down it, gun swinging lazily at his side. The fear had left him, suddenly and completely, like a buoy caught in the tide. He couldn't expect anything of what would come next. In fact, he didn't expect anything at all.

He reached the middle of the hallway. Clenched his jaw.

Behind him, the steel door of the hatch room buckled, and a rolling mass of bodies came crawling through. The air around them crackled and fogged, illogical shapes and motions converging towards the trapdoor on the ground.

Now was the time, he thought. There was the grenade, and he just had to jump on it.

He held up the pistol, plugged a finger in his ear, and fired. The sound exploded painfully through the tunnel, rippling the air like a slap to the face. The horde turned. Its mass moved. Shifted away from the hatch to the new sound, and with a bubbling wail somewhere between distress and fury, pursued.

Yule turned. Stuffed the gun in his pocket and ran as fast as his feet would carry him. Deeper and deeper, into the living jaws of the tunnel.

4:35

AMESVILLE, 1993

Trevor stood at the side of the road, hunkered down next to Cal's vehicle. He didn't want to call it a truck—it didn't look enough like one. The bed was taken up almost entirely by a large set of batteries wired up in parallel, leading to a large leaden box on top, while the rest of it was stripped away to the essentials: no windows or doors. With Cal's car waiting next to it, relatively normal if scratched and rusting, it looked almost ghoulish.

With a grunt, Cal came up from next to the truck, slapping the hood as he passed.

"That's four thirty-five," he said, glancing at his watch. "They'll be getting close now. Not much time—you got your brick?"

Trevor hefted the old stone his hand and presented it.

"Got it," he said. His voice was thin and raspy from nerves. Cal, after a moment's hesitance, put a steady hand on his shoulder.

"This is the easy part. Just put the brick on the gas pedal. Should shoot straight down the path, right into the factory," he said. Then, he paused, a kind of hard tiredness flickering across his aged face. "And the second that car is moving, you get out of here. You run into the tree line as fast as you can, and you don't stop until you can't hear what's out there anymore. Promise me that."

Trevor nodded, though the look of stony determination on his face was undercut by a noticeable crack of fear.

"I promise, man. I won't even look back, I swear," he said. And yet, Cal remained still. Staring, hand now resting on Trevor's shoulder as if letting go meant drowning.

"I mean it, Trev. I waited so long; I can't lose you now. Not again," he said. Then he let go and turned away, as if he was ashamed to hear his own admittance of it. Trevor grabbed his arm, gaze hardening.

"I can do it," he insisted, setting his jaw. Cal looked back at Trevor a moment, and the expression of grief on his face softened. He laughed a little, but it was something south of joy.

"I know you can. It's part of the reason I hate you so much right now— if you were a liability, I'd just tell you not to be here," he said. They both smiled weakly at each other, as if to prolong the idea that neither of them were really there. That things weren't the way they were, and that the lives they'd lived weeks and decades ago were still around. But as Trevor found his eyes drifting behind Cal towards the wood, he remembered, and knew they weren't.

"What about Jemima?" he asked. Cal's hint of a smile faded. When he next spoke, his voice was ashen, and gravelly. Like the years had suddenly piled on him.

"She'll follow the truck," Cal said. "As long as that thing keeps moving, she'll keep chasing it. I've seen it before."

He opened up the door to his car and glanced at his watch a second time, air whistling a little through his tightened lips.

"One minute 'til I have to go. Tell me the plan again," he said.

"Turn on the dog whistle at four fifty, brick on gas pedal, run like hell," Trevor replied. Cal nodded.

"Got it," he said, shifting nervously place as he glanced at his watch a third and final time. "I have to go. Just… just stay safe, alright? Don't fuck around, just keep yourself away from danger."

"I will," Trevor replied. Cal gave him a weak smile.

"Make sure you come back, traveler," he said. Trevor gave him an ashen smile.

"I *never* never come back," he finished. With that, Cal swung into the driver's seat and shut the door. The car juddered to life, slowly rolling across the road. With a final nod shared through the window, the car sped up across the concrete, and disappeared into the darkness. Trevor listened to the sound of it fade, until eventually there was nothing but the night around him.

Alone in the bare night, he waited. Minute by minute, time closed in.

"Yule! Yule!" she cried at the ceiling, voice cracking. But there came no reply. Leslie's hands flew to her face, a guttural moan of distress rattling up from her chest.

She could hear them, up above. Banging against the ceiling, gathering at the hatch, and then... a gunshot. Movement. She stood in the middle of the tunnel, frozen in place, listening with her hands still clutched tight against her cheek.

Moving away. He was leading them away.

She groaned again and tottered back, ankle throbbing from the fall. She couldn't even hear them anymore; they had gone somewhere deeper. And she... she was alone. Somewhere else. She turned in place, considering the space around her with wide eyes.

Another tunnel. Better lit, and modern. All plastic and chromed steel. No signs, nothing. Just her, all alone again. And Yule, was, he...

Her knees buckled beneath her, and she dropped. One hand shot out to catch herself on instinct, the other clutching at her chest. The world spun. Nausea reared in her belly. He was dead. Or dying someplace, or about to die.

She felt like she had to scream, yet it wouldn't go, like a hot stone caught in her chest burning from the inside out.

Beep, beep, beep.

– 361 –

Mid-sob, she stopped. The digital watch chimed in unfamiliar electronic tones on her wrist, cutting through the fog of panic to jolt her awake. Sharp, like a needle.

Ten-minute warning. Four forty on the dot.

And she was the only one around to hear it. Or was she? For in the seconds that followed, Leslie realized she felt almost at home in the tunnel hum. She was used to it. Like a second heartbeat, ever present and all around her, the way it had been for what felt like a lifetime. The freeing feeling that this wasn't anything new.

She'd been that way for weeks. Months. Trapped underground, not knowing where the end was. The last few months had been an exercise in enduring suffering ten minutes at a time. What difference would ten minutes more make?

Her hands clenched on the shotgun, eyes drawn to the side of the tunnel, and the thick cables bolted to the concrete. Black and rubbery, stamped with little signs in white ink.

She knew them. She could hear them, if she closed her eyes. She'd listened to them a hundred times over, lying alone in the dark space of the bunker. Power wires, which inevitably led to a source.

Four forty, she thought. Ten minutes of following. Running. She could handle that. She had to.

Otherwise, what was the point of it all?

Beep, beep, beep.

Four forty chimed on Trevor's watch, synthetic noise clean and clear against the organic sound of night around him. He silenced it quickly and padded from his hiding place, running awkwardly towards the truck.

"I can do this," he repeated under his breath. "I can do it."

He tumbled awkwardly through the truck door, giving a final glance to the gently swaying wood. He fumbled with the ignition, sweaty fingers slipping slightly on the keys as they twisted, and the truck chugged to life.

Trevor held his breath. The brick stood ready in his free hand, the other hovering above a large red switch taped to the dashboard. Waiting like tempting bait, to wake the night and call the monsters out.

And he could do it. He had to; he knew he had to. He would. His thumb slid over the switch, and the batteries in the truck bed hummed to life. A loud whine crackled from the box on top, rising higher and higher in pitch until Trevor couldn't even hear it anymore.

And then, the world fell silent. The insects, the birds, the deer. All of it. Like an invisible hand had snatched them all from the face of the earth, leaving only the groaning wind behind.

Then, it came. The sound. A roar mixed with a guttural, wrenching moan. Quietly at first, some place far in the distance. But closing in. Nearer by the second. *Her.*

A chill ran up Trevor's spine, and he threw himself from the driver's seat. He pushed down hard on the gas, brick holding it fast. The truck bucked forward and Trevor pulled back, tumbling into the dirt. Dazed, he leaped to his feet.

The truck was already rolling down the road. Gaining speed, carrying its grim cargo further away with every passing second. And Trevor could hear Jemima getting closer. When another howl came, the trees shivered. Trevor turned on his heel and began to run, hurtling towards the tree line in the opposite direction. He'd done it, he thought. He'd done his job, and now all he had to do was what he promised. Just keep running. Run, and don't look back.

But as he reached the tree line, Trevor froze. He moved to turn, then to run, then to turn again. He was in danger, he could feel it, but... he couldn't hear the truck anymore. He glanced over his shoulder, and somewhere behind the throb of anxiety, his heart sank.

The truck had stopped. Not crashed, just *stopped*, right in the middle of the road, a hundred feet away or so. He could make it all out with growing horror as the scene connected itself in the bare moonlight. The bounce of the suspension, rocking itself back to sleep. A pothole, lying a way behind. And the brick, thrown from the pedal into the middle of the road.

The noise came again. Closer now, much closer, near enough that birds scattered, and unseen bodies fled. Trevor stood rooted to the spot. A single, low note of terror erupted from him and tumbled through the air towards his shaking feet. And then... nothing. As if he'd broken through a terminal barrier of fear, to a space beyond it.

As he moved, Trevor realized he didn't feel like he was doing anything at all. As if his body was moving on its own and he was just watching it, from some numb, sunken place. Didn't even try to pick up the brick as he climbed into the driver's seat. It all just... happened. The terror was so elevating that he found himself thinking with perfect clarity, only of the goal, only of the situation at hand.

The truck had to move.

He pressed the gas, and the truck leaped forward. All around him the forest was an explosion of sound, things flying and fleeing in every direction. The trees shivered and shook as a curdled roar slopped from the undergrowth.

As the truck picked up speed and began to hurtle down the road, Trevor glanced in the rearview. Far behind, a bank of bushes split like overstuffed skin, as something huge and invisible burst from the undergrowth.

⁓

Seconds and minutes. That was all she thought about as she ran lopsidedly through the tunnel, trying to balance with a throbbing ankle and the weight of the gas can. The tunnels here were larger, more spacious and with moving air in them, but the principle remained the same. There was always the hum. Always the electrical veins, reaching toward metal and plastic arteries. All she had to do was follow, find, and slice them open.

She glanced at her watch. Eight minutes.

The hallway turned a corner, then to a large metal door. Leslie skidded to a halt, wincing as weight bounced on her foot. Her eyes turned immediately to the steel frame, trained on a little strip of red-tipped plastic inset into the metal. No time to wonder, she thought.

She pulled, hard. The lever came down, and immediately the walls around her began to vibrate and shudder. With a slow *tuk, tuk, tuk* the door raised and slid up into the ceiling to reveal what lay behind.

The room beyond was vast, roof soaring high overhead in a tangle of cables and black steel struts, walls pocked by banks of machine panels. A metal walkway led up and out to one end, but otherwise it was windowless and doorless, save for where she had entered, the air alive with the low, threatening growl of electricity.

What caught her attention immediately were the glass cubes. A dozen of them lined the central space, plugged umbilically to the ceiling by tangled columns of rubbery wire. Every so often a jolt of electricity lit the smoked glass.

Something in her head connected.

Power, she thought, *he was using them for power. Living fuel, if you could call it living at all.*

With one hand, she unclasped the jerry can from a belt loop. Beside her, a monolith structure of lights and dials ran up the walls, swathes of wires linked up to it like suspended jellyfish tentacles. It'd do.

Clumsily, she unscrewed the cap, and the smell of gasoline boiled in vapor tones from inside. Without hesitating, she swung the container in a hard arc, gas smearing in ribbons across the machinery. All the while Volatiles howled and shrieked in their glass cubes, sparking and glittering with electricity like caught storms.

Leslie threw the spent container to the floor and pulled out a beaten-up old lighter. The box lid clicked open, scarlet flame dancing in place above the wick.

She held it up to eye height and sucked in a deep breath, vision wandering to her free hand, and the blinking watch readout.

Four forty-five. Five-minute warning. *Time to light it all up*, she thought, grip tightening.

The booming noise came sooner than she expected. Like she'd dropped the lighter without realizing. But there were no flames. No blaze of glory. Just the sound of a broken metal case dropping to the floor beside her, the little fire gone dead.

Leslie frowned. Her head was buzzing. Something was wrong she thought—suddenly she felt numb, like she was drunk. When she tried to move the fingers on her right hand, there was only a sensation like hot pins. It was only as she saw the lighter lying on the floor, and the shiny new bullet hole in its side, that Leslie realized what had happened.

Slowly, almost dreamily, her hand drifted into view. She widened her eyes, mouth agape but silent. It was curtained with blood, running from a tangle where two of her fingers had been.

Finally, as if jolted awake, she screamed.

The forest flew by, awash with the sounds of panic. Trevor felt his hands seize on the wheel; little hairs stood upright at attention. He could hear it behind him now, not just the roaring but the steady *ka-thud, ka-thud, ka-thud* of its feet in the dirt.

He pushed harder on the gas pedal, as if the extra force would will the truck to go faster. In the rearview mirror he saw nothing behind him, except for a trail of smoking footprints slammed into melting concrete. And it looked like they were getting—

SKKKKRTSKK.

Metal wailed as something collided with the truck's bumper. The entire vehicle lurched and weaved, suspension trying desperately to keep up with its own momentum. Trevor yelled and tried to wrench it back under control, tried to keep it straight, but the wheels had a different idea.

Trevor felt like he took in everything that happened next in slow motion: the tilt of the vehicle as it spun one-eighty on the road. The sound of gravel clacking against the hood as the thing chased him.

As the headlights turned upon it, they seemed to bend. Distort a little around an unseen mass, whose shape was only suggested by the occasional bolt of bright electrical discharge. Even then, Trevor could barely think what it might look like. All he could see for sure were the footsteps, wreathed in smoke. Long and distorted, with more than four feet.

While his mind was busy seeing, his body simply acted. The time it took for his hand to swerve the truck into reverse felt much longer than a second, and it was only as it began to pull away again that he realized how fast they were going. Jemima let out a bubbling roar, and the night rang in reply.

The truck headlights began to flicker madly, twitching as if they wanted to turn away from the horror approaching. Trevor gritted his teeth. He could see the footsteps coming, he could see where they were going, maybe if he just—

The wheel jerked. The truck groaned again and pulled wide, re-orientating itself forward. The headlights seemed to follow the path of the unseen beast as it overshot its target and slammed into the ground, skidding madly in an attempt to stop itself and continue the chase.

Trevor wasted no time. He hit the lever, pushed the gas, and the engine screamed back to strained life, choking and gasping inside the hood as it passed through the dust cloud.

Trevor felt something like relief bloom in his chest. It was short lived.

With a dull thud, the truck jerked and pulled again. Trevor glanced out the side, just in time to see what remained of the right rear tire flying off into the blind dark. A limb had caught it on the way past, severing it and a bundle of wires, which had now disappeared into the toxic glow of electrical fire.

But Trevor didn't stop. The thought never occurred to him, not even then, only to go faster, as if to escape the flames on his back and the beast at his heels. But without its tire, the truck was crippled. Lurching in fits and starts, pulling hard to the right. Terror boiled cold in his chest, hands shaking, gut turning.

But he never stopped.

The road crested a small hill, and suddenly something bright fell into his vision. Far beyond the reach of the flickering headlights, the cold glow of floodlights waited at the end of the road. The factory. Trevor heaved on the gas and sped up, knuckles white on the steering wheel as the truck tried to buck out of control again. The fire widened and spewed a black cloud out behind him like a cloak.

Unnoticed in his panic and cloaked by the wall of sound, his watch beeped out a five-minute warning, hoping the distraction with the car would do its job.

Leslie cried out, clutching her mutilated hand at the wrist. Blood streamed down to her forearm, spouted from what remained of her index and middle fingers. The lighter lay useless on the floor, fuel blown out and flame dead.

Another shot rang out through the room, and this time she reacted. Twisted on her heel, injured hand still pointing up towards the ceiling. With a cry of pain and surprise she fell behind one of the cages for cover.

Through the smoked glass, she could see a man on the other side of the room. Descending down the metal walkway, a pistol drawn up and ready. A stab of pain rattled through her hand, keeping her somewhere above unconsciousness. The feeling of the cold air on bare bone felt like needles. She cried out again, this time more desperately, panic rising in her throat.

She tried to bring the shotgun up, but her hand was too slick with blood to grip it. As she fumbled, the man fired again, bullets thudding into the steel siding. Leslie gritted her teeth and tried to see through the nerve haze, swaying even as she leaned against the cage. She recognized him, she knew him—from that night in the trailer. Something white hot flared in her chest. The man who was going to break her fingers.

And he was saying something. Shouting at her. She couldn't tell what it was, it all just sounded like water moving inside her ear. Squeezing as tight as her mangled hand would allow, she brought the shotgun up and fired. The kickback alone was enough to make her drop it again. The pellet cloud went wide, hitting a wall some ways away.

With growing horror, Leslie realized she couldn't aim anymore. Even if she could fight through the pain, she couldn't hold it properly. And the yellow-toothed man was coming, approaching down the stairs, ducking between cages. All around them the Volatiles shook and slammed against the glass, whipped up into a frenzy by the noise and light.

Gasping for breath, Leslie looked down at the gun on the floor. This wasn't working. How many shells did she have left? Fuck, she hadn't been counting, how many shots had she fired?

A popping sound blipped her eardrums as another shot barely missed, burying itself in the side of the cage. He was nearly on her now. One more row, one more corner, and he was going to kill her. He was going shoot her, and then… oh god, oh shit, oh shit.

Her eyes darted downward. Stopped. Something new presented itself: tiny white lines on the glass, sprouting upwards from a bullet wound on the frame. A stem growing from a lead seed, illuminated by the electrical writhing of the creature inside.

There was no plan. Not really. Only an urgent knowing, like the need to swim against a drowning tide.

Gasoline on the ground. All she needed was a spark, and the cubes were full of them.

She gritted her teeth and cried out, heaving the shotgun up onto her knee. Couldn't aim, but she didn't need to.

The muzzle flare lit up her vision. A cloud of lead pellets fuzzed through the air, so fast they seemed only to flicker a moment in the middle of the room. But although their path lay invisible, their destination wasn't. That was clear enough in the snowflake-shaped crack in the cage glass opposite. She fired again, and another appeared below it.

Again, and once more until the trigger stopped resisting. The shotgun fell from her grip and she clutched at her wrist, spent and blinded by pain. The yellow-toothed man emerged from his cover and swept across the room, with all the speed and confidence of a man who knew he was the only one in the room with ammunition.

Inside the damaged cube, the sparking Volatile shifted. Heaved, the noise of its impact deadened by the thick walls.

Ka-thud, crack. Ka-thud, crrkkrack...

Daisy crept closer and closer, footsteps slapping wetly against the tile.

Ka-thud, crrrkkkccsskk...

She could hear him. Splashing up through the gasoline. All the way down the walkway, almost upon her, passing the cage with the snowflaked glass and-

With a ringing shatter, the glass screamed and tore itself open.

An impossible mass birthed itself from the weakened window and scrambled onto the floor, heaving and sparking violently. From her place on the floor, Leslie watched as a single, thread-like arc of electricity, leapt from the Volatile's impossible form to the shiny pool of gasoline on the ground.

The yellow-toothed man stepped back and opened his mouth to yell, but it was lost in the roar of fire igniting. Immediately the air was thick with the stink of burning plastic and seared chemicals. As if woken by the flame, Leslie leaped to her feet. She backed away from it, circling back around the cage to run up the side of the room, no feeling of victory, just the need to get out, to run up the stairway and be free, to live.

And yet as she went, she found her head turning. When she reached the bottom of the stairway, she stopped. The vicious, angry thing in her compelled her eyes into the fire, to make out the shape of Daisy, waving. Flailing. Then falling, disappearing into a bank of bright flames like a stone tossed into a lake.

Her mutilated hand shaking in midair, she looked down at her watch, burning wall reflected in the glass screen. Four fifty on the dot.

She almost smiled, before the glow sank. A shadow shifted across the watch face, and Leslie's eyes widened as she realized it was not her own.

AMESVILLE, 1993

Of all the things Cal had seen, the things he'd uncovered, only the silence unnerved him still.

It was particular, and rare. The absence not only of voices and human sounds, but of everything. No animals, no wind, nothing daring to break the oppressive stillness, as if the whole world feared to make itself known to whatever waited inside.

The factory was quiet, he thought. A quiet like he'd never heard.

He came to a stop between two hallways, split in opposite directions. He stuck a shaking hand into his pocket, rooting around for a familiar crumpled shape.

The map was mismatched and old. Copied from a dozen others, drawn and redrawn as he'd watched the factory being built. It wasn't the easiest or most efficient way to do it, and there were things he'd missed— but it told him enough. Where the major hallways led, where the stairs were. And where he'd watched reinforced metal being buried deep beneath the main building.

That was where Carnassus was keeping the time machine. He'd bet his life on it, and that bet meant going left.

He put the map away and continued onwards, trying to quieten the sound of his breathing. The carpet muffled his footsteps, but Cal was painfully aware that it could just as easily work against him. At each junction and every few feet, he would glance quickly behind to mark any pursuit, heard or not. He wasn't sure if a lack of it made him feel more or less on edge.

Carnassus hadn't been absent before. Right from the moment he'd arrived in town with his white suit and dead eyes: watching the construction, waiting at the drop-offs, overseeing everything that could come into his quiet kingdom. And yet here, now, on the eve of his fall, he was nowhere to be seen. It filled Cal more with dread than hope: he'd learnt better than to believe in good luck. The danger was the only thing that was real.

Down he pressed. Descended a large steel staircase and pulled another hard left, delving further into the fold of thick steel walls and vinyl danger signs. He was getting close, he could feel it; the air felt uneasy down there. Unsettled by something otherworldly.

His suspicions were all but confirmed when he reached the corridor's end, and he was confronted with the door. Right where it should have been, and just as intimidating as he'd imagined: a huge slab of rectangular steel stood inset into the wall, valves and seals gripping the side like clutching hands. A chrome combination dial stuck out of the center, flanked by a series of reinforcement rings. Cal looked it over for a moment, and then down to his watch.

He sucked air through his teeth and resisted the urge to tense up. Trust the guy to go secure—predictable, ultimately, but time consuming. But he had time, and if he didn't, he'd have to find it someplace.

He slung his backpack onto the floor and pulled a battered stethoscope from the mess inside. The deathly quiet of the bunker muffled as he affixed the ear buds, replaced with the crackle and heave of his own breath dancing on his eardrum. He pressed the little metal disc against the vault door, fingers teasing at the chrome dial.

He held his breath. Listened out for the chirp of ball bearings falling into place, as quiet and unobtrusive as a final gasp.

⁓

They weren't fast, but they didn't slow down. Not really, no matter what he threw in their path, they just kept coming. Yule didn't know how long he'd been running. A minute? It felt like an hour. Slow and fast at the same time.

Halfway down a hallway, there was a reverberating clunk somewhere in the walls as the generator ran out of fuel. Immediately, the harsh fluorescent lighting dimmed to a dull red glow, the color and brightness of an old scab. Yule stumbled and nearly tripped as the corridor seemed to disappear, eyes unadjusted to the disorientating gloom. But the horde never stopped.

Slowly, panic rose in his throat. The realization that although he'd managed to put a corridor length between them and him, he was tired. The breath burned in his lungs, legs cried out for rest, to stop. But he couldn't. He could hear them, more of them all around him, crawling through the tunnels like twitching insects. They emerged from shadows and side corridors, vents and test rooms. And although they were slow, their numbers kept swelling. Closing in.

He hadn't thought it would be like this. Maybe it was why jumping on the grenade seemed so easy, it was over fast. But this was slow and alarming. Like being choked by bedsheets.

He turned a corner and skidded to a halt. A door lay open before him, and in the corridors beyond, it was darker. Fewer lights. A good place to die terrified and confused.

Yule stood a moment, perfectly still, frozen before the threshold.

It felt like a choice. Stay and die, or run. But then, why was he running at all?

At once a yawning, terrible realization came over him: he didn't intend to die. He never had. And that took his diversion with the gun from 'heroic sacrifice' to 'dumbest plan possible'.

"Fuck...fuck fuck fuck you *dumb* motherfucker..." he muttered, weight shifting from heel to heel, filled from the toes up with a new, desperate energy. He glanced over his shoulder, unthinkable shadows pooling at the other end of the hallway as the horde pressed ever closer.

Ride or die, he suppose. Hard fight or long night. Yule turned and plunged into the darkness without a second thought.

The chase was something new and infinitely more panicked now. Urgent and clawing, not just the will of a body to live but the mind inside it as well, drunk on the terrifying prospect of oblivion. The new part of the tunnel was not only totally black, but partially collapsed as well, escape routes blocked by sheets of dirt and rock. Yule whirled madly in the darkness, a rat in a maze, only knowing as far as he could see.

They had followed him in. He hadn't looked back again, but he'd heard them, keener now in the dark. He didn't know if they used sight, or sound or what, it didn't matter. They were still coming. That meant he had to keep going, but he was still at a major disadvantage. Searching feverishly through the blackness, not daring or even able to look behind him at the unthinkable silhouettes.

He tore through a doorway and down a hall. Then, stopped. His feet skidded on the filthy tile as he swung the flashlight up and down, as if what he was seeing could be a trick of the shadows. But it wasn't.

The way was blocked.

A malformed pile of rock stood in the doorway, held together by dust, and spilled out over the floor like a makeshift burial mound. Yule leaped forward and dug at it with his hands, but most of it held fast, sharp fragments too painful to scratch away at. Again and again he pulled, until he felt his fingers and palms start to bleed, but still the rock stood firm.

Behind him, a bubbling howl echoed through the hallway. Yule looked over his shoulder, wide-eyed, just in time to see a long glowing arm grope around the corner. He let out a groan of fear and turned back around, flashlight scanning madly for something, anything that might help.

But the hallway had no more doors, and no windows. No hatches in the roof. No way out.

In a momentary twitch of panic, Yule's light turned upward. Immediately, instinctively, his eyes latched onto the one thing out of place.

There was a small hole, up near the corner of the doorframe. Jagged with sharp stones and stripped wires, it was barely child sized. But it'd have to do, he thought, grasping at the unforgiving slope as he climbed towards it. At the top, he pulled his shirt up around his nose and head and tried to squeeze through. But it was no good: the stones were too jagged and cropped together, he couldn't fit his shoulders through. He grunted and pulled himself out again, glancing back behind. He wished he hadn't.

There were at least six of them. Halfway down the hallway at varying levels, groping wildly in the dark with long, spindled limbs. Some crawled, some lurched, it was hard to tell. A great gibbering mouth became a bundle of kicking legs and reaching fingers.

With a desperate cry of alarm, Yule crushed his arm through the hole. Rocks scored flesh on its way through, but he didn't care, didn't think about the popping sensation of stone puncturing skin as he tore away to widen the exit with his free hand. Slowly, agonizingly, he pushed his head, a shoulder, his ribs through the gouging tunnel, kicking and flailing with what little strength he had left.

From behind him, he heard commotion. The sound of shifting limbs grasping at the bottom of the pile. Desperately, he pushed. Wriggled and pierced himself on the knife-pointed stones, inching his waist, his legs...

Something burned. Something white hot, boiling rubber sizzling against his heel as a Volatile reached out and touched his foot, going to grasp him, to pull him back through and—

With a final cry he pushed and fell forward, rolling down the pile on the other side. He lay there for a few seconds, moaning and running his hands over his skin. Everything felt slick, and warm. He couldn't feel much below his left ankle. But although the Volatiles were already digging and pulling at the dirt on the other side, but they couldn't quite break through. Not yet.

Slowly, Yule lifted his head up and opened his eyes. His finger slid on the flashlight button and the light winked to life. Revealed the room, and in doing so, stamped all hope to dust.

It was another dead end. A *true* dead end, no doors, just walls. No way out. He was trapped.

He lay there for a moment, stunned. He expected it to make him afraid, but it didn't. That was it, he thought: there wasn't any pain about it, no weight of decision, just... it. The grenade, however delayed, finally blowing up underneath him. Maybe he was just too spent to be sad about it, or maybe knowing he wasn't getting out made everything else seem trivial. He didn't even feel angry that he'd dared to hope he'd live through it a few minutes before.

Didn't matter if he was sad, he thought. He was going die, no matter how he felt about it.

A spatter of half-burned dust fell down onto his cheek, and Yule spluttered. Then he grimaced and clenched his fists. It occurred to him, strange and perverse as the thought seemed, that the only thing that mattered now was the way he went. He didn't want to do it choking on concrete.

Inch by inch he crawled deeper into the dark space, pulling himself upright against the wall. The sound of the approaching doom seemed far away. All he could hear was himself, breathing.

He didn't wonder what death would be like. Even if he wanted to be poetic about it, he couldn't, because all he could think about was how dry his mouth was. The chase and the dust had dried it all out, right down to the stem of his throat.

He wished he had a drink. Didn't want to die thirsty.

He guessed he'd have to.

Yule turned his head a little to check how much time he had. The glow of the Volatiles was getting brighter as they pulled more of the blockage away, blue flicker illuminating the dead room at random intervals. Slow progress, but they'd get through eventually.

He shifted. Stretched, and grunted as open wounds rubbed against themselves. Better get comfortable, he thought, letting his head fall back. That ended up being a mistake, as the back of his skull banged painfully against something sticking out of the wall.

Blinded by the unexpected pain, Yule clutched at his head, groaning. It was only as something landed on his bloody nose that he opened his eyes again. With a shaking hand he plucked it off, pulled up the flashlight, and furrowed his brow.

It was a leaf. Small and waxy green, shaped like an arrowhead. Slowly, his eyes tracked upwards to the space above his head. He squinted. Something in his belly turned.

There was a hole in the ceiling. And specks of light beyond, fifteen or twenty feet above him. A mass of branches and leaves grew through it, peeking in like curious onlookers.

His hand fell away from his face and collided with something that lay unnoticed on the floor next to him. Yule recoiled and looked down; the object lit up in the flicker of Volatile lights. A hatch, blackened and torn from its hinges. Yule stared at it for a moment as if he couldn't believe it was there.

A way out. There was a way out.

His hand felt blindly behind him on the wall and froze. He could feel a rung. He turned around on all fours and squinted through the darkness, terrified his senses had betrayed him. But they hadn't: there were more of them, blackened with soot and barely visible, leading all the way up the wall, *all the way up to the hole in the roof.*

At the other side of the room, a mass began to pull itself through the collapsing gap. But Yule was grinning.

He didn't feel any pain as he stood up. He felt the effort, but not the wounds. No foot throbbing as he planted it firmly on the ladder, red-soaked hands gripping tight on the rungs. All he felt was the climb. The sensation of the undergrowth as he sank his fingers into it and pulled, arms pressing hard into the rim of the hatch as he crawled up through the obscuring branches and leaves. Up, and up, until finally he felt fresh air kiss his face. The sensation of cold movement against the sticky slickness of his skin, the razor tingle of a chill breeze in his cuts. He kicked his way out of the bush and fell to the floor, gasping.

When he opened his eyes, he saw the night sky. Arrayed out in front of him like the rasping sparks of a lit matchstick, frozen in time.

Despite himself, he laughed. He was alive, he thought. Goddammit, he was alive. He lay there for some time, catching his breath and waiting for adrenaline to stop bouncing on his nerves. Through the hole, he saw the Volatiles swarm around the ladder, limbs wrapping over the rungs in an attempt to follow. But the metal bars glowed and melted, turning to hot, useless liquid in their grip, trapping them below.

As Yule watched them, the thrill of living slowly faded. Replaced instead by the insistent pressure of the life he'd returned to.

The others were at the factory, he thought. He had to get back there, somehow. Someway. With a long grunt of discomfort, he dragged himself to his feet again, and leaned up against a tree.

Just had to take a second. No use living if he was going to run off into the wilderness and die, he just had to think... what could he see? What could he hear?

He closed his eyes and listened out into the dark. Past the echoey howl of Volatiles swarming below, and the deadened whisper of crickets hiding in the wood. He pushed harder, tried to drag himself from the dead plane of panic but it was like climbing from a pool fully clothed. What could he hear?

Something on the breeze, Yule thought. The rumble of tires on ill-kept blacktop. A road, he thought, opening his eyes. And he could tell the direction. He stumbled through the bushes, following the hard slope of the earth until it opened up to bare road. He nearly fell as he clambered up onto it, a lone figure on the thin strip of bareness.

A light winked around the corner and bloomed into a full headlight glare. Yule held up his hands, waving them weakly above his head, not considering the fact he was torn up and covered variously with ash, filth and blood. The car screeched to an abrupt halt maybe five feet away from him and the driver's side door opened. An awkward-looking man with thick black glasses pushed his way out, hand clutching at his coat against the cold.

"Jesus, are you alright?" he asked, looking him up and down. "What happened? Christ, we gotta get you to a hospital!"

"Were you going out of town or into town?" Yule asked, slowly lowering his hands. The man screwed up his face a little, as if he'd been replied to in gibberish.

"Huh?"

"The direction you were going. You leaving Amesville or going towards it?" Yule repeated, slightly louder, if only so he could hear himself above the pronounced ringing in his ears.

"I was just coming out of town, been a big blackout," the man replied, glancing back the way he came. "Is this something to do with that? Did you crash your car out here?"

Yule made a note of the direction and slipped a hand into his pocket.

"I gotta borrow your car," he said, pulling out the gun. "I promise I'll bring it back, in like, an hour, but I need it."

The man blinked at the pistol, went pale, and clutched harder at his jacket.

"What?" he asked, dumbstruck with fear. Yule screwed up his face and rubbed a smear of blood from his brow.

"Look, man, I get it. I know this sucks, it's not a usual habit for me, I just... I really need your car, and I'm gonna bring it back, so just stay here, alright?" he said, slowly stepping around the man. The man tried to say something in reply, but nothing came out, even as Yule pulled himself into the driver's seat. The car crawled forward and the man leaped back out of its path, as if he expected Yule to plow into him at high speed. Instead, Yule inched a little past him, and rolled down the window.

"Seriously," he repeated. "I'll be back to return this, and I'll... I dunno, I'll put fifty dollars in the glovebox or something. *Don't move.*"

With that, Yule stepped on the gas, and the car went screaming into the night.

~

With a final click, the dial seized. Somewhere behind its face panel, the door's mechanism bloomed. It swung out with a resounding boom and lights turned on in the room beyond, revealing the monster hidden inside. As he entered, Cal stopped despite himself, and stared at it.

It was grotesque. A central console stood black and glossy, the lifeless eye of a deformed giant knotted to the ceiling, growing out of the wall like a cabled tumor amidst tangled black struts. The design was different, Cal thought, but he could see the logic in it. He'd read over Van Hallan's prototypes so many times, it looked like a variation—the capacitive dropper, the gradient coils, all the usual components were there but it was all much, much bigger. Capable of far more than Van Hallan's arcade machine device.

But still similar, he repeated in his head. Recognizable. That was all that mattered, he thought, pulling open a panel. The work was relatively simple: take the heavy car battery and its leads from the backpack, attach them at the right points to shudder the Hallanite into moving without waking its hungry belly. Easy.

The clips crackled, and with a sputter of sparks the monitor flickered to unsteady life.

"Okay... okay, okay," Cal repeated under his breath as he straightened back up, eyes cast over the information on the screen. Frequency levels. Intended input voltage.

His job was straightforward, he thought. Put the machine on the right settings and wait for the mother of all jump starts to arrive. It almost sounded cushy, if you didn't mention the giant invisible monster.

Somewhere in the filtered background, he realized he could smell gasoline smoke. The mark of a job well done, down below. And though part of him felt triumphant, the rest was taken up by the weight of the fact it was now his turn.

He unlatched a red button and pressed, priming the circuits. The screen flashed up with a power warning as the Hallanite fuel stirred inside. It was ready, he thought. Already processing what he needed it to, just waiting for enough charge.

They were doing it, he thought. They were winning.

"Turn around," said a voice from behind him. Cal froze, one hand at his pistol and the other up in the air, half surrendered. He turned, inch by inch, trying to take in everything he could before he met eyes with his enemy. But he wasn't prepared for what he saw, or the way it chilled him to the bone.

Carnassus stood like a specter by the door, his perfect whiteness inter-rupted by a ragged figure. Held tight by his forearm, Leslie let out a pained yelp, and a pistol barrel dug a little tighter into her temple. Her hand grasped at nothing, useless short of leaving bloody stump prints on Car-nassus' sleeve. Cal set his jaw at the sight of her and tried desperately to keep his eyes on the threat. Carnassus stared back, doll-like eyes dead and focused.

"I wondered what you'd look like," he said, lips curling into a disdain-ful smile. Like he was looking at roadkill. Cal glanced back down at Leslie, but her eyelids were fluttering. Trying to keep her aloft above the dark precipice of sleep.

"Leslie. Leslie, listen to me, this is going to be okay. I planned for this," he said, raising his voice a little. "Where did he get you?"

Leslie's eyes parted droopily.

"S-stairs... Five m-m-inute—" she began. But the words disappeared into a choked yelp as Carnassus grasped her harder by the neck, his eyes tightening to dead, predatory slits.

"Not her. Me, now," he said, adjusting his grip on the gun. "We're going to talk."

"Let her go, then," Cal replied. Carnassus' smile diluted a little, minor pleasure bleeding into contempt.

"I feel you'd be less communicative if I did. I was looking forward to a conversation with you," he said, dead gaze unmoving despite the shifting of his lips. "I've been waiting for this, you know. Patiently. *Avidly*. It's been like a puzzle, everything that happened at the trailer. Mister Wittey's brains on the wall, Leslie O'Neil escaping into the night, the continued resistance...I went into town over and over to see what was out of place, look at people's faces. I've never seen you before."

"I'm not that social," Cal replied, glancing at the watch on his raised hand. Christ, where was Trevor?

"But you seem to know a lot about me. About what I'm doing here. How is that?" Carnassus insisted, voice airy yet razor sharp. Cal set his jaw. He needed to stall.

"I've watched you ever since you got to Amesville, and even before that. I watched you build this factory, excavate the tunnels, and I know exactly what this place used to be because I saw that, too," he said.

Carnassus didn't move. Maybe something curious inside of him twinged, but Cal couldn't tell. When he next spoke, the words were balanced and monotone.

"What's your name?" he asked. Cal smirked.

"I'm not in the phonebook. You won't be able to just turn back time and erase me in my bed."

Carnassus considered the answer for a moment and inclined his head a little. Cal felt the weight of his dead gaze fall away from him, flicking downwards towards his gun.

"That means I'll have to deal with you now, then," he said, pulling the trigger.

The truck swerved and cried out in pain, axle keeling on its injured tire. Trevor jerked the wheel again, slithering a jagged path over the road.

Another blow hit the bed and more batteries went flying. Jemima burbled and fell back a few feet, unseen limbs slamming loudly into the road as the truck lurched forward to build up speed again. Trevor kept his eyes on the way ahead, fixed somewhere beyond himself by the rush of terror.

He could see the lights. He was so close.

A single shot rang out through the room. Cal didn't hear himself cry out through the ringing in his ears, but he felt it. In his belly and his throat, bouncing in his head. Even if he knew it was coming, even if he thought it could be fixed, he still couldn't have prepared himself for it. The sheer horror of seeing Leslie's head snap to the side. How her eyes fluttered and rolled back as her body went limp and fell to the floor. How after it fell, it simply lay motionless and dead, save for the slow clench and unclench of her hand, grasping at nothing.

Cal barely even noticed the gun's barrel dancing in the air, pointing to a new destination. The only real clue another shot had even fired came only when he felt a sudden, boiling heat in his gut. Cal looked down, his hand unconsciously clasping against the sensation. When he turned his palm up to the ceiling, he found it was slick with blood.

He looked up again at Carnassus, face pale with disbelief. Carnassus was just staring at him. Not happy, or even angry, just looking. Cal's knees buckled and he fell back against the machine. The pain was getting unbearable now, growing through his ribcage and down his side.

Carnassus walked towards him, shoes clicking on the ground. Cal tried to reach for his own gun, but moving his arm caused him too much pain everywhere. It just made him slip further and further down. Carnassus loomed over him a moment, before a gloved hand descended. Strong, slender fingers wrapped tightly over Cal's upturned face, and shoved. With a cry of surprise Cal toppled to the side and slammed into the rubber matted floor. Carnassus turned his attention to the machine, looking it over as if Cal wasn't even there anymore.

Teeth gritted, Cal began to drag himself backwards. He groaned in agony with every new movement, but he didn't stop. Tried to keep his head above the watery adrenaline rush, keep his thoughts going. Concentrate. The time machine had a ten-foot effective radius, he thought, fingernails digging at the floor. Ten feet, that was all. His life, all of their lives, for just a few more agonizing seconds of space to cross.

When he finally stopped, he let out a choked scream and rolled over, hands clutching tight at his gut. Carnassus clicked his tongue impatiently and turned around, white arms draped almost lovingly over the machine behind him. Cal could barely make out his features for blurriness, but he could feel the eyes. Two cold needle points floating in deep, observant darkness.

"It's over," Carnassus said calmly. "Whatever you were here to do, it's failed. I want you to know that."

"Maybe. Yeah, maybe. But I'm still breathing, right?" Cal panted, easing back a final inch. Carnassus smiled, but his expression was utterly without warmth. The pantomime of joy, hiding something drooling and hungry behind it.

"Only until I know everything I need to," Carnassus replied. Cal sucked in a shallow breath and tried to focus. Forget that he could see Leslie's hand in his peripheral, contorted at an odd angle towards the ceiling. He just had to keep stalling, even now. Play whatever hand he could.

"You could have won months ago, you know." He coughed. "Could've, but you didn't."

Somewhere in the blur, he saw the dead eyes twitch. Surprise, maybe. Or self-interest. It was hard to tell without the fine details, but he could see enough to know Carnassus hadn't been expecting it. Yet still, his voice lost none of its measured tone.

"Is that so?" he said. Cal nodded, and propped himself up a little more. The pain was starting to leave him now, and he felt cold. At any other time that would've been a worst-case scenario, but this time it was probably for the best. It wouldn't stop him.

"Yeah. If you'd have just left the town alone, nobody would have noticed. I wouldn't have noticed. But you couldn't just leave it all alone, you had to make it perfect. Over and over, problem after problem, just chasing this perfect sequence of events that you didn't even need," he said, a harsh, pained chuckle rasping from his throat. "World's not perfect. You try and make it perfect and that's when people start noticing."

Carnassus waited, then sighed. He almost seemed genuinely disappointed.

"Show an animal the sunset, all it sees is the glow," he said, going into his pocket. "The only people who see beyond that are The Branch, and it's obvious enough that they didn't send you. Otherwise, you wouldn't have made your big assault with gas canisters, and children."

Cal coughed, and tried to turn it into something close to a laugh.

"So they're what scare you? The Branch?" he asked. Carnassus brought something box-shaped out of his pocket, slender fingers teasing with dial settings on the back.

"You're trying to bait animal tendencies that don't exist. It's weak. The final resort of someone without a better plan than chance," he said.

"Chance got me pretty far. And if chance could do all this, maybe you're just not as smart as you think you are," Cal replied. Carnassus' eyes narrowed, holding back something sudden and vicious. His fingers tightened ever so slightly on the box.

"Chance got you a dead girl and a fatal wound in your belly. Chance got you failure. Even if this factory burns to the ground, I can start over. Take the Hallanite, build another machine in some other savage little town," he said, voice almost dripping with venom. "All that bloodshed, all that suffering, and all you've managed to take from me is my time and energy. I've already got an infinite supply of the first. And when I pull more Volatiles out of those tunnels, I'll have the other, too."

He twisted a dial sharply on the back of the lead box, which began to hum. Gently and sweetly, like tree boughs in the wind. Carnassus smiled.

"But you won't be around to see that," he said, fingers curling around the latch.

⁓

The truck bounced as it went from uneven road to concrete. Trevor yelled at the top of his lungs, nerves screaming at him to brake but his concentration unwavering, keeping his path rigid.

With a sound like brittle thunder, the truck rammed through a chain-link panel and careened into the factory parking lot. Trevor's rush of adrenaline was brief, replaced by a singular pulling sensation in his head as all the blood swerved to one side. Capitalizing on its sudden slowing, Jemima tore into the back of the truck, tossing it to and fro like a chew toy, ripping at the body, the batteries, the wires.

The smell of burning plastic thickened, stinging his eyes and throat. Another blow, more metal screeching. The truck was slowing down.

He had to do it. Had to make it count, he couldn't fail now. Not on success' doorstep.

With a final yell, Trevor yanked on the steering wheel. The world became weightless for a moment, churning around him like air bubbles in an upturned plastic bottle. That was soon replaced by a painful thrashing sensation as the truck rolled, battering him against the interior. He didn't feel how hard it hit him, on his neck, his head, his face. Maybe that was for the best.

When it stopped, he could at least feel that he was upside down. Didn't have the energy left to unbuckle. The world looked... well, he couldn't see it anymore. It was all dark. It felt like burning in his lungs, the kind coughing wouldn't help. There was fire, somewhere, he thought. But he couldn't see it.

He felt like all he could do was hear. The sound of Jemima tearing into the truck, before the battery hum of powered Hallanite went silent. Then, wet breathing, and the bobbing of some massive, invisible head in the dark.

When the roar came, it was deafening. Filled up his head with pressure and color. A red, wriggling howl all guttered up in shifting throats. Then, no sooner had the cry begun, there was movement. The rumble of asymmetrical limbs on the floor, rushing away. Dimly, quietly, Trevor heard doors break inward somewhere across the lot.

Despite himself, Trevor smiled. It had worked, he thought. He wasn't late... was he? Late for what? What had he been here to do, he couldn't... he could hear a bell, in his ears. Pulsing. Maybe he was going to be late, for... class, if... if he didn't... get...

He coughed one final time, then hung still. Heard no more.

The walls shook, and Carnassus reacted immediately. As he looked around for the source of the sudden noise, his fingers slipped from the Eraser Box and the deadly light died.

Cal smiled. His vision was starting to fade, but that was okay. He'd felt this before. It was all okay.

Vision was always the first to go. Then touch, and that was getting along too. The pain in his gut had dulled from excruciating brightness to a low glow of agony. It was the only thing he could feel anymore, but barely.

Hearing was last. That was the best for him. Meant he could hear the unsteady *ka-thud* of footsteps, raising to a howling pitch as Jemima rushed through the halls, her prize steadily pulsing a few feet away. Carnassus didn't run, just like Cal had predicted he wouldn't. Carnassus wasn't a runner, and he didn't need sight to know those dead eyes were still on him.

"I'll see you in ten minutes," Cal said with his final breath, smiling.

Something huge entered the room, and he heard no more. But then, the thousand hooks descended, strong enough to pierce the veil of numbness, stronger than he'd ever felt. As death came, he found himself beyond sense, beyond space. Riding a torn cascade, as time itself wriggled around its own horizons, unfolding and twisting before it reversed.

The room lay still and empty, just as it had ten minutes before. The glacial hum of time faded, leaving only the sound of Carnassus' heavy breathing to fill the empty space. The door, closed and locked, stood firm to shield him from outside noise. Only him, and the gentle *tick, tick, tick* of the clock on the wall.

He staggered a little, fighting waves of nausea to stay steady. The feeling of a thousand hooks still burned in his skin and, looking up expectantly, he realized he was alone. His thoughts swam, just as they always did when time bent backwards.

Had to think. Something... something had come into the room, he thought. Something huge and glowing, that had run past him, and towards...

Carnassus turned around, and his eyes widened.

The machine was dead. Ripped apart by the energy surge. It hung from its array like a butchered carcass, oily blood pooling on the floor below. Parts of the metal shell had melted into oozing trails, some still glowing and stinking.

He looked to the clock. Four forty-five. Turned back ten minutes exactly.

No. No, this couldn't be happening.

Carnassus felt something like red hot glass in his blood. He ran to the door and ripped the plastic lever cover off its hinges, slamming a fist into the emergency unlock button. As soon as the panels eased out of place, he threw himself against the steel, struggling like a starving beast to shoulder through the gap. His dead eyes widened, teeth bared.

"Animals," he repeated, as if the word were poison. "Filthy, fucking animals!"

He'd clean the world of them, he thought as he began sprinting down the hall. He'd put them all down.

04:49
AMESVILLE

Cal hardly knew what guided him through those hallways. He hadn't ever really gotten a handle on it, knowing whenever time had turned back. Felt like déjà vu, but more dense and anxious. A dreamlike intuition refined from red pressure. All he knew was that it pointed him on the opposite direction to the time machine, and down into the concrete belly of the beast. He found the doors unlocked and the final one wide open, as if someone had recently passed through. Although probably not *too* recently: now it was a shrieking portal, wreathed in bitter smoke and screaming in gunshot tones.

He threw his backpack to the ground and drew out his pistol, rushing in without a second thought. As he entered, a hot flash seized in the air. A rolling lake of fire erupted down below, licking at rows of glass cubes. But Cal's eye was immediately drawn to something at the burning lake's edge, silhouetted by the glow.

"Leslie!" he cried, rushing down the metal walkway below. "Leslie, get out of here! Run!"

He was so close now, step after step rattling on the metal walkway. His heart pounded, every breath pushing to get to her and answer to the red pressure in his head, lungs rebelling against the toxic air. Far below, Leslie turned, and somewhere through the smoke their eyes met.

Gunfire erupted from behind him, and two bullets spat fragments as they collided with the walkway. Cal turned to see Carnassus loping down the stairs towards him, hair flying around him in the hot air. His once-perfect mask was twisted into an ugly tangle, pure fury painted in porcelain. He fired a third time, bullet blinking through the air a moment before it thudded through Cal's shoulder.

White hot pain painted itself through his arm. He stumbled and cried out but didn't fall. Instead he raised an arm, a marionette on adrenaline strings. Fire winked from the gun barrel.

Carnassus fell back against the railing, his pistol clattering between the steps and down to the floor below. With a free hand he squeezed at his arm, wound already seeping dark red through white fabric.

But it didn't stop him. No. Like a man possessed, Carnassus rushed down onto the walkway, injured arm swinging uselessly as he threw himself forward. His forehead collided with Cal's nose and he crumpled back, walkway swinging as he hit the floor. Before he could react, Carnassus was on top of him, free hand thudding over and over into his throat and chest. Every time he breathed the wind was knocked from him, hands weakly trying to halt the fists.

But Carnassus was strong. His dead eyes were wide and hungry, baying silently for blood inside their sockets, open completely to reveal the awful blackness inside of them. With a final grunt of rage Carnassus brought a fist down on Cal's face, slamming his head into the steel.

Cal's eyes rolled. Darkness was creeping into his peripherals. He tried to fight, but he couldn't. He was too dizzy, too weak, too old. Helplessly trying to move as Carnassus shifted on top of him and drew out something long and shiny from his pocket. The blade pressed on Cal's chest as Carnassus leaned forward, his soft voice loud in Cal's ear.

"It could have been so beautiful," he whispered, "more than you animals deserved."

He sat up and raised the knife above his head, knuckle white on the handle. His doll eyes reflected nothing but fire against their glassy blackness, and with a final, desperate cry the knife came down towards Cal's chest, cutting through the air and—

"Ollie?" came a voice. The knife halted, barely an inch from the killing blow.

Carnassus' face fell. Softened, like he had suddenly forgotten where he was. Warmth, unaccustomed and alone in the cavernous internal black, flickered to life somewhere behind his mask.

With a grunt of pain, Cal looked up. At the end of the walkway, the double doors lay open. Yule stood a few feet in front of them, empty handed, his face a mixture of confusion and profound disappointment. Carnassus stared at him, expression lightening until it was nothing more than child-like surprise. Something innocent. When he spoke, his voice faltered.

"Yule?" he asked.

The was no reply. There wasn't time, before the gunshots screeched into him. One, two, three lead slugs popped against the back of his grimy white suit in puffs of torn fabric. Carnassus' back arched and he let out a strangled cry of surprise, knife clattering to the floor beside him. Then, his expression softened into one of disbelief, hands patting gently against the front of his suit. Blood swelled in pools between his fingers, blooming from beneath.

With a soft sigh, Carnassus' expression went neutral. He stared off into nothing as he slid off Cal and fell onto his side, hands still gently feeling over the rapidly growing stains on his jacket. A few feet behind, Leslie lowered the gun, her eyes fixed on his body. Cal couldn't tell what she was thinking—the pain was too bad to concentrate.

Leslie came over and pulled insistently at his sleeve, weakly struggling to pull him upright, gun tucked into her belt.

"Come on, you have to get up," she said, eyes turning fearfully to the fire below. "We have to go!"

Cal turned his head a little. The fire below was spreading, and more Volatiles had sprung from their cages. It was hard to tell if they were burning, or if the flames affected them at all. They looked almost at home in the heat haze, swirling limbs dancing between red tongues as they groped blindly around, electrical discharge all but wasted. Beside him, Carnassus let out a shaking breath.

"Cal! What do we do?" Leslie repeated, trying to pull him up, panic in her voice. Cal sat up; eyes still fixed on Carnassus' form on the ground.

"Nothing, I think…" he said, eyes fixed on Carnassus' living corpse, "…I think we've done it."

Yule's feet clattered on the walkway as he rushed over, slowing as he reached Carnassus' body. He stood over him, eyes wide and mouth open. Like he couldn't believe what he was seeing. Carnassus' eyes fluttered a little and came into focus. No hate or malice stained his gaze, as if death had surgically cut those parts away, and left only the warmth behind. Dwindling, faltering, but undiluted.

A gloved hand rose up to gently run its fingers over Yule's face, as if Carnassus couldn't believe he was real. Like he was seeing a dream.

"Y-Yule…you look…you l-look the s-same as when…" he repeated, voice shaking. "W-where… where did you g-g…?"

His hand fell to his chest, and his eyes dimmed. The words tumbled to nothing in his dying breath, a final soft gasp pushing a thread of blood past his lips and down his cheek. Yule bit his lip and put a hand to

Carnassus' chest. He muttered something to himself Cal couldn't hear, and Ollie never would.

There was a resounding boom as something set explosively alight below, and a column of flame boiled up into the air. The stairs near the ground had started to warp and melt, Volatiles swarming at the bottom like blind cockroaches. Cal put a hand on Yule's back, trying not to stumble.

"We have to get out of here," he said, already breathless without moving. "Leave him."

Yule nodded and straightened up, mouth opening to reply. Then he saw the dark streak of blood plastered through Cal's clothes and running down his arm.

"Oh, shit. Shit, what happened?" he said, moving to rip up part of his shirt. "That's a lot of blood, man. We have to get you to a—"

"No time. We have to go now, or we'll all die down here," Cal said, staying his hand and pointing to Leslie. "Help her."

They formed an injured herd, limping across the walkway towards the door. Cal followed behind Leslie and Yule, already out of breath a few steps in. His hand clutched weakly at his shoulder wound, fingers feeling numb.

The truck skidded to a halt, dead wheel biting into the dirt. Trevor, panting, turned around to see... something. Something he'd been running from. At least, it felt like he had, but the night was empty and still. Only the truck's idling engine struck to break the silence, carrying off boldly into the dark.

He sat back in the driver's seat and let out a strained gasp of relief, tension running out of him in shudders. His nerves were frayed, but he couldn't remember why. That was a good thing, right? He turned his eyes towards the factory, and felt a smile cut into his dusty cheeks. In the distance, illuminated on the bare parking lot by harsh floodlights, he could see ragged figures.

They'd done it, he thought. It was over. His feet flew through the dark as he pushed his way out onto the road and ran towards them with all his might.

The exit run was dreamlike and blurred by the pain haze. As he went, Cal felt like his legs were bicycling against nothing, like the halls were on some conveyor belt rotating around him in place. Sometimes he would see Leslie and Yule turn a corner, and despite the delirium he found himself smiling.

He'd done it, he thought. They'd all lived through it. No lives traded.

He stopped by the front door, fresh air settling on his face. Like the feeling of first waking after a long sleep. Leslie and Yule stood some ways away in the parking lot, beckoning him out, but he didn't move. He couldn't. He felt like a stripped wire giving up the last of his current. Brittle, and empty. He'd lost a lot of blood back there.

Out in the distance, a figure ran across the road towards them. Cal smiled, and something in him went out. The last person in danger, now safe. The satisfaction of a final duty fulfilled.

The wind was cold, he thought. Colder than he remembered.

The ground rose up to meet him as he collapsed.

HELLO, GOODBYE

AMESVILLE, 2002

The day was clear and bright. And although in the reeds and grass, insects buzzed their wings and chirped atonal tunes, the birds didn't sing. As if they too noted the silent crowd below, arrayed in formation around a long wooden box.

The photograph at its head was old but didn't seem that way. In all the years that followed, the photo had just become his face. The one plastered on posters and news reports, ageless. The years drew past, but inside that frame he never felt a day. His dated, ugly sweater never got dirty and his smile never got tired. Even as the world lost interest, he was still waiting there. The boy who never got a chance to grow old and tarnished.

Not like the man stood beside it. He looked older than he was, aged by grief and guilt. Could've looked worse, and the lines on his face suggested he had. But though his brow was cracked and his hands raw from wringing, he stood tall. A man who was healing, even if the wounds still bled. He looked at the photograph for a moment before turning to the small crowd.

Terry had gotten used to the cameras over the years. Now he barely noticed them peppered in like dead eyes amongst the crowd. He tried not to look at them as he spoke, and it was easy. As long as Pam was in the front row, it was easy.

"Thank you all for coming out," he said, voice clear on the cold air, "and thank you to everyone for your kind words at the church. I, ah…"

He trailed off, drawn to the cameras in the crowd. The world watching through a blind lens. He felt his heart begin to pound in his throat before something caught his eye. Movement, in the front row.

Pam was smiling at him. Just smiling. But suggested in it were a thousand remembered conversations, and hundreds of sleepless nights. It reminded him he was here, even though deep down, sometimes he felt as if he wasn't there at all. Or hadn't been, once. He took a deep breath through his nose, and felt the anxiety tingle out through his fingers, imagining it bouncing around in his hands just like the shrink had told him to.

Just say what you mean, he thought. *It was a mistake not doing it while he was here, don't keep things in now.*

"I thought a lot, about what I was gonna say today. About how good a kid he was, or how much joy he brought to the people around him. But, for the past nine years, we've talked about that a lot. And it at least gives me a little joy that so many people around the country were touched by Cal's life, and were inspired to offer us support in our darkest times. We've, ah, talked a lot about those, too," he said. He took another deep breath, and exhaled. Sparks in the fingers.

"But as many of you have said, today isn't about the past. It isn't about holding onto what could have been. It's about the future. And although my wife and I will never give up hope that one day Cal is going to walk through our door again, we can't wait our whole lives for it. And even if he never..."

He trailed off. Even now the suggestion burned in his throat like a brooding coal. Old, yet ever painful even as it cooled. Terry closed his eyes and centered himself. It was okay that he couldn't say it. He knew that.

"Wherever he is now, we hope he's safe. Hope he's happy," he said. "I hope he knows that no matter what, we loved him with all that we were. That we still do. Thank you."

He stepped away, and Pam's hand slipped into his, just like always. He held it tight as the first pieces of dirt were thrown onto the casket. He closed his eyes and tried not to think about how they sounded. The way they drummed on the hollow coffin, in want of a body.

Those nightmares had come and gone. Today was a goodbye, he thought, and not just to the things he missed.

After the casket was covered up, all that remained was to say goodbye to the attendees. A few words, maybe a hug. He got the impression most of it wasn't for the cameras. The press didn't stick around long: after a few candid shots they packed up their equipment, as the outside world's interest officially moved elsewhere.

Terry spent some time alone, looking at the unfilled hole. Didn't know what he was meant to think about. The only thing that pervaded above the sadness was a strange, unspoken dread in his gut. That there was something utterly unexplainable about what had happened, but... he couldn't think what. Like he'd dreamed it.

A goodbye to all things, he thought. All things.

He turned away from the grave, eyes instinctively searching for Pam in the sparse crowd. He quickly found her, and the familiar silhouette she was talking to. He walked over, put a hand on the man's shoulder, and smiled. And he meant it.

"I know we said it back at the house, but it means so much to us that you came," he said. "God knows you've done your fair share of travel back here over the years, but I know this would've meant a lot to him."

"Yeah," Trevor replied.

He smiled at him, and it actually gave Terry a little comfort. Even if college and age had slimmed him down and stretched him out, there was something in that smile that remained ever youthful. The reminder of a chubby young kid, forever parading around his house like it was his. Pam drew Trevor in close for a hug, her thin hands pressing tightly against his back.

"We're having my sister over for dinner tonight," she said, breaking the embrace. "As usual, you're more than welcome. I'll probably make that, ah, that lasagna thing again."

She smiled, but her eyes were sad. Trevor sighed and hugged her again.

"I know," he said. "I miss him too."

Like clockwork, the goodbyes came. Pam and Terry, hand in hand, took one final look at the grave before departing. Trevor adjusted the lapels on his jacket and looked over the plot. Considered it for a moment, his face betraying no hint at what thoughts lay behind it.

As he turned to leave, someone caught his eye. Someone at the edge of a conversation, watching him. Without a word, they nodded to each other. She waved for a moment with a gloved hand, three of the empty fingers flexing a little in the breeze. The exchange only lasted until her father turned to talk to her, and she rejoined the conversation.

Trevor smiled to himself and walked away.

The way into town proper was quiet, just like he remembered it. The path was better paved and a few more cars rolled by than he expected, but the old road remained largely unchanged. By the time he reached Clarence Street the sun was already starting to dip towards the horizon, amber light spreading autumn chill through the air. Everyone on the street was headed elsewhere, away from shop fronts that still stood empty, turning to ash amongst the golden leaves.

His hands in his pockets, Trevor considered them as he passed. No matter how much things changed, he thought, some things refused. Just like the man sat on a bench below the monolith, waiting.

When Trevor sat down next to him, he barely stirred, good eye fixed on the unlit shopfront some feet ahead.

"Y'know, that place has had the same radio display in it since 1987," he said coolly. "That's crazy, right?"

Trevor smirked, and nodded.

"Anywhere but here? Yeah, I'd say it's pretty crazy," he replied. Silence descended again, the weight of unsaid things straining as it tried to lie flat between them on the cold air. Cal sighed deeply, gloved hands squeaking a little as they adjusted on the head of his cane. The long shadow of the monolith obscured his eyes.

"Did it go okay?" he asked hesitantly. Trevor nodded, eyes held stoically forward at the radio shop.

"It was good. Your uncle gave a hell of a speech," he said.

"And Aunt Pam?"

"She's alright. They're both surviving," Trevor replied curtly. Cal tensed his neck and leaned back against the bench, cane tip tapping gently on the asphalt.

"Can we not do this again?" he asked.

"I just think you should've said something to them," Trevor said, as if he could hold it back no longer. "They think you're dead, Cal. Really, *actually* dead."

"Good," Cal replied, voice hardening. "That's what's safest for them. A normal tragedy—"

"A normal tragedy's better than an unexplainable truth. I know. Just because I understand it doesn't mean I gotta like it, that's all I'm saying. But by now there isn't much I can say that hasn't been said already. I don't wanna fight about it," Trevor finished. Cal sighed again and ran a hand over his gnarled brow. For a moment it seemed the uncomfortable silence was ready to descend, before Trevor let his shoulders slump. Slowly, he leaned over and elbowed Cal gently in the ribs.

"It was really good though, man. You should've come along," he said. Cal chuckled, freed for a moment from the dark shroud of age.

"Somehow, I don't think anyone would believe I was deformed Uncle Edgar, come to pay my respects."

Trevor *hmmed* in mock thought and nodded, hands interlaced over each other in his lap.

"Maybe you're right," he said. "Guess it's kinda tacky, the whole 'hero watches his own funeral' thing."

They both laughed a little, then let it fade. The breeze rolled against them as it passed, turned slightly chill by the approach of night. Dusk filled gaps in the stillness, amber-like and perfect. And though people passed by and stirred the air, and although in the distance the trees still swayed in time to the wind, it all felt undisturbed. No unknown pressure deadened their ears. No sickly green light nor smell of ozone crept amongst the leaves.

Cal turned his head to look at Trevor and then grunted, settling back into the bench.

"You don't have to be here all the time, y'know," he said, gesturing with his cane. "Not that I'm complaining, but... you don't. You know that, right?"

Trevor screwed up his face and turned to him, bemused.

"Yeah, I know that, so what?" he asked, laughing a little. Cal frowned and turned his eyes back to the radio shop. His hands tightened on his cane.

"You went to Princeton because it was close—"

"And, y'know, one of the best schools in the country."

"—and then every vacation, every break, you're here. Every year, no matter what you're doing, you come back," Cal insisted, gesturing to the empty street. "There's a whole world out there Trev, and it's just... The whole point of what happened was to make sure you weren't trapped in Amesville forever."

The statement hung in the air between them for a moment, before Trevor ran a hand through his hair.

"I guess this is a bad time to tell you I took a job in Philly, huh?" he said, smirking. Cal hissed through his teeth and shook his head. But he laughed, even if it was clear he hated what he'd just heard. Good old Cal.

"You're a son of a bitch, Trevvy," he muttered, laying his head back against the monolith.

"It's not just for you. Mom's here too," Trevor replied, settling back to look at the old radio shop window. There was a brief pause, and when Cal spoke his voice was low and gravel toned.

"I feel like you're not saying something here," he said. Trevor exhaled deeply.

"Have they been back again since last time?" he asked. For a moment the evening seemed to turn bitterly cold, and although it soon righted itself, the stain of it remained. The invisible silhouette of The Branch, unknown and yet ever present.

Cal shook his head.

"No. At least, none that I've seen. Cameras are telling me nobody's even been near the tunnel entrances for about a year now."

"And they're all still filled in? The holes?" Trevor asked.

Cal nodded.

"Checked them all last week, just in case. Nothing's getting out," he said. Trevor considered the statement for a moment, breath uncoiling a little in his chest. Even now, when he talked about it, he felt like a scared kid again.

"By all accounts, The Branch lost interest too. It's just us that know the truth now," Cal insisted.

"And Leslie, and Yule," Trevor said. Then, he caught himself, and a look of concern washed over his features. "He wasn't at the funeral. Nothing's happened to him, right?"

Cal laughed, and it clacked like rocks in his throat.

"No," he said, shaking his head, "nothing's happened. He's just doing me a favor right now. Out of town."

"What kind of favor?" Trevor asked, narrowing his eyes a little. Cal shrugged.

"Nothing dangerous. Think of it as enforced vacation. He half killed himself helping me mop up the mess, hadn't left town in years... I decided maybe it would be a good time for him to go see the USA of the future. A one-man road trip," he said. Trevor folded his arms and chuckled under his breath.

"Still annoying you that much, huh?" he said. A frustrated grunt popped from Cal's lips, unconscious and unstoppable, his shoulders dropping as the exhaustive weight of diplomacy fell away.

"You know he looks at people's door mats to see how often they get visitors? I mean, who does that?" he said. Trevor's smirk cracked open into a smile.

"I'm starting to see why it's a favor now," he said. Then, he turned his eyes towards the sky, orange sliding to red as the sun kissed the horizon. He brushed off the top of his slacks and cleared his throat; the universal symbol for the end of a conversation approaching. Cal noticed and perked up.

"So, what are your plans for tonight?" he asked.

"Dinner with your aunt and uncle at eight," Trevor replied, getting up. "So before you ask, yeah, I'll be free after that to come over. I'll bring beer."

Cal smiled, and began to slowly climb to his feet. Trevor didn't steady him on an arm, even when his weaker side looked as if it would stumble. No matter how much he needed help, Cal had always hated it just the same.

"Good. Good, that's… good," he said, smiling but out of breath. "Just give me a call before you arrive, maybe ten minutes or so. I've got a surprise I think you're gonna like, but I wanna have it set up first."

Trevor scoffed smugly, and Cal threw up his hands in confusion.

"What?" he said. Trevor smirked again.

"You sit there and talk about progress but is this big surprise something new in your life other than a forty-nine-inch TV?" he asked. Cal looked at the ground.

"It's actually fifty inches," he said quietly. A moment of tense silence passed, before Trevor burst out laughing. Cal laughed too, and for yet another second they were caught somewhere out of time. Just the two of them, together, made ageless by joy. As the laughter died down, Trevor gave Cal a thoughtful smile, and unfolded his arms.

"You're lucky that kicks ass, otherwise my point still would've stood," he said, turning to go. "I'll give you a call before I head over. But only if you promise we're not gonna watch *Basket Case* again."

He made it a few feet before a voice stopped him.

"Trev?" Cal called from behind him. Trevor turned around, now a few feet away and able to take in Cal for all he was. The faded gray suit and the prosthetic mask. The cane, and the cracked features.

And yet somehow, stood there in the evening light, Trevor could tell unmistakably that it was him, just like he always had. It was something in the eyes, he thought. Something young, and familiar. Cal adjusted his grip on his cane and looked thoughtfully at the monolith for a few moments, before making eye contact again.

"I know all the stuff I said earlier made it sound like I'm not, but I'm really glad you're here. I'm always really glad," he said. Trevor took a few steps forward and put his arms around Cal in a tight embrace.

"Me too," he said.

They stood there a few moments. Two specks adrift in the honey glow of evening. The street lay still, emptied by chill and without witness for the few words they exchanged there. They were simply lost in the wind, to tumble and fall amongst the grass, secret and unheard. And even as they parted, disappearing as darkness rolled over the sleeping landscape, the words remained. The ghost of a day remembered long after time had shifted it, and a reminder that no matter how much the world changed, some things remained.

A leaf tumbled on the wind and danced around the Clarence Street monolith. Bright with eggshell white paint, freshly replaced once the original message had been washed away. Familiar in its form and striking in its newness.

"*Who took Cal Greenwood?*" it asked.

OLD GOLD

STATE ROUTE 379, 2002

The gas station was the only thing for miles. Baked into a long stretch of highway cutting straight through the formless Nevada heat, and surrounded on all sides by nothing. Inside, grimy plastic fan blades spun lazily on the ceiling, hardly stirring the thick air. The ribbons of a chugging AC unit waved in their corner like dancers on a string.

He pressed his palm up against the glass of the vending machine, and felt the chill run up through his hand. Cold was hard to come by so far from home. Not moving, he scanned through a row of magazines on the rack, some a few weeks old. Airbrushed women in red dresses stared back at him in a myriad of joyful poses. Somewhere near the back of the store, something fell, and nobody moved to pick it up. That kind of place, he thought.

He navigated his way through the aisles to the counter, where a cardboard display for caffeine pills blared at him in primary colors. He picked two boxes out and slid them onto the counter towards the teller. She was pretty, he thought. Blonde and kind of docile looking, but then again in heat like this, maybe that was the way to go.

She smiled at him, and for a moment he felt old defenses spring up. Old rules. He must've made some kind of expression in the end, because she at least looked away without laughing.

"Can I get you anything else?" she asked, punching numbers into the till.

"Uh, yeah," he said, nodding absentmindedly to the rows of cigarettes behind the counter as he rifled for change, "could I get a pack of Old Golds as well?"

The girl at the counter furrowed her brow at him and cocked her head.

"I don't think we carry that brand. I've never heard of it," she said, glancing over her shoulder. Yule laughed, more to himself than her. It always came through in the little things, even after all this time.

"Sorry. Force of habit," he said, waving his hand to get her attention. "I'll just take Newports."

The girl smiled and nodded.

"Now *those* we've got," she said, turning around to pick them out. Yule laid his hands out on the counter and grimaced internally. The heat was in everything, he thought. In the walls, in the air, even in the hard plastic tabletop. Couldn't get away from it.

"You traveling?" asked the teller, as she turned back around and tossed a white cardboard packet next to the caffeine pills. Yule nodded and mustered a polite smile, trying to ignore the fact that the only alternative out there was sleeping behind the gas pumps.

"Yeah. Didn't get away from home much before, so I'm just kind of going everywhere that's connected by road," he replied, noting the digital readout and handing her a wad of bills. The teller nodded as she counted his change, smiling sweetly.

"Coulda guessed," she said, glancing at the caffeine pills. "Long journey from here?"

Guess there wasn't much company out in the middle of nowhere.

"Maybe. Depends how often the car gives out," Yule replied, glancing outside again. "You don't know how far Boonestown is from here, do you?"

The girl at the counter gave him an odd look.

"About a hundred fifty miles, give or take," she replied, eyeing him. "You're not one of those UFO people, are you?"

Yule laughed and help up his hands disarmingly.

"No. No, I'm not. Don't believe in that kind of thing. Just the next stop on my route," he said, picking up the cigarette packet. He smiled at her a final time and nodded. "Have a nice day."

She smiled back.

"You too," she said. With a final nod, Yule swam through the solid heat, stopping only for a moment to bathe in the weak column of cold beneath the air conditioner. But he couldn't linger long. Didn't have the time for it, even now. He had to go out again, into the hard heat and dry light. At least, for as long as it took him to get back to the car.

In the sparse few minutes he'd been away, the dash had already heated to the point of burning. As he turned out of the gas station and coasted down the empty road, he had to keep moving his hands on the wheel just to stop them from scalding. Christ, he hated Nevada, he thought as he punched the air conditioning to max.

After a few more miles he pulled to a stop at the side of the road, engine still running. He rolled the window down and winced as hot desert air slopped in through the gap, and onto his lap. At least it was better than standing out there, he thought, teasing a cigarette from the pack. He then took his wallet and propped it up on the dash, like a tri-fold frame on a mantelpiece. From the transparent pocket in the middle, his little niece beamed out at him, flanked by Ornell's grinning face. Yule ran a thumb over it, and a smile ghosted over his features.

"Uncle Yule. Hmph," he muttered, still wondrous at the novelty of it.

He sat there for some time; his cigarette hung lazily out of the window. His eyes scanned over the horizon and mirrors, back and forth, looking for movement. He wasn't sure what he expected to see, but there was nothing out there. Big nothing, vast nothing. Heat haze and rocks.

Nevada, he thought bitterly as he flicked the cigarette into the dust outside. Why did nothing weird ever happen someplace cold?

He rolled up the window and pressed on the gas again. The car became a lone moving dot on the landscape, passing soundlessly through the searing daylight. What little noise came from the tires was deadened by the warmth, and once he was gone there was nobody else around to hear it. Nothing saw him go, or even knew he was there.

And nobody saw the silhouette of the lone black van cresting the horizon some minutes later.

Following.

ABOUT THE AUTHOR

A former baby and future vengeful ghost, Jacob Close holds an MA in history from the University of Edinburgh and was shortlisted for the Allen Wright Award for Arts Journalism in 2015. He also writes for a living, and considering that you're reading this right now, we can both assume it's going at least moderately well.

Despite what his monsters suggest, he firmly believes the universe is a fascinating and beautiful place. Which is lucky, because that's where all of his things are.